THE LONG RIDE BACK

ED GORMAN

THE LONG RIDE BACK

LEISURE BOOKS NEW YORK CITY

LEISURE BOOKS ®

May 2004

Published by

Dorchester Publishing Co., Inc.
200 Madison Avenue
New York, NY 10016

ISBN 0-8439-5227-X

The name "Leisure Books" and the stylized "L" with design are trademarks of Dorchester Publishing Co., Inc.

Printed in the United States of America.

Visit us on the web at www.dorchesterpub.com.

TABLE OF CONTENTS

A Disgrace to the Badge

HERE LIES MICHAEL JAMES BRADY
ONLY THE LORD IS PERFECTION

Around ten o'clock, Deputy Jack Corey heard the scraping on the back of the jailhouse wall and knew he had a visitor.

Johnny Hayden was bringing provisions to his drinking partner Mike Brady. The provisions would be a pint of bourbon to get Brady through the night in his cell, the same cell Corey had tossed him into an hour ago. Happened every time Brady visited the jail, which was frequently. Brady was the town bully, a mean, reckless drunk who would, everybody knew, kill somebody someday. But his father was a powerful merchant and so about the worst punishment anybody was willing to inflict on him was a

1

night rolling around in the vomit and piss of cell two, where the drunks stayed.

Couple things about this particular night.

One being that Jack Corey was a little old to be a night deputy. Night deputies were usually strapping youngsters eager to break a few knuckles on the faces of such men as Mike Brady. But Corey was none of these things. He was a worn forty-one-year-old man who'd known nothing but law his entire working life. And most of his working life he'd also known, all too well, the bottle. Which accounted for him working in so many towns. Till the bottle got him fired. At his age, this was his last chance. And as of tonight, he'd failed it. Twenty-eight days dry, he'd been, on this new job in Dodge. Then tonight he stole a pint from a rummy in an alley and drank the quarter-inch or so that remained. This was around eight. Right now, he shook pretty bad. You know the way some folks wait for the cavalry to appear on the hill and come to their rescue? Well, Jack Corey was waiting for a whiskey bottle to come strutting in the door and come to *his* rescue.

The second thing was his concern that the town marshal would pay him a surprise visit. He'd done that a couple times. He knew all about Corey's bottle problem and so he kind of spot-checked him. The town marshal and his wife would be at the opera house or maybe a barn dance or maybe just out enjoying the spring weather—and then all of a sudden, there they'd be. The wife would always bring Corey a pastry or piece of bread slathered with jam, something that would make the visit seem social. But Corey knew why they popped in. They were testing him. And tonight he would fail the test. Sure as hell they'd smell the liquor on him—

the marshal had a nose a hunting dog would envy—and then what would happen to forty-one-year-old Jack Corey?

He was grateful for the distraction Johnny Hayden gave him. He raised himself from his desk chair, touched his holstered Colt .45 as if to make sure it hadn't run off and left him the way his wife had that time, and then he went out into the sweet chill spring night.

You couldn't give Hayden any points for being subtle. From somewhere he'd borrowed a ladder, which now leaned against the wall next to the open barred window three-quarters of the way up.

"Evening, Johnny."

Another man might have jerked around, scared, when he heard the deputy approaching him. Not Hayden. Hayden was secure in knowing that just about whatever kind of trouble he got in, old man Brady could and would get him out of. Hayden was young Brady's keeper and had been since they'd gone to grade school together. It was, from the outside, a curious relationship. Mike Brady humiliated Hayden every chance he got. He had knocked him out, spat on him, stolen various girlfriends, called him unforgivable names—and Hayden stuck by him. But Hayden was being paid a healthy stipend every month to keep Brady in check. Hayden always pulled Brady back from the kind of disaster not even the old man could fix. Without his watchdog Hayden, Brady would have been hanged long, long ago. Not a week went by that Brady wasn't suspected of some kind of trouble, often enough hanging kind of trouble.

"Evening, Deputy," Hayden said. He was a strong, beefy man given to dark suits and gentlemanly manners. He had a solemn face except for a certain irony in the dark gaze, a

3

weary acceptance of all things human. "I assume you know what I'm doing, Deputy."

"He doesn't need any more tonight."

"But he's asked for it. And that means I've got to give it to him."

He started down the ladder and reached the dirt.

"In fact, I've *already* given it to him."

"Yeah, how d'ya like that, you bastard?" Brady shouted from inside.

Hayden took the stepladder down. "The livery let me borrow it. I need to get it back to them."

They started walking to the street. Hayden carried the ladder.

"You ever get tired of waiting on him?"

Hayden smiled. "You really expect me to answer that?"

"Smart man like you, you could get yourself a good job."

"Smart but lazy, I'm afraid."

"Oh?"

"My folks are shirttail kin to the Bradys. They were always nice to us. I got used to their kind of high life. On my own, I couldn't live anywhere near so well. But I've got my own little apartment in their barn out on the estate and a hell of a nice monthly wage. And I don't want to give it up."

"You don't want a wife?"

"I'm twenty-three. Plenty of time for that."

Corey looked up and down the street of false-fronts. Just about everything you wanted to find you could find in Dodge. Daytime, for the legitimate things a feller wanted. Nighttime, for the things a feller didn't necessarily want to talk about. There had been a time when Corey had loved the sounds and scents and heady alcoholic feelings of nighttime, the laughter of whores mixing with the snappy rhythms of the player piano and the bawdy fun of the banjo. But there'd always been a wife to go home to in those days, after he was done drinking and whoring. But then one day she *wasn't* there and she was never there again and something terrible had happened inside of Corey then—his heart had been cut out by his own hand—and it was still terrible and it would *always* be terrible. And he couldn't even tell you for sure what it was. Just that it changed then and the bottle problems started and he wasn't the same old Corey anymore. Not at all.

"I should take that pint from him."

"Who said anything about a pint?" Hayden said. "I brought him a fifth." He laughed. "You think a Brady would settle for a pint?"

"He'll be some fun tonight. A whole fifth."

"He can get pretty abusive."

"He sure can."

"But at least you got him locked up."

"Yeah, and his old man's gonna be all over the marshal tomorrow about how hard I hit him. But he was strangling that gambler pretty good. A minute or so more, he would've killed him."

"You're right. The marshal's going to hear about it from Frank Brady himself. But hell, he won't put up much of a stink."

"He won't?"

Hayden leaned close, as if confiding a secret. "He'll raise some hell to keep Mike off his back. But old Frank knows how Mike is. And he's sick of it. Sick of paying out money to all the people Mike beats up. And paying for all the saloons Mike smashes up. And always having people snicker about Mike behind Frank's back. Snicker and hate him. Mike's wife is sick of it, too."

Mike Brady's wife. A sullen rich girl named Debra who would be even richer when the old man died and Mike came into the entire estate.

"She's tired of him whoring," Hayden said. "Breaking up saloons and things like that, she doesn't mind. But the whoring—she sees that as a reflection on herself. That she isn't woman enough to hold him."

"Sounds like you've got a real nice groups of folks out at the mansion."

Hayden smiled again. "Like I said, Deputy, I sleep in an apartment over the barn. It's a very nice place. I don't have to be around any of them."

Then he was off, carrying his ladder down the street.

Brady, tonight's only prisoner thus far, started in as soon as Corey got back to his office.

Another half hour, Corey would make his rounds again. There might be a few drunks but mostly there'd be merchant doors to check, that would be about as eventful as the evening would likely get.

Brady gave him the full show. Sang dirty songs off-key. Called him names. Threatened to kill him. Dared him to come back there and fight like a man. He puked a couple of times. He was a skilled puker, knew how to clean himself out so he could keep going for another round. They had a Mexican wash out the four cells in the mornings. They paid him a good wage to do so.

Corey had his own concerns. He kept thinking about that fifth Hayden had brought Brady. The fountain of youth, that bottle was—or the illusion of youth anyway. When you felt better physically and didn't have the burden of your grief and remorse and when it was easy to imagine pretty gals swooning over you and fierce men running away in shamed fear.

So many things in a bottle like that. Music. And sweet memories. And hope. And dreams.

And maybe—best of all—not giving a shit. Not having any gnawing fear that you'd lose a job or that somebody had called you a name or that you'd do something foolish and embarrass yourself.

Not giving a shit. That was the ultimate blessing a bottle like that could bestow on you.

He went back there just before he made his rounds. He felt better. It was nearly midnight. The marshal and his wife wouldn't be popping in tonight. Too late. The marshal was a man of strict and stringent habit. Up at five A.M. every morning. In bed every night before eleven.

The cells smelled like a cesspool thanks to Mr. Brady here.

Brady, a scrappy tow-head, said, "You come in this cell with me, Deputy. Leave your badge and your gun out there and we'll fight like men."

"Why don't you shut up and go to sleep?"

Brady preferred light-colored suits and frilly shirts. Gambler's attire. He was handsome in a sullen way but the booze was starting to rob his face of its lines. Puffy, he was. Twenty-three and puffy as a thirty-year-old who'd been boozing since his teens.

Doubtful he'd be wearing this suit again. It'd gotten torn in his dust-up with the gambler. And blood had streamed down the back of his head and trickled in crusty ribbons down the silk rear of his vest. The crusted puke all over his shirt didn't exactly help, either.

7

And then Corey saw the bottle.

Must be a slow night for the kid, Corey thought. *Most nights he would've put half of it away by now.*

For there—a vision almost celestial in its splendor—there on the floor next to the cot on the right-hand side of cell two—there was the fifth that Hayden had brought Brady.

The bottle was nearly full.

"C'mon," Brady said, putting up his fists like a prizefighter, and describing a semicircle with his clumsy feet. "C'mon in here and I'll kick the living shit right out of you!"

But Corey had eyes only for the bottle. Brady was mere unintelligible babble in the background.

"I'm gonna take that bottle from you," Corey said.

"Yeah. You just try. You think I don't know why you want it? You're a rummy and everybody knows it. *That's* why you want it!"

Corey couldn't stop himself. He was beyond the point of trying. His entire consciousness, his entire existence was focused on that bottle. He'd do what he needed to to get it.

He drew his Colt.

He put his key in the cell lock.

"I want that bottle of yours, Brady."

Drunk as he was, Brady could still understand what the deputy was all about.

He hugged the bottle protectively to his chest, the way he'd hold an infant, and grinned. "This is mine, all mine, Deputy. And you can't have it." The more he teased, the louder his voice got.

"I said I want that bottle. I'm taking it from you because you don't need any more to drink."

Brady smirked. "Sure you are, Deputy. And I'll bet you wouldn't even *think* of taking a drink of it, would you?"

"Give it to me."

He put his hand out.

Brady got even sillier, hugged it tighter and tighter, and started to rock it back and forth. "Poor little bottle. Poor little lonely bottle." Eyes watching the deputy all the time he was doing this. Knowing just how his mocking little show here was making Corey even crazier.

This time when Corey put his hand out, he saw that it was trembling. His mouth was raw with dryness. He could taste the liquor on his tongue; he could feel the mercy—*I don't give a shit anymore, you can't hurt me and I can't hurt myself anymore, and I don't give a damn if I'm a falling-down drunk or not*—the mercy the mercy the mercy—he could feel the mercy the golden bottle would bestow upon him.

And then, giggling, enjoying the holy hell out of himself, Brady took the bottle and tossed it up into the filthy air of the cell.

"No!" Corey cried, picturing drunken Brady missing the bottle as it fell back to him.

But he didn't miss.

"That was a close one, wasn't it, Deputy? That son-ofabitch coulda splattered all over the floor!"

Giggling all the while.

"You give that bottle here," Corey said, moving toward the man.

"You take one more step, Deputy, and I'm gonna smash this bottle against that wall back there. And you won't be able to stop me."

"You give it here."

So dry; so desperate.

Corey started to reach for it.

Brady took it by the neck and arched the bottle so that it was only inches from the wall. He hadn't been exaggerating. He could easily smash the bottle before Corey could stop him.

"Ummmm," Brady said. "Bet you can taste that liquor in your gut now, can't you, Deputy? And this is good stuff. Not like that mule piss you drink. This here's the brand my old man drinks. And he drinks only the best, believe me."

He made the mistake of falling in love with his words, Brady did. That's what gave helpless Corey the sudden advantage. Here's Brady thespianizing like some traveling-show ham and having such a good time at it that he didn't pay attention to business—said business being, at the moment, keeping himself and his bottle out of the clutches of the deputy.

Corey actually hit him a lot harder than he intended, too. It didn't take much to knock out a man as drunk as Brady was. But Corey kind of stumbled into the punch, *pushing* it sort of like, pushing it farther and faster than he meant to.

Two things happened at once.

The bottle went flying up in the air. And Brady's head ricocheted off the wall in a way that turned Corey's stomach. The kind of glancing ricochet that could permanently cripple or even kill a man. Corey had seen it happen.

The bottle—

The bottle was just now descending. Corey pitched his drawn .45 to the cot and lunged to position himself beneath the tumbling, falling bottle.

For now, there was no concern about Brady. The world—the universe—could be found, sum and substance, in the sweet succor of the bottle's mahogany-colored elixir.

He caught it.

And just as he caught it, Brady started his struggle to his feet.

Thank God.

The bottle safe in his hands now, he could appreciate the trouble he'd have been in if Brady had been seriously hurt.

Brady put a hand to the side of his head and said, "What the hell happened?"

Corey had seen this before, too.

A blow on the head knocking some of the drunkenness out of a man.

"You don't remember?"

Before he could answer, Brady puked again.

Corey said, "I'm gonna get you a cup of coffee."

He was back in two minutes with a cup of boiling java. He slid it through the rectangle in the cell door. "Shit's hot. Be careful."

"You sonofabitch," Brady said. An offer of coffee hadn't made him any sweeter. "You're gonna be damned sorry you roughed me up."

"I didn't rough you up. You hit your head when I slugged you. And I slugged you because you wouldn't turn over the bottle Hayden brought you."

Brady glared at the bottle in Corey's hand. "I figured that was mine. You can bet your ass I'm gonna tell the marshal you took it from me."

Brady was on the edge of many things—still drunk but getting sober in the worst sort of way, sick to his stomach and the possessor of a large knob on the side of his head, said knob radiating pain throughout his skull. And confused of memory and barbed-wire pissed about being pushed around by a rummy deputy.

But Corey was fully sick of Brady by now.

The way Corey saw it was, he'd take the bottle up front to his desk and have himself a good strong one. One. That was all. Then he'd go make his rounds and then, if he was of a mind, he'd take another one. One. He'd wrap the bottle in his coat and take it home when his shift ended next morning and if the marshal complained about Brady's bottle being stolen, he'd just say, *He was so drunk he don't know what he was talking about, Marshal.* And the marshal would most likely believe him.

"Get some sleep."

"I just can't wait for our time to come, Deputy, you know that? Just me and you. I just can't wait."

Then he was puking again.

Corey wondered what the hell he'd had for dinner.

He did as planned. Went up front, sat the bottle down on his desk as if it were a religious icon and just stared at it for a few exquisite moments. Probably hadn't had whiskey this good but three, four times in his entire life.

And then it was time.

Open the bottle.

Pour about an inch-and-a-half into his glass.

And then sit back all comfortable in his chair and enjoy some of the finest whiskey the good Lord had ever visited upon mankind.

Just one drink.

Voices:

(Male): He's a disgrace to that badge.

(Female): He killed poor Mike. No doubt about it.

(Male): And he'll pay for it, Debra. Don't you worry about that.

(The female began sobbing.)

Corey's way was to open one eye and kind of peer about and see if this was the sort of world he wanted to have anything to do with.

Usually.

But not today. Today, he instinctively *knew* that this was a world he didn't want to have anything to do with. That "disgrace to his badge" remark for one thing. And even worse that "He killed poor Mike" line.

Mike inevitably being Mike Brady. The prisoner he was guarding—or should have been guarding—all those long and now murky hours before he began to partake not just of one drink but many, many drinks.

And then that final male comment: "And he'll pay for it, Debra. Don't you worry about that."

No, sir, he didn't need to open an eye to know that this world was an extremely hostile one.

But then hands shook him roughly. And when that didn't succeed in getting his eyes open, somebody splashed a pail of icy water across his face.

"On your feet."

His eyes were open now. He wished they weren't.

"On your feet."

Marshal Beck, tall, wide, white of hair and mustache, imposing in the way an angry minister is imposing, said, "You're under arrest, Corey."

Corey managed to find his voice.

"For killing Mike Brady."

Then he saw the three others: old man Brady, Debra Brady the widow, and Hayden.

"I didn't kill him."

"Oh no? Care to go back and have a look at him in the cell?"

"It'll go easier on you if you just admit it," Brady said. "You got in a fight and hit him a little too hard. He got under your skin was all. Mike—God love him—he got under a lot of people's skin. I think we can see to it that the charges are dropped to second degree. You can be out in eight years. That sure beats a rope."

At which point, the widow Debra swooned with grief and said in her ice-blonde way, "We were going to start a family next year. He was going to quit drinking and everything."

Brady took her in his long, strong arms and sheltered her from the world.

This was some alternate realm he'd awakened to. Last time he'd seen Brady, Brady had a headache and was sick to his stomach was about all. The worst thing Corey had done was come up here and get passing-out drunk. The bottle responsible was still on the desk in front of him. Drained.

He became aware of his clothes. His head and his shirt were soaked. He said, "Let's go see Mike Brady."

All this craziness. He didn't know how long he could handle it. Beneath the water, he'd started to sweat and sweat good.

Mike Brady was sprawled on the cot. He was starting to get stiff now. The large bruise on the left side of his forehead was split down the center, like a fruit that had been halved. Blood had poured from it, streaking most of his face.

"That's the one that killed him," Hayden said.

"We'll let Dr. McGivern tell us which one killed him," the marshal said, "tomorrow at the inquest."

Hayden looked, not without sympathy, at Corey. "Mike was in an evil mood last night. Even by his standards, I mean."

"That's when he really scared me," Debra said, all finishing-school proper in her blue taffeta dress and jaunty feathered hat. Then: "God, the stench in here. Don't you ever clean this out, Marshal?"

The lawman frowned. "Do you know how ridiculous that question is?" He had his pride and not even the Bradys could intimidate him out of it. "By now, the Mexican has usually swamped out every cell. But given that your husband decided to stay longer than expected, the Mexican couldn't get in to do his work."

"She didn't mean anything by that," Brady said gently. "She's just upset."

The marshal nodded, as if he understood. But his harsh blue gaze said he didn't understand at all.

Around three o'clock that afternoon, Corey was lying in his cell, rolling himself a cigarette, listening to a couple of Negroes in the next cell talk sweetly of old St. Louis and life on the riverboats, when Marshal Beck came in with a stumpy little gal whose fierce little face scared the hell out of Corey. The Angel of Death couldn't be any more frightening.

"This is Sara Wylie and she's going to be your attorney."

"A woman?" Corey said.

"You have something against women?" she barked at him.

"No, ma'am," Corey said.

"I've won my last fourteen cases and saved three men from the gallows. I don't need to justify my existence to you, Corey. But I thought I'd tell you that for the record."

She had to know how her record would affect him. Suddenly the idea of a gal attorney was fine.

"The inquest starts in fifteen minutes," Marshal Beck said. "I'll let you two have a room in the courthouse for half an hour after it's over."

The inquest was brief and brutal.

Judge Holstein (what a monicker to get stuck with, imagine all the jokes the poor bastard had had to put up with all his life) laid out the circumstances of Mike Brady's death—between his stomach-churning bouts of hacking up sincerely green phlegm—and then called the doctor to the stand.

"Could you tell us how Michael James Brady died?"

"Yes, sir. A blow to the head. The forehead, more specifically."

Corey couldn't wait to tell his gal attorney that he'd accidentally put a goose egg on the side of Brady's head. But he had nothing to do with the business on Brady's forehead. Of that he was positive.

"Could Michael James Brady have tripped and inflicted that wound on himself?"

"Possible. But unlikely. There's a goose egg on the side of his head, too. That makes it look like he'd been in some kind of altercation."

The judge smiled. "By altercation you mean fight?"

"Yes, sir, I mean fight."

The judge looked out at the eager, trial-happy faces of the townsfolk who'd come here. He had to be re-elected soon and he liked to show people he was just folks. "I never use those big words myself. I didn't have the opportunity you had for education, I'm afraid, Doctor. So in my court, please use the language of the common folk."

"What an asshole," Sara Wylie whispered to Corey. Right then and there he decided he not only trusted her, he liked her, too.

Twenty minutes later, the inquest was finished when the judge said, "It looks as if we're dealing with a homicide here. I'll leave it up to our good friend the county attorney to proceed with the information we've given him today."

As the others left the courtroom, Corey sat there and said, "I think I'm in trouble."

"You sure you didn't kill him?"

"Yeah. I am."

"Give me till morning."

"What happens then?"

"Well, either my plan works or it doesn't."

"And what plan would that be?"

"No sense in getting your hopes up, Mr. Corey. You just go back to your cell now and get some sleep."

Educated people are always advising you to "examine your life." Didn't somebody famous once say, "The unexamined life isn't worth living"? Well, that's well and good if you've lived a decent life. But when you've spent your years inside a bottle—model ships aren't the only thing you can slide inside an empty whiskey bottle—you find that examining your life can be a very painful experience.

All the fights he'd picked; all the whores he'd whored with; all the ways he'd cheated, bullied and lied to the various town councils he'd worked for; all the jobs he'd gotten fired from. And most especially, the fine and lovely woman all his drinking and whoring and cheating and bullying and lying to had driven away.

17

That last one always made him feel cold and empty. And tonight in his jail cell, he'd never felt colder or emptier.

It was funny. About the only thing he *hadn't* done in his life was what he was now accused of—killing Mike Brady.

To everything else, he had to plead guilty as charged.

At seven o'clock in the morning, Corey woke up to find the marshal and young Sara Wylie standing in front of his cell door.

The marshal slid the key in and Sara, obviously happy to be saying it, said, "You're free to go. The doctor decided that Mike Brady's death was an accident after all."

"But he said there was no way—" Corey started to say.

"Well, that isn't what he's saying now," the marshal said. "Now do you want out of that cell or not?"

Corey grabbed his boots. Stomped them on and stood up. The marshal handed Corey his jacket, his gun. And then presented him with some paper money and a ticket.

"What's this?"

"Traveling money. And a train ticket. You'll be leaving town at noon. Which isn't very long from now."

"You're running me out of town?"

The marshal frowned and looked at Sara Wylie. "Miss Wylie, would you take this ingrate down to the café and try to explain to him how lucky he is not to be charged with murder?"

She led him quickly away, like an angry mother dragging a very, very bad child off for punishment.

"Why'd he change his mind?"

"He being who exactly?"

"He being the doctor who said it couldn't have been an accident."

"Because I talked to Mr. Brady late last night."

"Brady ain't no doctor."

"True, but Brady runs this town. And this town includes the doctor."

The breakfast business was still strong in the smoke-infested café. Corey had to keep rolling cigarettes in self-defense. The young lawyer lady looked hog-happy.

"You mean he told the doctor to change his mind?"

"That's right."

"Why'd he do that?"

"Because I told him if he didn't, I'd drag every man, woman and child that his son had ever abused onto the witness stand and we would destroy the Brady family name forevermore, to quote Mr. Poe's raven."

"And he went for it?"

"Of course, he went for it. What choice did he have? He's a businessman. He has to worry about his reputation. You get a couple rape victims up there—one of them I'm told was only fourteen when Mike Brady attacked her—and Brady's got himself some real trouble. So he decided that he'd just have to live with the fact that you killed his son. But he does want you on that train."

"Wait a minute. I didn't kill his son."

She made a funny face. "You didn't? Really?"

"You think I did?"

"Well, he was locked in his cell and you were the only one with the key—so who else could've killed him?"

"Anybody who came in there and saw me passed out and decided to settle a score with Brady."

"Gee, I thought for sure you killed him."

19

"I'm sorry to disappoint you."

"I wouldn't've held it against you. He deserved to be killed."

He patted his pockets. "I don't know how I'm gonna pay your bill."

"It's been taken care of."

"It has? By who?"

"By Mr. Brady. He says as long as you're on that noon train and never come back to town, he'll consider it money well spent. He said seeing you would just remind him of his son."

She stood up. "I've got to go meet a client."

Corey was still unhappy she'd marked him as the killer. "You think he killed somebody, too?"

She laughed. "No, but I do know for a fact that he burned down two barns and had some kind of carryings-on with one of Mel Fenwick's sheep."

A number of pretty ladies got on the coach in which Corey rode. They also wore summer-weight dresses and picture hats. Most of them carried carpetbags.

He tried to lose himself in their presence. Usually the sight of a pretty lady took him to a realm of ecstatic fantasies. He wanted romance as much as sex. He wanted that feeling of blind stupid glee he'd felt all those early years with his former wife.

But all he could concentrate on were the facts that a) Brady had ordered the doctor to change his autopsy report, b) Brady had ordered charges dropped and c) Brady had given him money and a ticket out of town, on the stipulation that he never return again.

Now that didn't sound right, did it?

All Corey could think of was what Hayden had told him that time, that Hayden, old man Brady and wife Debra had all turned against Mike. Could no longer tolerate him.

What if one of them had killed him?

He could think of no other reason for the charges being dropped and himself being pushed out of town.

A drunk remembers things sometimes, even after the worst of blackouts. What if Brady was afraid that Corey's memory would come back? What if Hayden had snuck in and killed Mike? Or even the old man? Or even Debra?

The train pulled out.

Corey was present in body only.

His mind was still back in town somewhere.

Four-and-a-half hours later, he left the train and went into the depot there and bought himself a ticket back to town. He had been many things in his life but he'd never been a killer. And by leaving town that was the impression he'd created.

His first stop was the general store where he bought writing supplies. He sat in the café and wrote out his letters. A lot of people stared at him. They assumed, just as that young lawyer had, that he'd killed Mike Brady. By now, the whole town knew that old man Brady had seen to it that Corey wouldn't be charged for it, not if he left town. So what the hell was he doing sitting in the café?

There was an old drunkard who did errands for folks during his few sober hours of the day. Corey gave him a dollar and told him where the letters were to be delivered. Hayden, Debra or old man Brady killed Mike Brady. The letter was designed to force the killer to reveal himself or herself.

21

He'd just sent the drunkard on his way when he saw the marshal walking toward him.

"You musn't recognize a gift from God when He puts one in your hand, Corey. Old man Brady doesn't want you here."

"I won't be here tomorrow morning. I just want everybody to know I didn't kill Mike Brady."

The marshal snorted. "You think anybody gives a damn if you did or not? They're just glad somebody did."

"Yeah but I don't want nobody thinkin' it was me. I don't kill people, Marshal. Never have, never will, not unless it's to save my own life."

The marshal glanced around the busy street. "You'd better keep out of sight, Corey. Old man Brady sees you, Lord knows what he'll do."

"Somebody's bound to tell him, anyway. I haven't exactly been hiding since I got back."

The marshal shook his head. "It's your life, Corey. All I know is I would never have come back here."

Corey shrugged. "I guess I just ain't as afraid of Brady as you folks that've lived around him for a long time."

"You get on his bad side, Corey," the marshal said, "and you'll be afraid of him soon enough. You mark my words."

He walked off down the street.

Corey got sick of people staring at him. There wasn't any particular ill-will in their stares, they were just curious about him. But as a drunkard, and a man who'd done some terrible and foolish things while trapped inside the bottle, he was tired of being a curiosity, of being sniggered at, whispered about, pointed to. A lot of elbows had been nudged into a lot of ribs when Corey walked by.

The saloon called, of course. Shot her silk skirt to reveal a good three inches of creamy white thigh, with the implied promise of showing even more as soon as he *answered* her call.

But he knew better. Knew that this was a lady who, for all her considerable and undeniable charms, had brought him only grief, sorrow and shame. Not her fault, really. His. For being so weak.

He found a good, lonely, grassy section of riverbank and sat there all afternoon, rolling cigarettes and napping a little and listening to the rush and roar of the downstream dam. He idly played loves me, loves me not with a number of flowers. He lost six times in a row. But on the seventh time he won so he gave up the game. He wasn't even sure who he had in mind, loving me and loving me not, maybe his former wife or maybe some dream girl, but it was fun to play. No matter how old and used-up a man got, loves me, loves me not was always fun to play.

The killer came at eight that night, right up on the ridge that sat above the dam.

Corey sat on a boulder, waiting to see which of the three he'd sent his letter to would show up.

> I SEEN YOU GO INTO THE MARSHAL'S
> OFFICE THE OTHER NIGHT AND KILL MIKE BRADY.
> I WILL TELL THE JUDGE IF YOU DON'T MEET
> ME AT THE DAM AT EIGHT O'CLOCK TONIGHT.

The moon was high, the breeze was so sweet-scented with spring it half drove a man crazy, he was so happy with the flowers and the river and the blooming trees and the smell of grass, he just didn't know what to do with himself.

Hayden saw him and came over.

"You're not very smart, Corey, you know that?"

"I guess that's about the only thing nobody's ever accused me of being. Smart."

"Old man Brady gave you a train ticket and money. You should've kept going."

"You killed him."

"What makes you say that?"

"I sent you the letter. You showed up, didn't you?"

Behind him, another voice said, "I showed up, too, Corey. Does that mean *I* killed him?"

A new scent, a lovely, elegant and somehow elegiac scent, was on the breeze now. A rich woman's perfume. Debra Brady came from the shadows into the moonlight.

"What're you doing here?" Corey said.

"Hayden's right," she said. She wore a white blouse and vest and black riding pants. Knee-length riding boots lent her a rich-girl air. Poor girls couldn't afford boots like that. But her voice, her manner was gentler than he remembered it. "I wish you would've just kept on going."

They stood together now. He wondered what he'd wondered when he'd talked to Hayden the other day. Wondered if there was some romantic connection between Hayden and Debra.

"Did you kill him?" Corey asked.

"What's so important about knowing?" Hayden said. "Hell, man, just walk away from it."

"I don't want people to think I'm a killer."

Hayden smirked. "They think you're everything else."

"Maybe so. But not a killer."

"Oh, what the hell," said a third voice. "We may as well

24

tell him. There isn't a damned thing he can do about it, anyway."

And from the same shadows where Debra had stepped, now stepped old man Brady.

"What're *you* doing here?" Corey said.

"Your letter. Now why the hell'd you go and write that stupid damned letter?"

"Because I want to know."

Old man Brady, who was built like a New York professional wrestler, low to the ground, wagon-wide, and possessed of a face that could intimidate Satan, came closer to Corey and said, "You already know all you need to know. He's dead and you didn't kill him."

"People don't believe that."

"People here. But you don't live here, Mr. Corey. Or you won't soon as you get on that train and stay on it. California's nice."

"I was actually thinking some about California."

"Good. Think a lot more about it. There's a train leaving here in an hour. There's still time to get yourself a ticket."

"Did you kill him, Mr. Brady?"

Brady sighed, pawed at the front of his business suit. He didn't look comfortable in a suit. Too confining in both the physical and spiritual sense.

Brady looked at Debra and Hayden. Then back at Corey.

"He raped a girl."

"I know about that," Corey said.

"This one you don't. He raped my niece's daughter. Thirteen years old. She's pregnant. My own son did that."

"He doesn't need to know all this, Mr. Brady," Hayden said.

"Hayden couldn't deal with it," Brady went on. "And neither could Debra. And neither could I. I don't know what was wrong with him. Some folks said I spoiled him and I guess I have to admit I did. But that don't mean spoiled kids go out and do the things he did. There was somethin' else wrong with him. That's why I had to have Hayden with him all the time. With my niece's daughter—"

"He knocked me out," Hayden said, "and then went into their house. She was in there alone, sleeping."

"You want to know how he died, Corey?" Brady said. "We had a meeting—Debra, Hayden and myself—and we drew straws. The one with the longest straw killed him. It didn't happen right away. We had to wait until the right time. We didn't mean to get you involved. We figured on hitting him when he was in his cell. Figured it'd look just like an accident. But then the doctor and the marshall got all hot and bothered and blamed you for it. I'm sorry it happened to you, Corey. I really am. But that's why I made the doctor change his mind and call it an accident."

Corey said, "So which of you killed him? Who drew the longest straw?"

Three passive faces stared at him. And then every one of them smiled.

Brady said, "You ever tell anybody about our little talk, Corey, and we'll just deny it."

"You ain't gonna tell me which one of you killed him?"

"No," Brady said, "we sure ain't."

All the way to California, Corey kept changing his mind. One minute he'd think it had to be Hayden. Then he'd think that it had to be old man Brady. And then he'd wonder—could a woman have done it? Why not? A ball bat or a small length of iron. Either one could do the job. Just lay it swift and hard up against a man's forehead and—

But then he'd get tired of his guessing game for a while and he'd roll himself a smoke and look out the window at the rivers and mountains and endless plains of the frontier.

California would mean a new start for him and he wasn't going to mess it up, the way he'd messed up so many other new starts. He was sure of it.

Deathman

The night before he killed a man, Hawes always followed the same ritual.

He arrived in town late afternoon—in this case, a chill shadowy autumn afternoon—found the best hotel, checked in, took a hot bath in a big metal tub, put on a fresh suit so dark it hinted at the ministerial, buffed his black boots till they shone, and then went down to the lobby in search of the best steak in town.

Because this was a town he'd worked many times before, he knew just which restaurant to choose, a place called "Ma's Gaslight Inn." Ma had died last year of a venereal disease (crazed as hell, her friends said, in her last weeks, talking to dead people and drawing crude pictures of her tombstone again and again on the wall next to her death bed).

Dusk and chill rain sent townspeople scurrying for

home, the clatter of wagons joining the clop of horses in retreat from the small, prosperous mountain town.

Hawes strode the boardwalk alone, a short and burly man handsome except for his acne-pitted cheeks. Even in his early forties, his boyhood taint was obvious.

Rain dripped in fat silver beads from the overhangs as he walked down the boardwalk toward the restaurant. He liked to look in the shop windows when they were closed this way, look at the female things—a lace shawl, a music box with a ballerina dancing atop, a ruby necklace so elegant it looked as if it had been plucked from the fat white neck of a duchess only moments ago.

Without his quite wanting them to, all these things reminded him of Sara. Three years they'd been married until she'd learned his secret, and then she'd been so repelled she invented a reason to visit her mother back in Ohio, and never again returned. He was sure she had remarried—he'd received divorce papers several years ago—and probably even had children by now. Children—and a house with a creek in back—had been her most devout wish.

He quit looking in the shop windows. He now looked straight ahead. His boot heels were loud against the wet boards. The air smelled cold and clean enough to put life in the lungs of the dead.

The player piano grew louder the closer to the restaurant he got; and then laughter and the clink of glasses.

Standing there, outside it all, he felt a great loneliness, and now when he thought of Sara he was almost happy. Having even sad memories was better than no memories at all.

He walked quickly to the restaurant door, pushed it open and went inside.

He needed to be with people tonight.

He was halfway through his steak dinner (fat pats of butter dripping golden down the thick sides of the meat and potatoes sliced and fried in tasty grease) when the tall man in the gray suit came over.

At this time the restaurant was full, low-hanging Rochester lamps casting small pools of light into the ocean of darkness. Tobacco smoke lay a haze over everything, seeming to muffle conversations. An old Negro stood next to the double doors of the kitchen, filling water glasses and handing them to the big-hipped waitresses hurrying in and out the doors. The rest of the house was packed with the sort of people you saw in mining towns—wealthy miners and wealthy men who managed the mines for eastern bosses; and hard, scrubbed-clean working men with their hard, scrubbed-clean wives out celebrating a birthday or an anniversary at the place where the rich folks dine.

"Excuse me."

Hawes looked up. "Yes?"

"I was wondering if you remembered me."

Hawes looked him over. "I guess."

"Good. Then you mind if I sit down?"

"You damn right I do. I'm eating."

"But last time you promised that—"

Hawes dismissed the man with a wave of a pudgy hand. "Didn't you hear me? I'm eating. And I don't want to be interrupted."

"Then after you're finished eating—?"

Hawes shrugged. "We'll see. Now get out of here and leave me alone."

The man was very young, little more than a kid, twenty-one, twenty-two at most, and now he seemed to wither under the assault of Hawes' intentional and practiced rudeness.

"I'll make sure you're done eating before I bother you again."

Hawes said nothing. His head was bent to the task of cutting himself another piece of succulent steak.

The tall man went away.

"It's me again. Richard Sloane."

"So I see."

The tall man looked awkward. "You're smoking a cigar."

"So I am."

"So I take it you're finished eating?"

Hawes almost had to laugh, the sonofabitch looked so young and nervous. They weren't making them tough, the way they'd been in the frontier days. "I suppose I am."

"Then may I sit down?"

Hawes pointed a finger at an empty chair. The young man sat down.

"You know what I want?" He took out a pad and pencil the way any good journalist would.

"Same thing you people always want."

"How it feels after you do it."

Hawes smiled. "You mean do I feel guilty? Do I have nightmares?"

The young man looked uncomfortable with Hawes' playful tone. "I guess that's what I mean, yes."

31

Hawes stared at the young man.

"You ever seen one, son?"

The youngster looked as if he was going to object to "son" but then changed his mind. "Two. One when I was a little boy with my uncle and one last year."

"Did you like it?"

"I hated it. It scared me the way people acted, it made me sick. They were—celebrating. It was like a party."

"Yes, some of them get that way sometimes."

Hawes had made a study of it all so he considered telling Sloane here about Tom Galvin, an Irishman of the sixteenth century who had personally hanged more than 1,600 men. Galvin believed in giving the crowd a show, especially with men accused of treason. These he not only hanged but oftentimes dismembered, throwing arms and legs to the crazed onlookers. Some reports had it that some of the crowds actually ate of the bloodied limbs tossed to them.

"You ever hang two at once?"

"The way they did in Nevada last year?" Hawes smirked and shook his head. "Not me, son. I'm not there to put on a show. I'm there to kill a man." He took a drag on his cigar. "I don't want to give my profession a bad name."

God knew that executioners, as a group, were unreliable. In seventeenth-century England, the executioner himself was put in a jail cell for eight days preceding the hanging—so officials would know he'd show up on time and sober.

"Will you sleep well tonight?"

"Very well, I hope."

"You won't think about tomorrow?"

"Not very seriously."

"How the man will look?"

"No."

"Or how the trap will sound when it opens?"

"No."

"Or how his eyes will bulge and his tongue will bloat?"

Hawes shook his head. "I know what you want, son. You want a speech about the terrible burden of being an executioner." He tapped his chest. "But I don't have it in me."

"Then it isn't a burden?"

"No, son, it isn't. It's just what I do. The way some men milk cows and other men fix buggies—I hang people. It's just that simple."

The young man looked disappointed. They always did when Hawes told them this. They wanted melodrama—they wanted regret and remorse and a tortured soul.

Hawes decided to give him the story about the woman. It wasn't the whole story, of course, but the part he always told was just what frontier newspapermen were looking for.

"There was a blonde woman once."

"Blonde?"

"So blonde it almost hurt your eyes to look at her hair in the sunlight. It was spun gold."

"Spun gold; God."

"And it was my duty to hang her."

"Oh, shit."

"The mayor of the town said I'd be hanging a woman but I never dreamt she'd be so beautiful."

"Did you hang her anyway?"

"I had to, son. It's my job."

"Did she cry?"

"She was strong. She didn't cry and her legs didn't give out when she was climbing the scaffold stairs. You know, I've seen big strapping men just collapse on those stairs and have to be carried all the way up. And some of them

33

foul their pants. I can smell the stench when I'm pulling the white hood over their eyes."

"But she was strong?"

"Very strong. She walked right over to the trap door and stood on top of it and folded her hands very primly in front of her. And then she just waited for me to come over there."

"What was she guilty of?"

"She'd taken a lover that spring, and when her husband found out he tried to kill her. But instead she killed him. The jury convicted her of first-degree murder."

"It doesn't sound like first-degree to me."

"Me either, son. But I'm the hangman; I'm not the judge."

"And so you hanged her?"

"I did."

"Didn't you want to call it off?"

"A part of me did."

"Did she scream when the door dropped away?"

"She didn't say anything."

"And her neck snapped right away?"

"I made sure of that, son. I didn't want her to dangle there and strangle the way they sometimes do. So I cinched the knot extra tight. She crossed over right away. You could hear her neck break."

"This was how many years ago?"

"Ten."

"And obviously you still think about her."

It was clear now the angle the young journalist would be taking. Hangman kills beautiful woman; can't get her out of his mind these long years later. His readers would love it.

"Oh, yes, son; yes, I still think about her."

The excitement was plain on the man's young face. Hangman kills beautiful woman, can't forget her. This may just have been the best story he'd ever had.

He flipped the cover of his pad closed. "I really appreciate this."

Hawes nodded.

The young man got up, snatched his derby from the edge of the table, and walked to the rear where the press of people and smoke and clatter was overwhelming.

Hawes took the time for another two drinks and half a Cuban cigar and then went out into the rain.

The house was three blocks away, in the opposite direction of the gallows, for which Hawes was grateful. A superstitious man, he believed that looking at a gallows the night before would bring bad luck. The man would not die clean, the trap would not open, the rope would mysteriously snap—something. And so he didn't glimpse the gallows until the morning of the execution.

Hawes came this way often. This town was in the exact center of the five-hundred-mile radius he traveled as an executioner. So he came to this town three or four times a month, not just when he had somebody to hang here.

And he always came to Maude's.

Maude was the plump giggling madam who ran the town's only whorehouse. She had an agreement with the sheriff that if she kept her house a quarter mile away from town, and if she ran her place clean, meaning no black whores or no black customers, then the sheriff would leave her alone, meaning of course he would keep at bay the zealous German Lutherans who mostly made up the town. Maude gave the lawman money but not much, and every once in awhile he'd sneak up on the back porch where one of the runaway farm girls she employed would offer the sheriff her wet glistening lips.

He could hear the player piano now, Hawes could, lonely on the rainy prairie night. He wished he hadn't told that pipsqueak journalist about the blonde woman because now Hawes was thinking about her again, and what had really happened that morning.

The house was a white two-story frame. In front, two horses were tied to a post, and down a ways a buggy dun stood ground-tied.

Hawes went up to the door and knocked.

Maude herself opened it. "Well, for shit's sake, girls, look who's here."

Downstairs there was a parlor, which was where the player piano was, and the girls sat on a couch and you chose them the way you did cattle at a livestock auction.

Hawes always asked for the same one. He looked at the five girls sitting there watching him. They were about what you'd expect for a midwestern prairie whorehouse, young girls quickly losing their bloom. They drank too much and laughed too loud and weren't always good about keeping themselves clean.

That was why he always asked for Lucy.

"She here, Maude?"

Maude winked at him. "Just taking a bath."

"I see."

"Won't be long." She knew his tastes, knew he didn't want to stay downstairs with the girls and the piano and the two cowboys who were giggling about which girls they'd pick. "You know the end room on the hall?"

"Right."

"Why don't you go up there and wait for her?"

"Good idea."

"You'll find some bourbon in the drawer."

"Appreciate it."

She winked at him again. "Hear you're hanging the Parsons boy in the morning."

"I never know their names."

"Well, take it from me, sweetie, when he used to come here he didn't tip worth a damn. Anything he gets from you, he's got coming." And then she whooped a laugh and slapped him on the back and said, "You just go right up those stairs, sweetie."

He nodded, mumbling a thank you, and turned away from her before he had to look directly at the small brown stubs of her teeth. The sight and stench of her mouth had always sickened him.

He wondered how many men had lain in this dark room. He wondered how many men had felt his loneliness. He wondered how many men had heard a woman's footsteps coming down the hall, and felt fear and shame.

Lucy opened the door. She was silhouetted in the flickering hall light. "You want me to get a lantern?"

"That's all right."

She laughed. "Never known a man who likes the dark the way you do."

She came in, closed the door behind her. She smelled of soapy bath water and jasmine. She wasn't pretty but she kept herself clean and he appreciated it.

"Should've just left my clothes off, I guess," she said. "After my bath, I mean."

He could tell she was nervous. The darkness always made her like this.

Wind and rain spattered against the window. The fingers of a dead branch scraped the glass, a curious kind of music.

She came over to the bed and stood above him. She took his hand and pressed it lightly against her sex. She was dry and warm.

"You going to move over?"

He rolled over so there was room for her. He lay on his back and stared at the ceiling.

As usual when they lay there, Lucy smoked a cigarette. She always hand-rolled two or three before coming to see Hawes because many times the night consisted of talk and nothing more.

"You want a drag?"

"No, thanks."

"How you doing?"

"All right, I guess."

"Hear you're going to hang a man tomorrow."

"Yes."

Next to him, she shuddered, her whole naked skinny body. "Forgive me for saying so, Hawes, but I just don't know how you can do it."

"You've said that before."

She laughed again. "Yes, I guess I have."

They lay there silent for a time, just the wind and the rain pattering the roof, just the occasional glow of her cigarette as she dragged on it, just his own breathing.

And the darkness; oh, yes, the darkness.

"You ever read anything by Louisa May Alcott?" Lucy asked.

"No."

"I'm reading this book by her now. It's real good, Hawes, you should read it sometime."

"Maybe I will."

That was another thing he liked about Lucy. Where most of the girls were ignorant, Lucy had gone through fourth grade before running away, and had learned to read. Hawes could carry on a good conversation with her and he appreciated that. Of course, she was older too, twenty-five or so, and that also made a difference.

They fell into silence again.

After awhile he rolled over and kissed her.

She said, "Just a minute."

She stubbed her cigarette out and then rolled back to him and then they got down to it seriously.

The fear was there as always—could he actually do it and do it right without humiliating himself?—but tonight he had no trouble.

He was good and hard and he got into her with no trouble and she responded as if she really gave a damn about him, and then he climaxed and collapsed next to her, his breath heaving in the darkness, feeling pretty damn good about himself as a man again.

She didn't say anything for a long time there in the wind and rain and darkness, smoking a cigarette again, and then she said, "That's why she left you, isn't it?"

"Huh?"

"Your wife. Why she left you."

"I'm not following you." But he was in fact following her and he sensed that she was going to say something he didn't want to hear.

"That time you got drunk up here in the room."

"Yeah? What about it?"

"You told me about your wife leaving you."

"So?"

"But you wouldn't tell me *why* she left you. You just kept saying 'She had a good reason, I guess.' Well, I finally figured out what that reason is."

He was silent for a time again, and so was she.

Obviously she could sense that she'd spooked him and now she was feeling bad about it. "I shouldn't have said anything, Hawes. I'm sorry."

"It's all right."

He was feeling the loneliness again. He wanted to cry but he wasn't a man given to tears.

"Me and my big mouth," Lucy said, lighting another cigarette.

In the flash of flame, he could see her face. Soft, freckled, eyes the blue of a spring sky.

They lay in silence a long time.

She said, "You angry at me, Hawes?"

"No."

"I'm sorry I said anything."

"I know."

"I mean, it doesn't bother me. The way you are."

"I know."

"It's kind of funny, even."

"It isn't funny to me."

And it hadn't been funny to his wife, Sara, either. Once she figured out the pattern, she'd left him immediately.

"How'd you figure it out?" he asked.

"I just started keeping track."

"Oh."

"But I won't tell anybody. I mean, if that's what's bothering you."

"I appreciate it. You keeping it to yourself, I mean."

"You can't help the way you are."

"No; no, I guess I can't."

He thought of how angry and disgusted his wife Sara had been when she'd finally understood that he was impotent all the time except for the night before a hanging. Only then could he fully become become a man.

The snap of the trap door; the snap of the neck. And then extinction. Blackness; utter, eternal blackness. And Hawes controlling it all.

In the wind and darkness, she said, "You ever think about how it'll be for you personally?"

"How what'll be?"

"Death."

"Yeah; I guess so."

"You think there're angels?"

"No."

"You think there's a heaven?"

"No."

"You think there's a God?"

"No."

She took a long drag on her cigarette. "Neither do I, Hawes. But I sure wish I did."

From down the hall, Hawes could hear a man laughing, then a woman joining in. The player piano downstairs was going again.

"Would you just hold me?" Hawes said.

"What?"

"Just hold me in your arms."

41

"Sure."

"Real tight."

"All right."

She stubbed out her cigarette and then rolled back to him.

She took him in her arms with surprising tenderness, and held him to her, her soft breasts warm against his chest, and then she said, "Sometimes, I think you're my little boy, Hawes. You know that?"

But Hawes wasn't paying attention; he was listening to the chill rain on the dark wind, and the lonely frantic laughter down the hall.

The wind grew louder then, and Lucy fell silent, just holding him tighter; tighter.

Mainwaring's Gift

He had been nine hours riding to get here, Mainwaring had, and now that he was here, he wondered if he should have come at all.

Stover was little more than two blocks of false fronts, a railroad depot, telegraph lines, and a big livery stable to handle all the drovers who came through here in the hot months.

Not even on Christmas Eve was the plain ugliness of the little town softened any. The covered candles that should have given the main street a soft glow only succeeded in showing up the worn look of the buildings and the hard, hostile faces of the people. Stover was a boastfully religious town where no liquor was served except at one hotel and a man should know better than to trouble the ladies. There were long-standing tales of men who had done such and had found themselves hanging wrist-tied and black-tongued from a tree next to the winding river to the west.

A church half a block away was furious with yellow light and even more furious with a choir singing Christmas songs. Out here on the prairie the little white box split the night with its light and sound.

Mainwaring's horse sounded lonely coming down the street, its metal shoes striking the cold-hardened ground and smashing through occasional patches of silver ice. The horse smelled of manure and sweat. Mainwaring probably didn't smell much better.

Mainwaring was a cowhand when he could be and a farmhand when he needed to be. The hell of it, here in the Territory of 1892, was that with all the bank failures, tending sheep and pigs and crops paid a lot more than tending beeves. Too many big beef men had gone bust for bankers to climb right back on.

Most of this year, his thirty-sixth, Mainwaring had spent on sixty-three acres raising shell corn and soybeans and okra. He had been to town here twice, once in March when one of the other farmhands was afraid he'd come down with cholera (but hadn't), and the other to celebrate his birthday. For only the second time in his life, Mainwaring, who'd been raised to believe in the Bible himself, had found his way to a bottle of rye. Most of that night was fuzzy but he did remember making the acquaintance of a certain woman and that was what brought him here tonight. Though he'd written her several times since going back to the farm, he'd received no reply. He figured that maybe he'd use the night of Christmas Eve to sort of accidentally see her. Maybe in his drunkenness he had offended her in some way. He hoped not.

At the end of the first block he found the hotel where he'd met the town woman.

The lobby was nearly as bright as the church. Piney-smelling Christmas decorations hung from walls and doors, and a holiday tree that seemed to be near as high as the church spire stood in one corner, casting off the warm yellow-blue-red-green hues of Christmas candles.

The people in the lobby were about what you'd expect, relatively prosperous-looking folks in three-piece banker suits and silk and organdy dresses. Only prosperous people could afford such clothes.

Within thirty seconds of him entering the lobby, a glass of hot apple cider was thrust into Mainwaring's hand by the desk clerk, a stout man with a walrus mustache, a bald and shiny head, and a genuinely friendly manner.

As he handed Mainwaring the cider, he squinted one eye and said, "You look familiar."

Mainwaring, who was usually too embarrassed to talk when he was in gatherings like this—he was well aware that he was a yokel and that these townspeople were his betters—muttered something about spending his birthday here last spring.

"Why, that's wonderful!" said the desk clerk. "I hope you enjoyed the festivities!" he said, poking Mainwaring playfully in the ribs.

Then, abruptly, the clerk stopped himself, looked around at the other guests, who were just now starting to sing more Christmas favorites, and said, "My God, you're the one."

"The one?"

"This is an unbelievable coincidence."

"What is?"

"That you're here."

"It is?"

"Tonight of all nights."

45

"What is?"

Even though he knew the cider to be nonalcoholic, Mainwaring wondered if somebody might not have put something in this fellow's drink because he just wasn't making any sense.

The desk clerk looked even more furtive now, as if he were afraid somebody might overhear their conversation. He took Mainwaring by the sleeve and drew him closer to the counter. "You came to see her, didn't you?"

"Who?"

"Who? Why Jenny, of course."

Mainwaring felt like a ten-year-old. His face got hot with blood at the implication linking them together. "Well," he said.

The clerk whispered even more softly. "Believe me, friend, you don't know how glad she's going to be to see you."

"She tell you so?" Mainwaring felt his head and heart thrum with excitement, though he tried to give the impression of being indifferent.

The clerk stared at him. "You don't know, do you?"

"Know what?"

"What happened to her."

"I guess maybe I don't."

The clerk leaned into him and nodded toward the group of people now starting to sing "Silent Night." "The people here have been awful to her."

"They have?"

"They point and they whisper and they condemn."

"Condemn?"

"Most all of them."

"But why?"

The clerk shook his head. "My God, man, can't you figure it out?"

He felt dense and more of a yokel than ever, Mainwaring did. But no matter how he berated himself for being stupid, he couldn't figure out what this man was talking about.

"Do you remember what you did that night?" the clerk asked.

Mainwaring tried a grin. "Got a little drunk."

"But that's all you remember?"

Mainwaring shrugged.

"She wasn't what she pretended to be," the clerk said.

"Huh?"

"Jenny. Don't you remember when she came into the saloon in the back there."

Mainwaring thought back and then flushed once more. "Oh. Yes. I sort of do now."

"She pretended to be a scarlet lady."

"Yes."

"But she wasn't."

"No, I didn't think so."

"She's the daughter of a man who was hanged here about a year ago for rustling some cattle. She went a little crazy after that and took to drink and wandered the streets here and gave everybody the impression that she'd become a lady of easy virtue. Sometimes she'd go out to where the mob hung him that night, and she'd stand under the tree and call out for her daddy as if he were gonna appear to her and answer." The clerk shook his head. "He never did, of course. Appear, I mean. But Jenny went right on cozying up to men and enjoying herself, so that she'd become a scandal in a town that was supposed to be without scandal. They threw her out several times but she kept coming back, kept cozying up to men in the saloon back there. But she never actually did anything with any of them."

"No?"

"No. Not until that night with you, that is."

"With me?"

"With you. She told me later on, after I'd given her some coffee and a cigarette, that she'd done it with you because there was an innocence about you that she liked and trusted. Something in your eyes, she kept saying." The clerk frowned. "Well, now that I've met you, I'd have to say you *are* a mite innocent—or something."

Somehow, Mainwaring didn't feel he was being complimented. "So what happened to her?"

"What happened? What do you think happened, fellow? She got with child. And that made her even more of a scandal. She'd walk everywhere, this unmarried woman with child, and say hello and nice day and how're you doing just as nice as pie, just as if nothing was wrong at all."

"They didn't like that, the townspeople?"

"Didn't like it? They tried threatening her out of town, and bribing her out of town, and even dragging her out of town. You know, they didn't feel it was fitting for a woman like her to show herself to our children."

"They didn't, huh?"

"Nope. But it didn't do any good. She was just as obstinate as ever. She might be gone for a day or two, but she always showed up again. Always. Then the accident happened and there wasn't much they could do, and still call themselves Christians and all."

"Accident?"

"Out near the tree where her daddy was hung."

"What happened?"

"Stagecoach. Running a couple hours late as usual and top speed. She'd been under the tree and wailing and carrying on the way she usually did, and she didn't hear the stage in the road and it ran her down."

"My Lord."

The clerk paused, his jowly face fallen into a look of despair. "She almost lost the baby. Would have if I hadn't took her in, put her in a guest room on the third floor. That's where she's been ever since."

Mainwaring raised his slate-blue eyes to the sweeping staircase before him.

"She's gonna have the baby any time now."

"She got a doctor?" Mainwaring asked.

The clerk glowered. "Nope. Only doc in town's afraid to help her because the good Christian people hereabouts won't like it. Oh, that isn't what he says, of course—he's got some other cock and bull explanation—but that's what it comes down to."

Mainwaring said, gently, "So what're you gonna do?"

The desk clerk popped his Ingram from the watch pocket of his vest and said, "Any time now, a granny woman from a farm ten miles north of here is comin' by. She's going to help her."

Mainwaring said, "You're trying to tell me this baby is mine, aren't you?"

The desk clerk laughed without humor. "Well, it took you a while to figure out what was going on here, but maybe it was worth the wait." He nodded to the stairs. "Come on."

The room was in the rear, next to a fire exit.

The desk clerk stopped him outside the door. "I'm going

49

in and talk to her a minute. Then I'll come and get you, all right?"

Mainwaring nodded.

While the clerk was gone, Mainwaring went over and looked out the back window. The night was black and starry. A quarter moon cast drab silver light on the small huddled town. Only the singing from the lobby below and the church nearby reminded Mainwaring of what night this was. He was still trying to make sense of this. He had come into town to see Jenny—all innocent enough—and now he was being told he was a father.

"She's ready for you," the clerk said when he came back. He closed the door behind him. "She's real sick, though. I wish that granny woman would get here."

Mainwaring went inside. He saw immediately what the desk clerk was talking about. The frail, blanched woman who lay belly-swollen and sweating in the middle of a jumble of covers was not the pretty fleshy girl of the spring. She had the look of all dying animals about her. Mainwaring felt scared and sick, the way he'd gotten just recently when he'd seen a foal dying in the barn hay a month ago. Animals, especially young and vulnerable animals, were Mainwaring's way of beating the loneliness of hardscrabble prairie life.

She lay on her back with her hands folded on her belly. Sweat had made her blond hair dark and her gray skin sleek.

He walked up to her and put his hand out and touched her folded hands.

"Hello," he said.

She opened her eyes then and he saw immediately how far gone she was.

She smiled, "I told him you'd come. Somehow."

"I came all right."

"Oscar said he told you about me and the baby."

"Oscar?"

"The desk clerk, Oscar Stern. You believe him?"

"That I'm the father?"

She nodded.

"Yes, ma'am, I do." His hat in his hand, gripping it now, he said "I hope I didn't—force you into anything that night."

"You didn't." She sounded as if even speaking were difficult. "I got your letters."

"You did?"

"Yes."

"How come you didn't write? I sat there in my cabin at night and thought you didn't want nothing more to do with me."

She closed her eyes. "I guess I was afraid you wouldn't believe me. I figured you'd think that maybe some other man . . ."

She convulsed then, her fragile body threatening to snap in two. She moaned and he saw her eyes begin to dilate.

He turned and opened the door. "That granny lady here yet?" he asked Oscar Stern.

Just as Oscar was about to speak, a short woman in some kind of cape came up the stairs. She had a pipe in one corner of her mouth, a furious glare in her brown eyes, and a curse coming from her lips.

Suddenly, Mainwaring saw what she was angry about.

Right behind her came a tall, severe man in a cleric's collar and three hefty women in their holiday finery.

The granny woman pushed past Mainwaring and the desk clerk and went inside.

The minister spoke first. "Oscar, even though you're of another faith, this town has striven to abide our differences. But we've warned you all along what would happen if you permitted this woman to have her child within these city limits."

Oscar Stern said, "Even though I'm not a Christian, Pastor, I'm trying hard to act like one. Somebody's got to care for that girl."

"Not in this town they don't," said one of the ladies.

"We have a wagon downstairs," the minister said. "We plan to take her out to the Kruse farm where a midwife there will take care of her. We just don't want a . . ."

"We don't want an unmarried woman having her child in our town," said another of the women. "What kind of example do you think that sets?"

The minister was getting himself ready for another round of rhetoric, patting his silver hair and swelling his chest, when Mainwaring stepped forward.

"Anybody tries to move that woman," he said, "I'll get my rifle and kill him on the spot."

"My Lord," said the third woman. "Who is this man?"

"I happen," Mainwaring said, "to be the father."

Grave looks of displeasure crossed the faces of the four visitors. The minister looked as if he wanted to spit something awful-tasting from his mouth. He looked Mainwaring up and down and said, "I must say, you're just about the sort of man I would have expected to be the father."

"You get out of here now," Mainwaring told them. "Oscar Stern owns the hotel and it's his rules we abide by here."

One of the women started to say something.

Glaring, Mainwaring pointed his finger at her as if it

were a weapon. The woman looked outraged and then she looked frightened.

"After tonight, Oscar," the minister said, "you may as well put this place up for sale. You won't be living in Stover much longer. I can promise you that."

The religious entourage left.

The granny woman, who had obviously been listening, stuck her head out the door and said, "One of you lazy-bones get in here. I need some help."

Birthing was scissors and thread and cloverine salve; birthing was sulfur and wine of cordia; birthing was cutting the cord and tying it off and dressing the baby; birthing was taking all the afterbirth, including the umbilical cord and placenta, and burying it out in the alley. After all this, the granny woman greased the infant's navel cord with castor oil and then added some powder to the oil.

During all this, Mainwaring sat in the room, terrified and joyous simultaneously, jumping up whenever the granny woman summoned him, carrying hot water and clean rags, ointment and liniment and salve.

When it was all over, when the infant was revealed to be a girl and Jenny herself was collapsed into an exhausted sleep, the granny woman left the child with Oscar and took Mainwaring out into the hall.

"You can see what's going on in there."

"Ma'am?"

"Jenny. She's dying."

Mainwaring felt colder than any winter night had ever made him feel. There was the unaccustomed sting of hot tears in his eyes. He said, "I love her."

"Right now, it's that little girl you've got to worry about."

"But—"

The granny woman said, "I know you love Jenny, son. But now, that don't matter. It's that child that matters."

Mainwaring went back inside the room. The granny woman gave him the infant and then left the room.

For half an hour Mainwaring sat next to the bed with dying Jenny. Occasionally she'd mutter something deep in the down-fathoms of her sleep, something that had the word *daddy* or *father* in it.

When the baby squalled, Mainwaring shushed and rocked it, thinking of all the tiny animals he had befriended over the years. This was the tiniest and most special animal of them all. His own daughter.

Finally, Jenny opened her eyes. Her mouth was parched and she could barely speak, but she spoke anyway. She smiled and looked up and touched their little girl there in Mainwaring's arms and said, "My daddy said she's beautiful."

Mainwaring said nothing.

"I saw my daddy just now. He's waiting for me."

Mainwaring felt the tears again and held the baby tighter.

"I'm sorry for how all this happened," Jenny said. "I should've written you back."

Mainwaring just shook his head.

"I want her to love you as much as I love my daddy," she said.

"I'm gonna give her every reason to love me," Mainwaring said. "I'm gonna be the best daddy she could ask for."

Jenny put her long, slender hand to Mainwaring's

cheek. "You're not the smartest or the prettiest man I ever saw, Mainwaring, but I honestly do believe you're the best. And that's why I'm so glad I'm leaving her in your care."

He wasn't sure when she died—whether it was when she sighed and her entire body trembled; or when her face turned away from her little girl, toward the wall; or when her hand stretched out briefly in the air as if she were taking an unseen hand in her own—but when he leaned down to kiss her forehead and felt the stone coldness there, he knew.

He sat with his child in his arms, not even noticing how she cried now, just gently rocking her and looking at the dead woman, feeling occasionally the tears in his eyes and the hard unbidden lump in his throat.

After a time, Oscar Stern and the granny woman came back in. The granny woman saw to Jenny and the infant, and Oscar saw to Mainwaring.

"Where you going tonight, son?"

Mainwaring shook his head. "I'm not going to stay here. Probably start back for the farm."

"You think you can handle that infant?"

"The owner's got a wife and a young daughter. They'll help."

Oscar frowned. "Don't blame you for wanting to get out of this town. I'll be leaving it myself soon enough."

Mainwaring put out his hand. "I want to thank you."

"I should be thanking you, Mainwaring. You brought Jenny and me together, and she was one of the few decent people I've known in this place."

Mainwaring went back inside the room. Alone there, the door closed, he knelt beside the dead woman and held her hand for a long and silent time. There were no tears now, nor any unbidden lump in his throat, just his wonderment at her goodness and her grace, and his wish that he'd had time to know her well and love her as all his life he had longed to love a woman.

He stood up, went out and said good-bye to Oscar and the granny woman, and then he set off with the child.

Just as he was leaving town, he heard the church bell celebrate another birth on this night nearly two thousand years ago, and he wondered if people so soured by righteousness and so empty of compassion would love even Jesus if he were to come back.

He rode on, Mainwaring did, hard into the dark night and on Christmas morning crested a hill from which he could see the farm below. He could see smoke from its chimney and hear children singing carols. Farmers from all over the valley had gathered in this house.

Just before he took the horse down the rocky hill, he looked at his swaddled baby and smiled. During the night he had realized that he did, after all, have a woman to love.

His daughter.

Dance Girl

At the time of her murder, Madge Tucker had been living in Cedar Rapids, two blocks west of the train depot, for seven years.

After several quick interviews with other boarders in the large frame rooming house, investigating officers learned that Madge Evelyn Tucker had first come to the city from a farm near Holbrook in 1883. At the time she'd been seventeen years old. After working as a clerk in a millinery store, where her soft good looks made her a mark for young suitors in straw boaters and eager smiles, she met a man named Marley who owned four taverns in and around the area of the Star Wagon Company and the Chicago and Northwestern Railyards. She spent the final five years of her life being a dance girl in these places. All this came to an end when someone entered her room on the night of August 14, 1890.

A Dr. Baines, who was substituting for the vacationing

doctor the police ordinarily used, brought a most peculiar piece of information to the officer in charge. After examining Madge Evelyn Tucker, he had come to two conclusions—one being that she'd been stabbed twice in the chest and the second being that she had died a virgin.

One did not expect to hear about a dance girl dying a virgin.

Two months later, just as autumn was turning treetops red and gold and brown, a tall, slender young man in a dark Edwardian suit and a Homburg stepped from the early morning Rock Island train and surveyed the platform about him. He was surrounded by people embracing each other—sons and mothers, mothers and fathers, daughters and friends. A shadow of sorrow passed over his dark eyes as he watched this happy tableau. Then, with a large-knuckled hand, he lifted his carpetbag and began walking toward the prosperous downtown area, the skyline dominated by a six-story structure that housed the Cedar Rapids Savings Bank.

He found a horse-drawn trolley, asked the driver where he might find a certain cemetery, and sat back and tried to relax as two plump women discussed the forthcoming election for mayor.

For the rest of the ride, he read the letters he kept in his suit coat. The return address was always the same, as was the name. Madge Evelyn Tucker. Just now, staring at her beautiful penmanship, tears formed in his eyes. He realized that the two women who had been arguing about the present mayor had stopped talking and were staring at him.

Rather than face their scrutiny, he got off the trolley at the next block and walked the remaining distance to the cemetery.

* * *

He wondered, an hour and a half later, if he had not come
to Cedar Rapids on the worst sort of whim. Perhaps his
grief over his dead sister Madge was undoing him. Hadn't
Mr. Staley at the bank where Richard Tucker worked suggested a "leave of absence"? What he'd meant, of course,
was that Richard was behaving most strangely and that
good customers were becoming upset.

Now Richard crouched behind a wide oak tree. In the
early October morning, the sky pure blue, a chicken hawk
looping and diving against this blue, Richard smelled grass
burning in the last of the summer sun and heard the song
of jays and bluebirds and the sharp resonating bass of distant prowling dogs.

It would be so pleasant just to sit here uphill from the
place where she'd been buried. Just sit here and think of
her as she'd been. . . .

But he had things to do. That was why a Navy Colt
trembled in his big hand. That was why his other hand
kept touching the letters inside his jacket.

By three P.M. the man had not come. By four P.M. the man
had not come. By five P.M. the man had not come.

Richard began to grow even more nervous, hidden behind
the oak and looking directly down at his sister's headstone.
Perhaps the man had come very early in the morning, before
Richard's arrival. Or perhaps the man wasn't coming at all.

A rumbling wagon of day workers from a construction
site came past the iron cemetery fence, bringing dust and
the smell of beer and the cheer of their worn-out laughter
with them. Later, a stagecoach, one of the few remaining
in service anywhere in the Plains states, jerked and jostled

past, a solitary passenger looking bored with it all. Finally, a young man and woman on sparkling new bicycles came past the iron fence. He saw in the gentle lines of the woman's face Madge's own gentle lines.

I tried to warn you, Madge.

His remembered words shook him. All his warnings. All his pleadings. For nothing. Madge, good sweet Madge, saw nothing wrong in being a dance girl, not if you kept, as she always said, "your virtue."

Well, the doctor had said at her death that her virtue had indeed remained with her.

But virtue hadn't protected her from the night of August 14. It hadn't protected her at all.

Dusk was chill. Early stars shone in the gray-blue firmament. The distant dogs now sounded lonely.

Crouched behind the oak, Richard pulled his collar up and began blowing on his hands so the knuckles would not feel so raw. Below, the graveyard had become a shadowy place, the tips of granite headstones white in the gloom.

Several times he held his Ingram watch up to the light of the half-moon. He did this at five-minute intervals. The last time, he decided he would leave if nothing happened in the next five minutes.

The man appeared just after Richard had finished consulting his watch.

He was a short man, muscular, dressed in a suit and wearing a Western-style hat. At the cemetery entrance, he looked quickly about, as if he sensed he were being spied upon, and then moved without hesitation to Madge's headstone.

The roses he held in his hand were put into an empty

vase next to the headstone. The man then dropped to his knees and made a large and rather dramatic sign of the cross.

He was so involved in his prayers that he did not even turn around until Richard was two steps away. By then it was too late.

Richard shot the man three times in the back of the head—the man who had never been charged with the murder of Richard's sister.

On the train that night, Richard took out the letter in which Madge had made reference to the man in the cemetery. Cletus Boyer, the man's name had been. He'd been a clerk in a haberdasher's and was considered quite a ladies' man.

He met Madge shortly after she became a dance girl. He made one terrible mistake. He fell in love with her. He begged her to give up the taverns but she would not. This only seemed to make his love the more unbearable for him.

He began following her, harassing her, and then he began slapping her.

Finally, Madge gave up the dance hall. By now, she realized how much Cletus loved her. She had grown, in her way, to love him. She took a job briefly with Greene's Opera House. Cletus was to take her home to meet his parents, prominent people on the east side. But over the course of the next month, Madge saw that for all he loved her, he could never accept her past as a dance girl. He pleaded with her to help him in some way—he did not want to feel the rage and shame that boiled up in him whenever he thought of her in the arms of other men. But not even her assurances that she was still a virgin helped. Thinking of her as a dance girl threatened his sanity.

61

All these things were told to Richard in the letter. One more thing was added.

Whenever he called her names and struck her, he became paralyzed with guilt. He brought her gifts of every sort by way of apology. "I don't know what to do, Brother. He is so complicated and tortured a man." Finally, she broke off with him and went back to the taverns.

As the train rattled through the night, the Midwestern plains silver in the dew and moonlight, Richard Tucker sat now feeling sorry for the man he'd just killed.

Richard supposed that in his way Cletus Boyer really had loved Madge.

He sighed, glancing at the letter again.

The passage about Cletus bringing gifts of apology had proved to Richard that Boyer was a sentimental man. And a sentimental killer, Richard had reasoned, was likely to become especially sentimental on the day of a loved one's birthday. That was how Richard had known that Cletus would come to the cemetery today. A sentimental killer.

Richard put the letter away and looked out again at the silver prairie, hoarfrost and pumpkins on the horizon line. A dread came over him as he thought of his job in the bank and the little furnished room where he lived. He felt suffocated now. In the end, his life would come to nothing, just as his sister's life had come to nothing, just as Cletus Boyer's life had come to nothing. There had been a girl once but now there was a girl no longer. There had been the prospect of a better job once, but these days he was too tired to pursue one. Dragging himself daily to the bank was easier—

The prairie rushed past. And the circle of moon, ancient and secret and indifferent, stood still.

The world was a senseless place, Richard knew as the train plunged onward into the darkness. A senseless place.

Guild and the Indian Woman

That was the autumn President Chester Alan Arthur fought hard for higher tariffs (or at least as hard as President Chester Alan Arthur ever fought for anything), and it was the autumn that Britain occupied Egypt. It was also the year that Leo Guild, a bounty hunter who sometimes described himself as a "free-lance lawman," pursued through the northeastern edge of the territory a man named Rogers. It was said that Rogers had killed a woman in the course of a bank robbery, though by all accounts the woman had been killed accidentally when Rogers tripped and the gun misfired. Guild did not care about the "accidentally" part. The owners of the bank were offering a $750 reward for Rogers. The spring and summer had not exactly made Guild a rich man, so finding Rogers became important. The search went two months and one week and ended in a town called Drayton, where there had been a recent outbreak of cholera, eighteen citizens dead, and three times as many sick. On a public notice listing the dead, Guild saw Rogers's name. But not being an especially trusting man, Guild went down the board sidewalk between the one- and two-story frame false fronts, alongside the jingle and clang and squeak of freight wagons and farm wagons and buggies, and found the local doctor's office.

Guild sat in Dr. McGivern's waiting room while, from behind the door, he heard McGivern giving instructions to a man who coughed consumptively. Guild touched the knife scar on the cleft of his chin and then rubbed his leg, still stiff from a boyhood riding accident. The injury caused him to limp slightly, especially now that gray November cold had set in.

He sat on a tufted leather couch across from a matching chair and beneath two paintings of very idyllic Indians looking noble in profile at breathtaking sunsets. The territory had not been kind to Indians (and for that matter, Indians, except perhaps for the Mesquakie, had not been kind to the territory), so it was unlikely you'd find such specimens as these in the paintings. On a table in front of the couch was a row of books held upright by bookends molded into the shape of lions' heads. Books by Longfellow, Hugo, Browning, and Tennyson shared space with medical books entitled *The Ladies' Medical Guide* by Dr. S. Pancoast, *Science of Life or Creative and Sexual Science* by Professor O. S. Fowler, and *Robb's Family Physician*. In a corner of the waiting room a potbellied stove glowed red with soft coal behind its grates.

The door opened and a stubby man with watery eyes and filthy, shapeless clothes emerged. He needed a shave and a bath. With the coast-to-coast railroad tracks and another cycle of bank failures, the territory was home to many men like him. Drifting. Dead in certain spiritual respects. Just drifting. Guild knew he was cleaner and stronger and smarter, but he was probably not very different from this man. So he was careful not to allow himself even the smallest feeling of superiority.

"You take this syrup for seven days and get all the rest you can and you'll be fine," Dr. McGivern said, following his patient into the waiting room. He was a tall, slender man in a three-piece undertaker's suit. He had the prissy mouth and pitiless eyes of a parson. He was pink bald and had a pair of store-boughts that gave his mouth an eerie smile even though he wasn't smiling at all. Guild, who tended to like people or not like people right off, did not like the doctor a whit.

The doctor put out his hand, and the coughing man put some coins in the doctor's palm.

"You sure it ain't the consumption, then?" the man said, obviously afraid.

"If it is, you'll know soon enough," the doctor said. His voice was as hard as his eyes. The patient had wanted something to be said softer. More reassuring. There was nothing soft about the doctor at all.

After the man left, the doctor pulled out a gold watch from his black vest pocket, consulted it importantly, and said, "I have a meeting at the bank in ten minutes." He pointed to his inner chamber. "Let's go in and have a look at you."

"I'm not here on medical business," Guild said. His dislike of the man was obvious in his voice. Maybe too obvious. Guild thought about the drifter who'd just left, thought about his fear. The doctor could have set his mind to rest.

Hell, that should be a doctor's most important duty, anyway, even more than dispensing medicine. Setting minds to rest.

Now the doctor dropped all semblance of patience. "You don't look like a drummer, and I'm through buying cattle for my ranch. So just what would your business be?"

"I want to make sure a man died."

"What man?"

"Lyle Thomas Rogers. Cholera. Few weeks ago."

"You're a relative?"

"I was trying to locate him."

"Now there's a nice ambiguous sentence."

Guild looked back at the books on the table of the waiting room. The doctor was obviously an educated man, and spoke like one.

"Your business is what, exactly?" the doctor said.

"I'm a free-lance lawman."

"Meaning?"

Guild felt as if he were five years old and being challenged by a teacher. "Meaning, sometimes I track people."

This time the store-boughts really did smile. "My God, what vultures you people are. You're a bounty hunter." The doctor stuffed his watch back into his vest pocket and laughed. His laugh was hard, too. "You were tracking this Lyle Thomas Rogers, but death cheated you out of a bounty, is that it?"

"Then you buried him?"

"I did indeed." He spoke now with obstinate pleasure.

Guild fixed his Stetson back on. He wanted to go down the street to the restaurant and have sausage and eggs and fried potatoes, and then he wanted to go over to one of the saloons and have a single shot of bourbon, and then he wanted to leave town.

Guild was about to thank the doctor for his time when the door opened up and a small Mesquakie Indian woman came in. She was barely five feet. She was probably in her sixties, or maybe even her seventies. She was dressed in a shabby gingham dress and a shawl. She wore tawny scuffed leather moccasins and thick green socks. She had a small, fierce nose and disturbing, dark eyes. She had so many facial wrinkles, she reminded Guild of the monkeys in the St. Louis Zoo.

"Ko ta to," the doctor said, pronouncing her name with a precision that was a bit too educated to seem comfortable. "What are you doing here?"

Guild got the odd impression the doctor was afraid of the woman.

Then he knew why.

From inside her shawl she took a Colt Peacemaker, nine long silver inches of barrel, and proceeded to put two bullets in the doctor's face, and two more in his chest.

McGivern barely had time to scream before he slumped to the floor.

The small room, with its flowered wallpaper and comfortable hooked rugs, felt alien now. Gunsmoke lent the air tartness, and the gunshots, so many and so close, had deafened Guild momentarily.

He started to draw his own Navy Colt, but the Indian woman said, "It is not necessary. It was only McGivern I wanted to harm." She handed Guild the Colt and said, "You will walk with me to the sheriff's office?"

The sheriff was named Lynott. He was fifty something, as tall as Guild, white-haired. He wore an impressive silver star on the flap pocket of his gray wool shirt, and an identical star on the front of his brown Stetson. Apparently he wanted you to make no mistake about who was sheriff in Drayton.

He poured Guild's coffee into a tin cup and then handed it over across the desk and said, "You going to take your eyes down from my wall?"

"It's my business," Guild said, referring to the rows of wanted posters the sheriff had thumbtacked to a section of the green east wall. The sheriff's office was a busy place. A civilian Negro drug bucket and mop along and scrubbed the already clean floors while deputies in khaki pushed sad and angry prisoners into and out of the cell block, most likely back and forth to a nearby courthouse. Behind Guild in the big, clean offices sat a deputy with his feet up on the desk and a Winchester .22 repeating rifle in his lap. Another deputy worked laboriously over a typewriter using two fingers.

Lynott said, "I want you to think real careful."

"Hell."

"What?"

"She didn't say anything, Lynott. Nothing that meant anything. You've asked me four times."

"She just walked in and looked at him and shot him?"

"That's about it."

"But not a word more?"

"She asked me if I'd walk her over here."

"Now, why the hell would Ko ta to want to shoot the doctor?"

"Go ask her."

"She's sittin' back there, and she won't say a word. I sent in a priest, I sent in a minister. I sent in a female newspaper editor, and she won't say a word. Not a damn word."

"She got any kin?"

Lynott shrugged. "There's a small group of wickiups near

69

up the boots. Mesquakies. Harmless, pretty much. Guess I'm gonna have to ride up there." Lynott looked very unhappy.

The deputy with the Winchester in his lap said, "They're still out there." From where he sat, he could see out the window.

Lynott said to Guild, "The whole town's upset. Take a look out the window."

Sighing—he wanted to leave; he'd been here nearly three hours now—Guild drug himself to his feet and looked out through the barred window and saw several small groups of citizens along the two-block expanse of board sidewalk. Some of the men wore homburgs. Some of the women wore sateen wrappers. It was getting to be a fancy place, Drayton was. Most likely the town would be like this—everybody whispering, speculating—until the old lady was sent to prison.

"He pretty popular?" Guild said, coming away from the window.

"Nope."

"Thought docs usually were."

"Cold type."

Guild thought about McGivern, recalling the way he'd treated the drifter. "Guess he was." Guild stayed on his feet, finished his coffee.

Lynott said, "I'd like you to stay around for at least the night. Inquest'll be tomorrow morning. All the goddamn rules and regs we got in this territory, I've got to be sure and do this right."

"I'm kind of flat. Hotel rooms cost money."

"Not when your cousin owns the hotel."

"Meaning the cousin would put me up free?"

"His name's Pete. Tell him you're my guest."

"I won't argue against a bed and clean sheets."

Lynott smiled. "Who said they'll be clean?"

The Parker House surprised him. Not only were the sheets clean, there were attractive young housemaids with courteous manners. Posters advertised a viola concerto by one Mrs. Robertson after supper. Being three weeks from a tub, Guild took advantage of the sheriff's largesse by taking a cigar and a magazine and then sitting in a hot, sudsy tin tub for half an hour. Such moments could sometimes be perilous because they gave him too much time to think, to remember. Stalking a man four years earlier, he'd made a terrible and unforgivable mistake. By accident he'd killed a six-year-old girl. A jury had reluctantly found him not guilty. Guild wished he could render the same verdict unto himself, but as his nightmares and vexations proved, he could not. Occasionally, though he was a Lutheran, he went to Catholic Confession, and sometimes that helped. Sometimes.

He ate a combination of breakfast and lunch and then went out into the streets. Guild always knew when there'd been a killing in a town. Despite the way Eastern papers liked to depict the territory, a terrible reverence was paid to murder here, and one could see that reverence—part anger, part fear (any death reminded you of your own), part excitement—on the faces of even the children.

As he made his way to a saloon down toward a spur in the tracks, he watched dead brown leaves scratch across the broad sidewalk, and he watched how people huddled into their heavy winter clothes. He wondered where he was going to spend the winter.

A railroad maintenance gang filled most of the saloon, farm kids mostly loud in their lack of book learning and zest for what they saw as "the city." They kept the player piano going and they kept the bartender going and they kept the single percentage going, several of the more eager ones dancing dances that made up in intensity what they lacked in grace. The percentage girl just looked sad. Guild felt uncomfortable watching her. Sometimes you wanted to help people. Usually there was nothing one could do. The sawdust on the floor needed sweeping out and replacing. It was tangy with hops and vomit. A drummer in a black double-breasted Chesterfield coat and a bowler sat at the end of the bar cadging slices of ham and cheese and slapping them with a curious precision to wide white slices of potato bread. Hard wind rattled the single glass window. Guild, standing at the bar, felt alone and old.

Guild had had two schooners and a shot of house bourbon, more than he'd intended for this time of day, when a voice said, "I understand you were the last person to see my father alive."

When he turned around, he saw one of those rarities—a son who looked an exact replica of his father. Usually the mother got in there somewhere—tilt of nose, color of eyes—but not in this case. The son was maybe thirty and already pink bald, and he carried himself with the same air of formality and peevishness his father had. He even wore the same kind of black three-piece suit. People grieved differently. Apparently for this man, anger was the worst part of the process because he looked as if he were barely able to keep himself under control.

Guild said, "I'm sorry about your father."

"I appreciate that." His tone said that Guild was wasting his time. "But I'm wondering what he said."

"He didn't have time to say anything."

"He just died?"

"He was shot with four bullets very quickly." Guild did not care for the son any more than he had the father.

"How about the Indian woman?"

Guild decided he was being unfair. Maybe these questions were the only way he could deal with his father's death. Guild said, "Why don't I buy you a drink and we'll leave the sheriff to figure it out."

"I'd really like an answer to my question."

"About the Indian woman?"

"Yes."

"She didn't say anything, except would I walk her to the sheriff's office."

"You're sure?"

"I'm sure."

Then the man did the damnedest thing of all. Obviously without meaning to, he sighed and smiled, as if a great and abiding relief had just washed through him. Then he said, "My name's Robert McGivern, Mr. Guild, and I'd be happy to have that drink with you."

Before suppertime, Guild decided to take a nap. He'd had many more drinks with Mr. Robert McGivern than he'd intended. McGivern was a strange one, no doubt about it, and one reason Guild had wanted to drink with him was to see when he'd break and show some simple human loss, but he hadn't. He'd talked about his importing business and he'd talked about his beautiful wife and his two beautiful children. He'd talked about the trips to New York City he took twice a year, and he'd talked about the territory someday becoming a state. But after finding out that neither his father nor the Indian woman had said anything to Guild, young

73

McGivern seemed to lose interest in the subject. Guild wondered what McGivern had been so afraid might be revealed.

Spindly branches rasped against the window glass as the November night deepened. Guild kept the kerosene lamp burning low. The light was a kind of company. He slept for an hour. He had a dream about the girl. She was dead now and in another realm. She stretched out her hand for Guild. He was afraid to take it. He wanted to take it but he was afraid. When the knocking came and woke him, he recalled the dream precisely, but he had no idea why he'd been afraid to take her hand. None at all.

He took his Navy Colt from the nightstand, stood up in his red long johns, and walked across the floor in the white winter socks he'd put on after bathing that morning. "Yes?" he said.

"Mr. Guild?"

"Yes."

"My name is Wa pa nu ke."

The name was Mesquakie. "What do you want?"

"I want to ask you some questions about my grandmother. She is the one who killed Dr. McGivern."

"Just a minute."

Guild went over and pulled on his serge trousers and then his boots. Then he went over to the bureau and poured water from a clay pitcher into a clay basin. He washed his face. He took a piece of Adams Pepsin Celery chewing gum, folded it in half, and then put it in his mouth. He picked up his Navy Colt again, and then went to let the Mesquakie into his room.

Wa pa nu ke turned out to be a chunky man in his twenties with a bad complexion and dark, guilty eyes. He wore loose denim clothes that accommodated his bulk. Guild could see that his ornate moccasins were decorated with deer's hair for the cold. He sensed a deep anger buried in the young Indian man, but he also sensed a curious temerity. It was not good to be red in a white man's world. Guild supposed it was that simple.

In five minutes Wa pa nu ke made his case very clear. He believed that his grandmother was perfectly justified in killing the doctor.

"That's probably not a very smart thing to say out loud, at least not in Drayton," Guild said. He had turned the kerosene lamp up. Shadows gave the room a kind of beauty.

"If only my sister would tell me what happened."

"Your sister?"

"Yes, my mother died years ago of consumption. My grandmother raised us. She was like our mother. Something happened over the past five months, but my sister and grandmother would not tell me what. And I was gone during most of it."

"Gone where?"

"A railroad job. The Rock Island has Indian gangs."

"I see."

The Mesquakie glared at Guild. For the first time Guild sensed the man's pride. He was here to ask a favor—that was becoming obvious—but he did not much like asking white men for favors. Not much at all.

"The sheriff should talk to your sister," Guild said.

"In the first place, my sister will talk to no one. No one. In the second place, even if my sister told him something, he would not believe her. She's a Mesquakie."

Guild got out his pack of gum and offered Wa pa nu ke a stick. The Indian declined.

75

"I need your help, Mr. Guild."

"There really isn't much I can do."

"I have asked about you. You are a 'free-lance lawman,' I am told."

Guild smiled. "That's something of a misnomer, I'm afraid. Sometimes people don't like the phrase 'bounty hunter.' Sometimes I don't like it myself. So I say 'free-lance lawman.' It doesn't mean anything."

"I'd like you to come out in the morning and talk to my sister. All she does is sob. She just keeps saying that she would like to help my grandmother, but that my grandmother would be angry if she tried."

"You really should talk to Lynott."

"I've told you about Lynott."

"It's not my concern."

"I have money saved from the Rock Island."

Guild sighed. The young Indian was as busted as Guild himself was. But he was willing to give it up. What choice did Guild have?

"Tell me where your wickiup is?" Guild said.

"Do you want to be paid now?"

"How much you got saved, kid?"

"Eighty dollars."

"I'm going to try something first, and if that doesn't work, then I'll ride out to your wickiup. I'll want ten dollars."

"Only ten? I don't understand."

The Indian was as poor as Guild. "You don't need to."

For dinner Guild had steak, boiled potatoes, cabbage, sod corn, and beer. This was served in the cramped but nicely appointed dining room of the Parker House. He was smoking an Old Virginia cheroot and enjoying the way the light from the yellow brass Rochester lamps played off the red hair of a woman dining across the way. Then Lynott came in wearing his two badges (coat and Stetson) and came over and sat down at Guild's table. Lynott smelled of cigarettes and winter.

Guild said, "I was going to look you up tonight."

"I take it Wa pa nu ke came to see you."

"How'd you know that?"

"I listened to him talking to his grandmother in the jail house."

"You always eavesdrop that way?"

"Judge wants me to. Says what I hear can help him make a case he might not be able to otherwise."

Guild shrugged. "Makes sense."

"So you going to?"

"Going to what?"

"Help him?" Then Lynott nodded with his big badge-covered Stetson. "You got another cheroot?"

"You're the one gainfully employed, and I'm handing out the cheroots," Guild said wryly. "You'd think I was running for office." He set one down and Lynott took it.

Lynott lit up with a lucifer. He made rings exhaling. He said, "I don't really give a damn if you want to get involved, but it won't change the outcome any."

"You're not curious?"

"About why she shot him?"

"Yep."

"Nope."

"Why not?"

"It'd just keep things stirred up, an investigation." He had some more of his cheroot. It seemed to give him pleasure. He said, "Anyway, as I said, it won't change any-

77

thing. You saw her shoot him in cold blood, right?"

"Right."

"And you're willing to testify to that, right?"

"Right."

"So who gives a damn why she shot him. She just shot him and that's it and that's all."

Guild said, "You know the son well? Robert?"

Lynott surprised him by flushing. Guild hadn't even been fishing particularly. But there it was. No reason at all for Lynott to get disturbed by the mention of the young McGivern, but he was very much disturbed.

"Some, I guess."

"We had some liquor today. He talks about himself a lot. One of the things he talked about was how important he was, what with being majority stockholder in the bank and all. Is he important?"

"I guess." Lynott still looked uneasy. His cigar didn't seem to give him any pleasure. He kept touching his chest as if he had pains or gas. In the hazy yellow of the Rochester lamp he seemed old now, his hair very white, the skin of his face loose and sad.

"Is he important enough that if he asked you not to investigate, you'd oblige him?"

"That supposed to mean something?"

"It means what it means."

"No reason for us not to be friends, Guild." Lynott smiled. "You being a 'free-lance lawman' and all."

"I didn't like him."

"Robert?"

"Yep."

"Don't much myself."

"Then why help him out?"

"I'm fifty-eight. Drayton's supposed to retire me in two years with a pension. I've got a signed contract to that effect. Why jeopardize that—especially when lookin' into it won't change anything, anyway? She shot him and you're the witness and the subject's closed."

Guild wanted another bourbon, but he recalled the state of his finances. He said, "Since I provided the smoke, how about you providing the next drink?"

Lynott grinned. "Sure. My cousin Pete serves me free, anyway."

Guild said, "Maybe it's time I get myself a cousin named Pete."

In the morning Guild followed the directions Wa pa nu ke had given him. Guild rode at a trot along a stage road through the plains where everything in the light of the low gray sky looked forlorn, grass and sage and bushes all brown. Frost silvered much of the ragged undergrowth. Hermit thrushes and meadowlarks sounded cold. Guild huddled into his wool coat, collar upturned. His roan's nose was slick where snot had frozen. In five miles the terrain changed abruptly. The ground rose into scoria buttes of red volcanic rock. Below, where two magpies perched on an old buffalo skull, lay a valley. He brought the roan to the edge of it, and there on the red rock surface below (he had read newspaper speculation that the surface of the moon would look like this), he saw the wickiups. There were seven of them. They were shabby structures made of brush and saplings. You could smell prairie dog on the air. The Mesquakies, impoverished, ate prairie dogs frequently. Guild led the roan carefully down through the small, loose, treacherous rocks.

79

A malnourished mutt joined him soon, yipping at the roan. Then three Mesquakie elders appeared. They wore heavy clothing that was a mixture of white man and red man. They each wore huge necklaces made of animal bone and teeth. The eldest carried a long, carved stick that appeared to be a cane. He came up to Guild's roan and said, "You are the man Wa pa nu ke told us about?"

"Yes."

"Then would you leave, please? We are old here, and we do not trouble the white man. We do not want the white man to trouble us."

"I would like to see his sister."

"She has been ill for two months. She is ill even yet."

A few more Mesquakies drifted from their wickiups. They looked as old and malnourished as the dog who had snapped at the roan.

Guild dismounted. For effect he took his Winchester from its scabbard. Winchesters had a way of impressing people. Particularly old people with no defenses.

"I can only ask you not to speak with her," the elder of elders said.

Guild pointed with his rifle. The only wickiup from which nobody had come lay on the edge of the small settlement. "Is that hers?"

The elder of elders said nothing. There was just the sound of the wind making flapping sounds of the saplings on the wickiups. The roan whinnied and snorted. There was no other sound except high up, where the wind sounded like a flute in the red volcanic rock.

Guild went past the elders to the wickiup, where he suspected he'd find the girl.

She lay on a pile of buffalo skins with more skins over

her. She was pale and sweaty. She trembled in the unmistakable way of cholera. Guild did not want to stay. Not with the virulence of cholera. But apparently she was getting better, because if it was going to kill her, it likely would have done so by now. The girl was perhaps in her late teens.

Guild said, "Your brother sent me."

She opened dark eyes that were vague with sickness. She was too toothy to be pretty, but she had very good cheeks and sensual lips.

"Will they hang my grandmother?" the Indian girl asked.

"I don't know. That could depend on what you tell me."

"My grandmother does not wish me to talk about it. She says it is a shameful thing. What I did and what the doctor did."

Obviously she wanted to tell him, had already hinted, in fact, at the course of her words. Guild said, "I heard her sob last night."

"My grandmother?"

"Yes. It was terrible, hearing her that way."

The Indian girl began to cry, and Guild knew his lie had worked.

"I should be the one who sobs—for what I have done, and for what the doctor did to my infant."

"Your infant?"

Wind threatened to tear the brush and sapling cover from the wickiup. The Indian girl used a corner of the place as her toilet, too weak to go elsewhere. Guild wanted to be outside the darkness and odor of this place.

"Yes," the Indian girl said. "Two months ago, when my brother was still away, Dr. McGivern helped me deliver my son."

"Where is your son now?"

81

"He is dead."

"How did he die?"

The Indian girl began weeping.

Four hours later, in Drayton, Guild rode his roan to the livery and then went straight to Lynott's office. The inquest was scheduled for three o'clock.

When he walked into Lynott's office, he saw a dozen well-dressed citizens, mostly men and mostly with cigars, sitting in straight-backed chairs around Lynott's desk. A fat man, whose gray, spaded beard lent him a satanic cast, sat in black judge's robes and brought down a gavel.

Guild slipped into a chair in the back row and listened as the proceedings began.

As Lynott had said, there wasn't much to debate. Guild was called and asked by the judge if the Indian woman known as Ko ta to had indeed murdered the doctor in cold blood. Guild said yes. He started to say something else, but then he saw Lynott and the judge exchange a certain kind of glance, and he knew that Robert McGivern could count not only the sheriff but also the judge among his good and true friends.

The inquest was over in twenty minutes.

"You think they'll hang her?"

"Don't know."

"I want your promise they won't. Otherwise I'll tell what I know."

"I've never been partial to threats, Guild."

Guild and Lynott stood outside the sheriff's office. As early dusk neared, the street traffic seemed in a hurry to go to its various destinations. He could smell snow on the wind. In these parts blizzards came fast.

Guild said, "You know what went on here. Why she killed him. Who's to say she wasn't right? At least she shouldn't die for what she did."

Lynott signed. "I guess I'd have to say you're right about that. That she shouldn't have to die."

"He was a goddamn killer, and the worst kind there is, and you know it."

Lynott dropped his eyes. "I know it. I won't dispute it." He sighed, touched a leather-gloved hand to the star on his coat. "I'll see that she doesn't hang, Guild. I promise you that. Now maybe it's time you ease on out of town."

Guild nodded to Robert McGivern, who was just emerging from the door with a very beautiful woman in a black dress, veil, and shawl. The rich always knew how to dress for funerals.

"I want one minute with him," Guild said.

"I don't want him hurt. You understand me?" Lynott's tone was angry.

Guild said, "He'll sign your pension checks, won't he?"

"I don't want him hurt."

"Just get him over here."

So Lynott went down the boardwalk and tipped his hat to Mrs. McGivern and whispered something to young Mr. McGivern and then nodded back to Guild.

Even from here, young Mr. McGivern looked scared. Lynott had to give him a little push. Mrs. McGivern seemed very confused by it all. She scowled at Guild.

Guild took his arm enough to hurt him and then said, "I'm going to walk you over to that alley, and if you don't go with me, I'm going to shoot you right here. Do you understand me?" He spoke in a very soft voice.

83

"My God, my God." was all young McGivern in his three-piece could say.

Guild took him over to the alley and then went maybe twenty feet into it, behind the base of a wide stairway running up the back of a brick building, and Guild made it fast. He hit McGivern four times exactly in the ribs, and then three times exactly in the kidney. He felt a great deal of satisfaction when he saw blood bubble in McGivern's mouth.

"What the hell did you think that Indian girl was going to do to you, kid? She was just as ashamed of the fact that you got her pregnant as you were. Only you had to go to your old man and whine about it, so your old man wanted to make sure that nobody ever knew—certainly not the respectable folks around here—so he offered to deliver the baby for you, didn't he?"

McGivern, still sick and terrified from the beating he'd taken, could only nod.

"He smothered the baby, McGivern. Your old man, the doctor. He killed that baby in cold blood. That's why her grandmother shot him, and you know it. Ko ta to would have kept your secret, McGivern. She really would have."

He had been holding McGivern up by the coat collar. Now he let him drop to the hard mud floor of the alley. McGivern was crying and trying to vomit.

Guild left the alley then, and started toward the livery.

Lynott fell into step next to him. "I told you not to hurt him."

Guild stopped and eyed the other man without pity. "Somebody needed to hurt him, Lynott."

Guild went the rest of the way to the livery by himself.

Anna and the
Players

At least they didn't have her running out and getting
lunch for them anymore, Anna thought. That in itself was
a sort of promotion.

She yawned.

As the lone female on the ten-man Cedar Rapids Police
Department in the year of Our Lord 1883, police matron
Anna Tolan had spent the previous night studying the
work of a French criminal scientist named Marie Françoise
Goron. The field was called criminology and both Scotland Yard and its French counterpart were expanding it
every day. Using various methods she'd learned from
Goron's writings, Anna had solved three murders in the
fourteen months of her employment here. Not that anybody knew this, of course. Two detectives named Riley and
Czmeck had been quick to claim credit on all three cases.

Anna yawned again. Her sweet landlady, Mrs. Goldman,
had come to her door late last night and begged Anna to

turn off the kerosene lamp and get some sleep. "You push yourself way too hard with this police thing, Anna."

Yes, and for what reason? Anna thought. It was doubtful she'd ever be promoted to full police officer. There were people in town who thought it was sinful for her to be on the police force at all. A woman. Just imagine. Tsk-tsk. They even stood before the mayor in city council meetings and quoted scripture to her that "proved" that God didn't want women police officers. Apparently, God had opinions on everything.

Thunder rumbled down the sky. The chill, rainy October morning was at least partly responsible for Anna's mood. Rain affected her immediately and deeply, made her feel vulnerable, melancholy. Even as a child back on the farm near Parnell, Anna had been this way. Rain always brought demons.

"There's a lady up front who won't talk to me," a male voice said. "Said she wanted to talk to the one and only Anna Tolan."

The half-bellow, the smell of cheap cigars and the dog-like odor of rain on a wool suit meant that Detective Riley was leaning in the door of Anna's office in the back of the station house.

"Something about ghosts," Riley said.

Anna turned in her chair and looked at him. Fifty pounds ago he'd been a good-looking man. But early middle-age hadn't been kind to him. He looked puffy and tired. Ten years ago, he'd pitched a no-hit game against Des Moines and had been town hero for several years following. Now, he looked like the bloated uncle of that young man, only the faintest resemblance showing.

"Ghosts?"

"That's what she said."

"Nice of you to give it to me."

Half the cops were nice to her and helped her in every way possible. They recognized her for the competent law officer she was. This, thank God, included the Chief. The other half gave her all the cases they didn't want. But she was glad to get even the bad ones, because otherwise her day would consist of checking the jail three times a day, walking around town in her light blue pinafore and starched white blouse and asking merchants if everything was going well with them—no break-ins, no robberies, nobody harassing them. One of the reasons that Cedar Rapids had grown so quickly was that it knew how to attract and keep businesses. Twenty-five thousand citizens. More than four hundred telephones. Electricity. In two or three years, there'd even be steam trolleys to replace the present horse-drawn ones. There was even an opera house that featured some of the world's most notable theatrical attractions. Chief Ryan once said, "It sure doesn't hurt to have a pretty little slip of an Irish girl—and with beautiful red hair yet—talking to the merchants to see that the town keeps them happy. It sure doesn't, Anna."

"I thought you wanted any cases we gave you," Riley said. "If you want me to, I'll give it to somebody else."

"I'm sorry. I'm just in kind of a crabby mood today."

"Trace Wydmore bothering you to marry him again?"

"I wish you'd leave him alone. He's a decent man."

"If he's so decent, why don't you marry him?"

"That really isn't any of your business."

"Tell him to give me some of his money. He's got plenty to go around, that's for sure."

Trace Wydmore was intelligent, handsome, pleasant,

fun and kind. He was also very, very rich. About every three months, even though they'd long ago quit seeing each other, Trace would suddenly reappear and ask her to marry him. She felt sorry for him. But she didn't love him. She liked him, admired him, appreciated him. But she didn't love him.

She changed the subject. "You're right, Riley. I *do* want the case. Thank you for giving it to me. I guess I'm just in a bad mood. The rain."

"You and my old lady," he said. "If it's not her monthly visitor, it's the weather. There's always some reason she's crabby." Then he waggled his fingers at her wraithlike and made a spooky noise. "I'll go get the ghost lady."

Her name was Virginia Olson, a bulky, middle-aged woman with a doughy face and hard, bright, not terribly friendly blue eyes. She cleaned rooms at the Astor Hotel, a somewhat seedy place along the river. She wore a pinafore, not unlike Anna's in cut and style, but stained and smudged with the indelicacies of hotel guests. When she talked, silver spittle frothed up in the corners of her mouth and ran down the sides of her lips. She said, "Oh, I seen her all right."

"Anthea Murchison?"

"Anthea Murchison. Right in front of my eyes."

"She's been dead over a year now. Her buggy overturned over in Johnson County and she went off a cliff."

"I don't need no rehash, miss," she said. "I read the papers. I keep up."

"Then if you keep up," Anna said, staying calm and patient, "and if you think it through, what you're saying is impossible."

"That a dead woman was in the hotel last night? Well, she was."

Anna sighed. "Exactly what would you like me to do?"

"You're just as snooty as the men officers. You try'n give the coppers a tip and look what you get."

"I'm sorry, Mrs. Olson."

"Miss Olson."

"Miss Olson, then."

"Not that I never had no chances to be a *Mrs.*" She sucked up some of the frothing spittle.

"I'm sure you had plenty of chances."

"I wasn't always fat. It's this condition I have. And my hair used to be black as night, too. But then I got this here condition."

"I'm sorry. Now, if you'll just tell me—"

"She wore this big picture hat. You know what a picture hat is?"

"Yes." They were fashionable these days, hats with huge brims that covered half a lady's face.

"She also had some kind of wig on when she came in the hotel. That's why I didn't recognize her. Her disguise. But I was goin' to my own room—the hotel gives me room and board except the food is pig swill—anyway, later on I'm goin' to my room and I seen her door was partly open and I just happened to glance inside and there she was without her hat and her wig and I seen her. Anthea Murchison. Plain as day."

"Did she see you?"

"I think she must've because she hurried quick-like to the door and practically slammed it." She paused to suck up some more spittle. Anna wondered if the spittle had anything to do with the woman's "condition."

Ed Gorman

"You'd seen the Murchison woman before?"

Miss Olson smirked. "You mean when she was alive?"

"Yes."

"Oh, I seen her all right. Plenty of times."

"Where?"

"The hotel. That's why I recognized her so fast. Her and her gentleman friend used to come up the back way."

"When was this?"

Virginia Olson thought about it for a time. "Oh, six, seven months before she died."

"How often did they come there?"

"Once a week, say."

"They didn't check in at the front desk?"

"No. They had—or she had, anyway—some kind of deal worked out with Mr. Sullivan. The manager. Poor man."

"Poor man?"

"The cancer. He weighed about eighty pounds when they planted him. Liver. He was all yellow."

"That's too bad."

"No, it isn't."

"It isn't?"

"I mean, I didn't want to see him die that way—I wouldn't want to see *any*body die that way—but he was a mean, cheap bastard who never did a lick'a work in his life."

"I'm sorry to hear that. But let's get back to Anthea Murchison."

"They were havin' it on."

"I gathered that. Did you know who he was?"

"I almost got a look at him once. But he always moved real fast. And he wore this big fake black beard and this big hat that covered a lot of his face."

"Like her picture hat?"

90

"I never thought of that. But you're right. It was sorta like a picture hat except it was for a man. Like somethin' you'd see on the stage. I guess. That a villain would wear or somethin'."

She took a railroad watch from the pocket of her pinafore and said, "I got to get back. I'm just here on my break."

"I still don't know what you want me to do, Miss Olson."

"Come over there and look at her. See if it ain't Mrs. Murchison in the flesh."

The woman wasn't going to be Mrs. Murchison, of course. But it'd be better than just sitting here on this gloomy morning. And on the way back, she could swing past the jail and make one of her morning inspections. Make sure things were being run properly. Chief Ryan prided himself on his jail. He wanted it clean, orderly and without a whisper of scandal. He hoped to run for mayor someday, Chief Ryan did, and he didn't want some civic group pointing out that his jail had been some hell-hole like something you'd see in Mexico. Their jails were much in the news lately. A lot of men died mysteriously in those jails.

"I'll walk back with you," Anna said, standing up.

"I got to hurry," Miss Olson said. "Mr. Sanford's worse than Mr. Sullivan ever was. Now Mr. Sanford, I sure wouldn't mind seein' him get the cancer. I surely wouldn't."

Hotel rooms always saddened Anna. She'd seen too many suicides, murders and bad illicit love affairs within their walls. One problem with being a copper was that you generally saw the worst side of people, even in a nice little town like Cedar Rapids. The grubby hallway of the Astor's third floor told her that the room she was about to see

91

would be grubby, too. The Olson woman had gone back to work.

The hallway offered eruptions of sounds on both sides—tobacco coughs, singing-while-shaving, snoring and gargling, presumably with "oral disinfectant" as the advertisements called it.

Room 334. Anna put her ear to it. Listened. Silence. Just then a door down the hall opened and a bald man in trousers, the tops of long johns, and suspenders peeked out and picked up his morning paper. He gave Anna a very close appraisal and said, "Morning."

Anna smiled, wanting to remain silent, and nodded good morning back.

She put her ear to the door again. If the woman inside was moving around, she was doing so very, very quietly. Maybe the woman had gone out the back way. While the desk clerk had assured Anna that the woman had not come down yet this morning, he obviously didn't know for sure that she was in her room.

Anna knocked gently. Counted to ten. No response. Knocked again. And still no response.

Sounds of doors opening and closing on all three floors of the hotel. Morning greetings exchanged. Smells of cigarettes, pipes, cigars. Men with leather sample bags of merchandise carted out here from points as distant as New York and Cincinnati and Chicago suddenly striding past her in the hall. A quarter to eight and the business day just beginning.

Anna knocked again.

One of the officers friendly to her had given her a couple of tools resembling walnut picks. Showed her how to use them on virtually any kind of door. He'd also given her several skeleton keys. She could get into virtually any room or house.

The room was about what she'd expected. Double bed. Bureau. Faded full-length mirror hanging on a narrow closet door. Window overlooking the alley on the east side of the hotel. What wasn't expected was the woman in bed. She lay in a faded yellow robe, with her arms spread wide. She was otherwise naked. Somebody had cut her throat. There was a necklace-like crust of dried blood directly across the center of her neck.

The woman was Anthea Murchison.

Anna's first instinct was to hurry downstairs and send somebody to summon the Chief. But then she forced herself to calm down. She wouldn't get much of a chance to scientifically appraise the room—the way her idol Goron would want her to—with other cops there.

She spent the next twenty minutes going over everything. In the purse, she found various documents bearing the name Thea Manners, obviously the name the Murchison woman used during the past year. But where had she been? What had she been doing? Anna inspected the bed carefully, looking for anything that might later prove useful. She found red fibers, hair strands that looked to belong to Anthea Murchison, a piece of a woman's fingernail. She checked Anthea's fingers. A slice of her right index fingernail had broken off. The piece Anna held fit the maimed nail perfectly. A couple of times, Anna noticed the small, odd indentation in the wooden headboard. She took a piece of paper and held it tight to the headboard. Then she scribbled lead over the indentation. It showed a symbol: H. The style was rococo, and a bit too fancy for Anna's tastes. She put the paper in her pocket. Then she started in on the floor. Down on her hands and knees. Looking for curious footprints, or something tiny that might have been dropped. She found a number of things worth dropping in the white evidence envelope she'd made up for herself. A plain black button interested Anna especially. She checked it against Anthea's clothes in the closet. There was no match. The button belonged to somebody else. The way fashions were getting so radical these days—an Edwardian craze was sweeping the country—it was impossible to know if the button had come off male or female attire.

Fifteen minutes later, the room was filled with police officers. Anna was pretty much pushed aside. She went downstairs to the porch and stood there looking out at the street. The rain had let up, but the overcast, chill autumn day remained. Wagons and buggies and surreys and a stray stagecoach or two plied the muddy streets. Somewhere nearby, the horse-drawn trolley rang its bell. Then she realized that the trolley could take her very close to where she needed to go.

She hurried to the corner. The trolley stopped for her. On a day like this one, the conveyance was crowded; bowlers on men, bustles on women bobbed as it bounced down the bumpy streets. Horse-drawn taxi cabs were busy, too. The rain had started in again.

Ten years ago, the large red barn had housed two businesses, a blacksmith and a farm implement dealer. It now housed The Players, a local theatrical group that did everything it could to create controversy, and thus sell tickets. Kevin Murchison was a dentist by day but at night he oversaw production of the plays. His partner was David Bailey, a medical doctor. The men had much in common. They were in their early thirties, literary, handsome and were widely held to have slept with half the women, married or not, who took roles in the various plays. Kevin was tall and pale and blond; David was short and dark and not without an air of not only malice but violence. His bedside manner was rarely praised. In fact, it was well known that most of the other doctors in town regretted ever letting him practice here. One practiced in Cedar Rapids only at the sufferance of the docs already in place. Many were called; few were chosen. David Bailey was generally regarded as a terrible choice.

The playhouse was empty when Anna arrived. She stood at the back of the place, listening to the rain play chill ancient rhythms on the roof of the barn. The stage was set up for a French bedroom farce advertised outside as "DEFINITELY NAUGHTY!"—THE NEW YORK TIMES. Who could resist that? Word was this was the most successful play of the past three years, so successful in fact that both dentist and doctor were thinking of quitting their respective practices and joining The Players full-time.

"It's lovely, isn't it?" The voice definitely male but practiced and just this side of being "cultured."

She turned to find three people standing there: Dr. Murchison, Dr. Bailey and Bailey's gently beautiful wife, Beatrice.

Anna said, "You've done a nice job."

Murchison said, "The finest theater outside Chicago."

Beatrice actually blushed at the hyperbole. "Or so we like to think, anyway."

There was no clue on their faces or in their voices that they'd heard about their friend Anthea. She was probably at the undertaker's by now.

Murchison, whose Edwardian suit complemented his clipped good looks and slightly European curly blond hair, said, "I'm sure you're here about Anthea."

So they did know.

"It's terrible," Beatrice said.

"I hope there'll be an investigation," Bailey said. His stocky form looked comfortable in Levi's and work shirt. The odd thing was, Murchison, who looked almost effete, had been raised on a farm. Bailey, who'd come from Boston money, could have blended in with a crew of railroad workers. "I was the one who pronounced her dead. I've got my reputation to think of." Then he made an awkward attempt to touch his hand to Murchison's shoulder. "I'm sorry, Kevin. You're grieving and all I can talk about is my reputation."

There was something rehearsed about the little scene she'd just witnessed. Or was there? Theater people—or so she'd read in one of Mrs. Goldman's eastern magazines—sometimes carried their acting over into real life. *Ham* was the word Anna wanted.

"Did any of you see her last night?"

"No," said Murchison. "I wish I had. My God, I have so many questions for her." Tears filled his eyes and Beatrice, tall, regal Beatrice, took him in her arms and held him.

"Why don't we step into the office?" Bailey said. "We can talk there."

Theater posters lined the walls of the small office with the roll-top desk and the long table covered with leaflets for the present production. *Uncle Tom's Cabin, The Widow's*

Revenge, A Cupid for Constance were listed as forthcoming. The Players were an eclectic bunch. They mixed tame fare with the occasional bedroom farce and seemed to be surviving quite nicely these days.

"She was dead when we put her in the ground," Bailey said. "I'd swear to that."

"You'll have to, Doctor. There'll be a lot of questions about the autopsy report you signed."

A tic troubled his right eyelid suddenly. Anna said, "You didn't see her last night?"

"I believe I already answered that question."

"I'd appreciate you answering it again."

"Neither of us saw her last night," Beatrice said as she came into the office. "Poor Kevin's lying down in his private office." She went over and took a straightback chair next to her husband's. "We worked at the theater until nearly midnight and then went home and went to bed."

"I see."

Beatrice smiled. "I was just wondering if you're even authorized to ask us questions. I remember you had some trouble with the city council and all."

"The Chief will back me up, if that's what you mean." Then, "I'm going to ask for the grave to be disinterred this afternoon."

"And why would you do that?" Bailey said.

"I want to see what's in the coffin."

"Well, obviously *Anthea* won't be." Bailey said. His eye tic was suddenly worse.

"How did Anthea and Kevin get along?"

"Just wonderfully," Beatrice said.

"There were a lot of rumors."

Beatrice smiled. "Of course, there were rumors, dear.

This is a rumor kind of town. Anybody who shows a little flair for anything even the slightest bit different from the herd—well, rumors are the price you pay."

"Then they were happy?"

"Very."

"And there was no talk of divorce?"

"Of course not."

They weren't going to cooperate and Anna knew it. They had pat little answers to turn aside all her questions. And that was all she was going to get.

She stood up. "Where's Dr. Murchison's office?"

"Just down the hall," Beatrice said. "But he really does want to be alone. He's very confused and hurt right now."

"I'll keep that in mind," Anna said. "And thank you for your time."

As she was turning to the door, Bailey said, "You've been incredibly insensitive. I may just talk to the Chief about it."

"That's up to you, Dr. Bailey."

They stared at each other a long moment, and then Anna went down the hall.

Just as she reached Murchison's door, she heard a female voice behind it say, "Oh, Kevin, why lie about it? You sleep with all the ingenues and then get tired of them. That's what's happening to us. You're tired of me but you don't want to hurt my feelings by telling me."

"I just need some time to—think, Karen. That's all. Especially after this morning. My wife and everything."

"You should be grateful to her," Karen said. "She gave you a perfect excuse for not seeing me tonight." By the end, her voice had started to tremble with tears. "Oh, I was stupid to think you were really in love with me."

Anna had always been told that in amateur theater

groups, the real drama went on offstage. Apparently so. She hated to embarrass Karen by knocking now but she had work to do. She knocked.

Murchison opened the door quickly, obviously grateful for any interruption. But he frowned when he saw Anna. "Oh, great, just what I need. More questions."

"I just need a few minutes, Dr. Murchison."

The word "ingenue" had misled Anna into picturing a slender, somewhat ethereal young woman. While Karen was still an exquisite-looking woman, her years were starting to do damage—the face a bit fleshy, the neck a bit loose, the high bustline a bit matronly now. She was a fading beauty, and there was always something sad about that. There was a wedding ring on Karen's left finger. But it was the other thing she kept touching, fingering—a large ornamental ring that was most likely costume jewelry.

"I'll talk to you tonight," Murchison said, "if Miss Tolan here doesn't put me in jail for some reason." He didn't even try to disguise the bitterness in his voice.

Karen whimpered, pushed past Anna, and exited the room.

"I suppose you heard it all while you were standing by the door," Murchison said, "and will run right down to her husband's office and tell him." Anna suspected that this was the real Murchison. The mild man she'd met earlier had been a mask.

"I don't even know who her husband is," Anna said.

"Lawrence Remington," Murchison said. "He has a very successful law practice in the Ely Building. On the second floor, in case you're interested." He smirked. "I only commit adultery with the upper classes. I guess I'm something of a snob." He took out a packet of Egyptian cigarettes.

Nobody was more pretentious than certain amateur theater types. "She's not as beautiful as she used to be. But Remington doesn't seem to notice that. He's insanely jealous."

"Maybe he loves her."

But love didn't interest him much. He merely shrugged.

"I'm told that you and your wife were on the verge of divorce at the time of her supposed death."

He glared at her. "You don't waste any time, do you? Have you ever thought that I might be grieving? Here I thought my wife was dead—and then she suddenly turns up. And now she's dead again." She could see why he produced the shows instead of starred in them. He was a terrible actor.

"Did you see her last night?"

"I've already told you no."

"What if I said somebody saw her slipping into your house?"

He didn't hesitate. "Then I'd say you're lying."

Sometimes the trick Chief Ryan had taught her worked. Sometimes it didn't. She tried a trick of her own. "I found a cuff button in your wife's hotel room."

"Good for you."

"I'm sure you'd be happy to let me look through your shirts."

He met her eye. He seemed to be enjoying this, which did not do much for her police officer ego. "Would you like to go to my place and look through my shirts?"

Once again, she changed the subject, now uncertain of herself and the direction of her questions. "The night clerk said he saw a man going up to her room late last night." One last attempt to trap him.

"Oh? Maybe you'd like me to stop by so he can see me."

He laughed. "I'll cooperate with you any way you want, Miss Tolan. I have nothing to hide."

Maybe he didn't, after all. Or maybe he was clever enough to offer himself up this way, knowing she wouldn't call him on it. She felt slow-witted and dull. She was sure she'd been the brunt of many jokes told after-hours at The Players' notorious wine parties. She was just glad Chief Ryan wasn't here to see this sorry interrogation. She wanted to be home suddenly, in Mrs. Goldman's parlor, listening to Mrs. Goldman's stirring stories about the Civil War, and how the ladies of Iowa had worked eighteen-hour days making bullets and knitting sweaters and stockings and mittens for their Union husbands and sons and brothers. Mrs. Goldman said that they'd even loaded up the steamboats when no men could be found.

She angled herself toward the door. "I guess I'll be going now."

"I was just starting to have fun." Then, "You're very pretty, Anna. Have you ever thought of trying out for one of our plays?"

She knew she was blushing. His compliment had cinched his victory. He'd reduced her status from detective to simple young woman.

"I'll talk to you later," she said, and hurried out of his room. He laughed once behind her—an empty, fake laugh that was yet another example of his bad acting.

Anna was about to walk out through the front door when she heard the weeping in the deep shadows to the side. She squinted into the gloom and saw nothing. But the weeping sound remained constant. Anna made her way carefully toward the far wall. A shape began to form. Karen Remington. She paused long enough to say, "Do you have a cigarette?"

Good girls don't smoke. Anna wanted to say. Or so her farmer parents had always told her, anyway. And Anna couldn't get away from their influence, much as she wanted to sometimes. Any woman she saw smoking a cigarette, she automatically downgraded socially if not morally. "I'm afraid I don't smoke."

"I must look terrible. My makeup."

Anna smiled. "Actually, I can't see you very well."

The Remington woman laughed. And that made Anna like her. "If that's the case, I should probably stay here the rest of my life. In the shadows. Then I won't have to see how old I'm getting." She paused, snuffled tears, daubed a lace handkerchief to nose and lips. "I've always read about women like myself—that's why I can't stand to read Henry James, I see myself in so many of his silly, middle-aged women. Vain and desperate." More snuffling. "I told myself that The Players would be good for me. My son was off to Princeton, my husband was always busy. I felt— Oh, it's all such a cliché. You know how I felt. So I decided to help out with publicity. Then I helped with costumes. Then I tried out for a part in a play. And then I got involved with dear Kevin. You know the funny thing? He not only seduced me—though of course I *wanted* to be seduced—he convinced me to give him money. And large amounts of it. My husband was furious when he found out. Even threatened to divorce me. I actually think he resented the money even more than he resented my being unfaithful. He's not a generous man. But I didn't care. Kevin and I were going to run off and start another theater someplace. I wanted to go east, to be nearer my son. Kevin led me to believe—"

"Nasty Kevin," a male voice said on the other side of the gloom. "Nasty, nasty Kevin."

It was Kevin, of course.

"I didn't 'lead her to believe' anything, Miss Tolan. She believed what she *wanted* to believe."

"Unfortunately," the Remington woman said, "that's true."

And promptly began sobbing again, even more violently than before.

Soon enough, Anna was on the trolley, headed downtown once again. The sun was out now; the temperature was up in the forties. Anna looked longingly at the stately buildings of Coe College, Main Building and Williston Hall, as they were known. She hoped to take classes there someday. She's seen photographs of college girls in crisp spring dresses. How intelligent and poised and professional they looked. Her secret dream was to be one of them. Anna Tolan, college girl.

Anna had no trouble with Chief Ryan. He understood exactly why she wanted the Murchison woman's coffin dug up. Judge Rollins, who could sometimes be a problem, also understood and approved her request.

At four that afternoon, Anna, Chief Ryan and two scruffy gravediggers stood over Anthea Murchison's gravesite. The air was fresh, cleansed by the recent rain, and the gravestones glistened as if they'd been scrubbed. Some of them dated as far back as the late 1700s, when some Frenchmen down from Green Bay, Wisconsin, had started trading iron kettles, cloth and knives for some of the Ioway Indians' animal skins. An influenza outbreak had killed at least a dozen of the French traders.

"If there's a body in there, Anna," Chief Ryan said. "I want you to look away. Otherwise, it'll stay in your mind the rest of your life."

Chief Ryan was every bit as grandfatherly as he sounded, a big, broad, gray-haired man with the red nose of a drinker and the kind eyes of a village priest. His grandparents had come from County Cork two generations ago. Every Ryan male since had been a law officer of some kind.

"I'll be fine, Chief."

"You're not as tough as you think, young lady."

Remembering her wretched questioning of the glib Kevin Murchison, she had to silently agree.

The exhumation went quickly. The gravediggers knew their business. When they reached the wooden coffin with the cross in the center of the lid, the taller of the two jumped down into the grave with his crowbar. He was able to balance himself against the walls of the grave and open the coffin lid.

He pried it up and flung it back. "Empty, sir," he shouted up to the Chief.

When they got back to the station, Anna found a man waiting for her. She saw him around town frequently but didn't know who he was or what he did.

He doffed his derby and said, "My name is Peterson. Pete Peterson. I sell insurance."

"This is a bad time to sell me anything, Mr. Peterson."

He smiled. He had a boyish face emphasized by the youthful cut of his checkered suit. Salesmen, or drummers as they were popularly called, had come to favor checks. They felt that the pattern put people in a happier frame of mind than, say, dark blue or black. "I'm here about Anthea Murchison."

"Oh?"

"My company issued her a life insurance policy for fifty thousand dollars eight months before she died."

"Oh," Anna said, catching his implication instantly.

They sat in her office for the next hour. The day shift was winding down. Men called goodbyes to each other. The handful of night-shifters came on, their leather gun-belts creaking, their heavy shoes loud on the wooden floors.

"Insurance fraud is what we're looking at," Peterson said. "If we can prove it."

"Why couldn't you prove it?" Anna said. "The coffin was empty. And Dr. Bailey signed the death certificate. He had to know she wasn't dead."

"I think it was for that theater of theirs."

"The money, you mean?"

Peterson nodded. "The way I understand it, they couldn't get any more investors. They'd borrowed everything they could. The theater was going under."

"So they staged Anthea Murchison's death."

"And collected fifty thousand dollars."

"Your company didn't investigate?"

"Of course, we investigated. But as you said, we had a signed death certificate. There was no reason to go into an all-out investigation. We didn't spend all that much time on it. Now, it's obvious we were defrauded."

"They'll probably try to leave town."

"If they haven't already."

"I'm not sure how long I can hold them on what we have now, though."

"But we *know* what happened, Anna."

105

"Yes, we know it. But can we prove it? Defense attorneys are very creative people, Pete."

"Don't I know it. They've helped cheat my company out of millions of dollars." Whenever he spoke of the company, his tone became downright reverent. Like a cardinal invoking the name of the Vatican.

"I need to talk to the Chief about all this. Pete. There's also a murder investigation going on. He'll want to move carefully."

"What's he afraid of?"

"What he's afraid of, Mr. Peterson," Chief Ryan said, walking into Anna's office, "is that you'll get your fraud case all resolved, and we still won't know why Anthea Murchison came back to town last night—and why one of them killed her."

Peterson frowned. "So you're not going to arrest them?"

"Not right now," Ryan said, "and I don't want you approaching them, either. You understand?"

"My company isn't going to be happy."

"I'm sorry about that, Mr. Peterson," Ryan said. "But that's the way it has to be for a little while longer."

Mr. Peterson's checkered suit seemed to fade slightly in intensity. Even the magnificently bogus gleam in his eyes had dulled. His company wasn't happy, and neither was he.

"Now, if you don't mind, Mr. Peterson, Anna and I need to get back to work."

Mr. Peterson dragged himself to his feet. He looked weary, old. He took his faded suit and faded eyes to the door and said, "I'll have to go and send my company a telegram, I guess." And with that, he was gone.

A moment later, Chief Ryan said, "The mayor wants me to put Riley on the case."

"I figured that would happen."

"You know this isn't my decision. But there's an election coming up and he doesn't want to have an unsolved case like this hanging over his head." Ryan smiled. "But nobody can stop you from working on the case on your own, Anna."

Their usual bargain had been struck. Anna worked on the case and secretly reported back to the Chief.

Anna smiled. "I guess I do have a little time on my hands tonight."

"Glad to hear it."

After dinner with Mrs. Goldman. Anna took the evidence up to her room and started sifting through it. Goron had instructed would-be detectives to store all evidence in the same box, and to tag it alphabetically. Fingerprints were beginning to play a role in law enforcement. Even though officers in the United States were still skeptical of such evidence—and no court would allow it to be used—Goron insisted that all pieces of evidence remain as pristine as possible. She also insisted that fingerprints were the surest way to identify a killer. Find a print on a murder weapon and you had your man.

Anna worked till after midnight. On her bed was the button she'd found on Anthea Murchison's hotel bed, the sketch she'd made of some strange footprints on the hotel room floor, a cigarette made of coarse tan paper and heavy tobacco leaves, a man's comb with gray hair in it, a drinking glass across which were smeared two or three different sets of fingerprints, and then the curious H marking she'd found on the headboard of Anthea's hotel bed. The trouble with all her evidence was that she couldn't date it. It might have been in the room for a month. Even the cigarette butt didn't tell her anything decisive. A sloppy cleaning woman might have left it behind a few weeks ago.

There would be no trouble proving that the owners of The Players had perpetrated a fraud: proving that one of them had perpetrated a murder might be something else again.

Kevin Murchison had planned on only one drink at the River's Edge. He had four in less than an hour. On an empty stomach. Which was not exactly brilliant. With the law now having him under suspicion—even that stupid insurance investigator Pete Peterson should be able to figure things out now—he needed to remain sharp and clearheaded.

But somehow his fear (Oh, he'd do just dandy in prison, wouldn't he?) and self-pity (Why shouldn't a nice decent fellow like himself be able to get away with a little fraud now and then? Insurance companies had lots of money, didn't they?) and loathing (He hated the taverns of Cedar Rapids; all the silly yokel chatter; never a word about theater life or the latest Broadway scandal, which Kevin kept up on via *The New York Times*, however dated it was by the time it reached this little hellhole of a burg.)—somehow his fear, his self-pity and his loathing forced him to drink more.

By the time he was ready to walk home, he had to make himself conscious of his gait. Didn't want to appear drunk. Drunk meant vulnerable, and oh, how that pretty little piece of a police matron or whatever the hell she was would love to get him when he was vulnerable.

The autumn dusk was chill and brief and gorgeous, the sky layered in smoky pastels of gold and salmon. His Tudor-style home was dark when he reached it. He'd let the last of his servants go shortly after Anthea's "death." He could no longer afford the pretense. Anyway, he needed the town's sympathy—the bereaved husband and all that—to allay suspicion that Anthea's death had been suspicious. People in a place like Cedar Rapids were never sympathetic to people who had servants.

He reheated this morning's coffee and then went to the north wing of the house, where the den was located. He'd just touched a match to the desk lamp when the smell filled his nostrils. He wanted to vomit.

She lay over by the fireplace, the fire poker next to her fine blond head. The tip of the poker gleamed with her blood.

He knelt next to her. Once or twice, he reached out to touch her. But then stopped himself. He didn't want to remember her flesh as cold. In life, it had been so warm and supple and erotic. He had never loved anyone as much as he'd loved Beatrice. They'd been planning to run away tonight, leaving her husband David Bailey to explain things to the police—the insurance fraud and Anthea's murder last night.

Now, he knew who had murdered Anthea. David Bailey. Anthea'd stopped by the house here late last night and demanded more money, said she'd been living in New Orleans but had run out of money. They'd been planning to divorce anyway at the time they faked her death—so she took one-third of the insurance money and fled, and they put the rest of the money into the theater. He'd lied to her last night and said he'd get her more this morning. Anything to get rid of her. So, apparently, she'd next gone to visit and blackmail Bailey. And he must have killed her. As he'd killed poor Beatrice tonight. Bailey, a jealous man for all his own unfaithfulness, had likely learned about Beatrice and Kevin. And killed her for her betraying him.

He wasn't given to tears and so his sobs were fitful. He leaned in. He couldn't help himself. He kissed her cold dead lips.

And then he stood up and knew what he had to do, where he had to go.

Right now, nothing else mattered. Nothing else at all.

"You could've killed Beatrice," Anna said.

"No, I couldn't," Murchison said. "I loved her too much."

"So," the Chief said, "you admit to the insurance fraud."

"Yes, of course. I've told you that already. We were just trying to save the theater."

"But not to murdering your wife," Anna said.

"Or Beatrice," the Chief said.

It was near midnight in the small back room of the station the police used to question suspects. The room was bare except for a few fading dirty words prisoners had scribbled on the wall from time to time.

Kevin Murchison had gone to Anna's and told her what happened. His version of it, anyway. Then she'd taken him downtown and used the telephone to call the Chief and ask him to come down, too. She still got a thrill every time she used the telephone. They'd spent the last two hours going over and over Murchison's story. The atmosphere wasn't hostile but it was certainly intense. The dancing light of a kerosene lamp threw everything into soft shadow.

"Who do you think killed them, then?" Anna said.

"I've told you that already."

"I wish you'd quit saying that," the Chief said, lighting his pipe with a stick match. "We're well aware we keep asking you the same questions over and over."

"It's damned annoying is what it is."

"So," the Chief said, "who do you think killed the two women?"

Murchison glared at him. Sighed. "I've told you and told you. David killed them."

"Why would he kill them?"

"He's got a terrible temper. Anthea must've seen him last night and demanded money. The same way she did from me. He got angry and killed her."

"But why would he kill Beatrice?" Anna said.

"Because he found out about us. Not only that we were lovers but that we were running away together."

"And so he killed her?" Anna said.

"You'd have to see him lose his temper to understand how easily he could kill somebody. He's terrifying when he's like that."

A knock. The Chief said, "That's probably Henning, Anna. Why don't you take it? I'll keep on questioning our friend here."

"I didn't kill either of those women," Kevin Murchison said, sounding like a sad little boy. "I really didn't."

Anna opened the door. Henning was one of the older officers, a big, bald man with bushy eyebrows and a chin scar from a long-ago altercation with a hobo. Anna stepped out into the hall. "Bailey wasn't at home."

"Did you find a train schedule?"

Henning nodded, handed her a pamphlet.

"Thanks," she said.

"I need to make my rounds."

She nodded. There was a train leaving for Chicago in forty-five minutes.

She opened the door and peeked in and said. "I'm going over to the train depot."

"Good idea," the Chief said. "You know where my Navy Colt is. Take it."

"I probably won't need it."

"Take it, anyway."

While Anna didn't much like firearms, the Chief had turned her into a fair marksman. She preferred to think of herself as a Goron-type of peace officer. "Brain power" Goron often said was more important than "brute power." But she reluctantly went into the Chief's office, went to his desk, opened the wide middle drawer, and took out the Navy Colt.

Cedar Rapids had a crush on its train depot, one of those crushes that made folks just about absolutely goofy. Some folks would bring their own chairs to the depot just so they could sit and watch trains arrive and depart all day long. Other folks even brought picnic lunches, just to sit and watch the panoramic show that trains put on. People loved everything about trains, the bold colors of the engine cars, the gray billowing smoke, the stink of coal, the smell of oil, the clatter of couplings. They were especially interested in the fancy dining cars and parlor cars. "The envy of sultans!" as one advertisement boasted. They liked to see exotic strangers disembark. New York people or Chicago people or Boston people, fancy people stepping down to stretch their legs before the train roared away again, women in huge capes and big important hairstyles, and men in dove-gray vests and top hats and spats, money and culture and a self-confidence that Cedar Rapids folks could only daydream of.

Because the temperature had dipped several degrees, most of the waiting passengers were inside the depot, on the benches close to the potbellied stove. The fog had discouraged them, too; a damp, thick, gritty fog. There weren't many people inside, mostly drummers on to the next burg, derbys down on their faces as they snored off weariness and whiskey.

She searched all the obvious places inside. Bailey wasn't in any of them. She described him to everybody she saw. Nobody had seen him. Not even the ticket seller recalled seeing him.

She'd been there fifteen, twenty minutes when the drunk came reeling in. She'd arrested him a few times. His name was Henry. He'd used so many aliases neither he nor the police were sure of his last name. He was mostly a small-time grifter preying on elderly folks. He was a decent-looking man but you couldn't tell it beneath the layers of grime and bar liquor.

He went over to the ticket window. Moments later, he was shouting at the ticket man. Anna went over.

"Where the hell is he?" Henry wanted to know.

"Where is who?" the ticket man said several times. "I don't know who you're talking about."

"That doctor."

"What doctor?" Anna said.

Henry turned awkwardly and glared at her. He looked to be near collapse, the final stages of this particular bender. He'd stay dry for a few months, working his grifts, and then do another bender again for five, six weeks. "You got no call to arrest me."

"I just want to talk to you."

"That's what you said las' time."

For a drunk, he had a good memory. She took his elbow, angled him away from the ticket window. "Who's the doctor you're looking for?"

"None of your damn business. I got rights, you know."

"You keep it up, Henry, and I *will* arrest you. Now who's the doctor?"

He needed a shave, two or three baths, and his dirty black suit needed all sorts of sewing. He glared silently at her as long as he could. Then he sighed and said, "Bailey."

"I thought so. Why're you looking for him?"

"He promised me five dollars." Five dollars would buy a lot of bad liquor.

"For what?"

"For buying his train ticket."

So that's how Bailey had worked it. He knew the police would be watching the depot. "Where'd you see him last?"

Henry nodded eastward. "Out by the baggage carts."

The plan was becoming obvious. Bailey had sent Henry in to buy a ticket. That's why nobody had seen Bailey. Then he'd wait till the very last minute and jump out of the shadows and board the train. He'd hide somewhere aboard until the train was thirty, forty miles down the line.

"Where was the ticket to?"

"Chicago."

A good place to get lost in, Anna thought.

"He said he'd pay you five dollars?"

"Yeah. But he only paid me two. Said that was all the cash he had on him. I went over and started drinkin' and the more I thought of it, the madder I got. So I come back here."

"I appreciate this, Henry."

"You see him, you tell him he owes me three dollars."

"I'll tell him, Henry. Don't worry."

Things were working out for Bailey. A heavy autumnal fog was even heavier, rolling in, snaking silver across everything. You couldn't see more than a yard or so in front of you.

She started making her way down the platform. She'd decided to use the Chief's Navy Colt, after all. She gripped it tight in her right hand.

She heard somebody walking toward her. She ducked behind an empty baggage cart, one as large as a small horse-drawn utility wagon. She raised the gun, ready to use it if necessary.

An older couple, the Mayples, appeared out of the fog. Selma Mayples had on the tiny straw hat with the merry red band she wore whenever she left the house. Stout Sam Mayples was carrying a small suitcase. Selma must be visiting her sick sister in Rock Island again.

After they passed, she resumed her search. She walked up and down the platform twice, searching in, under and around anything that looked even vaguely like a hiding place. She had no better luck outside than she'd had inside.

She was just about to give up when she heard a horse neigh somewhere in the gloom. The cabs. This late at night, there'd be only one cab working. But a couple of the drivers always left their cabs here. The livery was close by. They'd just walk their horses over in the morning and they'd be ready to go.

She found the shapes of three empty cabs down by the wagons. In the fog, the wagon beds resembled coffins. She had her gun drawn, ready.

Night sounds. Player piano music from a tavern somewhere. The rail-thrumming buzz of a distant train. Fog-muted conversation from inside the depot.

She walked up to the first wagon. Checked out the bed. Empty. Moved on to the second wagon. Also empty.

Was just moving to the third wagon, when he suddenly lurched from the murk—the smell of whiskey, the rustle of his wool suit—and brought the handle of his six-shooter down on the side of her head. But she'd just been turning away from him and so the impact of his blow lost most of its effectiveness.

Bailey made the mistake of trying to hit her a second time. He moved too far in and this time—despite the pain he'd inflicted—she was ready for him. He found himself facing the barrel of her Colt.

"Give me your gun."

He hesitated. Then she put the barrel of her weapon directly against his left eye and slowly eased back the trigger.

"Your gun."

He handed her the gun.

"The Chief wants to talk to you," Anna said.

"For what?"

"For killing Anthea last night, and your wife Beatrice tonight."

She couldn't see him well enough to read his expression. But when she mentioned Beatrice, an animal cry seemed to stick in his throat. "Beatrice? Beatrice is dead?"

"You don't know anything about it, of course?"

"My God. You're talking about my wife. I would never kill her."

She thought of Murchison saying essentially the same thing about his own wife's death. They were both apparently reading from the same bad play.

"I didn't kill her, Anna. I really didn't."

"We'll talk to the Chief about that."

She took his shoulder, turned him around so that he faced the depot. "We'll walk to the depot then take the alley over to the station. Just remember I have a gun."

"He must have done it."

"Who?"

"Kevin. He thought she loved him. She must've changed her mind and then he killed her. He was never satisfied with just seducing them. They had to fall in love with him, too." His words were bitter yet tired, the force of them fading in the fog. "The way he got Karen Hastings to fall in love with him. He thought that was such a conquest."

"Who's Karen Hastings?"

"You met her yesterday. At the theater. In Kevin's office."

"I thought her name was Remington."

"Oh—sorry. Hastings was the name she used at the theater. It was her maiden name."

"C'mon, now. Move."

"But I didn't do anything. I really didn't."

"You're part of an insurance fraud if nothing else."

She nudged him with the gun.

The tracks thrummed louder now. The train was approaching. Passengers were drifting to the platform, carrying carpetbags and suitcases and even a trunk or two. This late at night, and the fog so heavy, the festive air common to the depot was gone. The passengers just wanted to get on board and be gone. A couple of Mesquakie Indians shivered inside the colorful blankets they had wrapped around themselves.

And then Anna saw the woman they'd just been talking about, Karen Remington. She was just now hurrying out the depot door to the platform. She wore a vast picture hat that did a good job of concealing her face, as the Russian-style greatcoat concealed her figure. Anna wouldn't have recognized her but Bailey did. "Karen!"

The Remington woman swung her face away from Bailey and tried to hurry to the edge of the platform. Obviously, she didn't want to be seen. Bailey started to reach out for her but Karen Remington raised her hand to keep him away.

And when Anna saw the large, pale hand—and the ring with the H on the large, pale hand—she remembered the indentation on the headboard in Anthea Murchison's hotel room. A ring had put that indentation in the headboard, probably when the hand was flung against the wood as the killer was wrestling with Anthea. A ring with the letter H on it. Karen Hastings Remington was the killer Anna was looking for.

It was dawn before Karen Remington told Anna and the Chief what had really happened. When Karen learned that Anthea was back in town, she was afraid that Anthea would steal Kevin back. So she killed her. Then when Kevin spurned her for Beatrice, she decided to end his life in an especially nasty way—kill the woman he loved, and see to it that he was hanged for that murder.

Anna used the new typewriter to pound out a confession for Karen Remington to sign. By this time, Karen's blustery husband was in the station making all sorts of threats to the Chief and talking about what an outrage it was to even *suspect* a woman of such high reputation of murder. He even summoned a few more of his firm's lawyers to come to the station and badger the Chief.

Anna reached home about noon. Mrs. Goldman fed her warm tomato soup and a cheese sandwich. Anna took the latest Nick Carter suspense story upstairs with her. She didn't get much further than the part where Nick disguised himself as a blind Chinese wise man so he could infiltrate the Tong gangs that had been plaguing the city.

Nick would have to wait. So would everything and everybody else. She slept.

The Old Ways

For Norman Partridge

There had been a gunfight earlier in the evening, but then, in a place like this one, there usually were gunfights earlier. And later, for that matter.

The name of the place was Madame Dupree's and it was one of the big casino-drinking establishments that were filling the most disreputable part of San Francisco in this year of 1903. The Barbary Coast was the name for the entire district and, yes, it was every bit as dangerous as you've heard. Cops, even the young strong ones, would only come down here in fours and sixes, and even then an awful lot of them got killed.

The way I got this job was to get myself good and beaten up and tossed in an alley behind the Madame's. One of her men found me and brought me to her and she asked me if I wanted a job and since I hadn't eaten in three days I said yes and so she put me to work as a floater in her casino. What I did was walk around with a few hundred dollars of Madame Dupree's money in my pockets and pretend to be drunk. Inevitably, rubes would spot me as an easy mark and invite me into one of their poker games. Thanks to a few accoutrements such as a holdout vest and a sleeve holdout, I could pretty much deal myself any cards I wanted to. Eighty-five percent of my winnings went back to Madame Dupree. The rest I kept. Not bad pay for somebody who'd been raised on an Oklahoma reservation and seen three of his brothers and sisters die of tuberculosis before they reached eight years of age. I'd gotten my memory back and wished I hadn't.

What Madame Dupree didn't say—didn't need to say, really—was that an Indian was a perfect mark because he was held to be the lowest form of life in these United States, even below that of Negro and Chinaman. What rube could possibly resist taking money from a drunken Indian? Or, for that matter, what Indian could resist? You saw a lot of red men along the Barbary Coast, men who'd worked or stolen their way into some money and now wanted to spend it the way white men did. The Barbary was about the only place in the land where no distinction was made among the races—if you had the money, you could have anything any other man could have. This included all the white girls, some of whom were as young as thirteen, though this particular summer a wave of various venereal diseases was sweeping the Barbary. More than six hundred people had died so far. A Methodist minister had suggested in one of the local newspapers that the Barbary be set afire with all its "human filth" still in it. I wasn't sure that Jesus would have approved of such a proposal, but then you never could tell.

Tonight's gunfight pretty much started the way they all do in a place like this.

On the ground floor, Madame Dupree's consisted of three large rooms, the walls of which were covered by giant murals of easy women in even easier poses. As you wandered among the sailors, the city councilmen, the crooked cops, the whores, the pickpockets, the professional gamblers, the farmers, the clerks, the disguised ministers and priests and even the occasional rabbi, the slumming socialites, and the sad-eyed fathers looking for their runaway daughters, you found gambling devices of every kind: faro, baffling board, roulette, keno, goose-and-balls, and—well, you get the idea.

Tonight a drunken rube suspected he'd been cheated out of his money. And no doubt he suspected correctly. He got loud and then he got violent and then as he was being escorted out one of the side doors by a giant Negro bouncer with a ruffled white shirt already bloody this early in the evening, he made the worst mistake of all. He pulled his gun and tried to shoot the bouncer in the side. And the bouncer responded by drawing his own gun and shooting the man's gun away. And then the bouncer threw the man through the side door and went out into the dark alley.

Everybody who worked here knew what was going to happen next. Every bouncer at every major casino in the Barbary had a specialty. Some were especially good with knives and guns, for instance. This man's specialty was his strength. He liked to grab the top of somebody's head with his giant hand and give the head a violent wrench to the left, thereby breaking the neck. I'd seen him do it once and I couldn't get the sight out of my mind for a couple of weeks afterward. The funny thing was he was called Mr. Stevenson because late at night, at a steak house down the street, he read Robert Louis Stevenson stories out loud to anybody who'd listen. Mr. Stevenson told me once, "I was a plantation nigger and my master thought it'd be funny to have a big buck like me know how to read. So he had me educated from the time I was six and a couple of times a week he'd have me come up to the house and read to all his friends and they just couldn't believe I could read the way I did." That gave us something in common. An Oklahoma white man who ran the town next to my reservation put me through two years of college. I probably would have finished except the man dropped straight down dead of a heart attack and his son wasn't anywhere near as generous.

That was how Mr. Stevenson and I were the same, the education. How we were different was his physical strength.

After Mr. Stevenson finished with the rube, I got myself a good cigar and wandered around in my good clothes, weaving a little the way I did to let people know that I was a drunken Indian, and I got pulled into three different games in as many hours. I won a little over four hundred dollars. Madame Dupree would be happy—at least she would be if she'd gotten over her terrible cold, which some of us had come to suspect was maybe something more than a cold. Be funny if one of the owners died of venereal disease the way their girls and their customers did.

Around ten, I saw Mr. Stevenson working his way over to me. He wore his usual attire, a bowler perched at a rakish angle on his big head, his fancy shirt with the celluloid collar, and a sparkling diamond stickpin through his red cravat.

"You catch a drink with me?" he said as he leaned over the table where I was playing.

"Something wrong?"

He nodded. He had solemn brown eyes that hinted at both his intelligence and his anger.

"Five minutes."

"You know that coon?" one of the rubes said after Mr. Stevenson had left.

"Met him a little earlier. Why?"

The rube shook his head. "Scares the piss out of me, he does. I heard about how he snaps them necks." He shuddered. "Back in Nebraska, you just don't see things like that."

I finished the hand and then joined Mr. Stevenson at the bar. As always, he drank tea. He took his job very seriously and he didn't want whiskey to make him careless.

I didn't much worry about things like that. I had a shot of rye with a beer back.

"What's up, Mr. Stevenson?"

"Moira."

"Oh."

There was a group of reservation Indians who had collected in the Barbary over the past two years or so. Maybe a dozen of us, all employed in various capacities by the casinos. One was a very beautiful Indian girl who'd been called "Moira" by the Indian agent where she'd grown up. Mr. Stevenson was sweet on her, and in a terrible way. He'd go through periods where he couldn't sleep; you'd see him standing in front of her cheap hotel, staring up at her window, doing some kind of sad sentry duty. Or you'd see him following her. Or you'd see him sitting alone in a coffeehouse all teary-eyed and glum and you knew who he was thinking about. Or I did, anyway. I'd gone through the same thing with Moira myself. I'd been in bitter love with her for nearly a year but then I'd passed through it. Like a fever.

Not that you could blame Moira. She was as captivated by another reservation Indian named Two Eagle as we were captivated by her. Did all the same things we did with her. Followed him around. Bought him gifts he didn't want. Wrote him pleading little notes.

Then they got a place and moved in together. Moira and Two Eagle, but word was things weren't going well. He was one of those Indians too fond of the bottle and too bitter toward the white man to function well. Kept a drum up in his room and sometimes in the middle of the night you'd hear it, a tom-tom here in the center of the Barbary, and him yowling ancient Indian war cries and chants. He was fierce, Two Eagle, and he seemed to hate me especially, seemed to think that I had no pride in my red skin or my ancestors. I returned the favor, thinking he was pretty much of a melodramatic asshole. I was just as much an Indian as he was. I just kept it to myself was all.

Only time I ever liked him was one night when I ran into him and Moira in a Barbary restaurant, real late it was, and Two Eagle gentle drunk on wine, and him telling her in great excited rushes about the old religions of ours, and how only the red man—of all the earth's peoples—understood that sky and sun and the winds were all part of the Great God spirit—and how a man or woman who knew how to truly speak to God could then address all living creatures on the earth, be they elk or horse or great mountain eagle, for all things and all creatures are God's, and thus all things in the world, seen and unseen alike, are indivisible, and of God. And he spoke with such passion and sweep and majesty that I could see tears in his eyes—as I felt tears in my own eyes . . . and I saw that there was a good side to his belligerent clinging to the old ways. But his bad side . . .

Moira liked white-man things. Back when she'd let me take her to supper a few times, we'd gone for a long carriage ride by the bay and she'd enjoyed it. Then we went up where the fancy shops were. She made a lot of little-girl sounds, pleased and cute and dreamy.

This was the part of her Two Eagle hated. By now he'd got her to dress in deerskin instead of cloth dresses, her shining black hair in pigtails instead of tumbling tresses, her face innocent of the "whore paint," as he pontifically called it. He worked as a bouncer in a place so tough it might have given Mr. Stevenson pause, and she worked behind the bar in the same place. Pity the man who got drunk and started sweet-talking Moira. Two Eagle would drag him outside and make the man plead for a quick death.

Now that I was over Moira, I didn't especially like hearing about either of them. But you couldn't say the same for Mr. Stevenson. He was as aggrieved as ever, all pain and dashed hope.

"She went out on him."

"Oh, bullshit."

"True," he said. "Few nights ago. They got into a bad fight and he kicked her in the stomach. He didn't know she was just startin' to carry a baby. Killed the baby and nearly killed Moira, too."

"The sonofabitch. Somebody should kill that bastard."

"You haven't heard the rest of it."

"I'm not sure I want to."

"He wants to cut her."

"Cut her?"

"The old ways, he says. What the Indians used to do back when I was on the plantation. When a woman went out on a man like that. You know—her nose."

"That's crazy. Nobody does that shit anymore."

"He does. Or at least he says he does. You know how he is. All that warrior bullshit he gets into."

"Where's Moira?"

"That's the worst part. She thinks she's got it coming. She's just waitin' in her room for him to come up and cut her. Says she believes in the old ways, too."

I shook my head. "That sounds like Moira." I took my pocket watch from my breeches. "I've got some time off coming. I can tell Madame Dupree I'm going for the rest of the night."

"You're tough, man, but you aren't that tough. Two Eagle'll kill you." He showed me his hands. How big they were. And strong. And black. "Fucker tries to cut her, I'll take care of him." He nodded to the front door, his bowler perched at a precarious angle. Sometimes I wondered if he had it glued to his bald head. "Let's go."

We went.

Making our way along the board sidewalks this time of night meant stepping over corpses, drunks, and reeking puddles of vomit and blood from various fights. Every important casino had a band of its own, which meant that the noise was as bad as the odors.

It was raining, which meant the boards were slick. But

we walked fast, anyway. Two Eagle had a couple of rooms on the second floor of a livery stable. Moira lived there, too. She'd waited a long time for him to marry her. I figured she'd wait a lot longer.

A drunken rube made a crack about Mr. Stevenson, but if the black man heard, he didn't let on. Just kept walking. Real quiet and real intense. Like he had only one thought in the entire world and everything else just got in the way. Moira can make you like that.

The Barbary looked pretty much as usual, a jumble of cheap clothing stores for drunken sailors, dance halls where the girls were practically naked, and signs that advertised every kind of whore anybody could ever want. There was a new one this month, a mulatto who went over four hundred pounds, and a lot of Barbary regulars were giving her a try just to see what it'd be like, a lady so fat.

Half a block away you could smell the sweet hay and the sour horseshit in the rain and the night. Closer, you could hear the horses roll against their stalls, making small nervous sounds as they dreamed.

We went up a long stretch of outside stairs. The two-by-fours were new and smelled of sawn wood, tangy as autumn apples on a back porch.

Stevenson didn't knock. He just kicked the door in and stepped over the threshold. The walls inside were stained and the floors so scuffed the wood was slivery. She'd put up new red curtains that were supposed to make the shabby room a home but all the curtains did was make everything else look even older and uglier.

Moira, sad beautiful Indian child that she was, sat in a corner with her head on her knees. When she looked up, her black eyes glistened in the lantern light. She wore a deerskin dress and moccasins. The walls were covered with the lances and shields and knives and arrows of Two Eagle's tribe. He liked to smoke opium up here and tell dream-stories about ancient days when the medicine men said that the bravest warriors had horses that could fly. But the toys on the wall looked dulled and dusty and drab. Every couple of weeks he had his little group of Barbary-area Indians up here, Moira had told me once. The last stand, I'd remarked sarcastically. But she hadn't found it funny at all.

"This is crazy shit, Moira," I said. "We're gonna get you out of here before he comes back."

She had wrists and ankles so delicate they could make you cry. She stood up in her red skin, no more than ninety pounds and five feet she was, and walked over to Mr. Stevenson and said, "You don't have no goddamn right to come here, Mr. Stevenson. Or you either," she said to me. "What happens between Two Eagle and me is our business."

"You ever seen a woman who's been cut?" I said. I had. The man always took the nose, the same thing the ancient Egyptians had taken, just sawed it right off the face, so that only a dark and bloody hole was left. No brave ever wanted a woman who'd been cut, so many of the women went into the forest to live. A few even drank poison wine to end it quickly.

She looked at Mr. Stevenson. "We don't have no whiskey left."

"So the nigger goes and fetches you some, huh?" he said in his deep and bitter voice.

"I need to talk to Jimmy here, Mr. Stevenson, that's all. Just ten minutes or so."

He brought up his big murderous hands and looked at them as if he wasn't quite sure what they were.

"Rye?" he said.

She smiled and was even more beautiful. "Thanks for remembering. I'll get some money from Two Eagle and pay you back."

"I don't want any of his money," Mr. Stevenson said, and fixed her with his melancholy gaze. "I just want you."

"Oh, Mr. Stevenson," she said, and gently touched her small hand to his wide, hard chin. Sisterly, I guess you'd say. She was like that with every man but Two Eagle.

"You don't let him lay a hand on her," Mr. Stevenson said to me as he crossed the room to the door.

I brought up my Colt. "Don't worry, Mr. Stevenson."

He glanced at her one more time, sad and loving and scared and obviously baffled by his own tumultuous feelings, and then he left.

"Poor Mr. Stevenson."

"He's a decent man," I said.

"Kinda scary, though."

"Not any more so than Two Eagle."

"I just wished he understood how I felt about Two Eagle."

"Maybe he finds it kind of hard to understand a man who kicks a woman so hard she loses the baby she's carrying—and then wants to cut her nose off."

"He didn't mean to kick me that hard. He was real sorry. He cried when he saw—the baby."

I went over to the window and looked out on the Barbary Coast. One of the local editorial writers had estimated that a man was robbed every five minutes in the Barbary. At least when it rained, it didn't smell so bad.

I turned back to her. "I want to put you on a train tonight. For Denver. There's one that leaves in an hour and a half."

"I don't want to go."

"You know what he's gonna do to you."

Her eyes suddenly filled. She padded back to her corner and sat down and put her head on her knees and wept quietly.

I went over and sat down next to her and stroked her head as she cried.

After a time she looked up, her cheeks streaky with warm tears that I wiped away with my knuckles.

"He caught me."

"It's not something I want to hear about."

"I was so mad at him—with the baby and everything—that I just went out and got drunk. Didn't even know who I was with or where I was."

"Moira, I really don't want to hear."

"So he came looking for me. Took him all night. And you know where he found me?"

I sighed. She was going to tell me anyway.

"Up in some white sailors' room. There were two of them. One of them was inside me when he came through the door and found me."

I didn't say anything. Neither did she. Not for a long time.

"You know what was funny, Jimmy?"

"What?"

"He didn't hurt either one of them. Didn't lay a hand on them. Just stood there staring at me. And the guy, well, he pulled out and picked up his clothes and got out of there real fast with his friend. It was their own room, too. That's what was real funny. By then, I was sober. I

131

tried to cover myself up but I couldn't find my clothes, so I went over and held Two Eagle just like he was my little boy, and then he started crying. I'd never heard him cry before. It was like he didn't know how. And then I got him over to the bed and I tried to make love to him but he couldn't. And he hasn't been able to since it happened, almost a week now. He's not a man anymore. That's what he said to me. He said that he can't be a man ever again after what he saw. And it's my fault, Jimmy. It's all my fault."

I wanted to hate him, or her, or myself; I wanted to hate some goddamned body, but I couldn't. It was just sad human shit and at the moment it overwhelmed me, left me ice cold and confused. People are so goddamned confusing sometimes.

She laughed. "You and Mr. Stevenson must have some conversations about us, Jimmy."

I stood up, reached back down, and took her wrist. "C'mon now, I'm taking you to the train."

"You ain't takin' her nowhere."

A harsh, quick voice from behind me in the doorway. When I turned I was looking into Two Eagle's insane dark eyes. I'd never seen him when he didn't look angry, when he didn't look ready for blood. He wore a piece of leather tied around his head, his rough black hair touching his shoulders, his gaunt cheeks crosshatched with myriad knife slashes. His buckskin outfit gave him the kind of Indian ferocity he wanted.

He came into the room.

"Why can't you be true to our ancestors for once, Jimmy?" he said, pointing his Colt right at my head. "Cutting her is the only thing I can do. Even Moira agrees. So why should you try to stop it? It's our blood, Jimmy, our tribal way."

"I don't want you to cut her."

His hard face smiled. "You gonna stop me, Jimmy?"

He expected me to be afraid of him and I was. But that didn't mean I wouldn't shoot him if I had to.

And then Mr. Stevenson was in the doorway.

Moira made a female sound in her throat. Two Eagle followed my gaze over his shoulder to the huge black man in the doorframe.

"You're smart to have him around, Jimmy. You'll need him."

Mr. Stevenson came into the room carrying a bottle of rotgut rye in one hand and a single rose in the other. He carried the flower to Moira and gave it to her. Then, without any warning, he turned around and backhanded Two Eagle so hard the Indian's feet left the floor and he flew backwards into the wall. The entire room shook.

Mr. Stevenson wasn't going to bother with any preliminaries.

He went right for Two Eagle, who was trying to right his vision and his breathing and his ability to stand up straight. He'd struck his head hard when he'd collided with the wall and he looked disoriented. Bright red blood ran from his nostrils.

Mr. Stevenson grabbed him and it was easy to see what he was going to do. Maybe he thought that this would ultimately give him his first real chance with Moira, killing Two Eagle by snapping his neck.

"No!" I shouted.

And dove on Mr. Stevenson's back, trying to pull him off Two Eagle.

But it was no use. I clung to Mr. Stevenson like a child. I could not even budge him.

By now he had his hands in place, one on top of Two Eagle's head, the other on the bottom of his neck—ready for the single wrench that would kill Two Eagle.

Two Eagle used fists, feet, even his teeth to get free, but Mr. Stevenson paid no attention. He was setting himself to perform his most magnificent act . . .

Moira shot him once in the side and then raised the gun and shot him once on top of the head. His hair flew off, a bloody black coil of curls affixed to the wall by pieces of sticky flesh and bone.

The funny thing was, he kept right on going, as if he refused to acknowledge what Moira had done to him.

Getting ready to snap Two Eagle's neck—

And then she ran closer, shrieking, and shot him again, and this time not even Mr. Stevenson could refuse to acknowledge what had happened. Blood poured from his ears.

An enraged Two Eagle was now able to bring his hands up and seize Mr. Stevenson's throat, holding tight, choking him, as the big black fell over backwards. Two Eagle riding him down to the floor and then grabbing the gun from Moira's hand.

Two Eagle put the barrel of the .45 to Mr. Stevenson's forehead and fired three times. Didn't seem to matter to him that Mr. Stevenson had died a little while ago.

With each shot, Mr. Stevenson's head jerked upward from the coarse board floor and then slapped back down.

Two Eagle was calling him nigger and a lot of other things in our native tongue.

Then he was done, Two Eagle, pitching forward and lying facedown on the floor, very still for a long time.

I got up and straightened my clothes and picked up my gun from the floor where it had fallen when I'd jumped on Mr. Stevenson.

Moira said, "You two shouldn't have come up here."

"I guess not." I nodded to Mr. Stevenson. "He was trying to help you was all."

"It wasn't none of his business and it ain't none of yours, either."

"I guess he didn't see it that way. Seeing's he loved you and all."

"A nigger," Two Eagle said, getting up from the floor suddenly. "A nigger, lovin' Moira. Maybe you think that's all right, Jimmy, but then you give up bein' a true man a long time back."

And then he went for me. Couldn't help himself. He still had all this fury and it had to light somewhere.

Some came at me, but he was stupid because he didn't look at my hand.

I felt his powerful arm wrap around my neck. I smelled his sweat and whiskey and tobacco.

He pushed me back against the wall.

And that was when I raised my Colt and put it directly to his ribs and fired three times.

He was dead before he hit the floor.

She was screaming, Moira was. That was about all I can tell you about my last few minutes in the room. She was screaming and Two Eagle had fallen close by Mr. Stevenson and then I was running. That's about all I can remember.

Then there was the night and the rain and I was running and running and running and tripping and falling and hurting myself bad but no matter how far or how fast I ran, I could still hear Moira screaming.

* * *

Week later it was.

I was back doing my nightly turn at Madame Dupree's, winning upwards of five hundred dollars this particular night, when I saw Lone Deer come in the side door by the faro layout.

She looked frantic. I figured it was me she wanted.

Being as we were waiting for some liquid refreshments at our table, I got up and went over to her.

When I reached her, she said, "She's goin', Jimmy. Leavin' us. Twenty-five minutes, her train leaves. I didn't find out till half an hour ago myself. Thought I'd better tell you."

"I appreciate it."

I suppose, like Mr. Stevenson, I'd had the idle dream that Moira and I would be lovers now that Two Eagle was gone. I didn't have to worry about any recriminations from the law getting in my way. A dead nigger and a dead Injun on the Barbary Coast don't exactly turn out a lot of curious cops. They're just two more slabs down at the morgue.

I'd figured I'd give it a few weeks and then go see her, tell her how what I did was the only thing I known to do— kill him to save my own life. And then I'd gentlelike invite her out for some dinner and . . .

But that wasn't to be. Not now.

Moira was leaving.

"You'd better hurry," Lone Deer said. And then took my arm and drew me closer. "There's something else I need to tell you."

Less than two minutes later I was running toward the depot. It was crowded and the conductor walked up and down all pompous as he consulted his railroad watch and shouted out that there were only a few minutes left before this particular train pulled out.

I found her in the very back of the last coach. The car was barely half full and she looked small and isolated there with the seats so much taller than she was. Moira. She'd always be a child.

I dropped into the seat next to her and said, "Lone Deer told me what you did."

"I wish she wouldn't have. I didn't want nobody to see me off."

"I love you, Moira."

"I don't want to hear that. Not with Two Eagle barely a week dead. Didn't I betray him enough?"

I'd seen the soldiers drag my grandfather from the reservation one day when I was very young. They were taking him to a federal penitentiary where he would die less than two months later at the hands of some angry white prisoners. I could still feel my panic that day—panic and terror and a sense that my own life was ending, too.

That's how I felt now, with Moira.

"But I won't betray him no more," Moira said. "You can bet on that."

"Is that why you did it?"

"Why I did it is none of your business."

I looked at her there in her black mourning dress and black mourning hat and black mourning veil, a veil so heavy you couldn't make out anything on the other side.

"No man'll ever want to bother me again. I made sure of that."

I was tempted to lift the veil quickly and see what she

137

looked like. Lone Deer had said that Moira had used a butcher knife on her nose and that nothing remained but a bloody hole.

But then I decided that I didn't want to remember her that way. That I always wanted her to be young and beautiful Moira in my mind. Every man needs something to believe in, even if he knows it's not true.

"You got a ticket, buck?" the conductor asked me. Ordinarily, I'd take exception to his calling me "buck," but at the moment it just didn't seem very important.

I leaned over and kissed Moira, pressing her veil to her cheek. I still couldn't see anything.

"Hurry up, buck. You get your ass off of here or you show me a ticket."

I squeezed her hand. "I love you, Moira. And I always will."

And then I was gone, and the train was pulling out, all steam and power and majesty in the western night.

Then I walked slowly back to Madame Dupree's where I got just as drunk as Indians are supposed to get.

Killer in the Dark

Tuesday 4:03 P.M.

The tall man in the dark city-cut suit says nothing. He is not unfriendly.

That is to say, he smiles when the others smile; he gives approving nods when the others do likewise. He picks up one of the ladies' magazines when it is jostled to the floor of the stagecoach. He even offers a stick match to one of the men who wants to light his cigar. But he does not join in any of the conversations. He seems distracted. He stares out the window. Every time one of the passengers mentions Tombstone, which lies just ahead, his dark eyes flicker.

4:09 P.M.

"I don't want to piss you off, Virgil."

"Well, it sure as hell isn't going to do me any good if you

139

lie to me, Sam. So tell me, what did the council say?"

"It wasn't the whole council."

"No?"

"It was just three out of four."

"That's a pretty good number."

"It don't matter what they said, Virgil. I shouldn't ought've brought it up in the first place."

When you were city marshal of a town as wild and dangerous as Tombstone, you needed loyalty from your deputies. The trouble with Sam Purcell was he took loyalty too far. From time to time he'd hear things that Virgil ought to know. But he wouldn't share them because he was afraid he'd hurt Virgil's feelings.

But he'd made a mistake.

He'd started telling Mal Bottoms, one of the other deputies, what he'd overheard at the town council meeting this afternoon. And Virgil had happened to be within ear distance.

So now Virg and Sam stood in the empty outer office with all the wanted posters and the smell of burnt coffee and Virg's Scottish pipe tobacco, and Virg said, "Tell me, Sam. And tell me right now."

Sam sighed. Sam was a champion sigher. In fact, Sam was far more articulate with his shoulders than he'd ever been with his tongue.

"Well, in a nutshell what they said was, and you know I sure as hell don't agree with it, was that maybe you were the right kind of town marshal for when a bunch of cowhands want to come in town and raise hell, but maybe you're not the right kind of town marshal for a manhunt."

"Meaning Bobby Gregg."

"Meaning Bobby Gregg. They said he's probably in Mexico by now."

"Not unless he has wings. Suzie Proctor was murdered less than thirty-six hours ago."

"Like I said, Virgil, it ain't me sayin this, it's the council."

"Three out of four."

"What the hell do they know anyway?"

"That all they said?"

"Pretty much."

Virg smiled. "Meaning there's somethin you left out."

"Well."

Now it was Virg's turn to sigh. He wasn't as good at it as Sam, but he gave it a good try. "I'm supposed to be lookin' for a killer, Sam. I believe—despite what the town council says—that he's hiding right here in Tombstone. Now I need you to tell me what else the council said and then I need to get back to work."

Sam made a face. "They said if Bobby Gregg gets away— Suzie bein' so popular and all—that they'll take your badge away whether Wyatt Earp's your brother or not."

"They said that, did they?"

"I didn't want to tell you, Virgil. But you made me."

"It's all right, Sam."

"You pissed off?"

"Not at you."

"I'm sorry, Virgil."

"I know you are, Sam. Now let's get back to work."

A few minutes later, strapping on his Colt and grabbing a Winchester, Virg Earp left the town marshal's office. He had three different posses looking for Bobby in the areas surrounding Tombstone. He kept on working the town it-

self. A lot of people smirked when he passed by. A few
even made jokes about him. Mostly that he was too lazy to
go out into the blistering desert sun and look for Bobby.

Nobody but Virg seemed to believe that Bobby was hiding somewhere in town here.

5:01 P.M.

He was an unlikely killer, Richard Turney. He ran one of
Tombstone's three newspapers. He'd been educated in the
East at Rutgers, and had seriously considered attending
Harvard Divinity School afterward. He would have made
a fine parson. But he decided he could be more effective as
a journalist. He worked for a time for the *New York Daily*
and the *Chicago Gazette*. He was the champion of the miners and their families and a favorite of the area's ministers,
priests, and one rabbi. Too many newspaper editors were
in the pockets of the rich and powerful. Not Turney. His
office had been raided, trashed, burned. He had been followed, threatened, shot. His wife Jean Anne had been as-
saulted and very nearly raped. And yet he kept on being
the spokesman for the poor, the weak, the sick, the men-
tally troubled, the Irish, Jews, colored, Chinese—and for
decent working conditions in the mines, where men died
every single day of the week and usually unnecessarily.

He hadn't wanted his affair with Suzie Proctor to become any more than friendship. And yet—taking on a life
of its own—it had. He had a lovely wife and two lovely
children. And most of all, he had his reputation for recti-
tude. Let other Tombstonians carry on as if they lived in a
whorehouse . . . but not Richard Turney.

But what use was a fallen sinner to his community . . .

or to himself? He'd tried to convince her to quit her job as his assistant, and quit sneaking off with him in the evenings. She was officially engaged to Bobby Gregg, who was a fine young man. Did she want to destroy her future with him? But she was adamant. She loved Richard. There was nobody else for her. Bobby was a child. Richard was a grown and wonderful man. A wonderful man who'd strangled her.

He'd crept home late, from dragging the body to the river. Jean Anne had been awake when he came in. Demanded to know what had happened. Listened in shock and terror as he'd told her all of it. A parson's daughter whose good looks—it was said—were utterly wasted on so religious a woman, she'd told Richard he must not confess. Because if he did, who would defend the poor and powerless of this area?

He got up several times during the night. Couldn't sleep. Wanted to go to the town marshal's office and confess. She awoke each time with him. Wouldn't let him go.

Walking the streets now was difficult for him. He wanted the forgiveness of every citizen, for he felt that his behavior—first his adultery, then the killing—surely required their understanding.

How could he live with this, even though suspicion had naturally fallen on Bobby Gregg, who had been seen arguing violently with Suzie three hours before the murder?

5:07 P.M.

The stranger was the last person off the stage. He stood in the dusty twilight looking around the legendary town with icy interest.

Boomtowns usually deserved their reputations. But men like the Earps—hired guns who wore badges—took care to see that such towns were safe for those who had to live there. You could whore it up and drink it up and gamble it up if you stayed in the places that the Earps owned. But anywhere else, they'd run you in fast. And your fine would help swell the town treasury, to which they were entitled to a goodly share.

He began to walk, a cheroot stuck in one corner of his mouth. With his dark suit, dark flat-brimmed hat, and dark-handled .44 riding in a dark leather holster, the stranger brought a funereal aspect to a part of town where most folks were dressed for partying. His younger brother had walked these same streets for the past few years after settling in here as a miner. The kid had kind of drifted around before. The stranger had been so happy to hear he'd taken a regular job, he'd bought the kid a whole bunch of new duds including boots, and put twenty-five Yankee dollars in an envelope too. He'd sent them to the kid for his twenty-first birthday.

He continued to walk, to watch. He did not walk unnoticed.

Sam, the deputy, took note of him when he walked down Main Street and stopped in at the telegraph office; Mal, the other daytime deputy, took note of him when he left and walked over to the Bountiful Hotel.

Sam went over to the telegraph operator and asked to see what message the stranger had sent.

Burt Knowles, the telegrapher, laughed. "He was foxin' ya, Sam. He wanted to see if anybody was followin' him. He just come in here and stood over in the corner smokin' that cheroot, and then he left. Then he got down to that corner where Mal picked him up, and he stood there and watched you come in here."

This was greatly amusing to Burt. Much less so Sam.

The stranger registered at the hotel and went directly to his room. He slid off his clothes except for his underwear, and then climbed into bed and started reading a book by Sir Walter Scott.

He decided he'd get a little reading done before the local law came to call.

The knock came thirty-five minutes later. The stranger recognized the man in the door immediately. Virgil Earp.

"I come in?" Virgil said.

"I wouldn't be foolish enough to stop you."

Virgil nodded and entered. "Just doing my job, mister. My responsibility to know who's in town and what their business is."

"Yes, I've always heard that Tombstone only lets the elite stay within its city limits."

Earp gave him a sharp look. "Nobody's claimin' we're angels here. But there's different kinds of bad men. Bad and real bad. The real bad ones we don't let in. Now, I'd like to see some identification if you don't mind."

The stranger, who was wearing his suit again, slipped a hand inside his suit jacket and pulled out a wallet. He handed it to Earp.

Earp looked through it and whistled. "You're a Pinkerton?"

"That's right."

"And your name is Ben Gregg?"

145

"Right again."

"You any relation to Bobby?"

"I'm his older brother."

"You know he's wanted for murder?"

"He didn't do it."

"How do you know?"

"I know Bobby. He's emotional, but he's not a killer."

Earp handed the wallet back. "I don't suppose you might be a wee bit prejudiced."

"He's my brother. I spent twelve years with him on an Ohio farm. I know how he reacts to things. He told me all about Suzie. How she'd agreed to marry him, and then backed out all of a sudden. And how he was going crazy."

"You saw him?"

"He wrote me."

"He must be quite the writer."

"He finished the tenth grade. He's a smart kid."

"He's also a killer, Mr. Gregg. I don't take any pleasure saying that to you. I really don't. I have brothers too, and I know what this must be like for you. The best thing you can do is help us find him. And then have him give himself up before somebody decides to play hero and shoots him— or a bunch of drunks get together and try to lynch him."

"He didn't kill her."

Earp walked back to the door. "I wish you'd help us, Mr. Gregg. You might save his life."

"Save his life until the territory can hang him, you mean."

"I don't make the laws. I just enforce them."

"Noble sentiment."

Earp opened the door, lingered. "You seem like a smart man, Mr. Gregg. It's hard to be objective in a situation like this. He's your own flesh and blood. You might think you're helping him—but maybe you're really hurting him. And yourself in the process. There are laws against aiding and abetting a fleeing felon, Mr. Gregg." He paused. "Even when the felon happens to be your brother."

Then he was gone.

6:03 P.M.

"How come Daddy is in bed?" twelve-year-old Ruth asked Jean Anne Turney. She seemed older than her calendar age, having the poise and elegance of her mother.

"He's not feeling well, honey."

"How come he doesn't feel well?" Nicholas Turney said. He was eight.

"He just has a little touch of something is all, sweetheart." She was a lovely, elegant woman—even in a much-washed and much-patched cotton pinafore she was elegant—with the features of classical statuary and eyes that sparkled with life. Until you studied them anyway. Some folks claimed to see a hint of madness there—all that religion she so deeply believed and espoused. Most pioneer stock had brought their religion with them. But they weren't about to let themselves become fanatics about it. Leave that to the Mormons.

"What's a 'touch' mean?" Nicholas wanted to know.

Jean Anne smiled at him. "Correct me if I'm wrong, but didn't we sit down here to have supper?"

He giggled. He loved it when Mommy played school-teacher. It was fun. "We sat down to eat. E-A-T."

"Correct," Jean Anne said. "Now, can you tell me *why* we're not eating?"

He giggled again. "Because we're gabbin'. G-A-B-B-I-N."

"That's right. Gabbing. You can't put food in your mouth while you're yapping." Jean Anne smiled. "I thought we were going to quit gabbing—*and* yapping—and eat our dinner."

Corn on the cob; potatoes; green beans. All from the garden Jean Anne tended to so devoutly.

"But first, let's say grace."

Jean Anne usually concentrated on each and every word of every prayer she said. Sometimes people just rushed through prayers, mumbling the words and letting their minds stray to other matters. What was the point of praying then? God wanted total attention. God wanted utter and uncorrupted devotion.

But tonight, as the children raggedly prayed their way through grace—she loved the sound of their small earnest voices; and surely God too must be pleased when He heard such pure and innocent voices—tonight she was no better than the mumblers she castigated.

She couldn't think of anybody but Richard; of anything but Suzie Proctor's death.

Forgive me O Lord, she thought. But I can't have this scourge brought down upon my children. If people know that their father killed her—accidentally or not—then they'll be marked for the rest of their lives, like a version of Cain's mark.

She tried not to think of her proper folks back East, her father a parson so respected that the Episcopal bishop declared him the finest church orator he'd ever heard. The scandal—adultery, death—would surely hasten his death. He had a bad heart and was already failing.

148

She had never told a serious lie in her life; and the few small lies she'd told she'd later admitted to, and asked the person's forgiveness.

But she knew this was one lie she would have to be part of for the sake of the children. Bobby Gregg was the man the mob was looking for. Bobby Gregg was the man who would have to stand trial for Suzie's death. She tried to convince herself she was doing the only thing she could. Bobby was single, had no roots, would probably not live long anyway, given his temper. He and Richard were good friends, pitching horseshoes whenever they had a chance, Bobby eating dinner here a couple of times a month. And Bobby was a good young man, but—but Richard, on the other hand, was the father of two, a successful businessman, and a man who brought the truth to all. She knew as a Christian that all lives were important . . . but (and forgive me, O Lord, if this is the sin of pride) aren't some lives more important than others in the scheme of things?

"My beans are cold," Ruth said.

"Gosh, I wonder why," Jean Anne said.

"Because we were yappin'," Ruth said, and looked at Nicholas.

"Huh-uh. We were gabbin', not yappin'," Nicholas said.

"It's the same thing," Ruth said.

"Huh-uh." Nicholas said. "Is it, Mommy?"

Are some lives more important in the vast scheme of things? Jean Anne knew she was treading on some mighty dangerous territory here. Playing God was what she was doing. Making decisions only the Good Lord Himself should be making.

149

But how could you look at these two wonderful children and not spare them the mark that would be associated with what their father had done?

But Bobby Gregg . . .

7:23 P.M.

Serena's brother Tom made ninety dollars a month as a bricklayer. Serena, all of seventeen, made $150 on average. Serena was a prostitute. Not that Tom knew. He lived in Denver. Not that her mama knew. Though she lived in the house with Serena, she was still suffering the effects of her stroke. She was not yet forty-five, but looked eighty, crabbed up in her wooden wheelchair. Sometimes she shit herself. Sometimes she talked in that slow, retarded way to phantoms and ghosts. And sometimes she sang this strange, melancholy, beautiful song in the clear, dear voice of the young woman she'd once been.

Serena worked right in Tombstone. There was one house that had been particularly good to her, so she'd pretty much stayed there. But she always came home. She worked four hours a night, and then went back to her mama's place for the night. She had a face and figure that could command so much money for so little work. Every man who came into Mama Gilda's wanted Serena. And who could blame them?

Tonight Serena was late for work. There'd be a battle with Mama Gilda. She'd begun to wonder if Gilda knew what was going on, with Bobby Gregg and all. Serena, who was in love with him, and had been since the very first time she'd ever seen him, had hidden him in the attic ever since they'd found Suzie Proctor's body. She believed Bobby—even if few others did—that he hadn't killed

Suzie. And she knew damned well that if Virg Earp (who had visited her more than a few times at Mama Gilda's) ever found Bobby, he'd do what he needed to to satisfy the public at election time. He'd made a big show against it—but he'd let a lynching take place. And he wouldn't indict anybody after it either.

Serena's mama had had a bad time just around dusk. She'd started throwing up and talking crazy. She'd also started running a hell of a fever. Serena—knowing that Doc Wright would just say to let the fever run its course—had spent nearly two hours with Mama before getting the old lady in bed and settled down for the night.

Now, a dinner of squash, peas, wheat bread, and apple pie filling a large plate, she climbed the stairs to the attic. She had the sensation of climbing into night itself. Except for a tiny window in the front of the house, no light liberated the attic. It was a prison of darkness.

She heard Bobby start as she reached the narrow square where the ladder ended. She heard him draw his six-gun. Bobby was scared, no doubt about it.

She walked slowly through the gloom, over to the small window where Bobby sat propped against the wall. She'd brought him a chamber pot a few days ago. The pot was starting to reek. When she had time later tonight, she'd empty it for him.

"You hear anything today?" he said. Then: "I really appreciate you doing this for me." He sounded so young, frightened. He'd told her at least a dozen times about a lynching he'd seen up to the Missouri border one time. How the man had screamed and sobbed until the noose finally broke his neck.

She couldn't see much of him, but the moonlight hinted at the strong lines of his face and the vulnerable beauty of his brown eyes. He was all man, Bobby was.

"The manhunt's still on if that's what you mean."

"What's Virg sayin' about me?"

"He still thinks you're in town."

"They still laughin' at him?"

"Sure. Most people think you're long gone." Then: "You better eat, Bobby."

She liked to watch and listen to him eat. He ate vulgar, jamming the food into his mouth without pause, and smacking his lips loudly and pleasurably. All this evoked a maternal feeling in her. That was it. He was her lover, but somehow he was her brother, too.

"They're gonna get me, aren't they?"

"Not if you stay here. I can protect you, Bobby."

She wouldn't mind spending the rest of her life like this. Someday, they'd give it up and wouldn't hunt for him anymore. And by that time, he'd be so grateful that he'd never leave. That was *her* fear. That he would run off. And so she did everything she could to convince him that he would certainly be lynched if he ever left this house.

"You just stay here. I'm going to see your brother tonight."

"My brother! He's here?"

"I wired him, Bobby. I figured you'd want me to."

"Good Lord, if anybody can figure a way out of this, it's him."

"I have to be careful about seein' him, though. Virg Earp is probably watchin' him pretty close."

"My brother," Bobby marveled. "My brother!" He sounded as if all his troubles had been swept away. He pulled her to him and kissed her. It wasn't the passionate, open-mouthed kind of kiss she wanted from him. It was more just a chaste brother-sister kiss right to the left of her mouth. But it would have to do for now. Bobby didn't love her yet. But by the time this whole thing was over and the real killer had been found, he'd be so grateful that he'd never leave her. Or, if the killer was never found, she'd keep right on hiding him, as she'd thought of earlier.

"I got to go now, Bobby."

"You tell him it's all up to him."

"I will, Bobby."

"You tell him they'd just love to lynch me."

The initial enthusiasm was waning. He was beginning to understand that Pinkerton man or not, his brother maybe couldn't stop the manhunt from taking its inevitable course.

"You just finish your supper and rest, Bobby."

"Sometimes I hear your ma down there singing to herself."

"It's pretty, isn't it?"

"Yeah, except it's sort of spooky too. And I don't mean that to give offense."

"I know what you mean. All the time I was growin' up, she called it her ghost song. That's sort of what it's like."

"Ghost song," Bobby said. "That's a good name for it all right."

6:43 P.M.

Ben knew about conducting a murder investigation. He'd spent an hour where they'd found the young woman's body. He got down on his hands and knees with a magnifying glass and went over everything he could that looked even vaguely useful. He found a variety of buttons, the butts of cigars and cigarettes, small scraps of paper, tiny pieces of broken bottle glass, and numerous other bits and scraps that he dropped into a plain white envelope. Virgil Earp apparently hadn't found any of this material interesting. Ben Gregg had had the advantage of training under Alan Pinkerton. Alan was much taken with the way Scotland Yard and its French counterpart used the idea of a "crime scene" in homicide. You staked out a wide area of ground where the body had been found, and then you carefully combed it for anything you could find. You never knew what would prove helpful to your investigators or the police or the district attorney. So you kept everything and cataloged it.

From time to time, he thought of something else too. According to the newspaper account, she'd been strangled. But then a heavy object had been used to smash in the side of her skull. It seemed an odd combination. If the killer had strangled her, wouldn't that be enough? Why then smash a rock against the side of her head?

Finished with his work, he went back to town and spent two hours talking to people who knew Bobby. None of them thought he was the killer. It was hard to know why they just saying this. Did they really believe it, or were they just saying it to make an older brother feel better? He learned nothing special from these interviews, except that Bobby's best friend in town was probably an "upstart" editor named Richard Turney. Turney was, in the parlance of many, a 'goody-goody,' but as one saloon enthusiast said in his smiley, slurry voice, "Them two, yer brother and that fuckin' big-mouth newspaperman, they're just about the two best horseshoe players in the whole territory. They get more people t'watchin them than them shimmy dancers do when they come here with the county fair every summer."

Turney's name was the only one that was repeated, which was why Ben Gregg was on his way to the Turney house right now.

He might find some answers there.

7:03 P.M.

The young ladies at Mama Gilda's glared at Serena when she came into the parlor. The three men in the room could feel their anger, and wondered what was going on. Then they saw Serena and didn't *care* what was going on. This beautiful, small, delicate creature with the exotic eyes and erotic mouth was the one they wanted. Their first choice anyway. Maybe that's what the other girls were so mad about. That they weren't as pretty or erotic as Serena.

Mama Gilda, a tiny woman with a big temper, pushed her way into the room and said, "I want to see you, young lady, and right now."

The other young ladies smirked with delight. Mama Gilda was finally going to give it to Serena. And it was way past time.

7:04 P.M.

Mike Craig's leg wasn't getting any better. It'd been broken in a landslide and then gangrene had set in somehow. Word was, he was going to lose it. Which meant he couldn't serve as Virg's chief deputy no more.

Virg hadn't decided on who Mike's successor would be. In truth, it would be hard to replace Mike. He was a red-headed Irishman who knew how to keep his temper and how to walk away from a whiskey bottle. The townspeople liked him and the deputies liked him. Hell, some of the prisoners in the lockup liked him. Mike had a million stories.

Sam Purcell meant to have the first deputy's job. He'd served three years with Virgil now, and had learned a damned good lot about being a good, sober public server.

He probably didn't have any real edge. Virg might well not choose him, in fact, which was why Sam was hiding behind the tree across the street from Serena's house on the edge of town.

As usual, Sam had paid a visit to Mama Gilda's Tuesday afternoon. He always collected Virg's share of the money Mama kicked back to him. That's when he'd overheard two of the girls running Serena down. Who does she think she is? She gets paid too much already, and now she isn't even showing up regularly? Sam asked Mama Gilda about this, and the madam acknowledged that Serena had indeed begun acting strangely lately. She works so few hours as it is, Mama Gilda said, and now the little bitch don't even show up for *them* half the time. She didn't have no idea why Serena had suddenly stopped showing up on time. Far as Mama Gilda knew, nothin' bad had happened, not there anyway. No man had mistreated her, none of the gals had stolen from her or beat her up, and she got her money full and on time just like always.

Which had given Sam his idea. Though not a lot of people knew it, Serena and Billy spent their free time together. Good Christian boy like Billy, he didn't want nobody to know, of course. What kinda upstandin' young man keeps company with a whore? It was one thing to visit her at Mama Gilda's and pay for it; but it's another thing entirely to keep *company* with a whore.

So tonight, he sees Serena coming late to Mama Gilda's and he remembers what them gals was chewin' on the other day, how Serena's been comin' into work late and not doin' like she ought to in general. Not like her, Mama Gilda had said, shakin' her head; not like her t'all.

Well, what could a young gal have gone and got herself all caught up in? Could be a rich man; could be some kind of venereal disease even a whore was embarrassed about; or it could be . . . hiding a fugitive.

What if Bobby was in her house somewheres?

Well, that's what Sam was doing here. Just ten, fifteen more minutes and the sun would start sinking, and he'd be sneaking across the road.

If he brought in Bobby Gregg, he'd be first deputy for sure.

7:10 P.M.

Stupid bastard.

Thinks Bobby doesn't see him.

Well, of *course* Bobby sees him. And sees him good too.

Saw him come up from the ravine and go hide behind the tree. He think Bobby's blind or what?

The thing now is, what's he gonna do next? Bobby wonders.

Is Sam gonna charge the house and shout for him to come out?

Or is he gonna try and sneak inside and real quiet-like check out every room in the house?

Bobby'd put money on sneaking inside. Sam fancies

himself a real foxy type. Fought in the war with a buncha farm boys and been sailin' bullshit stories about it ever since. Hear him tell it, Union Army didn't fear nobody as much as they did him.

Then Bobby feels unholy. He is a churchgoer, Bobby, and he has been praying his ass off ever since the manhunt started. He prays and prays and prays, and he feels holy and safe and good. And then he spoils it all by thinking bad thoughts about people and how much he dislikes them and thinks he's better than them and would like to do them harm, and then he doesn't feel holy anymore. He chased holiness away, and now he's just one more miserable desert rat.

No.

He takes it back.

I hope you come in here, Sam, and you don't find me, and you go back home to that Mex wife and kids of yours and you have yourself a real nice, real long life.

That's what's in my heart, Lord. It purely is.

But then he hears Sam on the back porch, sneaking in. Only way he could make any *more* noise was if he fell down into a buncha pots and pans.

Subtle, he ain't.

Then he hears the back door itself squawk open. Door swelled and doesn't fit frame right anymore.

He's inside, Sam is.

Searching.

Only a matter of time till he finds the attic.

O Lord, please keep Sam from finding me. Please, Lord. Please.

It still hurt where Mama Gilda slapped her. Serena sat on the bed in her room, touching her fingers tenderly to the sore spot on her gracefully carved cheek. Bitch probably put a bruise there.

The place was crowded tonight. Lots of whiskey, lots of laughter, lots of prairie flowers fading fast. That was her biggest fear. That somehow she'd wake up one morning and look like them. And it happened so fast sometimes. Take young Helen from Pennsylvania. Came West with her folks, who got killed in a sudden flood. Ended up working as a whore so she could support her two little brothers. Mama Gilda was good to her. Serena had to say that for the old bitch. Mama Gilda saw to it that the kids were put in school, that they found a nice little cabin to live in, and that Helen was home most nights before ten o'clock to tuck the boys in.

But wasn't nothin' Mama Gilda could do about Helen's looks. Year ago. Helen had been almost as beautiful as Serena. Fresh, young, and vital. A lot of her johns—especially the young cowhands—fell in love with her and asked her for her picture and things like that. But as with many of the girls, disease aged them fast. Bad luck of the draw, to be sure; but this bad luck seemed to come to so many of the girls. First, Helen had come down with just crabs, then with gonorrhea. And she was always catching colds and having influenza and getting the chills and then the fevers for no reason—not even the doctor—could see. And it had all taken its toll. Pale, tired, drab, she had worked her way down toward the bottom of popularity. No men, either young nor old, asked for her anymore, and Mama Gilda had begun to give her day work—helping clean and sew and do bookkeeping work (at least Helen had a bit of education and was smart, which was more than you could say for most of the other girls), the sort of jobs girls got if they were diagnosed with syphilis, Mama not allowing no girls with syphilis to cavort with her customers till the doctor said they couldn't infect nobody.

So far tonight, Serena had had two of her regulars, and they'd both said that she seemed in sort of an owly mood. She'd put on her best smile and forced herself to laugh a lot, but they knew better and she knew better. She'd worked them hard too, so they'd come faster.

She needed to be alone to think about Bobby. Now that she was away from the house, she saw how foolish she'd been. Somebody was bound to find him there. People were always coming over to drop things off for her mother. One of them was bound to see or hear something.

Why couldn't Virg Earp just find the real killer anyway?

She knew what that posse would do if they ever did find Bobby. All his nightmares about being lynched would come true.

At this point, his brother was his only hope. That's probably why she was so anxious. She needed to get out of here and go see his brother.

But the clock hands didn't seem to move. She was sure they hadn't moved in an hour.

A knock.

"It's me, Princess. Tom Peters."

"Hi, Tom."

"Are ya decent?"

"No, I'm not."

"Then I'll be right in."

It was the same joke he used every time he came to Mama Gilda's, and usually the idiocy of it made her smile despite herself. But not tonight.

She hurried to the mirror. She took pride in her job.

She fixed her hair from the last tumble on the bed, freshened her makeup, daubed on some more perfume.

If only helping Bobby was this easy.

But she had to help him before the lynch mob did.

7:36 P.M.

It made for a lonely portrait, the sight of Gregg the Pinkerton man in his shirtsleeves bent over a table where he'd spread out everything he'd found where the girl had been strangled, a flickering lamp his only companion. He was a city man and this was a nowhere town, and in his occasional sighs you could hear the pain that time had inflicted on him, and that he had sometimes inflicted upon himself.

The wife and two sons who had left him when it became clear that he would never give up this detective business and stay home like a real father. The illegitimate son he'd fathered a few years later, who'd smothered to death in his crib one night. The earnest if desperate attempt to reconcile with his wife—traveling by train mid-winter for six hundred miles—only to see her sitting in a restaurant with the man she intended to marry, the man he suspected she loved more than she'd ever loved *him*. Self-pity, self-hatred, a lonesomeness that was a physical ache sometimes—these were the detective's lot, redeemed only by his sense of humor about himself. Nobody could make better jokes about him than he could. And—for everybody's sake—he made such jokes often.

Thank God for detective work. It almost made up for the loneliness. It almost made him forget all the terrible mistakes he'd made in his personal life, not least of which was being such a miserable absent father to his boys. He

161

never would've said that out loud, of course, about detective work being his one true love. Might end up in an asylum if you said it loud enough. Hey, ain't that the guy who said he was in love with detective work? And there he'd be in one of those padded rooms where they slid your food in through a little flap in the bottom of the door. Don't want to get *too* close to the crazy man. Whatever he's got might be catching.

But he lived for the British magazines that detailed all the exciting new work being done in England and France. Fingerprinting was just coming into its own. No court had yet allowed it to be used as evidence, but that was only a matter of time. Phrenology—determining a person's criminal inclinations by the shape of his head—was fading in popularity, and that in itself was exciting. He'd always considered it useless. Scotland Yard was also beginning to create a file on every criminal they arrested. This might be the most important development of all, and Gregg was pleased to see that Alan Pinkerton—despite the reluctance of city cops to do it—was likewise creating his own files on criminals he apprehended.

The two items that interested him most now were a black button that appeared to have come from a dress jacket and two different boot heel prints. The ground there was clay and showed up prints pretty well. He'd gotten down on his knees and scratched a pencil over a thin piece of white paper. The designs on the boot heels showed clearly. There was one other heel design. A much smaller one. A woman's shoe. The heel had been worn down, but you could still see a faint V on it.

He went back to the button. It was the size of a cuff button on a suit jacket. While black was a reasonably popular color with men—easiest to dust off and clean—there were very few men who wore the color regularly. It was considered too hot for summer, for one thing. And too dour for any kind of festive occasion. He started making a list of men who wore black regularly. Preachers, mortuary men, town officials who had to go to a lot of funerals, and carriage-trade types who might get invited out to a fancy dance every once in a while. He could eliminate the latter as a category around here. There *weren't* any fancy dances. He could also eliminate town officials. Folks around here understood how hot it was. They didn't expect anybody to dress in black at functions.

But why would a preacher or a mortuary man be out where a young woman was killed?

He opened himself a pint of rye and pondered. Sometimes, pondering was a whole lot of fun.

8:07 P.M.

Nicholas said, "She's cryin' and she won't stop."

"Your sister?" Jean Anne said. And then realized that was one of those stupid little things people said without thinking. Who *else* would be crying but Ruth? "Where is she?"

"On the swing."

"You finish drying those dishes for Mama. I'll be right back."

"It's *her* turn to dry."

"Don't sass me now; don't you sass me, you understand?"

Nicholas was old enough, and savvy enough, to understand when his mommy was real serious about her threats. Sometimes she was just sorta half-serious and you could tell by her tone of voice that she didn't really want to do anything to you. But then there were times—as now—when he knew that strap wasn't far away if he didn't do *exactly* as she told him.

He took the dish towel down and started drying the dishes.

Jean Anne could hear her before she reached her. Crying bitterly into the last cool traces of daylight.

"Quit swinging, honey, I want to talk to you."

"I don't want to talk, Mama." And kept right on swinging, pigtails flying, the hem of her dress fluttering in the slight wind. She spoke through tears.

Jean Anne grabbed the swing. "What's the matter with you? Don't you do what your mama tells you to do?"

She had to grab the swing even harder to bring it to a full stop. A few times Ruth scuffed her shoes in the worn earth of the swing's path, slowing the swing even more.

"Now I want you to tell me why you're crying."

"I just think Gus is sick is all."

Gus was their sad-faced hound. He was older than Ruth. Jean Anne could see her daughter was lying. She said, concerned now because Ruth so rarely lied, "I need to know the truth. I can't be a good mama if I don't know the truth. You don't want the Lord to punish me for bein' a bad mama, do you?"

Ruth didn't say anything for a time, and then she lifted her sweet little face and looked at her mama. "I guess I just get scared sometimes. Like right before a storm."

Ruth was given to odd moods, moods that sometimes worried both her parents deeply. She did indeed get scared before storms; the smell, the suddenly brooding sky, the sharp decline in heat—she frequently hid under the bed. She was so grown-up in many ways—people often mistook her for sixteen or thereabouts—but there were still strong elements of the little girl in her too.

Ruth was silent. Cows, horses, a distant coyote, night-birds; the restive and restful sounds of a farm as night fell.

"Honey, what are you tryin to say?"

But Ruth, fighting back another round of tears, wouldn't listen. She jumped from her swing and took off running toward the pasture.

Leaving Jean Anne to wonder—what in the Lord's name had *that* been all about?

Nicholas came out the back door. "I'm done with the dishes, Ma. Will you draw pitchers with me later?"

"Yes," Jean Anne said. "Yes, I will."

Nicholas went back inside. He was such a good little boy, uncomplicated.

She wondered what was wrong with Ruth.

8:10 P.M.

He was starting to sweat, Sam was. He'd felt all right entering the house, but once inside, his balls started to shrink and his stomach started to knot and his asshole started to get tight and his breath started to come fast and ragged and the sweat started to pour off him. He felt like some Mex working the fields at high noon. That kind of greasy, filthy sweat.

The downstairs was empty. He'd gone through it room by room. Nothing. Dinner smelled good, though. For a whore, Serena knew how to run a house real good. Trouble was, by the time she was ready to settle down—all rotten-toothed and disease-scabbed like a leper—who the hell would want her? Who would want to stick his dick into a honey pot that had been fouled by so many other dicks?

No man with any sense; no man with any pride. No man Sam knew.

He had a piece of peach pie. Sitting right there just like he'd been invited, a nice little vase of flowers on the table and everything. And he was eating.

Now wasn't that the damndest thing you ever heard of?

This is a man who reads all the dime novels. Who has a very glorified ideal of what a deputy should think, do, and be.

And so what does the sonofabuck do when he sneaks into a house after a cold-blooded mad-dog killer?

He sits his wide ass down on a kitchen chair and helps hisself to a piece of pie. Peach pie. He would've preferred punkin (his word for pumpkin), but this is better'n nothin', that's for sure.

And it doesn't end there.

Because he eats another piece.

Serena's probably gonna wonder what the hell happened to her pie. Her ma is upstairs crippled. She sure as hell didn't come down here and get any. And (if Sam's hunch is right) Bobby Gregg is hiding in the attic, and *he* sure wouldn't've snuck down here either. For a piece of pussy, yes, maybe so. But not for no piece of pie.

But that's where Sam's wrong.

Because Bobby got to wondering upstairs what ole Sam was doin' downstairs. You sneak into a house, you check it out room by room, how long can it take you? Five–ten minutes at most. And that's if you're checkin' under the bed and in the closets and all that stuff.

And Sam's been in the house here a good twenty minutes. So what the hell's he up to?

No sense in waiting to find out.

No sense waiting up here liked a treed fox just waiting for the inevitable.

He's gonna surprise the sonofabitch.

Has to be very quiet. Can't put the attic ladder down. Too much noise. All he can do is take off his boots and hang from the open hatch, and drop to the floor in his socks and hope to hell Sam doesn't hear him.

But Sam is too busy eating to hear him. You can't shovel that much pie into your mouth without at least a little bit of it gettin' in your ears.

So here sits Sam shovelin' pie into his face.

And here comes Bobby sneakin' up on him in his socks.

And there squats this huge black fly on the last slice of pie left, and Sam reaches out to brush it away when he accidentally hits the slender vase and knocks it over on the table.

Except—

The spilled water in the vase runs backward because the table isn't level—runs right over the edge of the table and right on his crotch, and he's wearing these gray work pants and the soaking water make it looks like he pissed his pants.

And then—

There's this six-shooter pressing against the back of his head—

And Bobby says, "You just put your gun on the table, Sam, so I can see it real plain."

"Look at me, Bobby!" Sam says. "People're gonna say I wet my pants I was so scared of you. You kill me here, that's just what they'll say for sure! Then all the time my kids're growin up, their fuck-face little friends'll say your old man was so scared a Bobby Gregg he pissed his pants!"

"Just calm down!"

"This ain't no way for a man t'die, Bobby!"

167

"Dammit, Sam, I'm not going to kill you."

"You're not?"

"No, I'm not."

"Well, you killed Suzie Proctor."

"No, I didn't."

"You didn't?"

"No."

"Then who did?"

"You're the lawman. You tell me."

"You didn't kill her, why you holdin' gun on me?"

"Because I'm gonna escape. Because if I stay here you'll take me in."

"I got to. Bobby. It's my job."

"Well, you'd be takin' in the wrong man."

"Don't tell nobody, all right?"

"Tell 'em what?"

"You know, about me eatin' the pie and all."

Bobby grinned. "Eatin' pie and havin' wet pants. Guess that wouldn't make you look real good, would it?"

"My kids'd get teased somethin' awful."

"I think you're worried a little more about yourself than your kids."

"So what if I am?"

"I'll make you a deal, Sam."

"What kind of deal?"

"You give me a half-hour head start, and I won't tell nobody about the pie."

"Or my pants."

"Or your pants."

"Nobody?"

"Nobody. Not a single soul."

"I really am jus' thinkin' of my kids, Bobby."

"Guess I'll have to take your word for it, won't I?"

"You really didn't kill her?"

"I really didn't kill her."

Sam looked at the table. "So I sit here half an hour?"

"Yep. You don't holler for help and you don't go into town."

"There's a piece left."

"I see that."

"What if I ate that last piece?"

"I'll tell you what, Sam."

"What?"

"You don't holler and you don't run into town for half an hour, and I'll tell Serena I ate the whole pie myself."

"Ya will?"

"I will."

"The whole thing?"

"The whole thing."

"You think she'll believe ya?"

"Sure she will." Then: "That last piece looks mighty good, doesn't it?"

Sam smiled. "Now that you mention it, it sure does."

8:07 P.M.

Ben Gregg knew it was late to go calling, but he hadn't gotten around to talking to the Turney family. Maybe they could be helpful. Several people had mentioned that Bobby was a good friend of the family.

He passed down the streets of saloons and gambling parlors. There had been a time when such noises had been exciting to him. No arms had seemed warmer than those of a whore; no drink more nourishing than whiskey. But these things and his wanderings as a Pinkerton had cost him the only woman he'd ever loved, and his children. The detective's way of life was legitimate; the other things weren't. And now they offered him only bitter reminders of how foolish and young and empty he'd been.

A faint light pressed at the window next to Turney's front door. Townspeople went to bed later than farmers. Maybe he wouldn't be waking anybody up.

He knocked.

He looked around him at the hills. On the other side of them was the river where the young woman's body had been found. It came down to two things: Bobby needed an alibi, which he apparently didn't have; or Ben, or somebody, had to find the killer fast.

The man in the door had an Eastern quality that gave his grave but handsome face a real dignity. The wide forehead, dark, wary eyes, brooding brow, long nose, and wry mouth bespoke both intelligence and humility, not a combination you saw very often. People with brains flaunted them like young girls with their first bloom of breasts.

"Gosh, I thought I was seeing things," Turney said. "You look like your brother so much."

"Only older. Bobby doesn't have any gray in his hair yet. At least not the last time I saw him."

"Not yet he doesn't."

Ben put his hand out and the men shook.

Turney said, "Why don't you come inside. There's still some of the day's coffee left."

"That sounds good. Thank you."

As soon as he was inside, he saw a very pretty girl of twelve or maybe older staring at him from behind a blue curtain that no doubt hid a bedroom. She looked sadder than anyone her age ever should. He sensed she wanted to say something to him. She opened her mouth a few times tentatively. But no words came out.

The coffee was good. Jean Anne, a very good-looking woman, served it, and then she sat down with the men.

"I just hope Bobby gives himself up before they find him," she said.

"Then you're assuming he killed her?" Ben said. He didn't make it an accusation—as if she was betraying him—he just asked her a question.

"I, well, I—" Despite his gentle tone, his question had clearly rattled her. Then he noticed that her eyes had met those of the girl who was peeking out from behind the curtain. They shared some kind of secret.

"All she's saying, Ben," Turney said, "is that guilty or not, he has to avoid being caught by one of those posses. They'll lynch him for sure."

"Do you think he's guilty?" Ben asked.

Turney too looked flustered. "This isn't easy for us."

"He's our best friend," Jean Anne said, wiping floury hands on the front of her pinafore.

"He has supper with us two or three or three times a week," Turney said.

"And we sure don't think he *did* do it." Jean Anne said. "Not deep down anyway. Even despite the way things look."

Ben was troubled by their unease. Why should they be so nervous answering questions as straightforward as his? He wasn't trying to trick them or trap them. He was just trying to find out about his brother. But they were firing glances back and forth and tapping their fingers on the table and constantly shifting in their chairs. Alan Pinkerton drilled into the heads of his operatives certain telltale

171

signs to watch for during interrogations. The Turneys were displaying them all.

"He was here the night of the murder," Jean Anne said.

"Oh? How was he acting?"

They glanced at each other again.

"He was pretty down," Turney said. "The Proctor girl had told him she didn't want to marry him."

"He told you that?"

"Why, yes," Turney said. "I was at the office working on some papers. He'd been here with Jean Anne and told her all about it. Then when I got home, he told me all about it too. He was pretty drunk by then, though."

"He drink a lot?"

"Not much actually. And we don't keep anything on hand here in the way of liquor."

"But he was drinking here?"

Turney said, "He'd brought his own bottle of whiskey."

"Did he make any threatening remarks that night about the Porter girl?"

Another exchange of glances. Jean Anne shook her head. "Not really. I mean, it was obvious how hurt and angry he was. But no threats—or at least I can't remember any." She looked at her husband as she said this.

"I can't remember any threats either," Turney said.

"About what time did he leave?"

"Oh—" She nodded at her husband. "Do you remember?"

"I wasn't paying much attention, I guess."

"Just a guess."

"Maybe ten."

"Ten. And was he still drunk?"

Jean Anne shrugged. "Not as much, I think. I'd given him some coffee."

"Was he still talking about the Proctor girl?"

"Oh, no." Turney smiled for the first time. "By then, we were on the subject of politics."

"I see." Then: "So you were here the whole time?"

"Why, yes," Turney said, sounding surprised. Here they'd been talking about the evening, them relating how Bobby had been acting all evening, then all of a sudden Ben Gregg seemed to be questioning if Turney had even *been* here. "Why would you ask that?"

"Somebody thought they saw you about nine o'clock."

"Well, if they did, it was somebody who was peeking through my window."

"Who said that anyway?" Jean Anne said. She was angry.

"It doesn't matter. You said you were home."

"And you believe me then?"

"If it's the truth I believe it."

"I don't like the tone of that, Mr. Gregg," Jean Anne said. "We love your brother. He's like one of our own family. We're trying very hard to believe he's innocent. But we have to tell the truth. We have to say exactly what happened that night. You wouldn't want us to lie, would you?"

"No, I wouldn't."

"Well, there you have it then. My husband was home the entire night. If someone said they saw him anywhere else, they're wrong. And Bobby acted just the way we said he did. He was a lot soberer by the time he left and he'd quit talking about the Proctor girl."

He saw her again, the girl. Peeking out from behind the curtain. Again, and for a reason he couldn't explain, he felt that the girl wanted to say something to him. He wondered what. He was intrigued.

173

This time, her mother saw her too. "You get back in there and get to sleep, young lady."

She vanished.

"She likes to listen to adults," her father said. "She has a lot of curiosity."

Jean Anne smiled fondly. "She has my husband's mind. My son and I are bright enough, I suppose—but Richard and Ruth are the real brains in the family."

"Oh, now," Turney said. But he said it in such a way that Ben knew they'd had this particular little joust many times.

"So Bobby left and that was the last you saw of him?"

"Yes."

"And you haven't had any word from him since?"

"No."

Ben looked around the area by the front door. Turney's Wellington boots stood there. The Easterner had made no concession to the styles of the West. Given his Edwardian-cut clothes and his boots, he would have been right in fashion in downtown Boston. It was the first sign of vanity he'd seen in the anxious man.

Ben stood up. Walked to the window. "Right over that hill is the river where the body was found? You see anybody on the hill that night?"

Without looking at each other, they both shook their heads.

"Virgil Earp asked us about that," Turney said. "But we couldn't be much help to him there either."

"Didn't hear anything either, I suppose? Screams, anything like that?"

"Nothing, Mr. Gregg." Turney cleared his throat. "Nothing at all, I'm afraid."

Ben turned back from the window and as he did so, he made sure to knock his foot against one of Turney's Wellington boots. He bent down to right the boot, and in doing so took a close look at the heel. A V symbol was raised on the heel, the V for Victor Boots. It matched one of the heel patterns he'd traced on the muddy bank.

Turney said, "My wife bought me those for my last birthday."

"You've got a good eye for boots, Mrs. Turney."

"Thanks. I wanted to get something that would last."

"Well," Ben said, "I guess I'll be going. I've still got some work to do tonight." He didn't know if he had his killer. But he did know that he had somebody who'd been there that night.

Just as he was turning to the door again, he saw the girl—Ruth—watching him from behind. He'd never seen a girl so forlorn. She looked as if she'd been crying too. But it must have been silent crying, otherwise he would have heard her. As in most frontier houses, the rooms were very near each other.

"We're praying for Bobby," Jean Anne said.

"Night and day," said Turney.

"This may turn out all right," she said. "Sometimes the Lord surprises us."

"Yes," Ben said, "sometimes He does."

He opened the door. The night was cool. He wanted to be out in it. It promised a kind of clarity that would help him escape all the complicated lies he'd been treated to here.

Ruth was still watching him.

He said good night again and left.

175

Ed Gorman

Bobby aches when he sees the lights of town. So many pleasures a man takes for granted in normal times. Just the liberty of walking free and unfettered down the street. Or the pleasure of sipping a friendly beer in a saloon. Or watching town girls in their town dresses walk coyly past him.

It is a different world now that he is being hunted. At any moment somebody could step up and arrest him. Or open fire on him. The way the town hates him, nobody's going to complain if he gets shot in the back.

The alley is narrow and dark. He crouches behind a tree. Sweat stings his eyes. He smells rank from his time in the attic. He wants to reach the mouth of the alley across the street. That will bring him to a straight path to Richard Turney's house. Richard and Jean Anne are sensible people. And his best friends. They'll loan him money. Help him escape from town. That's all that's left him now. Escape.

He leans away from the tree. Looks down the street. All the houses dark or darkening now that bedtime nears. Another pleasure a free man takes for granted. His own bed and the freedom to luxuriate in peaceful sleep. A hunted man never sleeps. A part of his mind always stays alert to trouble.

He leans across the street and then keeps on running. There are long stretches of open road on the way to the Turneys. He has to keep low, move against the deepest darkness he can find.

Dogs and coyotes; wagons and trains. The noises keep up a running dialogue with the night.

But what if they turn him in?

But that's unthinkable. Not the Turneys. They'll know

he didn't do it. As religious as they are, they are generally not quick to judge people. They'll give their old friend time to explain himself, to be heard.

A horse.

Somewhere behind him.

Coming up fast.

He pitches himself in a leaf-littered gulley still muddy from last Monday's hard rain.

He rolls all the way down the leafy, shallow gully and then lies completely still. Sweat is freezing on him now. His breath comes in raw, painful gasps.

A posse man could have spotted him. Closed in. He listens for the horse to slow. Fortunately, the rhythm of the horse's hooves cutting into sandy earth remains the same. Wherever the rider is going, he's going in a hell of a hurry.

Heart pounding. Head aching. So unreal, all of it, him in this gulley, Suzie Proctor in her grave. God. So unreal.

He gives the rider plenty of time to vanish into the dark distance, and then he stands up, brushing leaves from legs, chest, hips, and legs.

He needs to hurry more than ever. The Turney home has begun to assume a magnificence well beyond its reality. There he will find nurture and acceptance and understanding; there he will find comfort and solace and help. If only he can travel these last few miles without being seen.

He runs on. For the first time in his young life, he finds himself feeling old. He's barely twenty-three, but he can feel the incredible stress all this exercise has put on him. Even two years ago—even with his smoking and drinking—this wouldn't have been anything for him. But now . . .

He runs on.

He is just starting to feel good about things—he *will* escape—he *will* ultimately be found innocent—

—when somebody opens up with a carbine.

He's running along a leg of the moon-dappled river when somebody from behind one of the birches lining this side of the shore starts firing.

One of the first three shots comes so close to his face that he can *smell* it.

Two more shots.

He dives and rolls. He doesn't know what else to do. Dive and roll, all the gunslingers always suggest in dime novels. That's about the only thing a man can do when somebody is ambushing him.

The only thing these supposedly knowledgeable gun-fighters don't mention in their stories is how hard diving and rolling is on the body. Solid earth doesn't give any when a human body collides with it.

He's just had to roll down a ravine. And now he's diving and rolling? Being a fugitive is damned hard work.

After his body has been jolted, rattled, and shocked enough, he crawls to his knees, gets behind a boulder, and begins to take a little target practice of his own. His assailant doesn't seem to realize that the moonlight makes him a reasonably easy target.

Bobby is gratified to hear the man cry out in pain.

The sweetest sound he's heard in some time.

8:48 P.M.

Ben Gregg was walking toward his hotel when he saw Virgil Earp hurrying from the town marshal's office. His mount was ready for him. He was about to swing up on it when he saw Ben.

He walked over and said, "Your brother was holed up at Serena's place."

"How'd you find that out?"

"My deputy, Sam. Your brother knocked him out."

"I take it he's on the run?"

"That's the way Sam tells it."

Ben nodded to Earp's horse. "You have any idea where he might be hiding?"

"Nope. I just hope I find him before the posse does."

"They still working this late?"

Earp shook his head. "The other two posses came in and gave up. They're pretty much tired of lookin' for him. But there's six or seven of the boys who're still lookin'. And now they're in town here. I guess they decided I wasn't so stupid after all, him holin' up at Serena's place all this time." He made a face. "The other thing is, they stopped off at a trail saloon about five miles east of here and drank most of the afternoon. They probably tied a pretty good mean on too."

"You could always call them in."

"Not where Suzie Proctor's concerned, Gregg. Just about everybody liked her and they sure want to see her killer caught."

"Maybe I'll look for him myself."

"How about you?" Earp said. "*You* got any ideas?"

"Afraid not."

"Well, if you find him, bring him in."

"I will, Marshal." And he would too. He'd rather take a chance with Earp and Earp's jail than with a gang of drunks.

* * *

Ben watched the marshal ride off and then went up to his room. The moment he opened the door, he knew that somebody was inside waiting for him. The perfume told him so.

"You need to keep the lamp off. For both our sakes."

"Who're you?"

"My name's Serena. I am in love with your brother."

"Where is he?"

"I'm not sure. But I have an idea."

"Where?"

She sighed. "Do you know the Turneys?"

"I just came from there."

"They're the only people in this town who'll help him."

"Besides you."

A hesitation. "I know I am in trouble. They already hate me here because I'm a whore. But I love him. I know that someday we'll have a family together. Or shouldn't I say that because I'm a whore?"

"Whore is a mental state."

"I don't understand."

He took his pipe from his suit jacket, tamped down the tobacco with his thumb, and got it going with a stick match. "In your mind and soul. If you feel like a whore there, then you are a whore. But if all that you give men is the use of your body—and you don't cheat them or hurt them or hurt yourself—then I reckon there're are worse things to be."

She laughed. "I should have you along when the town girls call me names."

"I'd be happy to go." Then: "Shouldn't you be at work?"

"I quit tonight."

"How'll you support yourself?"

"We're through around here anyway, your brother and I. We'll go somewhere else and start a new life."

He found it strange that a woman with such sure ideas wouldn't have come up once in his brother's letters. The kid was forever falling in and out of love, but he'd never once talked about Serena.

He said, "I'm going to ask you something and I'd appreciate an honest answer."

"All right."

"You think he killed her?"

"That Bobby killed Suzie?"

"Yes."

"No. No, he wouldn't do anything like that. Ever."

"He drinks."

"Yes."

"And sometimes he has a bad temper."

She looked cold, hard angry. "He didn't kill her."

"Good enough."

"Certainly you can't think he killed her."

"People always surprise me. Sometimes for the bad and sometimes for the good. It makes you lie awake some nights and just think about things."

"He didn't kill her, Mr. Gregg. He didn't kill her."

He said, "You'd better go. I'd better check out the Turneys' place again. He has to give himself up before that posse finds him."

"I'll go with you."

"No."

She stood up. "You can't stop me. If I want to follow you, I can. You might as well take me along."

He said, "I don't mean to hurt your feelings here, but are you sure my brother's in love with you?"

"Not yet, he isn't. But he will be and very soon now. Some men are just very slow learners, and Bobby is one of them."

181

He liked her more than he might have expected. She was a little hard, but she had an honesty and dignity he admired. It wasn't easy to have any self-respect in her chosen calling, but somehow she did. Nobody pushed her around or took advantage of her. But given Bobby's history with women, he wasn't sure she was going to get her man.

"You do exactly what I say."

"Fine by me," she said.

He looked out the window. "We'll have to go out the back way."

"Why?"

"Virgil Earp's got one of his deputies stationed across the street. I'm sure he's ready to follow us."

"What if there's a deputy in back?"

"Then you'll have to do a little dramatic presentation and divert him."

"What're you talking about?"

"You'll see."

9:09 P.M.

Turney was just putting the cat out for the night when he heard the scuffle of a boot on dry earth outside in the night. Alarmed, he looked hard to the right and saw nothing. Then he looked to the left.

"You've got to help me, Richard," Bobby Gregg said.

Turney hardly recognized the man. Sweat, dirt, mud, even leaves covered various parts of his body. Even from a distance of four yards, Turney could smell the sour body odors.

"They're looking for you, Bobby." He didn't know what else to say. He felt guilty. As if Bobby could read his mind, knew all about Jean Anne's notion to blame Bobby for the murder and keep Richard free. He swallowed hard. Bobby might have been a ghost, he'd rattled Richard so hard.

Gregg surprised him by smiling. "Hell, Richard, you think I don't know that?"

"Who's there, Richard?" Jean Anne said from inside.

Richard waved Bobby inside.

Bobby knew instantly that something was wrong. Soon as he stepped inside. The first thing was, they kept backing away from him. They were usually physical people. They patted shoulders, gave hugs, Jean Anne was even known to put a kiss on your cheek from time to time. But now they were wary of him, as if he was a disease-carrier. And they kept glancing anxiously at each other, as if responding to a secret only they knew. And then he realized what this was probably all about. Of course. They probably believed he'd killed her. Sure, that was why they were acting this way. You have a good friend for a number of years—a solid, honest, decent friend, one you think you know pretty well—and then he suddenly kills a woman. The woman he loves, no less. And so things change. He becomes a monster. And he's standing right in your own kitchen. Asking for help. No wonder they looked scared and nervous.

He said, "I didn't kill her. I want you to know that."

"Everybody sure thinks you did," Jean Anne said.

"Does that include you?"

Her eyes avoided his. "No."

He said, "It does, doesn't it? You believe I killed her and so does Richard here. That's why you're acting this way."

"We don't know what to think, Bobby," Jean Anne said.

"We kept telling people over and over you were innocent. But when so many people believe something—"

"When so many people believe something, it must be true, is that it?"

"Something like that," she said miserably. "You talk to him, Richard."

Richard said, "Maybe it'd be better if I fetched Virg Earp."

"They'd still lynch me. They'd go over him if they had to. Or hell, he might just let them hang me, an election comin' up and all."

"Then what's the alternative, Bobby?"

"Running," he said. "For right now that's the only alternative anyway. Running. But I need a bath and some fresh clothes and some money."

The look again, passing between them.

"We could get in trouble."

Bobby smiled. "Yeah, Jean Anne, you could get in trouble. But I could get lynched." In some ways, it was hard to believe that they'd ever been friends. He remembered so many good times with these people. Hell, he was the little boy's godfather. But that was gone from him now. They'd never be friends again.

"We could at least do that for him," Richard said. "Some fresh clothes. And some money. He could scrub up at the sink over there."

"I'd appreciate it," Bobby said.

"You might, but the law won't, Bobby. Earp'll get on us for helping you escape."

"We have to help him, honey, he's our friend."

"Some friend," Jean Anne said. "He kills a woman and then comes here and wants us to help him."

And it was then she figured out the way to handle this

whole thing. She had a Navy Colt in her drawer. She'd kill Bobby with it. There'd be reward money and the case would be closed. No more questions asked.

She sighed. "Oh, all right. I'm sorry if I sounded unfriendly, Bobby. I'm just scared is all."

"I really appreciate this," Bobby said. "It's the only chance I've got."

Richard found him clothes. Jean Anne set up the sink so he could give himself a good sponge bath. She went to the drawer with the gun. It was also where they kept their cash box. There were eighty dollars in there. Everything they had. She'd give Bobby thirty. It'd be good when her money was found on him. It would demonstrate that they really *had* been trying to help him escape. But had been forced to shoot him when he demanded every penny of their savings. Virg Earp would have no reason to disbelieve them.

She stayed in the bedroom until she heard Bobby dumping out the water he'd used to bathe in.

Then she hid the gun in the folds of her farm skirt and went out to face him.

9:30 P.M.

"You did that well."

"My hip hurts."

"Well, I just wanted you to know that I appreciated it."

"I just hope we're not too late."

Serena was hobbling. She'd gone out the back door of the hotel first. She made a big thing of being drunk and falling on her face. The deputy—never one to pass up a cheap feel—went to her assistance immediately. Filling his hands with her swelling breasts, he managed to get her to her feet and steady her. For which she was appreciative enough to touch her lips to his in a pretense of lusty drunkenness.

The splendid performance allowed Ben Gregg to sneak out the back door and clear of the deputy. Serena, hobbling because of the hip injury she'd suffered when she'd thrown herself gallantly to the ground, caught up with Ben ten minutes later.

Now they were near the railroad tracks that ran north-south. Far in the distance you could hear a train thundering down the tracks like some mythic nocturnal beast. Indian art often depicted trains with the totem-like faces of monsters, all red glowing eyes and steam pouring from nostrils and mouths. Indian children were no doubt told that if they did not behave, the train monster would get them.

"Trains scare me," Serena said.

"Why?"

She shuddered. "My uncle once saw a woman get her head cut off when she fell underneath a train. He used to tell us over and over about it."

"Just the kind of fella you'd like to have around."

They climbed a small, sandy hill. Below them, in a small, tree-ringed valley, lay the small, tree-ringed house of the Turney family, window-dark in the starry night.

Somebody was coming out the front door.

Ben had one of those moments when the brain refuses to accept the information the eyes are relaying.

Yes, this was a young man who did bear some resemblance to his brother Bobby. Yes, that strange kind of lope was the distinctive walk of the entire Gregg family. And true, the flat-brimmed dark blue Stetson looked unique even half-lost in the shadows this way.

But how could it be so easy? As a Pinkerton man, Ben Gregg was used to things being done the hard way. You walk to the rise of a small hill and there, not a hundred yards away, is the brother you've been desperately searching for?

No. Impossible.

But it was Bobby. No doubt about it. And the way Serena clutched Ben's arm confirmed what eye was telling brain.

And then something even more unlikely happened: Jean Anne Turney, devout Christian woman that she was, flung herself through the cabin door and screamed, "Bobby!"

Her intentions were as clear as the six-shooter in her hand. Just as Bobby was turning toward her voice, she was firing.

Then Ben heard himself shout: "Bobby! Bobby!" and was running down the hill with his gun drawn, firing at Jean Anne Turney before she could squeeze off any more shots.

Then Richard Turney ran out the front door crying, "Jean Anne, what're you doing? What're you doing?"

By now, Ben Gregg had reached the cabin and was kneeling down next to his brother. He shouted to Turney, "Get me a lantern!"

Turney didn't have to take the six-shooter from his wife. In a deep state of shock, her eyes looking off into some distance only she could see, she let the weapon drop from her fingers. He picked it up.

While Turney was getting a lantern, Ben said to Serena, "Would you go get Virgil Earp? Turney won't mind if you take one of his horses."

She hurried away.

Turney returned moments later with a glowing kerosene lantern.

Jean Anne rushed up to him as he stood over Bobby's body. "Is he dead? Did I kill him? Oh, Lord, I'm so sorry."

Turney handed the lantern to Ben. "She was doing it to protect me. I killed Suzie Proctor. But since everybody thought Bobby did, she thought nobody'd question her killing him."

Ben only half-heard what Turney was saying. He was more interested—at least for the moment—in Bobby's wound. It was high, in the shoulder. The blood flow was warm and thin. You could smell it on the chill night.

"How is he, Mr. Gregg?" Jean Anne said. "Oh, Lord, I'm so sorry. He was our best friend."

Bobby's eyes came open then and he said, "Yeah, best friend, all right. Some best friend." Ben had seen this many times. Somebody is shot, slips into unconsciousness, then suddenly comes to again after a few minutes.

"Should we take him inside?" Jean Anne said.

"I don't want to ever step inside your house again," Bobby said. He was strong enough to express anger with real passion.

Ben took off his suit jacket and laid it across Bobby blanket-style. He put Bobby's hat underneath his head, propping it up slightly. At least it wouldn't be lying directly upon the cold hard earth.

Ben stood up. From the doorway of the Turney home, Ruth watched them. He wondered if she could hear what was being said. That her father was the killer.

"You'll need to take care of things, Jean Anne," he said. She started to cry. Her face in her hands. Turney took her into his arms. "I'm so sorry for everything I've done," he said. "I've brought God's wrath down on myself—and now my whole family's suffering. I just pray that you can forgive me someday, honey. I just hope you can forgive me."

Ben kept putting off what he needed to do. Every time he was about to speak, one of the Turneys would say something very emotional and Ben would lay back again. During the last exchange, they moved downhill further, so that Ben couldn't hear them.

"I'm freezing my ass off down here, brother," Bobby said in the windy prairie night.

"Your girlfriend should be back with Earp and the wagon right away." He got down on his haunches and pulled his suit jacket up tighter around his brother.

"She ain't my girlfriend."

"She tells a different story. And anyway, you could do a lot worse. I like her."

Bobby grimaced with the pain from his shoulder. "Yeah, that's the hell of it."

"What is?"

"I like her, too. She kind of snuck up on me. I kinda knew Suzie was sneaking around on me, so I started spendin' time with Serena. I sure never figured it'd go anywhere, her bein' a whore and all."

"Mr. Gregg?"

He looked up. Ruth stood there. She said, "I'd like to talk to you."

"You be all right?"

Bobby nodded. "Can't get any colder than I am right now."

"You could always go inside."

189

"No way."

"All right. I'll talk to the young lady, then."

He stood up, knees cracking. Every once in a while he got the sneaking suspicion that one of these days he was actually going to get old.

You could see the sleep on her face. She'd apparently slept at least a while tonight. She was as pretty as her mother, her gentle face pale in the moonlight.

She said, "I killed her, Mr. Gregg."

He sensed the great grief in her. Her father a killer. The only way she could help him was to take the blame herself. An absurd story. But a profoundly touching one.

He drew her into the circle of his arm. "Your father wouldn't want you to go around saying things like that, honey."

"But I did kill her, Mr. Gregg. I really did." Her tone was as chill as the night. "I knew they were over there by the river. They went there a lot. Sometimes, I sneak out of the house and go for walks at night. And one night I saw them together. And then I saw them a *lot* of nights. You know, they say she was such a fine person and all. But she wasn't. She was destroying my family and she didn't care at all. That's why he strangled her. Because she wouldn't let him go. I watched him strangle her. I was hiding behind the tree where I usually did. And then after he ran off, I went down there. I'm not even sure why. I'd never seen a dead person before. Maybe I was just interested in that. But anyway, I went down there and when I was leaning over, she opened her eyes and started to get up. And I just started screaming all these things at her. About how she was ruining my folks and everything. And then I just picked up this rock and I hit her with it. I hit her twice, as a matter of fact. And then I dropped it and ran back up to the house."

He'd wondered why she'd been both strangled and then hit with a heavy rock. Now he knew why. He also knew that Ruth was telling him the truth. He said, "You wore the shoes you usually do?"

"Yes, why?"

"Mind if I see your heel?"

"How come?"

"I need to see if there's a V imprinted there."

The V was there, all right. Imprinted in the heel itself.

"You think they'll hang me?"

The way she said it, so dispassionately, he wondered for the first time if she might be insane.

"No; no, they won't hang you, sweetheart."

"I just wanted my dad to be home the way he should be."

"I know."

"My mom would never do anything like that to *him*."

"No; no, she wouldn't."

Then she was in his arms and starting to cry. "I know I shouldn't have hit her; I know I shouldn't have, Mr. Gregg."

He let her cry for a time, and then he called out to the people down the hill, "You need to come up here, Mr. and Mrs. Turney."

Soon after, Virgil Earp and a hospital wagon for Bobby showed up too.

Next Day, 2:37 P.M.

Serena sat in a chair next to Bobby's hospital bed. Ben stood on the other side saying, "It's a good thing you're my brother. Otherwise I would've charged Pinkerton rates."

"He thinks he has a great sense of humor," Bobby said.

"I should charge you too for all the peach pie you ate," Serena said. "You finished off the whole thing."

Bobby looked as if he was about to say something in his own defense, then stopped.

"What were you going to say?" she said.

"I can't say."

"You can't say what you were going to say? What kind of crazy talk is that?"

"I gave my word," Bobby said, thinking of Deputy Sam wolfing down the entire pie.

Older brother Ben patted his hand and said, "I need to go. Allegedly, my train leaves in another half hour."

"Allegedly?" Bobby said.

"You ever know a train to leave on time?" Ben said.

On his way to the depot, he ran into Deputy Sam carrying a pie to the hospital.

"This," Sam said, "is for your brother. I had my wife work all morning. It's peach."

"That's funny," Ben said. "Serena was just saying that Bobby ate this whole peach pie that *she* fixed."

"It's a small world, isn't it?" Sam said, and then took off scuttling toward the hospital.

A strange little burg, the Pinkerton man thought as he began walking toward the depot again. A strange little burg indeed.

The Victim

I suppose everybody in this part of the territory has a Jim Hornaday story to tell. See, you knew right away who I was talking about, didn't you? The gunfighter who accidentally killed a six-year-old girl during a gun battle in the middle of the street? Jim Hornaday. Wasn't his fault, really. The little girl had strayed out from the general store without anybody inside noticing her—and Hornaday had just been shot in his gunhand, making his own shots go wild—so, when he fired. . . .

Well, like I said, the first couple shots went wild and those were the ones that killed the little girl. Hornaday managed to kill the other gunfighter too, but by then nobody cared much.

There was a wake for the girl, and Hornaday was there. And there was a funeral, and Hornaday was there, too. He even asked the parents if he could be at graveside and after some reluctance they agreed. They could see that Hornaday was seriously aggrieved over what he'd done.

That was the last time I saw Jim Hornaday for five years, that day at the funeral of my first cousin, Charity McReady. I was fourteen years old on that chilly bright October morning and caught between grieving for Charity and keeping my eyes fixed on Hornaday, who was just about the most famous gunfighter the territory had ever produced. When I spent all those hours down by the creek practicing with my old Remington .36—so old it had paper cartridges instead of metal ones—that's who I always was in my mind's eye: Jim Hornaday, the gunfighter.

I killed my first man when I was nineteen. That statement is a lot more dramatic than the facts warrant. I was in a livery and saddling my mount in the back when I heard some commotion up front. A couple of drunken gamblers were arguing about the charges with the colored man who worked there. You could see they didn't much care about the money. They were just having a good time pushing the colored man back and forth between them. Whenever he'd fall down, dizzy from being shoved so hard, one of them would kick him in the ribs. For eleven in the morning, they'd had more than their fill of territory whiskey.

Now even though my father proudly wore the gray in the Civil War, I didn't hold with anybody being bullied, no matter what his color. I leaned down and helped the colored man to his feet. He was old and arthritic and scared. I brushed off his ragged sweater and then said to the gamblers, who were all fussed up in some kind of Edwardian-cut coats and golden silk vests, "You men pay him what you owe."

They laughed and I wasn't surprised. The baby face I have will always be with me. Even if I lived to be Gramp's age of eighty-six, there'll still be some boy in my pug nose and freckled cheeks. And my body wasn't any more imposing. I was short and still on the scrawny side for one thing and, for another, there was my limp, dating back to the time when I'd been training a cow pony that fell on me. I'd have the limp just as long as I'd have the baby face.

The taller of the two gamblers went for his Colt, worn gunfighter-low on his right hip, and before I could think about it in any conscious way, I was drawing down on him, and putting two bullets into his chest before he had a chance to put two in mine. As for his friend, I spun around and pushed my own Colt in his face. He dropped his gun.

I asked the colored man to go get the local law and he nodded but, before he left, he came over and said, nodding to the man dead at my feet, "I don't think you know who he is."

"I guess I don't."

"Ray Billings."

Took me really till the law came to really understand what I'd done. Ray Billings was a gunfighter mentioned just about as often as Jim Hornaday by the dreamy young boys and weary old lawmen who kept up on this sort of thing. The law, in the rotund shape of a town marshal who looked as if he were faster with a fork than a six-shooter, stared down at Billings and then looked up at me, smiling. "I do believe you're going to be famous, son. I do believe you are."

He was right.

Over the next six months I became somebody named Andy Donnelly, and not the Andy Donnelly I grew up being—the one who'd liked to slide down the haystacks and fish in the fast blue creeks and dream about Marian Parke when he closed his eyes at night, Marian being the prettiest girl in our one-room school house. This new Andy Donnelly, the one that a bunch of hack journalists had created, was very different from the old one I'd known. According to the tales, the new Andy Donnelly had survived eleven gunfights (three was the true number), had escaped from six jails (when, in fact, I'd never been in a jail in my life), and was feared by the fastest guns in the territory, Jim Hornaday included.

All of this caught up with me in a town named Drago, where I had hoped nobody would know me. I was two hours past the DRAGO WELCOMES STRANGERS sign, and one hour on my hot dusty hotel bed, when a knock came and a female voice said, "I'd like to talk to you a minute, Mister Donnelly."

By now, I knew that a man with a reputation for gunfighting didn't dare answer a knock the normal way. Propped up against the back of the bed, I grabbed my Winchester, aimed it dead center at the door, and said, "Come in."

She was pretty enough in her city clothes of buff blue linen and taffeta, and her exorbitant picture hat with the fancy blue ribbon. She was wise enough to keep her hands in easy and steady sight.

"Say it plain."

"Say what plain, Mister Donnelly? I'm Patience Falkner, by the way."

"Say why you're looking for me. And say it plain."

She didn't hesitate. "Because," she said, all blue, blue eyes and yellow hair the color of September straw, "I want you to kill him."

"Him. Who's him?"

"Why, Jim Hornaday, of course. Isn't that why you came

to Drago? Because you knew he was here? I mean, he killed your poor little cousin. You're not going to stand for that are you, an honorable man like yourself?"

I smiled. "You don't give a damn about my cousin. You're one of them."

"I think I've been insulted. 'One of them' . . . meaning what?"

"You damned well have been insulted," I said.

I swung my body and my Winchester off the bed, went over to the bureau where I poured water from a pitcher into a pan. The water was warm but I washed up anyway, face and neck, arms and hands. I grabbed one of two cotton work shirts and put it on.

"You know how old you look, Mister Donnelly?"

I turned, faced her, not wanting to hear about my baby face, a subject that had long ago sickened me. "What did he do to you? That's why you want me to kill him. Not for my little cousin . . . but for you. So what did he do to you, anyway?"

"I don't think that's any of your business."

"You don't, huh?" I said, strapping on my holster and gun. "He shoot up your house last night or something, did he? Or maybe you think he cheated your little brother at cards . . . or insulted your father at the saloon the other night. Last town I was in, somebody wanted me to draw down on this gunfighter because the gunny wouldn't pay his hotel bill. Turned out the guy who wanted to see me fight was the desk clerk at the hotel . . . figured I'd do his work for him." I shook my head. "Lots of people have lots of different reasons for us gunnies to shoot each other. Now, are you going to tell me your reason or not?"

I didn't make it easy for her. I slid on my flat-crowned hat and went out the door.

She followed me down the stairs, talking. "Well, I probably shouldn't tell you this but . . . well, he won't marry me. And he gave me his word and everything."

I smiled again. "And you want me to kill him for that?"

"Well, maybe my honor doesn't mean much to you," she said, out of breath as she tried to keep up with me descending the steps, "but it means a lot to me."

Down in the lobby, a lot of people were watching us. I said, "You're right about one thing, lady. Your honor doesn't mean one damn thing to me. Not one damn thing."

I walked away, leaving her there with the smirks and the sneers of the old codgers who sit all day long in the lobby, drifting on the sad and worn last days of their lives.

Patience Falkner wasn't the only one who told me that Jim Hornaday was in the town of Drago. There was the barber, the bootblack, the banker, and the twitchy little man at the billiard parlor—all just wanting me to know he was here, just in case I wanted to, well, you know, sort of draw down on him, as they all got nervously around to saying. Seems this fine town had never been the site of a major gunfight before and—just as Patience Falkner had her honor at stake—Drago had honor, too. They'd be right proud to bury whichever of us lost the gunfight. Right proud.

I was on my way to the saloon—being in dusty need of a beer—when a man said, "Wait a minute. I want to talk to you when I'm done here." He stood on the edge of the boardwalk. He had been busy jabbing his finger into another man's chest. He was a stout man in a white Stetson, a blue suit, and a considerable silver badge. After he got my attention, he turned back to the man he'd been arguing with. "Lem, how many damned times I got to tell you about that horse of yours, anyway?"

Horse and owner both looked suitably guilty, their heads dropped down.

"You know we got an ordinance here . . . any horse that damages a tree, the owner gets fined one hundred dollars. Now, I've warned you and warned you and warned you . . . but this time I'm gonna fine you. You understand?"

The farmer whose horse had apparently knocked down the angled young sapling to the right of the animal looked as if somebody had hit him in the stomach. Hard. "I can't afford no one hundred dollars, Sheriff."

"You can pay it off at ten dollars a month. Now you get Clyde here the hell out of town and keep him out of town."

"Don't seem right, folks fining other folks like that. God made us all equal, didn't He?"

"He made us equal, but He didn't make all of us smart. Fella lets his horse knock down the same tree three times in one month . . . that sure don't say much for brains . . . horse or man." He had an impish grin, the sheriff, and he looked right up at the horse and said, "Now, Clyde, you get that damned dumb owner of yours the hell out of here, all right?"

The farmer allowed himself a long moment of sullenness then took the big paint down the long, narrow road leading out of town.

"Looks like you were headed to the saloon," the sheriff said. "So was I." He put his hand out. "Patterson, Deke Patterson. I already know who you are, Mister Donnelly." Then the impish grin again. "You look even younger than they say you do."

Inside, I had had two sips of my beer when Patterson leaned and said, "I need to be honest with you, Mister Donnelly."

"Oh?"

"I grew up with Jim Hornaday over in what's now Nebraska. He's my best friend."

"I see."

"I wouldn't want to see him die."

I smiled. "Then you're the only one in Drago."

He laughed. "I saw Patience headed over to your hotel. She tell you they were engaged and then he broke it off?"

"Uh-huh."

"And she asked you to kill him?"

"Uh-huh."

"She tell you why he broke it off?"

"Uh-uh."

"Because he walked along the river one night and there on a blanket he found Patience and this traveling salesman. Sounds like an off-color joke, but it wasn't. Old Jim took it pretty hard."

"Don't blame him," I shrugged. "But it's no different in any other town. People always have their own reasons for wanting you to fight somebody."

The grin. "You mean, in addition to just liking to see blood and death in the middle of Main Street?"

"Sounds like you don't think much of people."

"Not the side of people I see, I don't." He had some more beer and then looked around. On a weekday afternoon, the saloon held long shadows and silent roulette wheels and a barkeep who was yawning. Patterson suddenly looked right at me. There was no impish grin now. All his toughness, which was considerable, was in his brown eyes. "He's hoping you kill him."

"What?"

Patterson nodded. "He's never been the same since he accidentally killed that little cousin of yours. For a long time, he couldn't sleep nights. He just kept seeing her face. That's when he took up the bottle and it's been downhill since. He keeps getting in gunfights, hoping somebody'll kill him. That's what he really wants . . . death. He won't admit it, maybe not even to himself, but the way he pushes himself into gun battles when he's been drinking . . . well, somebody's bound to kill him sooner or later. And I know that's what he wants because he can't get your little cousin out of his mind."

"I didn't come here to kill him, Sheriff. My reputation is made up. I got forced into three fights and won them, but I'm not a gunfighter. I'm really not."

He regarded me silently for a long moment and then said, with an air of relief, "I do believe you're telling me the truth, Mister Donnelly."

"I sure am. I didn't even know Hornaday was here."

"Then you don't blame him for killing your little cousin?"

"Some of my kin do, but I don't. It was accidental. It was terrible she died but nobody meant for her to die."

He asked the barkeep for two more beers. "One more thing, Mister Donnelly."

"You could always call me Donny."

"One more thing, then, Donny. And this won't be easy if you've got any pride, and I suspect you do. He's gonna try and goad you into a fight, but you can't let him. Because the condition he's in . . . the whiskey and all. . . ."

I stopped him. "I don't have that much pride, Sheriff. I don't want to kill Hornaday. Sounds like he's doing a good job of it himself, anyway."

We talked about the town and how it probably wasn't a good thing for me to stay much past tomorrow morning, and then I drifted back to my hotel and my room and there he sat on my bed, a man with an angular face marked with chicken pox from his youth. These days, he resembled a preacher, black suit and hat and starched white shirt. Only the brocaded red vest hinted at the man's festive side. He'd never been known to turn down a drink, that was for sure.

"You're her cousin?"

"I am."

"And you know who I am?"

"Yes, I do, Mister Hornaday."

"I killed her."

"I know."

"I didn't mean to kill her."

"I know that, too."

"And I'm told you came here to kill me."

"That part you got wrong, Mister Hornaday."

"You didn't come here to kill me?"

"No, I didn't, Mister Hornaday."

"Maybe you're not as good as they say, then."

"No, I'm not, Mister Hornaday, and I don't want to be, either. I want to be a happy, normal man. Not a gunfighter."

"That's what I wanted to be once." His dark gaze moved from me to the window where the dusty town appeared below. "A happy, normal man." He looked back at me. "You should want to avenge her, you know."

"It was a long time ago."

"Ten years, two months, one week and two days."

If I hadn't believed he was obsessed with killing poor little Charity before, I sure did now.

"It was an accident, Mister Hornaday."

"That what her mother says?"

"I guess not."

"Or her father?"

"No, he doesn't think it was an accident, either."

"But you do, huh?"

"I do and so do most other people who saw it."

He got up from the bed, the springs squeaking. His spurs chinked loudly in the silence. He came two feet from me and stopped.

The backhand came from nowhere. He not only rocked me, he blinded me momentarily too. He wasn't a big man, Hornaday, but he was a strong and quick one.

"That make you want to kill me?"

"No, sir."

He drove a fist deep into my stomach. I wanted to vomit. "How about that?"

I couldn't speak. Just shook my head.

He took a gold railroad watch from the pocket of his brocaded vest. "I'll be in the street an hour and a half from now. Five o'clock sharp. You be there, too, you understand me?"

He didn't wait for a reply. He left, spurs still chinking as he walked heavily down the hallway, and then down the stairs.

The next hour I packed my warbag and tried to figure which direction I'd be heading out. There was always cattle work in Kansas and right now Kansas sounded good, a

203

place where nobody had ever heard of me, a place I should have gone instead of coming here.

I was just getting ready to leave the room when I heard the gunfire from down the street. A nervous silence followed and then shouts—near as loud as the gunfire itself—filled the air. I could hear people's feet slapping against the dusty street as they ran in the direction of the gun shots.

I leaned out the window, trying to see what was going on. A crowd had ringed the small one-story adobe building with SHERIFF on a sign above the front door. A man in a brown suit carrying a Gladstone bag came running from the east. The crowd parted immediately, letting him through. He had to be a doctor. Nobody else would have gotten that kind of quick respect, not even a lawman.

I was turning back to the door when somebody knocked. Patience Falkner said, "Did you hear what happened?"

"Why don't you come in and tell me."

She didn't look so pretty or well kempt any more and I felt a kind of pity for her. Whatever had happened, it took all her vanity and poise away. She looked tired and ten years older than she had earlier this morning.

"Jim killed Sheriff Patterson."

"What?"

She nodded, sniffling back tears. "The two best friends that ever were." She glanced away and then back at me and said, "I should have my tongue cut out for what I said to you this morning. I don't want Jim dead. I love him."

She was in my arms before I knew it, warm of flesh and grief, sobbing. "I wasn't true to him. That's why he wouldn't marry me. It was all my fault. I never should've asked you to kill him for me. And now he's killed the sheriff. . . . They'll kill Jim, won't they?"

There was no point in lying. "I expect they will. Why'd he kill him, anyway?"

She leaned back and looked at me. I thought she might say something about my baby face. "You. You were what they were fighting about. Jim told Patterson that he'd called you out for five this afternoon. Patterson told him to call it off but Jim wouldn't. Jim was drinking and angry and Patterson gave him a shove and . . . Jim took his gun out and they wrestled for it and it went off. Jim didn't mean to kill him but. . . ."

"Where is he now?"

"Nobody knows. Ran out the back door of the jail."

I shook my head. This was a town I just plain wanted out of. I eased her from my arms, picked up my Winchester and warbag, and walked to the door.

"You're leaving town?"

"I am."

"Then . . . then you're not going to fight him?"

"No, ma'am, I'm not."

"Oh, thank God . . . thank you, mister. Thank you very much."

"But if you're going to say good bye to him, you better find him before that crowd does."

Even from here I sensed that the crowd was becoming a mob. Pretty soon there would be liquor, and soon after that talk of lynching. The territory prided itself on being civilized. But it wasn't that civilized. Not yet, anyway.

I'd paid a day in advance so I went down the back stairs of the hotel. The livery was a block straight down the alley. I paid the stocky blacksmith with some silver and then walked back through the sweet-sour hay-and-manure smells of the barn to where my mount was waiting to be saddled.

I went right to it, not wanting to be detained in any way. Kansas sounded better and better. I had just finished cinching her up when somebody said, "You probably heard I killed the sheriff, Donnelly. He was my best friend."

The voice was harsh with liquor. I turned slowly from the mount and said, "Little girls and best friends, Hornaday. Not a record to be proud of."

"I didn't say anything about being proud, cowboy. I didn't say anything about being proud at all."

The men in front had overheard our conversation and had walked through the barn shadow to get here quickly. There were three of them. They were joined moments later by Patience Falkner.

"Jim . . . ," she started to say.

But his scowl silenced her.

We stood in the fading light of the dying day, just outside a small rope corral where the six horses inside looked utterly indifferent to the fate of all human beings present. Couldn't say I blamed them. Hornaday eased the right corner of his black coat back so he could get at his gun quick and easy.

"Even if you don't draw, cowboy, I'm going to draw and kill you right on the spot. That's a promise."

"I don't want this fight, Hornaday."

"What if I told you I killed that cousin of yours on purpose?"

"I wouldn't believe you."

"I killed my best friend, didn't I?"

"That could have been accidental, too."

By now there were twenty people filling the barn door, standing in the deep slice of late-afternoon shadow.

"You've got to fight me," Hornaday said. "A reputation like yours. . . ."

"You need to get yourself sober, Hornaday. You need to take a different look at things."

"I'm counting to three," Hornaday said.

"Like I said, Hornaday, I don't want this."

"One."

"Hornaday. . . ."

"Two."

"Jim please . . . ," the Falkner woman cried. "Please, Jim. . . ."

But then he did just what he'd promised. Feinted to his right, scooped out his six-shooter, and aimed right at me. What choice did I have?

I was all pure instinct by then. Scooping out my own gun, aiming right at him, listening to the shots bark on the quiet end of the day. His knees went and then his whole body, a heap suddenly on the dusty earth. Nobody moved or spoke.

I just stood there and watched Patience Falkner flutter over to him and awkwardly cradle him and then sob with such force that I knew he had just died.

The blacksmith went over and picked up Hornaday's Colt, which had fallen a few feet away. He picked it up, looked it over. He'd probably talk all night at the saloon how strange it felt holding the same gun Jim Hornaday had used to kill all those men.

Then he said, "I'll be dagged."

"What is it?" I said.

The blacksmith glanced around at the curious crowd and then walked the gun over to me.

"Looks like you performed an execution here today, mister," the livery man said.

He handed me the gun. All six chambers were empty. Jim Hornaday had fought me without bullets.

They got the Falkner woman to her feet and led her sobbing away, and then the mortician brought his wagon and they loaded up the body and by then the deputy sheriff had finished all his questions of the crowd and me, so I was up on my roan and riding off. I tried hard not to think about Hornaday and how I'd helped him commit suicide. I tried real hard.

Gunslinger

He reaches Los Angeles three days early, a scrawny forty-eight-year-old man in a three-piece black Cheviot suit made of wool and far too hot for the desertlike climate here. He chews without pause on stick after stick of White's Yucatan gum. He carries, tucked in his trousers beneath his vest, a Navy Colt that belonged to his father, a farmer from Morgan County, Missouri.

As he steps down from the train, a Negro porter accidentally bumping into him and tipping his red cap in apology, he takes one more look at the newspaper he has been reading for the last one hundred miles of his journey, the prime headline of which details President Teddy Roosevelt's hunting trip to the Badlands, the secondary headline being concerned with the annexation by Los Angeles of San Pedro and Wilmington, thereby giving the city a harbor. But it is the third headline that holds his interest:

DIRECTOR THOMAS INCE, NOW RECOVERED
FROM HEART TROUBLE, STARTS NEW PICTURE
THURSDAY WITH HIS FAMOUS WESTERN STAR
REX SWANSON.

Today was Monday.

He finds a rooming house two blocks from a bar called The
Waterhole, which is where most of the cowboys hang out.
Because real ranches in the west have fallen on hard
times, the cowboys had little choice but to drift to Los
Angeles to become extras and stunt riders and trick shoot-
ers in the silent movie industry. Now there is a whole
colony, a whole sub-culture of them out here, and they are
much given to drink and even more given to violence. So
he must be careful around them, very careful.

In the street below his room runs a trolley car, its tin-
gling bell the friendliest sound in this arid city of 'dobe
buildings for the poor and unimaginable mansions for the
rich. It is said, at least back in Missouri, that at least once
a day a Los Angeles police officer draws down on a man
and kills him. He has no reason to doubt this as he falls
asleep on the cot in the hot shabby room with its flowered
vase lamp, the kerosene flame flickering into the dusk as
his exhausted snoring begins.

In the morning he goes down the hall, waits till a Mexican
woman comes out of the bathroom smelling sweetly of
perfume, and then goes in and bathes and puts on the
things he bought just before leaving Morgan County. A
bank teller, he is not particularly familiar with real Western attire, but he knew it would be a mistake to buy his
things new. That would mark him as a dude for certain. He

had found a livery up in the northern edge of the county that had some old clothes in the back, which he bought for $1.50 total.

Now, looking at himself in the mirror, trying to be as objective as he can, he sees that he does not look so bad. Not so bad at all. The graying hair helps. Not shaving helps. And he's always been capable of a certain blue evil eye (as are most of the men in his family). Then there are the clothes. The dusty brown Stetson creased cowhand-style. The faded denim shirt. The Levi's with patches in knee and butt. The black Texas boots.

For the first time he loses some of his fear.

For the first time there is within him excitement.

In his room, before leaving, he writes a quick letter.

Dear Mother,

By the time you read this, you will know what I have done. I apologize for the pain and humiliation my action will cause you but I'm sure you will understand why I had to do this.

If it were not for the man I will kill Thursday, you would have had a husband all these years, and I a father.

I will write you one more letter before Thursday.

Your loving son,
Todd

The next two days . . .

In the Los Angeles of the movie cowboy extra, there are certain key places to go for work. On Sunset Boulevard there is a horse barn where you wait like farmhands to be picked for a day's work; then there are a few studio backlots where you can stand in the baking sun all day waiting for somebody already hired to keel over and need to be replaced; and then there is Universal's slave-galley arrangement where extras are literally herded into a big cage to wait to be called. Five dollars a day is the pay, which for some men is five times what they were getting back in the blizzard country of Montana and Wyoming and Utah.

It is into this world he slips now, making the rounds, trying to get himself hired as an extra. If he does not get on Ince's set Thursday, if he does not get that close, then he will be unable to do what he has waited most of his life to do.

He is accepted. Or at least none of the other cowboys question him. They talk in their rough boozy way of doing stunt work—something called the "Running W" or the even more frightening "Dead Man's Fall" are particularly popular topics—and they gossip about the movie stars themselves. Which sweet young virginal types can actually be had by just about anybody who has taken a bath in the past month. Which so-called he-men are actually prancing nancies afraid to even get close to a horse.

All this fascinates and frightens him. He wants to be back home in Morgan County, Missouri.

All that keeps him going is his memory of his father. The pennies on Father's eyes during the wake. The waxen look in the coffin. The smell of funeral flowers. His mother weeping, weeping.

The Navy Colt burns in his waistband. Burns . . .

Late on Wednesday, near the corral on the Miller Brothers 101 Ranch where Ince makes his two-reelers, a fat bald casting director in jodhpurs comes over and says,

The Long Ride Back

"You five men there. Can you be here at sunup?"

He has traveled fifteen hundred miles and forty-one years for this moment.

Dear Mother,

   I never told you about where I saw him first, in the nickelodeon six years ago. He used a different name, of course, but I've seen so many photographs of him that even with his dyed hair and new mustache I knew it was him. I see now that his whole so-called "murder" was nothing more than a ruse to let him escape justice. He is not dead; he's alive out here . . .

   He is very popular, of course, especially with the ladies, just as he was back there. He is also celebrated as a movie hero. But we know differently, don't we? If Father hadn't been riding back from the state capital that day on the train . . .

   In the morning I go out to the Miller ranch where the picture is to be shot.

   It will not be the only thing being shot . . .

   Say hello to Aunt Eunice for me and think of me when you're making mincemeat pie next Thanksgiving.

   I think of your smile, Mother. I think of it all the time.

                              Your loving son,
                              Todd

All he can liken it to was his six-month stint in the army (six months only because of what the post doctor called his "nervous condition")—hundreds of extras milling around for a big scene in which a railroad car is to be held up and then robbers and good citizens alike are attacked by an entire tribe of savage Indians. It is in this way that the robber will become a hero—he will be forced to save the lives of the very passengers whom he was robbing.

The trolley car ran late. He did not sleep well. He urinates a lot. He paces a lot. He mooches two pre-rolls from a Texas cowhand who keeps talking about what a nancy the casting director in the jodhpurs is. The smoke, as always, makes him cough. But it helps calm him. The "nervous condition" being something he's always suffered from.

For two hours, waiting for the casting director to call him, he wanders the ranch, looks at the rope corral, the ranch house, the two hundred yards of train track meant to simulate miles of train track. There's even a replica of the engine from the Great Northern standing there. Everything is hot, dusty. He urinates a lot.

Around ten he sees Rex Swanson.

Rex is taller than he expected and more handsome. Dressed in a white Stetson, white western shirt with blue pearl buttons, white sheepskin vest and matching chaps, and enough rouge and lipstick to make him look womanly. Rex has just arrived, being dispatched from the back of a limousine long enough to house thirty people. He is instantly surrounded and in the tone of everybody about him there is a note of supplication.

Please Rex this.

Please Rex that.

Please Rex.

Rex *please*.

* * *

Just before lunch he sees his chance.

He has drifted over to a small stage where a painted backdrop depicts the interior of a railroad car.

It is here that Rex, in character, holds up the rich passengers, a kerchief over his face, twin silver Peacemakers shining in his hands. He demands their money, gold, jewelry.

A camera rolls; an always-angry director shouts obscenities through a megaphone. Everybody, particularly the casting director, looks nervous.

His father knocking a baseball to him. His father bouncing him on his knee. His father driving the three of them—how good it felt to be the-three-of-them, mother son father—in the buggy to Sunday church. Then his father happening to be on the train that day/so waxen in the coffin/pennies on his eyes.

He moves now.

Past the director who is already shouting at him.

Past the actors who play the passengers.

Right up to Rex himself.

"You killed my father," he hears himself say, jerking the Navy Colt from his waistband. "Thirty-seven years ago in Morgan County, Missouri!"

Rex, frantic, shouts to somebody. "Lenny! My God, it's that lunatic who's been writing me letters all these years!"

"But I know who you really are. You're really Jesse!" he says, fear gone once again, pure excitement now.

Rex—now it's his turn to be the supplicant—says, "I'm an actor from New Jersey. I only play Jesse James in these pictures! I only *play* him!"

But he has come a long ways, fifteen hundred miles and forty-one years, for this moment.

He starts firing.

It takes him three bullets, but he gets it done, he does what Robert Ford only supposedly did. He kills Jesse James.

Then he turns to answer the fire of the cowboys who are now shooting at him.

He smiles. The way that special breed of men in the nickelodeons always do.

The gunslingers.

A Good Start

"The last important outlaw in Oklahoma, Henry Starr, was the first bandit to use a car in a bank robbery."
—Jay Robert Nash, *Encyclopedia of Western Lawmen & Outlaws*

Sam Mines, the high sheriff of Pruett County, Oklahoma, was known to be exceptionally proud of three things—the forearm scar left over from a shoot-out with Tom Horn, from which both men had walked away; his 1914 Ford Model T; and his lovely seventeen-year-old daughter, Laurel, whom he'd raised alone for the past twelve years, following the death of his wife from cancer.

Pruett City, the county seat, was Mines's fiefdom. Like many towns of 15,000 at this point in the new century, Pruett City was caught between being a noisy old frontier settlement and a by-god real town with telephones, electricity, and a newspaper that came out three times a week.

Mines wasn't a mean man, but he was a tough one. If he caught you carrying a gun in his town, he'd run you in no matter who you were. A saloon fight would get you anywhere between three and five days in jail. And you'd pay for every penny of the damages you'd caused or you'd rot in jail. And if you, God forbid, ever struck a woman, be she your wife or not, you'd get the cell with the drunks, most of whom were eager for a fight. The lingering death of his wife had taught him about the strength and spiritual beauty and courage of womankind, and if you did anything to defile a woman—

On this particular night in early autumn, Mines slept the sleep of the just, a deep and nourishing sleep that would enable him to be the kind of military-style lawman he'd long been. Khaki uniform crisp and fresh. Campaign hat cocked just so on his bald head. His father's Colt in his holster.

A part of his mind was hoping for another spectral visit from his wife, Susan. He'd never told anybody, not even Laurel, that the ghost of his beloved wife appeared to him from time to time. He did not want amusement or pity to spoil the visits.

And then something woke him up.

Something he'd only imagined in the fancies of his dreams? Or something real? A lawman had enemies, and every five years or so—that seemed to be the cycle—somebody would get paroled out of prison and come back to town to start discreetly harassing the man who'd sent him up. Garbage dumped on the front lawn. Dirty words painted on the shed door. Threatening letters clogging the mailbox. All these things had happened to Mines.

Moonlight painted the windows silver.

A barn owl somewhere; the wind soughing the autumn-crisped leaves that crackled like castanets; a horse in the barn next door, crying out suddenly, perhaps in its sleep, perhaps out of sheer loneliness. Town people kept just one horse these days, that for the family buggy that was rapidly being replaced by Tin Lizzies. Mines imagined that the animals got awfully lonesome being the only one of their kind, unlike the old days when every family had two or three horses.

A sound.

A kind of . . . ticking sound.

Almost like the sound large hail makes.

He grabbed his Colt from the holster on his bedpost, dangled his feet off the bed, straightened the nightshirt sleep had wound round him, pressed bare feet to the chilly wooden floor. And proceeded to find out just what the hell was going on.

As he left the bedroom, he glanced at the clock on the bureau. He'd just assumed it was the middle of the night. But it was barely ten o'clock. He'd been asleep less than an hour.

What the hell was going on, anyway?

Sully Driscoll, at nineteen, had done some pretty dumb things in his life. And this one, he realized as he heard the pebble striking Laurel's window, had to be just about the dumbest.

But he couldn't help himself. She hadn't spoken to him for three days, not since she'd seen him sitting on the town square park bench with Constance Daly—which he sure as heck shouldn't have been doing—and by now he was so desperate to speak to her, he'd resorted to this crazy idea.

He'd even scrubbed beneath his nails extra good tonight, just on the off chance that she'd hear the pebble against her glass and sneak down and see him. Sully worked at The Automobile Emporium, one of Pruett City's three gas stations and automobile repair shops. And also the best. Sully pumped gas because the owner made him. His real love was fixing cars. Second only to Laurel's beautiful, heart-shaped face, the sight of an engine in need of work was the most fetching thing Sully had ever seen. But a lad sure did get greasy and oily working in, around, and under a car. So he'd washed up extra good tonight.

Quiet street. Deep moonshadows. And the gink of a nineteen-year-old firing pebbles at a window. If her father ever caught him—

And that was when Sully saw the ghost.

Coming around the corner of the house. And moving faster than he'd ever heard of a ghost moving before. And Sully was something of a ghost expert, having practically memorized every single short story by Edgar Allan Poe.

But it wasn't a ghost, of course. It was big Sam Mines in his nightshirt. With his Colt out. Huge white feet slapping through the dewy grass like rabbits.

Sully's first inclination was to run.

Maybe Sam hadn't gotten a good look at him yet.

But, no. Nothing much ever got past Sam.

Sully said, "Evenin', Sam." Trying to sound as casual as possible.

There were times when Sam was a splutterer. You didn't see it very often—usually Sam was so cool, ice wouldn't melt on him—but every once in a while he'd confront a situation that exasperated him so much he'd start asplutterin', spittle flying from his lips, eyes bugging out, the true deep red of rage discoloring his face.

But before he even had time to form a semi-coherent word, Laurel's window flew open—Now she opens it, Sully thought miserably—and Laurel leaned out and said, "What's going on down there, anyway?"

"It was my fault," Laurel said at breakfast the next morning.

"How was it your fault?" her father asked around a piece of fried potato.

"Because I wouldn't speak to him for three whole days and he was going crazy."

"That still doesn't give him any right to start throwing rocks in the middle of the night at your—"

"It was only ten o'clock. And they were pebbles, not rocks."

"Still."

"I shouldn't have gotten so jealous over Constance. He broke off with her before he started seeing me. And I've always been afraid that maybe he thinks he made a mistake."

"He's a grease monkey. He doesn't belong with a rich girl like Constance, anyway."

"Her father offered to set him up in his own garage."

Sam Mines glowered. "If he's not careful, I'll set him up in his own jail cell."

He took out his pipe and started filling the air with its wonderful aromas. This was the scent Laurel would always associate with her father. It was a breakfast and dinner smell, a meal finished, strapping Sam Mines leaning back in his chair and smoking his pipe, maybe a thumb hooked into a suspender, a curled charred stick match sitting on the saucer of his coffee cup.

But the light of this autumn morning was no friend to aging flesh, and as she looked at him, she saw that he was no longer "becoming" old (the way she'd preferred to think about it these last six or seven years). He'd arrived. He *was* old. Not by normal human being standards, perhaps. But certainly by lawman standards. Arthritis crimped his hands and knees and feet. And his blue eyes were somewhat vague when they looked at you. They weren't even as startlingly and deeply blue as they'd once been, as if age preferred to paint in pastels.

And Henry Starr was coming to town.

Everybody knew it but nobody said it.

Not to his face, anyway.

But down at the bank, where she worked as a teller, that was all anybody talked about or thought about.

Henry Starr, the first bank robber in the state to use a motorcar in his raids, was inexorably working his way toward Pruett City. You could follow his robberies with a southeast slanting line drawn on a map. Oh, he'd zig a little sometimes, and zag a little others, but the southeastern line didn't vary much. And someday soon, he'd be here. Mr. Foster, the bank's owner, had put on two extra shotgunned guards. He had a bad stomach, did our Mr. Foster, and he walked around these days popping pills and touching his stomach and grimacing.

And Dad would inevitably have a run-in with Henry Starr, who was known to love shoot-outs, as well he should, having won every darn one he'd ever been in.

She looked at her father now and fought back tears. He looked old and somehow little-kid vulnerable. The liver spots on his big hands resembled cancerous growths. His arthritis-cramped hand gnarled itself around his pipe.

Henry Starr, who was not unintelligent it was said, had likely sent a spy on ahead to look over Pruett City. And the report back would be obvious: the sheriff's an old man; he'll be easy pickin's.

Sam Mines consulted the railroad watch he always carried in his vest pocket. "Well, time for me to be—"

She smiled and took his hand. She wanted to jump up and hold him to her and never let him go. But she knew that such shilly-shallying would embarrass him. So she simply finished his sentence for him "—time for you to be pushin' off."

He smiled right back. "I sure wish you'd look around for another beau, Laurel. That grease monkey's never gonna amount to much, I'm afraid."

It had been funny with the whore last night. Usually, he would have made love to her without any hesitation. That's what whores were for, wasn't it?

But a certain thing he'd read in *The Police Gazette* crossed his mind just as he'd begun to unbutton his trousers—a thought so nagging that Henry Starr had buttoned right back up again and kicked the whore out of his hotel room.

The thought was this: a man named Max Bowen, whom the magazine called "the most successful bank robber New York City ever saw," attributed his astonishing run of fifty-three bank robberies over eight years before being apprehended to the fact that the night before a robbery, he abstained from both liquor and ladies. The way, said this Max Bowen, that prizefighters did.

And so there Henry Starr had been, unbuttoning his trousers, when the thought about abstinence struck him . . . and he'd immediately ordered the whore out of the room.

This morning, as he cranked up his Model T and waited for his lazy-ass gang to come tumbling down the hotel steps so they could drive on to Pruett City and rob the bank there, he wondered if he'd been stupid.

That whore sure was pretty. And sure did have a nice pair of breasts.

Henry Starr, not a reflective man, gave a few moments thought to how bank robbing had been not all that long ago. Horses instead of cars. And no federal agents on your ass unless you killed one of their own. And no telephones to make tracking you down all that much easier.

The car, especially, was a mixed blessing.

Here it was, for example, a perfectly fine autumn day, sixty degrees already at seven A.M., the engine should be performing very well, and yet he still had to crank the damned thing as if it was twenty below zero and the engine block was covered with snow and ice.

Not to mention problems with tires, muddy roads, and running out of gas.

The one nice thing was the speed.

You come bursting out of a bank with six or seven bags of cash, hop into the car, and in a few minutes you're tearing ass out of town at forty-five miles an hour—and God help anybody who gets in the way.

That was where the Tin Lizzie beat the hell out of any kind of horse you'd care to name.

The car finally kicked over.

And by that time his gang, yawning and toting huge mugs of steaming hot coffee, came hurrying down the stairs, knowing Henry was going to be damned mad about them sleeping in this way.

As soon as Sully Driscoll opened the police station door, he knew he'd made another mistake. One just as dumb as last night's mistake of pelting Laurel's windows with pebbles.

"Help you?" said Clete Mulwray, one of Pruett City's twelve deputies. He sat behind a large desk, seemingly lost in a sinkhole of paperwork.

"I'd like to see the sheriff."

"Any reason in particular?"

"I guess I really should just talk to him."

Mulwray shrugged, stood up. "Wait here." He disappeared down a short hall.

He sure wasn't friendly. Sully wondered if the sheriff had told him about what Sully had done last night. No—if he had, the deputy would be smirking.

Mulwray came back. "First door on your left."

Sam Mines wore his familiar crisp khaki uniform. His campaign hat was angled from the top notch of a hat tree. With all the glassed-in law books, the office looked as if it belonged to a lawyer.

Sam said, "Help you with something?"

"I came to apologize."

"You apologized last night."

"Yeah, but I couldn't sleep much. All I did was think about how stupid I was. So I came to tell you again."

Sam leaned back in his chair. He didn't invite Sully to sit down. His eyes were even unfriendlier than Mulwray's.

"You ever think you might be better off with Constance Daly?" Sam said.

Sully swallowed hard. Was this Sam's way of saying he didn't want Sully to see Laurel anymore?

"No, sir. I—I love Laurel."

"Laurel can't give you your own auto shop."

"I know that."

"And Laurel can't give you a big house and a nice fat bank account."

"I know that, too. But I happen to love Laurel."

Job couldn't have sighed any more deeply than Sam Mines did at that moment. He leaned forward, elbows on his desk, and said, "Sully, I'm going to tell you something. And it's going to hurt your feelings. And I'm sorry for that in advance. You're kind of brash sometimes—and you're so crazy over motorcars you make people laugh at you—but you're a decent, hardworking lad, and I really don't mind you at all."

"Is that a compliment?"

Old Sam smiled. "Yeah, I guess it is."

"Then thank you."

"But."

"There's always a but, isn't there, Sam?" Sully said, hoping to keep the conversation light.

"Yes, I'm afraid there always is." Sam glanced away, as if preparing himself to say something he was reluctant to say. "Sully, you're a decent boy. And my daughter loves the hell out of you. But I want to ask you something, and I want you to answer me honestly."

"All right." Sully knew this was going to be terrible.

"Do you think you can make much of a living working at that garage?"

Sully felt sick. "You mean she could marry somebody with a better future?"

"That's a good way to say it, I guess."

"Well, I—"

"I want the best for Laurel, Sully. You can understand that, can't you?"

"Well, sure, but—"

"I wish you'd think about it, Sully. I know it's not the way young people like to think about their futures—once upon a time I was just as hot-blooded as you are—but just think about what Constance could do for you. And what somebody like Andrew Stillson could do for Laurel."

Andrew was a thirtyish bachelor, and a nice enough guy, who ran the local apothecary. But he wouldn't make a good husband for Laurel—

"I'll think about it, sir."

"That's all I ask, son. And about last night— Don't worry about it. I got too mad by half. Like I said, I was hot-blooded myself once." He smiled. "That's just how men are built, I guess."

The newspapers in the state were after Henry Starr even more relentlessly than the lawmen.

And as he bumped and swayed along behind the wheel of his Model T, Starr thought of the lies they wrote about him and how they were purposely damaging his reputation.

There was a time when the Henry Starr name shone as brightly as that of Jesse James and the Dalton Brothers. Your first-class bank robber. A man that a lot of people secretly looked upon as a folk hero. The banks robbed people, didn't they? Then what was so wrong about robbing them right back? That was the attitude a lot of folks had.

Then came that damned robbery in Oklahoma City, and people had never again felt the same quiet admiration for Starr.

"Technically," Starr always said to his gang when he'd been drinking—and Lord were they long tired of hearing about it—"technically, I didn't shoot him in the back. I shot him in the side."

This was in reference to one Horace P. Puckhaber, manager of the State Bank and Trust, who had been about to throw a jar of ink through a side window so as to warn the people on the street that a robbery was going on inside the bank. Hopefully, the people would be smart enough to inform John Law.

At the exact moment he hurled the jar, Horace P. Puckhaber was standing with his hands held high, his back to Starr. Starr had his Colt trained on the man. Starr hadn't seen the plump little man earlier secret the jar into his meaty fist. In order to throw the jar through the window, though, Puckhaber had to turn sharply to his left. He would then—this was the only way Starr could figure out such a foolish but surprisingly brave act—pitch himself to the floor and roll away behind a desk for cover.

Now, wouldn't *you* shoot such a man in such a situation? Of course you would. What choice would you have? You had to stop him before that damned ink jar smashed the window, didn't you?

So here's how it actually happened:

Puckhaber, his hands up, seemingly being as obedient as a good dog, suddenly starts to turn to his left.

Starr sees the ink jar. Sees the window. Understands what's going on.

He shouts, "Drop that jar!"

Then it gets confusing. Because at first—for just one second—Puckhaber starts to carry through with his plan. He keeps turning left.

At which point, by instinct, Starr fires his gun.

But all of a sudden, before the bullet tears into him, he turns away again, his back to Starr.

Well, he *almost* turns back.

Here's why Starr says that the press is lying about him: If you look carefully at the fatal wound, you'll see that it is actually on the side of the man. Very near his back, true—within an eighth of an inch—but still, technically, in the side.

Making Starr, at worst, a *side*-shooter.

Now, a man can live with a reputation as a side-shooter. But not as a back-shooter. Even though many legends have, in fact, been back-shooters—including Wild Bill and all four of the Earps—the people who read the newspapers and the dime novels don't know of it. They believe that their heroes are simon pure, just as white-hatted and blue-eyed and pearly-teethed as the hacks say they are.

Starr has shot and killed eight men. And all of them bankers, which is pretty much like killing Indians or coloreds, which is to say not much of an offense at all according to the general populace of this particular time and place.

Starrs is *proud* of murdering eight bankers.

Were these the same type of whore who'd foreclosed on his very own parents in 1881? Proud of being a front-shooter.

And not at all ashamed of being a side-shooter.

He just wishes that the newspaper bastards would lay off him about being a back-shooter. . . .

Such were the thoughts of Henry Starr as he rolled toward Pruett City in his Model T.

* * *

Was there any machine so wondrous as a Model T? A miraculous instrument of gasoline tanks, acetylene headlights, inner-tube tires, and clutch, reverse, and brake. And was there any experience—excepting kissing Laurel—as much fun as spreading the innards out on a sheet and cleaning each one so that it performed to utter perfection?

That was how Sully spent the morning. George Adair, one of the wealthiest men in the area, had brought his son's car in for a quick clean-up. And had insisted that Sully do the work. More and more people asked for Sully personally. Hank Byers, the owner of the gas station–garage, was both flattered and hurt—flattered that he had the best garage man in town, and hurt that his own days as the reigning car expert had waned.

Usually, you could hear Sully whistling as he worked on cars. Who wouldn't whistle when he was doing—and doing well—exactly what God had put him on the earth to do?

But there was no music in his soul this sad day. Sam Mines had made it clear that he would not countenance a marriage between Laurel and Sully. And Sam was—whether or not he wanted to face up to it—in a position to discreetly undermine any wedding plans.

And Sully felt sure that was just what Sam would do.

Laurel taught school in the mornings. She was always home in time to fix her father his lunch.

Though today was sunny and perfumed with that most enchanting of scents—burning leaves and hazy hills—it was still nippy, so she fixed tomato soup, generous slices of cheddar cheese, and slabs of wheat bread. Food that would stick to the ribs and give you energy for this harbinger of winter.

Sam didn't mention last night until they were almost finished eating. "Sully stopped by to apologize again."

She smiled. "He wants you to like him, Dad. I want you to like him, too."

Sam frowned at his soup bowl.

"Something wrong, Dad?"

Sam sighed. "Well, I don't think *he* likes *me* very much right now."

She had been about to put the spoon to her mouth but stopped. Her father's demeanor had become troubling. She sensed that their comfortable little lunch hour was about to be spoiled. "Did you have an argument?"

"No, no argument."

"Well, what then?"

He leaned back in his chair. He looked nervous.

"You look as if you're afraid to tell me, Dad."

A kind of shame came into his expression. "Maybe I went a little too far."

She slammed her spoon down on the table. "Darn it, Dad. Tell me what you said to Sully. That's what we're talking about here, isn't it? Something you said to him rather than the other way around?"

The shame did not leave his handsome but age-wrinkled face. "I told him the truth was all, honey. The truth as I see it, anyway."

And then he told her what he'd said.

At the time the car pulled on to the drive, Sully was busy pounding nails into the leg of a wooden workbench that had gone all wobbly. He had a pocketful of nails and a hammer and was working fast as he could. He wanted to get back to his real calling: fixing engines.

He put the hammer down, wiped his hands on the bib overalls he wore to work in, and then proceeded out into the sunlight from the cool shadows of the garage.

Four men sat in a green Model T. There was a similarity of bulky body, of big-city suits, and of wide-brimmed dress hats that made him think of the covers of his favorite magazine, *Argosy*, whenever it ran a story about gangsters. The license plate read Oklahoma, all right, but that was the only thing local in the picture, which he was giving a quick study.

But that wasn't the only local thing, it turned out. When the burly driver spoke, it was with the familiar Okie twang that was Sully's own.

"Fill up the gas, kid."

Sully almost smiled. They were *imitating* the *Argosy* was what they were doing. Imitating the covers and the gangster silent pictures that were just starting to come into fashion.

Sully wondered if the driver had a crimp in his neck. The way he angled his head down, so that he hid virtually his entire face beneath the wide brim of his fedora— *No, not a crimp in the neck*, Sully realized. *The driver is hiding his face.*

"Yessir," Sully said.

And it was then that the driver seemed to forget himself. He raised his head just enough so that Sully could see his face and realize just who he was dealing with here.

Their eyes met, locked.

There was great, knowing rage in this man's gaze. The banality of his words had nothing to do with the hard anger of his brown eyes. "And check them tires, too."

Sully almost said, "Yessir, Mr. Starr."

But, thank God, he caught himself in time. If Starr knew that Sully had recognized him—

Laurel was raking leaves when she realized what she *really* should be doing. Talking to Sully. Telephone was no good because it was a party line and saying anything confidential over the phone—well, you might as well be done with it and just put it in the newspaper.

She rushed to the garage and climbed aboard her bicycle with the outsize basket for carrying groceries, with the outsize light for riding at night, with the outsize horn for getting tykes, squirrels, dogs, kittens, and raccoons out of her way as she was rolling along.

Dad was speaking for himself, Sully. I love him and I know he means the best for me. But he's wrong about you. I know how much you love working on cars, and that's what I want you to do for the rest of your life—for the rest of our lives. I don't want to go against my own father, Sully, but I will if I have to. One way or another, you and I are going to get married. I promise you that, Sully. On my sacred word.

And she would seal it—as did all the girls in the romance novels she wouldn't admit to reading or liking—with a kiss.

The kid recognized me, Henry Starr thought. No doubt about that.

With the all the Wanted posters everywhere, it was difficult to go anywhere without being recognized. That's why Starr had been thinking about leaving Oklahoma. He'd heard Missouri was good pickings for bandits—he himself preferred the romantic sound of "bandit" to the drab word "robber"—and maybe it was time to give it a try.

As for the kid who was just now starting to put gasoline in the car . . .

One of the boys in the backseat leaned forward and whispered, "That kid recognized you."

"I know."

"Maybe we should kill him."

"We kill a kid like that, we'll have every lawman in the state down on us. You think it's bad now, wait till we do something like that. One more killing in this state and they'll probably sic the damn army on us."

"Then what you gonna do?"

"I'm gonna tie him up and gag him."

At which point Henry Starr opened the door and climbed out of the car.

Laurel was relieved to see only one car on the drive. Sometimes when she popped in to see Sully, he was so busy he could barely give her enough time for a simple hello.

Maybe he'd have at least a few minutes, if the repair work inside the garage wasn't too much.

She was no more than thirty feet from the garage, just about to sound her horn so Sully would know she was here and maybe wave to her, when she saw the big man take the gun from somewhere inside his suit coat, walk up to Sully, who was pumping gas, and shove the gun into Sully's back.

A robbery!

"Sully," she cried out.

The man turned and looked at her now. And half a second later another man in the car came lunging out onto the drive and started running for her, pistol drawn and gleaming in the autumn sunlight.

"Get out of here!" Sully shouted to her. "Fast!"

But her hesitation undid her. For such a bulky body, the second man could sure run fast. He closed on her, pointed the gun right at her face, and then escorted her to the gas station.

She and Sully were prisoners.

Sam Mines got the call just as he was leaving the sheriff's office.

A lawman to the east told him, "Hotel people think Starr and his boys stayed there last night. The night crew didn't pick up on it, but one of the morning people saw four men around a Model T this morning and was pretty sure that it was Starr and his boys. That means he's on a direct route to Pruett City."

"It sure does," Mines said. "Thanks."

The last words Sully said to Laurel—just before one of Starr's men gagged him—was, "I sure wish you wouldn't've come out here, Laurel."

"I had to, Sully. I wanted you to know that my Dad wasn't speaking for me when he said all those things."

"Aw," Starr laughed. "Listen to 'em. True love."

Once Laurel and Sully were both bound and gagged, Starr and his men left the station, got in their car, and pulled away.

Sam Mines issued each of his three daytime deputies a shotgun. "I want two of you in front of the bank, out in plain sight where everybody can see you. And I want one of you on the back door. In plain sight."

"Shouldn't we try to ambush them?" one of his men said.

"Nope. Ambush would mean a shoot-out. A lot of people could get hurt. They won't see the two of you out front until they get close. And that's when I'll use my own car to pull up right behind them and order them to put their guns down."

"What if they start firing?"

"With three shotguns on them?" Sam said. "If they're that crazy, then so be it."

It was sort of funny, watching Laurel and Sully wiggle and waggle and wobble on their bottoms trying to extricate themselves from the ropes Starr's man had wound them up in.

Every once in a while, they'd try and talk around their gags. She was trying to tell Sully that she loved him. Sully was trying to tell her about the hopefully clever thing he'd done. He just hoped Sam could find out about it in time.

"The car kinda ridin' funny?" one of Starr's men said.

Starr sighed. It was always something with these guys. Someday he'd get himself a fine shiny new bunch of boys. Boys who weren't always complaining. Boys who weren't always second-guessing everything he said. Boys who were grateful to be in the presence of a man as notorious as Henry Starr. "The car is ridin' just fine. Now shut up."

He said this just after driving four blocks to the start of Pruett City's business district.

* * *

When the car came on the dusty drive, both Sully and Laurel looked up. If only the customer would come inside and find them—

This customer, whoever it was, was in a hurry.

Honked the horn not once, not twice, but three times.

He will come in and untie and ungag us, and Sully will grab the telephone and call Sam and tell him what he's done.

Hope gleamed in Laurel's lovely eyes.

They would be rescued at last.

She was sure of it.

And it was then, after a final frustrated honk, that the customer pulled away.

Within a few minutes, Sam's men took their places in front of and behind the bank. Sam had quickly called in a couple of auxiliary men who'd do anything as long as they got to wear badges. These two men set about keeping the bank street clear, rerouting people so they'd be out of the way if any trouble started.

Henry Starr had one of his few moments of peace. He liked Pruett City. There was something so pleasant about the tree-shaded streets and all the little white clapboard houses and cottages, the picket fences, the dogs and cats and tykes. He even cast an appreciative glance on the Lutheran church and its proud white spire that seemed to almost pierce the soft blue sky. Someday, when he retired . . .

"Hey, boss."

"Yeah?"

"You sure you don't feel nothin'?"

Starr did, but he didn't want to admit it. He was sick of their whining. Maybe he could *will* the obvious problem away by just not thinking about it.

He drove on.

This time the customer, a middle-aged lady in a bonnet, goggles, and long driving gloves, came in and expeditiously freed Laurel and Sully from their bonds. Sully jumped up and ran to the phone. The operator put him through to Sam's office. The man left behind said that Sam was out. Sully told him what he'd done and told him to get the word to Sam immediately.

A few minutes later, Sam was in his own car with two of his deputies in the back, shotguns at the ready.

The scene was just as Sully had predicted. Henry Starr and his boys were in the process of pushing their car off to the side of the street where they could fix the flat tire Sully had given them.

Starr's gang was in no position to grab their weapons. Or even run. Not when they were being covered by three shotguns.

With Starr, it was another matter. With the speed and force of a much younger man, he grabbed a lawman and got him in a choke hold that turned the officer's face a dark sick red. The man was dying on the spot.

Starr relieved him of his gun and then stabbed the barrel of it against the man's temple.

"You," Starr snapped at Sam. "You drive that car of yours over here. We're goin' for a ride."

Everybody could see the resentment on Sam's face.

What a way to wind down a career—helping a wanted killer escape.

But what choice did he have? The hostage was twenty-four years old and the father of three. Sam couldn't stand here and let him be sacrificed that way.

"Let him go," Sam said.

"Sure," Starr said. "That would make a lot of sense, wouldn't it? I let him go and you open fire. Now get your car."

Sam shook his head. He didn't have any choice. He would have to help this killer make his escape.

Or would he?

The shadows that had troubled Sam's eyes were gone suddenly. He walked almost jauntily to the car he'd kept running. Even if it meant that he had to give up his own life, he'd be damned is he'd help Starr escape.

He pulled the car up to Starr.

"Open the door," Starr said, meaning the passenger door.

Sam's jaw muscles bunched, and he muttered a lot of words the ladies wouldn't ever approve of. And then he pushed the door open.

Starr proved agile again. He flung the young deputy away from him and in the same motion, jumped in the passenger seat and jammed his gun against Sam's head.

"Drive," Starr said.

Sam drove. Boy, did he drive. And he knew just where he was driving to—at fifty-three miles per hour. Absolute top end.

"You ever seen what somebody looks like when the car he's in runs into a tree at this speed?" he shouted at Starr above the roar of the engine.

"You crazy bastard! Slow down!"

"About a block from here there's this old oak tree, Starr. It sits right on the corner. If you don't throw that gun of yours out the window, I'm going to drive us right into it."

"You won't kill yourself! Don't try and bluff me old man!"

"Won't I? Like you say, I'm an old man. I've had a good life. And I'll be damned if I'll help you escape."

Houses and trees and lawns began to sweep by as Sam kept the car at top speed. Buggies and carriages and bicycles all whipped out of his way, many of their occupants shaking fists at him after he'd passed.

"You got one block, Starr! Make up your mind. I'll be dead, but so will you." There wasn't any guarantee either of them would be dead—though there was a good probability they would be—but he didn't need to tell Starr that at the moment.

"Slow down!"

"It's comin' right up, Starr! Half a block!"

Starr saw the massive oak Sam was talking about. You could see him calculating his chances of surviving such a crash.

A quarter of a block now.

Sam gulped. Starr was a brave man in his way. Most men would've thrown their guns out a block ago.

Sam said a mental good-bye to his loved ones and began to angle the car toward the low curb so that the car would hit the tree at a solid angle. He wouldn't want to survive this kind of wreck anyway. It wouldn't be any kind of life being crippled or maybe without any mental faculties left.

And it was then that Starr screamed, "All right! All right! I'm throwing my gun out."

And just as Sam had been preparing to set his eyes on some angels—at least he hoped that was the general vicinity he was headed for—Starr flung his gun out the window.

And Sam, shaking, sweating, feeling a need to vomit, began the process of steering the car back onto the street and slowing down.

"So where did you get the nail?" Sam asked Sully later that afternoon. Sully, Laurel, and Sam had gone to the ice cream parlor for sodas. Sam hadn't had to tell them about his cleverness and bravery. By now it was all over town.

"Had it in my pocket. I'd been fixing up that old workbench I use. Had a bunch of nails in my pocket, matter of fact."

"You just might've saved a lot of lives," Sam said. "I was afraid Starr and his boys might panic when they pulled up in front of the bank and saw my men. These days, bank robbers do some pretty crazy things."

They talked for another twenty minutes, and then Sam said he had to get back to the office. As he was leaving, he said, "I guess maybe I'd better think some things through, huh, son?"

Sully smiled. "I guess so."

After he was gone, Laurel said, "That doesn't mean he's changed his mind."

"I know."

"But it's a start." Then she took his hand and caressed it. "A good start."

Enemies

Cedar Rapids, Iowa, 1893

Speaks should have known better. Hell, he was dealing with Harry Creed, and Harry Creed was one crazy son of a bitch.

"Where the hell you takin' me, Harry?" Speaks said.

"Oh, you'll see, you'll see," Harry Creed said, sounding like a kid teasing his younger brother. But at a hard-lived sixty-three, Speaks sure didn't look like any kind of kid.

The date was September 2, 1893. The place was Cedar Rapids, Iowa.

"We almost there?" Speaks said after they'd walked four more long blocks.

"Almost, almost." Harry Creed laughed.

These days Harry was dressing like a pirate. He wore a bandanna over his head, a golden ring on his right lobe, and he had a wee bit of a knife scar on his right cheek. Speaks wondered cynically if Harry had given himself that scar.

For all his bitching, Speaks was enjoying the day. This was one of those golden, lazy autumn days when the flat autumnal light of the sun seemed to penetrate to your core and warm your very soul. The air smelled of burning leaves, and there was no headier perfume than that, and the trees were so colorful they almost hurt the eye. He wanted to be a raggedy-ass kid again.

And just then, Harry Creed steered them around a corner and down a dusty alley.

Speaks was hot now, in his black suit coat and gray trousers, sweating. When they got where they were going he'd take the coat off. He was wearing a ruffled white shirt. He'd been doing a little gambling this year, and had decided to dress appropriately. His Navy Colt was back in his hotel room. Cedar Rapids had a full force of police. They'd throw your ass in the jug if they saw you sporting a handgun. The old days were long gone. Long gone.

The first thing he saw was the big red barn that said BLACKSMITH over the double doors. The first thing he heard was the shouts and curses of men who'd already been doing some drinking at ten o'clock on this fine fall morning. He could also smell blood, but he wasn't sure if it was human or animal. The scent of fresh blood tainted the air. He'd been around enough of it to recognize it instantly.

"You bring me to a cockfight?" Speaks said.

"Hell, no, man." Harry Creed grinned. "Somethin' a lot better than that."

And he just beamed his ass off right then. Speaks half expected him to start skipping at any moment. Skipping. A grown man.

The barn smelled of the smithy's fire and new-mown hay and horse shit. The smithy, a wiry little bald guy with a toothless grin and a wary eye, nodded them toward the back of the barn. His wary eye was fixed on Harry Creed's pirate getup. "You wouldn't happen to be Captain Kidd, would you?" he said, and winked at Speaks.

"Asshole," Harry Creed muttered as they walked to the back where maybe a dozen men stood in a circle, their hands filled with greenbacks just pleading to be bet. This was Saturday, and Friday, at least in most places, had been payday.

"You get the old Master in here, and I'll bet he gets through three of them little peckers in under a minute." The man speaking wore a cheap drummer's outfit and puffed on an even cheaper cigar. "And I got three dollars here to say I'm right."

Another man, a youth really, dressed in a blue workshirt and gray work trousers, said, "I'll see that three and make it four."

The other men laughed.

"This ain't poker, kid," one of them said.

Speaks still couldn't figure out what Harry Creed had gotten him into.

The barking dog got everybody's attention. It was a boxer, and a damned good-size one, and when it moved you could see its muscles move in waves down its back. Tear your damned leg off, this one would.

The men made loud cheering noises, as if a favorite politician had just walked into the barn.

"Master's gonna do it, aren't ya, boy?" said the young guy. "You're gonna make me a rich man, ain't ya, Master ol' boy?"

A couple of the men separated then and Speaks got his first look at the ring. It ran maybe three feet high, was metal, and was maybe four feet across. This was the kind of ring cockfighters used.

"Next batch!" a pudgy guy shouted as he came through the back door carrying a round, lidded metal can.

"God, I hate them things," one of the men in the circle said, and shuddered for everybody to see.

"What the hell's in the metal can?" Speaks asked Harry Creed.

But all Harry did was smile that stupid pirate smile of his. "Ain't you gonna be surprised?" he said.

As the man with the can reached the ring and started to pull the lid off, all the men, without exception, moved back. It was clear they wanted no part of whatever was in the can.

Master was in the ring now, crouched low, his eyes mesmerized by the can in the man's hands. Master's jowls flickered and snapped. Master knew what was in that can, all right.

The men got excited, too. Their eyes gleamed. Some of them made eager, lurid noises in their throats. In many respects, they were even more animal-like than the rats. Killing had never been something Speaks cared to see, even if the victim was an animal. In Houston once, admittedly carrying more than a few drinks around in his belly, he'd broken the nose of a hobo who was trying to set a cat on fire for the amusement of his pals.

The man was swift and sure. In a single motion he jerked the lid away and upended the can.

At least eight or nine fat, angry, filthy, tail-twitching rats fell to the floor of the ring. When they hit the floor they went crazy, running around in frantic circles, bumping into each other, trying to cower when there was no place to hide or cower at all.

Master was jubilant with blood lust.

He didn't need any encouragement.

He leapt upon the first rat, seizing the thing between his teeth, catching it just right so that when teeth met belly, blood spurted and sprayed all over Master's otherwise tan face. The way a burst balloon would spurt and spray.

Speaks had enough already.

This little wagering sport was called ratting. You bet on how many rats a dog could catch and kill in a sixty-second period. Ratting was even more popular in the East than out here. Easterners just didn't talk about it much. They always made you think that they were very civilized people and that you, a Westerner, were somehow heathen. But Speaks had been to New York a couple of times and he knew that civilization was not a dream shared by everybody. He'd seen a man cut out the eye of his opponent with a Bowie knife.

While Speaks was not partial to rats in any way, he still couldn't see torturing them this way. He didn't like cock-fighting, either, far as that went.

"Hey, where ya goin'?" Harry Creed said. "Master here just got goin'."

But Speaks just wanted out. Who the hell wanted to watch a dog get himself all bloody by killing rats when it was such a beautiful day outside? Life versus death; and at this point in Lyle Speaks's years, he always chose the way of life and not the way of death.

He was just turning around when he felt something press against the lower part of his back.

"You just walk out of here real nice and easy, Mr. Speaks," a voice whispered in his ear, "and everything's gonna be just fine. Just fine. You understand me?"

Speaks was wondering who it was. You lived a life like

Speaks's, it could be almost anybody, anybody from anywhere for almost any reason at all.

"You understand me, Mr. Speaks?" the voice asked again.

Speaks nodded.

If there was one thing he understood without any difficulty at all, it was having somebody hold a gun on him when he was unarmed. He understood it very, very well.

The gun nudged him around until Speaks was facing the double front doors of the barn. Then the gun nudged him right on out of the barn.

He didn't really get a good look at the guy until they were almost out of the alley, and the only glimpse he got then was by looking over his shoulder.

He was a kid. By Speaks's standards, anyway. Twenty-two, twenty-three at most. One of those freckled frontier faces with the pug nose and the quick grin that made them look like altar boys until you noticed the pugnacious blue eyes. Speaks had seen kids like this all over the West. Not knowing what they were looking for but somehow all finding the same thing: trouble. There used to be a lot more of this kind in the West, self-styled gunsels who strutted and peacocked all over the place, just trying to prove how tough they were. But that was the old West, when there were a lot of bona fide gunfighters roaming around, and when kids like this one always got themselves killed in saloons for saying the wrong thing to the wrong man. This kid was out of place and out of time, a decade too late to live out his dime-novel dreams.

A couple of times Speaks thought of trying a move or two on the kid, but he decided against it. These old bones weren't what they used to be, and his glimpse of the kid told him that he was dealing with a very serious pistolero, or whatever the dime novelists were calling punks this year.

"I'm going to make it easy for you," Speaks said.

"Just keep walkin'."

"I don't have much money, and I don't know where I can lay my hands on any, either."

"I don't give a damn about money."

"You will when you get to be my age, kid."

"Just shut up and keep walkin'."

Now they were on the sidewalk. In one of the newspapers that he'd read last night, an editorial had boasted that Cedar Rapids possessed seven hundred telephones, fifteen blocks of electric streetlamps, and more than a mile of paved streets. A lot of the sidewalks were still board, though. Like this one.

"They're onto you."

"Who's onto me?" the kid said.

"The people. They can see you got a gun on me."

"Bullshit."

"Look at their faces, kid. These aren't dumb people. One of them's gonna get a cop."

The kid went for it, not right away maybe, but after a minute or so. He started watching the faces of the passersby, the women in big picture hats, the men in fancy Edwardian-style duds, the farmers with their sun-red faces and hat-white foreheads. Speaks could sense the kid's step falter as he started to watch passing faces closely. Falter, and make him vulnerable.

Speaks wheeled around. The kid was right-handed, so Speaks came in left, fast, under the arc of the kid swinging his gun around.

He got the kid in the ribs with his elbow and in the groin with his fist. The kid folded in half, and Speaks ripped the gun out of his hand.

Speaks knocked off the kid's fancy-ass cowboy hat, grabbed him by the hair, and dragged him all the way back to the alley.

"My hat!" the kid kept saying, as if Speaks had taken his magical talisman away. He didn't seem to notice that in the meantime Speaks was tearing out a good handful of his hair.

Speaks found a wall and threw the kid up against it and then, to send him a clear and unmistakable message, started slamming the kid's head against the wall, never once letting go of the greasy hair.

Three, four, five times the kid's head came into slamming contact with the wall until finally his eyes rolled back, and the kid started sliding to the dusty alley, whereupon Speaks kicked him in the chest for good measure. Holding a gun on an unarmed Speaks was not the way to curry favor with the big man.

"Who the hell's this?" said the pirate.

Speaks looked over at Harry Creed and sighed. "What's the matter, they run out of rats?"

Speaks wished his traveling buddy Sam November was here. He'd be able to shoo Harry Creed away. But Sam was up visiting a sick relative in the Decorah area, which was why they'd traveled up the Mississippi from New Orleans in the first place. So now Speaks was stuck with a punk who meant him harm, and the antics of Harry Creed. He'd come here to see an old friend, Keegan, but now he wondered if he should've come here at all. Harry Creed was not somebody he wanted to spend any time with. And the punk just made things worse.

"Them rats really bothered you, huh?" Harry Creed giggled. "You shoulda seen yer face, Lyle boy. You was whiter than a frozen tit."

The kid was just coming around.

"Who's this?" Harry Creed said.

"Don't know yet," Speaks said. "But I sure aim to find out."

In Cedar Rapids, the courthouse was on an island in the middle of town. The original inhabitant of the island, back in the Indian days, had been a horse thief whose luck ran out years later in Missouri, where he was hanged. Local folks never tired of telling this tale. When asked if it was really true or not, this unlikely tale, the residents of the town would point you to the public library and tell you to go look it up. And by God, if it wasn't true, as the books verified, a horse thief had been the first resident of what later became the town. How was that for a rough beginning?

A number of taverns lined the streets two blocks north, giving a good view of the island and, farther down, the ice works.

Harry Creed went and got them beers while Speaks shoved the kid into a booth at the back of the place. It was a choice seat. Hot wind carried the smell of the outhouse through the screen door. The men playing pinochle didn't seem to notice Speaks, or the smell.

"Who the hell are you?" Speaks asked.

"None of your business."

"Kid, I don't need much of an excuse to kick your ass, so you'd better start talkin'."

The kid sighed. "My name's Pecos."

Speaks laughed. "Pecos, huh?"

"Yeah, what's wrong with that?"

"Kid you got farm all over your face, and your twang puts you in Nebraska. So how the hell do you get 'Pecos' out of that?"

But before Pecos could answer, Harry Creed sat the beers down and they proceeded to drink.

"Guess what his name is?" Speaks said to Harry Creed.

"His name?"

"Yeah."

"Now, how the hell would I know what his name is?"

"Take a guess."

Harry Creed shrugged. "Jim?"

"Nope."

"Bob?"

"Uh-uh."

"Arnell?"

"Pecos."

"Oh, bullshit," Harry Creed said.

"Ask him."

Harry Creed took another sip of brew. "What's your name, kid?"

"Go fuck yourself."

"I'd be watchin' my mouth if I was you," Harry Creed said. Then he grinned. "With all due respect, I mean, Mr. Pecos."

"You assholes think this is funny, huh?" Pecos didn't wait for an answer. "Well, it won't be so funny when your friend Chris Keegan gets here and I get him in a gunfight."

"Aw hell," Speaks said. "That's what this's all about."

"What's it all about?" Harry Creed said.

"His name and wearin' his holster slung low like it is," Speaks said. "This dumb kid thinks he's a gunfighter."

"Not thinks," Pecos said, "am."

Speaks made a sour face and shook his head. "Kid, there haven't been any gunfighters since they shut down the trail towns ten years ago. And most of what you hear about gunfighters is bullshit anyway."

"Not about Wild Bill," Pecos said.

"Especially about Wild Bill," Speaks said. "And the only reason Chris Keegan ever got into any gunfights was defendin' himself against kids like you who forced him into it."

"He killed twenty-two men."

Harry Creed snorted. "More like four or five, kid, and Lyle's right, he didn't want to get into any of them. Kid came up to him one night in Abilene and called him out. He woulda killed Chris, but he was so drunk he tripped over his own feet and Chris killed him."

"Yeah," Speaks said, "and another time Chris was standin' at the bar and he saw this kid comin' through the batwings and he saw this kid start to draw and that gave him plenty of warning, so he ducked down and turned around and shot the kid before the kid could clear leather. Didn't take a whole lot of brainpower to do that."

"Plus which," Speaks said, "Chris Keegan is a year older'n me, which'd put him right about sixty-four. Even if he used to be a gunfighter, he sure isn't anymore."

"I could still be the man who beat Chris Keegan," the kid said.

"You're a crazy bastard," Harry Creed said.

But a dangerous one, Speaks thought. He said, "That why you put a gun in my back? So I'd be sure to tell Chris about you when we meet his train tonight?"

The kid nodded. "That way he'd know I was serious. Real serious."

Speaks threw his beer in the kid's face.

Even the pinochle players glanced over to watch this one.

"Hey, Lyle," Harry Creed said. "What the hell you do that for?"

"Because I'm sick of this little prick."

The bartender came over. "You got trouble, take it outside."

"No trouble," Speaks said. "I'm just leavin', is all."

He stood up and did just what he said.

"You son of a bitch," the kid said as Speaks walked out the front door. "You son of a bitch."

The train was eight cars long, all passenger cars except for the caboose. Behind the windows Easterners sat staring imperiously at the small train depot. Not until they reached San Francisco would they be able to inhale civilized air again.

Chris Keegan looked fifteen years younger and ten years better than Speaks. They were almost the same age.

Keegan had always been something of a dude, and he was a dude still, what with the black silk gambler's vest, the flat-crowned Stetson, and black Wellington boots shined to blinding perfection.

Amy Keegan was a perfect match for her husband: blonde, poised, beautiful in a slightly wan way. Her dark blue traveling dress clung to curves that time had not ruined as yet. There was just a hint of arrogance in her eyes as she beheld Lyle Speaks. Clearly, she considered both her husband and herself his superior. Once again, Speaks wondered why this woman had ever taken up with Harry Creed.

Thinking about Harry Creed reminded him that Keegan was now married to a woman he'd stolen away from

Creed. Why hadn't Harry erupted at the simple mention of Keegan? Strange, he thought. Man stole a woman from me, I'd curse every time I heard his name. I surely would.

"How about a drink?" Speaks said.

"I'd really like to freshen up," Amy said.

Keegan said. "Why don't we freshen up a little first and meet you down in the hotel bar? I assume they have one."

"Yeah," Speaks said, "a nice one."

Speaks walked them back to the hotel. The lamp-lighters were at work, pushing back the night. Player piano music from the saloons. Violins from the Hungarian restaurant down the street. The steady *clop clop clop* of horses pulling fancy carriages toward the opera house. The dusk sky was vermillion and gold and filled Speaks with a sadness he couldn't articulate, not even to himself. Rainy days and dusk skies always did that to Speaks.

When they reached the hotel entrance, passing couples strolling the sidewalks beneath the round red harvest moon. Keegan said, "Oh, hell, honey, why don't I have a drink with Lyle here and then I'll come up to the room."

Speaks expected her to say no, but she surprised him.

"That's a good idea. Then maybe your dear old friend Speaks here can explain what Harry Creed was doing at the depot."

"Harry Creed?" Keegan said.

"He was standing at the west end of the platform," she said. "Watching us."

"Is Harry Creed in town?" Keegan said to Speaks.

"I'm afraid he is. Sam November ran into him up in Dubuque and told him we'd all be down here today."

The Long Ride Back

"He's not exactly Amy's favorite person," Keegan said.

"I don't want to be in the same town with the man," Amy said. "In fact, I think I'll change our plans, Chris. I think we should leave first thing tomorrow."

For the very first time since he'd met her ten years earlier, Speaks felt sorry for Amy Keegan. Tears shone in her eyes, and she looked genuinely frightened. Speaks wondered just what the hell Harry Creed had done to her, anyway.

Then, as if she sensed that this was one of the few times Speaks liked her, she said in a very soft voice, "Oh, why don't you two have your drink. I'll just go on up to the room." Then to Speaks, smiling sadly: "People will think I lead him around by the nose all the time."

"Oh, honey," Keegan said.

She really was crying now, gently.

"See you in a little bit," Keegan said, and kissed her good-bye on the cheek.

The tears had softened her face; and as he looked at her now, Speaks was almost rocked by her beauty.

"The last night the bastard raped her," Keegan said. "Then he broke her arm."

For all of Harry Creed's antics, for all of his prairie-boy affability, he was a treacherous and ruthless son of a bitch, part of a lower order of men who had drifted through the frontier scavengerlike, mostly as con artists who unburdened the dumb and the greedy of their money. But they had more sinister sides, too. They were arsonists and stickup men and hired assassins, too. Whatever was needed in a particular time and place, they would be.

255

"That's why she's the way she is," Keegan said. "Never lets me out of her sight, because she's scared he's going to show up sometime."

"What I can't figure out is how the hell she ever got with a man like Creed, anyway."

They were in the taproom of the hotel. Men in Edwardian suits and women in bustled dresses filled the room. The waiters wore starched white shirts with celluloid collars.

Keegan said, "Her father was a missionary to the Indians. Lutheran. She got some of that from him. She's always trying to save people. When we lived in Kansas City, she spent half her time working at the Salvation Army." He shook his head. "Well, you know Harry. Back when she was living over in Peoria, he met her at a temperance meeting and her husband had just died of influenza and she was very lonely and . . . well, she ended up marrying him. Didn't last long. Four months, I guess." He made a face. "He made her do all kinds of filthy things I'd rather not talk about. And he beat her up all the time, too." He made a fist. "Nearly every night."

"You never went after him?"

"She won't let me. She's afraid he'll kill me. I mean, a fair fight, guns or fists . . ." He shrugged. "But you know our Harry. It wouldn't be a fair fight. He'd be up to something."

Just then Speaks looked up and saw Amy coming toward them.

"I decided I'd rather be down here with you two," she explained as she sat down. "I got a little scared upstairs all alone. Knowing Harry's in town."

Keegan hadn't been exaggerating her fear. She looked agitated, all right.

Then she said gently, touching Keegan's hand, "I'd really like to leave tomorrow morning."

He nodded. "That's what we'll do, then." To Speaks: "Sorry, Lyle."

"I understand." Speaks looked at Amy. "I would've run him out of town if I'd have known what he did to you, Amy."

"He's always lurking someplace," she said.

"This has happened before?"

"Oh, sure," she said. "He's shown up several places over the past five or six years, hasn't he?"

"Yeah," Keegan said, "and he always leaves little reminders of himself. A note. A photograph of the two of them. Only time I ever called him on it, he denied it, of course. You know Harry."

"Yeah," Speaks said, "unfortunately, I do."

They drank through two hours of conversation, good conversation, fond memories of a good friendship, once they found out about Harry Creed, anyway. Keegan asked after Speaks's wife of five years, Clytie, and Speaks told him they were still very happy together in Montana. Ranching, he said, was agreeing with him.

Amy contributed, too. The booze took away her slight air of superiority. She was just a good woman then, and Speaks could see how they loved each other and took care of each other, and he was happy for Keegan. Keegan was one of the good ones. Despite his years as a reluctant gunfighter, he was a peaceful, fair-minded, and decent man, and he deserved good things. There was no meanness in him.

Keegan had just ordered another round when Harry Creed came into the taproom.

Harry's pirate getup was gone. He wore a tweed coat,

white shirt, dark trousers. His hair was slicked back in the fashion of the day. He actually looked handsome, and for the first time Speaks could imagine Harry and Amy walking down streets together. He came straight over to the table, as if they'd been expecting him.

Amy bowed her head, wouldn't look up at him.

But Keegan looked up, all right. "You got sixty seconds to get out of here. Harry."

Harry Creed smirked.

"You try to do an old friend a favor and look what you get."

Speaks wasn't sure which old friend Harry was talking about, Amy or Keegan.

"Sixty seconds, Harry," Keegan repeated.

Amy still wouldn't look up.

"There's a kid, Noonan's his real handle—Lyle here met him this afternoon—and anyway, he wants to shoot it out with you, Keegan. Says you're the last gunfighter and he wants the honor of puttin' you away. I'm tryin' hard to talk him out of it."

Now it was Keegan's turn to smirk.

"I'll bet you're tryin' real hard, Harry. I'm sure you wouldn't want anything terrible to happen to me, us bein' such good friends and all."

"I'm doin' everything I can," Harry Creed said. "I just thought I'd let you know. I'd be very careful where you go tonight."

Then he looked at Amy.

"You're lookin' lovely tonight, Amy."

Her head remained bowed, eyes closed. She was trying to will him out of existence.

The waiter appeared.

"Will you be staying?" he asked Harry Creed.

"No, he won't be," Keegan said harshly.

The waiter set down their beers and left quickly.

"I'm gonna try'n talk him out of it, Keegan," Harry Creed said.

"You do that," Keegan said. "Now get the hell out of here."

"You sure do look pretty tonight, Amy," Harry Creed said. Then he laughed. "Not quite as pretty as when she was with me, of course, but she was a lot younger then." He glanced at Speaks. "By the way, the kid likes ratting a lot better than you do. I can hardly drag him away from the barn." He patted his stomach. "Guess he's a little younger than you are, Speaks."

That was Harry, always getting in the last line.

They sat in silence for nearly two minutes. Amy brought her head up and reached over and touched her husband's hand again.

"Someday you won't be able to stop me, Amy," Keegan said softly. "Someday I'm going to kill him."

"Then they'd hang you," she said. "And he's the one who should hang."

Speaks said, "I'm going to take care of the kid for you. You two just go ahead and have yourselves a good meal."

"Don't get into trouble," Amy said.

Speaks shrugged.

"I've been in trouble a few times before." He smiled. "And I probably will be again before they plant me."

Keegan frowned.

"I wish there was a train out of here tonight. I want to get out of this town."

"Just relax and enjoy yourselves," Speaks said. He took

out some greenbacks and laid them down on the table. "The next round's on me."

"Amy's right," Keegan said. "I don't want you to get into any trouble."

"I'll be fine," Speaks said, then shuddered inwardly. He'd be fine except for seeing the rats in the ratting cage. Kinda funny, the way you could feel sorry for something you hated. Speaks hated rats, and yet now he felt sorry as hell for them. He wasn't at all surprised that a punk like Noonan would enjoy ratting. He wasn't surprised at all.

He said good-bye and set off for the blacksmith's barn.

Two blocks away Speaks started hearing the dogs barking as they went after the rats. This was something he'd have to keep to himself, feeling sorry for the rats and all. People would think he was one strange cowpoke for taking the side of the rats.

The next thing he heard, this a block away, was the men. This time of night they were drunk, words slurred. But you could hear the blood lust in the timbre of their voices. They didn't much care whose blood it was as long as somebody excited them by bleeding.

Speaks went inside the barn and moved to the far doors where the crowd gathered.

Harry Creed and Pecos stood together, watching as more rats were dumped into the ring. They were at the back of the crowd, which made things easy for Speaks.

Pecos's face glowed with glee. This was something to see, all right. He even giggled like a little girl.

Speaks moved up carefully behind him, and then returned the favor Pecos had done for him that afternoon.

Speaks shoved his Colt hard against Pecos's back.

"We're going to turn around and walk outside."

Pecos looked over at Harry Creed. Creed saw what was going on. He nodded to Pecos.

The three of them went outside.

Pecos obviously figured he was going to get it first, but Speaks surprised him by turning around and kicking Harry Creed right square in the balls, then slashing the barrel of the gun down on the side of Harry Creed's head. Harry dropped to his knees.

"That's for what you did to Amy," Speaks said. "And this is so you don't get ideas about Pecos here doin' your killing for you." And with that he brought the toe of his Texas-style boot straight into Harry Creed's jaw. Harry had the good sense to scream.

Pecos he just pistol-whipped a little. Nothing special, nothing for Speaks to brag about or Pecos to bitch about, not for long, anyway, just enough so that Pecos had a couple of good-size welts on his face, and one very sore skull. There was a little blood, but again not enough to warrant bringing a reporter in.

Inside, the dogs went crazy. So did the crowd.

Harry Creed picked himself up. He was pretty wobbly. He started to say something, but then gave up. Very difficult to talk with a mouthful of blood.

"There's a train," Speaks said, "and it leaves in twenty minutes. I want you on it." This train was heading in the direction from which Keegan and Amy had just come.

"A train to where?" Pecos asked, trying to stand up.

"It doesn't matter where," Speaks said, "as long as you're on it."

Harry Creed, having apparently swallowed a mouthful of blood, said, "Amy gonna give you some of that nice sweet ass of hers, is she, Lyle?"

One punch was all it took, a straight hard shot to the solar plexus, and Harry Creed was sitting on his butt again.

"Maybe I should break your arm the way you broke hers, Harry."

"It was an accident."

"Sure it was, Harry."

"The bitch didn't appreciate nothin' I did for her."

"The train," Speaks said. "Be on it. Both of you."

"You son of a bitch," Pecos said as Speaks walked away. "You son of a bitch!"

Speaks went back to the hotel. Amy and Keegan were gone. Probably up in bed already. He had three brews, and then he was upstairs, himself.

He stripped to his long johns, the smell of his boots sour, meaning he'd have to powder them down inside again, and then he lay on his bed in the darkness, the front window and its shade silhouetted on the wall behind him.

He thought briefly of Clytie, waiting for him to return to their ranch in Montana. He wished Sam November would finish up his visit to his relatives so they could head back.

That was the last thing he thought before he fell asleep.

Somebody was pounding on his door so hard, all he could think of—now that he was starting to think clearly—was that there must be a fire.

"Hey! You in there!" a man's voice shouted.

Speaks was off the bed and at the door in seconds.

The man was familiar-looking somehow—then Speaks remembered. A man at the bar downstairs earlier that night.

"You know that friend of yours, the one with the pretty wife?" the man said. He had gray hair and muttonchop sideburns and a belly bursting the vest of his dark three-piece suit.

"What about him?"

"He's got trouble downstairs, mister. There's some punk kid tryin' to get him into a gunfight downstairs in the street." The man shook his head. "Hell, mister, we don't have no gunfights here. This is Cedar Rapids. We've got over seven hundred telephones."

"Son of a bitch," Speaks said. Then: "Thanks."

He got dressed in seconds and hurried downstairs.

Pecos had read way too many dime novels.

He stood spread-legged in the middle of the street, his right hand hovering just above the pearly handle of his Peacemaker.

He'd gotten a crowd surly enough, too. His kind always wanted crowds around. In the electric light of the new lamps, Pecos looked like a raw kid wearing his older brother's duds.

"I'm givin' you ten more seconds to draw, Keegan," Pecos said to Keegan's back.

He was slurring his words. He was drunk.

Speaks looked over at Harry Creed and scowled. No mystery here. Harry Creed had decided to let the kid do his killing. He got the kid drunk and pushed him out on stage.

Amy Keegan grabbed Speaks's arm when he reached the sidewalk.

"You hear me, Keegan?" Pecos said.

"He's callin' you out," Harry Creed said, "fair and square."

"My Lord," said the man who'd roused Speaks from sleep. "This is Cedar Rapids." He didn't mention the seven hundred telephones this time.

"He doesn't want to kill the kid," Amy whispered to Speaks.

Speaks nodded and then looked over at Keegan. He was standing with his back to his tormentor. You could see the anger and humiliation on Keegan's face. Obviously, a part of him wanted to empty his gun into the kid. But the civilized part of him—the part that had changed for the better under Amy's guidance—declined the pleasure.

Without turning around Keegan said, "Kid, I'm going to walk up these stairs and go into the hotel. And if you want to shoot me, you'll just have to shoot me in the back."

"You think I won't?" Pecos snapped.

Keegan couldn't resist.

"Even a punk like you wouldn't shoot a man in the back." And with that Keegan started up the stairs.

"You think I won't?" the drunken kid called out again. "You think I won't?"

Keegan took another slow, careful step up the stairs to the front porch of the hotel.

"Draw, you bastard!" Pecos shouted, weaving a bit as he did so, the alcohol slurring his words even more now.

"Shoot him, kid!" Harry creed said. "You gave him a chance! Now shoot him!"

Even boozed up the way he was, the kid was passing fair with a handgun.

His gun cleared leather before Speaks even noticed. The kid brought the gun up and sighted in a quick, easy movement and—

Speaks shot the gun out of his hand.

The kid cried out, dropping the gun and looking around, as if some dark demon had delivered the shot and not some mere mortal.

Speaks walked directly over to Harry Creed. Harry turned and started to move away quickly, but not quickly enough. Speaks grabbed him by the hair, got his arm around Harry Creed's throat, and then proceeded to choke him long enough to make him puke.

A few moments later Harry Creed was on his hands and knees like a dog, vomiting up chunks of the evening's repast.

For good measure and because sometimes he was—he had to admit—a mean son of a bitch, Speaks then kicked Harry Creed in the ribs twice.

Harry did a little more throwing up.

Speaks went back to Amy and Keegan and said, "C'mon."

Keegan said, "God, friend, I really owe you one."

Speaks took Amy by the arm and helped her up the stairs. "I want to get you two into your own room and then I'm going to stand guard all night."

"All night," Amy said. "Are you kidding?"

"No," Speaks said, knowing that Harry Creed would try something else later on. "No. I'm not kidding at all."

Speaks found a straight-backed chair and hauled it down in front of Keegan's door. He sat down and put his weapon in his lap and rolled himself another one of his sloppy, lumpen cigarettes.

He was just enjoying the first couple of drags when he heard footsteps coming up the hall stairs. Moments later, a cop appeared.

Out west they were wearing those kepi hats, the kind

favored by Foreign Legionnaires and other types of fancy-uniform complements. But Cedar Rapids would apparently brook no such foolishness. This hefty Irishman wore a blue coat and a blue cap and a dramatic star pinned on the chest of his coat. He carried a nightstick and wore a squeaking holster filled with a shiny Navy Colt.

"You the man in the gunfight?" he asked Speaks.

"There wasn't any gunfight."

"There almost was."

Speaks shook his head.

"Some punk named the Pecos Kid stepped out of line."

The big Mick grinned.

"The Pecos Kid, huh? In Cedar Rapids?"

"That's what he calls himself."

"So it's all over?"

"All over."

"You a Pinkerton man or something?" the Mick asked.

"No, why?"

"You're guarding the door."

"Oh. No, I just want to see that my friends get a good night's sleep."

"You think the punk'll be back?"

Speaks shrugged. "I just don't want to take any chances."

The Mick said, "Pecos, huh?"

Speaks smiled. "Pecos."

"Wait till I tell the boys."

In the silence again Speaks listened to the various sounds of humanity up and down the hall. A few doors away a couple was having enviably noisy sex. Then there was the man with the tobacco hack. And then there was the nightmare-screamer. And then there was the snorer.

The guy was sawing logs so loudly Speaks half-expected to hear the door ripped off its hinges.

Every time he got dozy, Speaks rolled another cigarette. By the fourth one, three hours after he'd applied the seat of his pants to the seat of the chair, he was really starting to get the hang of rolling smokes. Imagine, after all these years, he was finally learning to do it right.

He heard the noise then, and he knew instantly that Harry Creed had outfoxed him.

Creed knew Speaks was sitting in the hall. So Harry decided to shinny up the side of the hotel and go in the window.

The bastard.

Speaks burst through the door into darkness. He glimpsed shifting figures in the gloom, but that was all because just then somebody hit him very hard from behind with a gun.

Pain. Anger. Then a rushing coldness. And then— darkness. Speaks was out, sprawled on the floor.

Pain.

He wondered what time it was.

The hotel room was empty.

More pain. Then anger again as he remembered how Harry Creed had come up the side of the hotel.

Muzzy streetlight filled the window frame.

The town of Cedar Rapids was quiet.

Speaks pushed himself to his feet. He'd been out long enough for the blood on the back of his head to dry and scab over a bit.

He poured warm but clean water from the metal pitcher into the washing pan. He splashed water across his face and the back of his head.

Not until now had he seen the small white piece of paper on top of the bureau. He picked it up.

BARN

The one word.

Nothing more.

He wondered what the hell Harry Creed was up to now.

Moonlight lent the old buildings lining the alley a shabby dignity. A couple of cats sat atop a garbage can, imperiously noting Speaks's passing.

Only one of the smithy's doors was open now. The interior was completely dark.

A kind of metallic chittering sound reached Speaks's ears.

At first he couldn't fathom what could make such a noise.

But as he pushed into the barn, his gun leading the way, he had a terrible premonition of what he was about to see.

And of what was making that noise.

One of the rear barn doors was ajar just enough for Speaks to see the shape of the ring.

Keegan was in the ring. Or what was left of him, anyway. The rats had eaten most of his face. One of his eyeballs was already gone. They'd probably fought each other for the sake of eating it. Keegan's forehead glistened. Harry Creed had borrowed an old trick from the Indians. Cover a man in honey and let the rats at him. The rats had also eaten out Keegan's throat. They were working on his stomach and groin now. The air stank of fresh blood and feces.

He was about to fire at the rats, drive them away, when he felt a rifle barrel prod the back of his head, the wound inflicted earlier. He winced.

"Kind of makes you hungry, don't it?" Harry Creed laughed from the darkness behind Speaks.

"Where's Amy?" Speaks snapped.

"Ain't that sweet?" Harry Creed said. "He's worried about Amy. I knew he was interested in that sweet ass of hers. I just knew it."

He stepped out of the shadows. He was wearing his pirate getup again. He plucked Speaks's gun from him. "Pecos went and got hisself killed."

"I'm really sorry to hear that."

"Forced Keegan into a gunfight. Guess you were right, Lyle. Keegan killed Pecos right off."

"Then you tied Keegan to the ring."

Harry Creed shook his head.

"I love that woman, Lyle. I purely do. And she was my wife before she was his. I had to teach him a lesson, didn't I?" Then Creed smiled. "He didn't scream for very long. They killed him right off. I mean, there wasn't all that much pain for him, if that's what you're worried about."

"Where's Amy?"

"I guess that's for me to know," Harry Creed laughed, "and for you to find out. Now it's gonna be your turn, Lyle. You always did think you was a little better'n me. Now you're gonna find out otherwise."

Harry Creed nudged Speaks toward the pit.

"You get in there and sit down."

Speaks hesitated a moment. Not until a few minutes before had he realized how crazy Harry Creed really was. Speaks had no doubt that Creed would shoot him right now if he disobeyed.

Speaks looked in the pit at the rats swarming all over

poor Keegan. Poor Keegan was going to be poor Speaks in just a few more seconds.

"Climb in," Harry Creed said.

Speaks raised his leg, climbed into the pit. The rats were too busy feasting on Keegan to pay much attention to Speaks.

Speaks saw the honey pot then, stashed over in the shadows near the right side of the pit. It was about the size of a coffeepot.

"Start daubin' that stuff on your face and hands," Harry Creed said.

Speaks thought of refusing, but why die sooner rather than later? But it'd be better to be shot than to have rats rend you. It'd be much better.

The honey pot was a lidded ceramic bowl. Speaks took the lid off and plunged his hand deep inside.

Sticky honey oozed around his hand, sucking it ever deeper into the bowl.

"Now start rubbin' it on your face, Speaks."

For the first time a few of the scrambling rats looked over in his direction. The sweet smell of the honey pot was what did it. There was a whole new feast over here. Their eyes glowed red in the oppressive darkness.

Harry Creed came right over to the edge of the ring now.

"Start rubbin' it on your face, Speaks. You heard me."

Speaks had no choice. His hand dripping honey, he began to wipe the thick stuff on the angles of his face.

Already a few of the rats had drifted over and were starting to climb his legs. At this point, he could still kick them away. But not for much longer.

"Now sit down."

"No."

Harry Creed aimed the rifle right at Speaks's face.

"I said sit down."

Speaks had one chance, and if he muffed it he was going to be eaten alive the way his friend Keegan had been.

Speaks slowly sat down on his haunches.

More and more rats swarmed around him.

"All the way down," Harry Creed said.

Speaks reluctantly sat all the way down.

Now the rats were all over him, on his back and arms and legs. All he could think of was the illustrations he'd seen of *Gulliver's Travels*, a book Clytie had given him to read, all the tiny people walking up and down the giant.

A rat scrambling over his shoulder lashed out at Speaks's honey-painted face.

Speaks jumped half an inch off the pit floor and made a wild wailing sound in his throat.

"Scary little buggers, aren't they?" Harry Creed said. "Now lay down."

"What?"

"You heard me, Lyle. Lay down. Flat. On the floor."

"No way."

The bullet passed so close to his ear, he could smell the metal of it. A few of the rats scattered. Most continued to cling to Speaks. There were maybe two dozen of the things on him now.

"Lay down, you son of a bitch."

So Speaks lay down. The pit was so small that he had to prop his legs up on the edge of the ring.

Then he screamed.

The rats seemed to suddenly triple in number, and they were all over him, especially his head and hands.

The small honey pot was four inches from his right hand. He would have to be quick. And then he would have to roll away from where Harry Creed was likely to fire.

"My, these fellas sure have big appetites," Harry Creed said. "You and Keegan in one night. My, my."

A rat sank teeth into Speaks's left hand. Speaks sobbed with pain and terror and reached for the honey pot.

He caught Harry Creed right in the center of the forehead.

Then he rolled quickly to the right. Harry Creed staggered, then pumped three bullets into the exact spot Speaks had occupied only moments earlier.

Speaks jumped to his feet, rats hanging off of him as he did so, and lunged at Harry Creed.

He tore the rifle from Creed's hand and drove a punch deep into Harry's stomach. Harry doubled over. Speaks took the rifle and started clubbing Harry Creed on the side of the head until the man slumped forward into unconsciousness.

Once he had slapped and shaken the rats off of him the first thing he did was take the rope off Keegan's wrists and ankles and carry the ripped and bloody body out of the pit. Bleeding from his own bite wounds, he found a horse blanket and covered him with it.

His final act was to pick up the honey pot and empty it lavishly over the length of Harry Creed's face and body, back and forth, back and forth, until Harry was saturated with honey.

A few minutes later, Speaks found Amy up in the haymow. She'd been bound and gagged.

She was sobbing when she got to her feet.

"I'll never forget the screaming," she said, leaning on Speaks for support. "He died so slowly."

He let her cling to him, let him be her strength for a long moment. He kept seeing how Keegan's face had looked after the rats had finished with it. He wanted to slice a knife blade into his brain and cut out the memory forever.

"Where's Harry?" she said finally.

"Don't worry about Harry."

"You're going to turn him over to the law, aren't you?"

Grimly, with no hint of humor, he said, "Let's just say I've taken care of Harry in my own way."

They went down the ladder to the ground floor and then out the door. He steered her away from the ring so she couldn't see. Being a good Christian woman, she might try to talk Speaks out of what he was doing.

"We'll go to my hotel room and wash up," Speaks said.

"But Harry. Where's Harry?" Amy said. "Shouldn't we turn him over to the law?"

Harry Creed regained consciousness just then. Two, three, even four blocks away they could still hear him screaming.

"Oh, my God," she said. "You put the rats on him, didn't you?"

Speaks said nothing.

Just took her arm a little tighter and escorted her out of the alley.

After a block or so you couldn't hear Harry scream hardly at all.

Blood Truth

Kendricks put the toe of a pointed boot to Helms's ribs and nudged hard. "Wake up. We're off-schedule already," he said. All the time he talked, Kendricks kept his Remington aimed straight at the kid's chest. Walter Helms had killed a man in an argument over a poker game, and he wasn't the sort you took chances with.

They were up near the Canadian border, in Toole County, east of Sunburst. This was a chill spring morning, as you could tell by the silver glaze of ice over the stream below and the frost on the bunch grass and sagebrush. The sky was a porcelain blue and the sun promised to warm the land later on.

Kendricks had trailed Helms to a rooming house on the edge of a prairie town in Alberta. He'd caught him in bed with a nice-looking redhead who probably wasn't old enough to be legal. Right off, Kendrick had seen the kid's pride, how embarrassed he was to be apprehended in front of a woman. But Walter Helms had said only one thing as Kendricks brought him down the back stairs, and that he said softly: "My turn'll come, bounty hunter. You wait and see." There hadn't even been any anger in the threat. He seemed to be just stating a fact.

Walter Helms sat up in his blankets and tried to shake off sleep. His blond hair was matted against his skull and his chin was stubbly with a light beard. He needed a shave and he needed a bath, but Kendricks figured the authorities could worry about that. The good people of Chinook planned to try the twenty-one-year-old and then quickly give him a proper hanging.

"I didn't get much sleep," Helms said, looking around the small, crude campsite. The fire had burned out and Kendricks had pitched dirt over it. Everything had been packed up on their horses. Kendricks hadn't even left the tin coffeepot out. "I kept having nightmares."

"So I heard," Kendricks said. "You kept me awake, too." But that wasn't all that had kept Kendricks awake. He'd kept thinking about what the kid had asked him yesterday. Kendricks had said no right away, but now he wondered if he shouldn't say yes.

Helms stared up at him with his strange blue eyes. The kid's gaze always looked innocent and slightly hurt. That's what fooled people. His gentleness. "You'd have nightmares, too, if you knew there was a rope waiting for you." The kid was always a gentleman; almost unnervingly so.

Kendricks's tone softened some. "I guess I would, kid. I guess I would." He nodded to the horses. "We'd better get going. Like I said, we're running behind schedule."

* * *

During the morning they worked their way across a broad plain that eventually gave way to scattered foothills. They were near Willow Creek now, heading south.

Kendricks sat a dun and rode slightly ahead of the kid, whom he'd handcuffed to his saddle horn. The kid was a talker and Kendricks hated talkers.

"You like your job, Mr. Kendricks?" Helms asked around noon. That was one of the kid's many eerie habits. Here he was, a cold-blooded killer, but he always sounded as proper and respectful as a schoolboy. It seemed to be one of the reasons that young females seemed to find him so dashing and fascinating. In a land of crude, even vulgar men, the kid had real style.

"It's all right, I guess."

"I'll bet it's hard work. Being a bounty hunter, I mean."

Kendricks looked back at him and shook his head. "Not near as hard as being a killer."

For half the afternoon they skirted low foothills. Helms's roan picked up a rock, and so they had to stop while Kendricks tried to fix the shoe. In the war one of his jobs had been apprentice to a blacksmith. He had some luck and the horse was soon walking smartly again.

In another hour the sky changed abruptly. Black clouds replaced the blue sky. You could smell rain coming.

"You remember what I asked you yesterday, Mr. Kendricks?"

"I remember."

"Well, we're not more than a half mile from it. Right over that ridge and down along a creek bend. And there it sits."

"I'm sorry, kid. I can't do it."

Helms brought his horse up next to Kendricks. His blue

276

eyes showed innocence again. "You know what they're going to do to me, Mr. Kendricks. I only want to see her for an hour or so."

"Kid, I just don't think it's a good idea. And that's all I've got to say about it."

But the pain was back in the kid's gaze, and for some reason it struck Kendricks as genuine.

"Wouldn't you want to see your mother once before you died?" the kid said.

The rain started. It was hard, cold, numbing rain, and the horses hated it as much as their riders. This kind of weather always brought on Kendricks's arthritis. At forty-one, the former Helena lawman often got crippled fingers and painful knees from weather like this. And sleeping on cool ground wasn't going to make him feel any better, either.

They rode on. Kendricks thought things over. A farmhouse sounded good. Most likely, she'd feed them well and bed them down pleasantly, and in the morning they could set off fresh and dry and make the last leg of their journey in one long day's ride.

Kendricks fell back in the pounding rain and shouted above the din, "You sure your ma's the only one there?"

"I'm sure."

"Then let's head there."

Even in the dusk, even through the slanting silver rain, Kendricks could see the kid's grin. He looked like a twelve-year-old who just won a prize at the county fair.

The soddy sat in a small bowl of sandy earth, ringed on three sides by junipers. This was a Kansas-style soddy which meant that the sod blocks probably weighed as much as fifty pounds each, with wooden frames carefully set in place for windows.

Now, just after dark, the only light was a kerosene lamp flickering faintly against the glass.

They took their horses to a rope corral around back and Kendricks fed them hay. Helms watched this, his hands still cuffed.

Kendricks went up to the door first and knocked. Apparently the rainfall had drowned out all sound of them arriving. After a time the door opened and a short, slender woman, just as good-looking as her son, stood warily looking out at him. The kerosene lamp back-lighted her head and gave her graying hair, tied up into a knot in the back, the sheen of gold.

"Hello, Mom," Helms said, stepping into the lamp-glow.

No mistaking the sound the woman made. A sob of pure joy. Nobody would greet heaven with any happier voice.

"Come in, come in," she said after hugging him and kissing him several times. She seemed not to notice Kendricks.

Kendricks followed them inside.

In a poor soddy like this you didn't expect to find much in the way of furnishings. But you could tell that the woman had tried to improve her hardscrabble life by adding a worn carpet to the floor and strips of gingham to the rough walls. Patchwork quilts decorated two straw-filled mattresses. A wooden dry-goods box had been covered with a small festive scrap of red cloth and now served as a table.

Only when she got her son inside, into the light, did she see the handcuffs. Then she glared at Kendricks, her eyes filled with accusation. "No need to tell me what you are, mister," she said.

"He's not so bad, Ma," Helms said gently. "He's just trying to make a living the same as we all are." Again, Helms sounded not like a snarling killer but more like an educated and most genteel young man. "I'd appreciate it if you'd fix us some dinner."

But the woman still glared at Kendricks. "I'll fix you some food, Walter, but I'll be darned if I fix him any."

The woman, whose name, he learned, was Grace, heated up some prairie chicken in the three-legged "baker" that stood over burning coals. She dished potatoes and biscuits onto her son's plate.

As she did this, Walter lay on the bed, staring at the ceiling. Kendricks sat in a rocking chair. Every once in a while the chair would squeak when he'd lean forward, but most of the time there was just the sound of the rain hammering away at the soddy's roof. The fire and the smell of the food made Kendricks feel comfortable and lucky. His stomach rumbled and a kind of sickness came over him when he saw how full Walter's plate was.

Grace Helms set the plate on the bed. Walter sat up. He still had the cuffs on, of course. His mother had to cut his meat for him.

About halfway through his meal Helms looked up at his mother, who was now back at the stove, and said, "Now, Ma. This isn't like you. Treating guests this way."

"He's no guest, Walter. He's a bounty hunter. The lowest form of life there is."

"Then do it for me," Walter Helms said. "For me, dish him a plate of good prairie chicken and biscuits and potatoes the way you did for me."

She looked over at him from the baker where she was stirring the broth. "You really want me to?" She looked pretty then, and younger, not so prairie-hard as she had in the doorway.

"Yes, Ma, I really want you to."

So Kendricks got his supper, after all, including a cup of very bitter coffee.

Around nine o'clock the rain became sleet. It sounded as if pellets were being fired against the roof.

Grace Helms had set a kerosene lamp on the floor next to her son's bed. He immediately picked up a month-old issue of the Great Falls *Tribune* and started reading it.

To Kendricks she said, "I want you to know something, Mister. That's an educated boy there. He got through fourth grade and he knows how to read Sir Walter Scott with no help from his teacher."

Helms put the newspaper down and looked over at Kendricks. He smiled. "I don't think you've convinced our friend here that I'm a model citizen, Ma."

"Well," she said, "what does he know anyway?"

Helms went back to reading. Grace sat across from him in a matching rocking chair. She darned socks with amazing efficiency.

For a time Kendricks sat with his head back and his eyes closed. His .44 sat in his lap. His rough hand was never more than an inch away from the trigger. He dozed and he listened to the sleet. He still felt snug and lucky about being in here tonight. He just wished he could keep his eyes open. Dozing off in this situation could be dangerous. . . .

The next time he sat up straight, he heard Walter snoring in his bed. His mother was standing over him, looking down at him. Kendricks couldn't recall ever seeing a more perfect portrait of grief. Within a month her son would be hanged.

Seeing that Kendricks was awake, she turned around and came back to her rocking chair.

"He used to sit there," she said. She spoke gently now. Her fingers flicked over the darning. "In the chair where you are."

"Walter, you mean?"

She shook her head. "No; his father."

"Oh."

"Died when Walter was eleven. Consumption."

"I'm sorry."

"Walter and I, we both miss him." She glanced over at her sleeping son again. The newspaper had fallen across his chest. She smiled at Walter and then looked back at Kendricks. "I'm sorry I was so harsh when you came in."

"I understand, ma'am. This isn't an easy thing."

"He's a good boy."

"I'm not judging him, ma'am."

"But you're taking him in."

"It's how I earn my living. It's nothing personal."

She seemed to study his face. He felt sleepy. He probably looked sleepy, too. "Would you like a little more chicken?"

"No thanks, ma'am."

"Then some more coffee, maybe."

He rubbed at his face, yawning. "Coffee sounds real good. I'd appreciate it."

She filled his tin cup and brought it back to him. He heard this rather than saw it. His eyes had closed again and he'd tilted his head against the back of the chair.

When the coffee came, he sat up straight and kept blinking his eyes. He seemed to be having a little trouble focusing.

Thank God for the coffee.

Grace Helms sat across from him again, doing her darning, staring at him. "Did you ever think he may not have done it?"

"As I said, ma'am, I don't judge him. That's up to the jury and the court."

"He wrote me a letter. He said it was a fair fight. He said that the man had accused Walter of cheating and drew his gun on Walter. Walter didn't have any choice but to draw his gun and defend himself."

Kendricks sighed. Maybe knowing the real facts would help her in some way. "From what I'm told, Walter was dealing a marked deck. The man picked up all his chips and tried to leave the game. Walter shot him in the back. The man was a farmer. He was unarmed." He spoke as softly as he could.

She didn't say anything now. She just sat there in the lamp-glow, the wind whining, the sleet raking the roof, and looked at Kendricks as if he'd just spoken in a language incomprehensible to her.

Finally, in barely a whisper, she said, "Is that the truth?"

"It's the truth as far as I know it, ma'am."

And then he yawned again. He liked sitting here across from her. Despite her fear and bitterness there was a soft quality he liked about her. He could imagine holding her in his arms; not even sex, not at first anyway, just holding her.

"Do you have a family, Mr. Kendricks?"

He took note of the "mister."

He shook his head. "Back when I was a town marshal in Helena, I had a wife. She was shot one day during a bank robbery. Completely innocent. She'd just gone in to make a deposit."

The woman sighed. "That's terrible, Mr. Kendricks. I'm sorry."

"So I went after the men who did it. It took me eight months and three states, but by God I found them and I turned them over for trial."

She started staring at him hard again, as if she were trying to decipher something in his expression. "And you've been chasing bad men ever since?"

"Ever since."

She nodded to the bed. "You've got my boy confused with the kind of men who killed your wife, Mr. Kendricks. But he's not like that at all. Not at all."

He felt sorry for her. He'd seen this in the parents of so many killers, how you told them the truth—that Walter Helms's victim had been shot in the back—but somehow they forgot right away and went back to seeing their boy as somebody the law was picking on.

He yawned again, and that was when he knew. His head started spinning and the hand he put to the armrest of the rocking chair trembled. "The coffee," he said. "You put something in the coffee."

"He's a good boy," Grace Helms said.

He tried to push himself up from the chair but he didn't have the strength. He just kept yawning; and his head kept spinning.

"The coffee," he said again, feeling drool run down his mouth. Whatever she'd put in there was enough to knock him out entirely.

By the time he'd sunk full into the chair again, his breath was coming loud and ragged. Everything before his eyes was being swallowed up in darkness.

* * *

Just before he opened his eyes, Kendricks made note of two things. One, he had to pee pretty bad. Two, he had a headache that was like getting your skull sawed in half.

He opened his eyes.

In front of the door, Walter Helms was tugging on his sheeplined coat and strapping on the .44 and holster that had belonged to Kendricks.

Seeing that the bounty hunter was awake now, Helms said, "I was hoping for this, Kendricks." The young man's tone was different now. Gone was the almost toadying politeness. Cold rage filled his voice.

"You promised, Walter," his mother said, coming over to him. "You just git now and git fast. You can be fifty miles in any direction by the time he gets a horse."

But whatever was troubling Walter Helms was troubling him deep.

He lunged across the room and put the .44 into Kendricks's face. "You could've waited till I came downstairs and got me when I was alone, Kendricks. You didn't have to humiliate me in front of that girl."

So it was just as Kendricks had suspected. Helms had been angry over being taken while the girl was still with him. Some men were like that. To Kendricks it made no sense.

"Get up," Helms said.

"Walter," his mother said. She stood next to him, pawing at his sleeve like a frightened animal. "You just git gone now. You hear me?"

"He's going out the door with me," Walter Helms said.

Kendricks was still trying to come out of the sleep the

284

coffee had put him into. His head ached and buzzed and he was still having trouble focusing his eyes.

"I said come on!" Walter Helms said. He put the cold barrel of the .44 hard against Kendricks's forehead.

Kendricks stood up.

Because of the coffee all this had a certain dreamy quality to it. His knees felt wobbly. He felt as if he were about to pitch forward.

"No!" Grace Helms said.

But Walter paid her no attention. He waved Kendricks to the door and outside.

As Kendricks reached the Helms woman he composed himself enough to say, "Still think he's a good boy, Mrs. Helms?"

"None of your back talk, bounty hunter," Walter Helms said, and gave Kendricks a rough push into the night.

The rain and sleet were coming down so hard Kendricks's flesh felt as if it were being struck by very sharp and very tiny pins.

He could see almost nothing as he staggered through fog and sleet, starting to slip on the soggy ground that was becoming icy.

Somewhere behind him Walter Helms's voice barked for Kendricks to stop. But why give the little son of a bitch the satisfaction, Kendricks thought. He's going to back-shoot me just the way he back-shot that farmer. So I may as well keep on walking.

Which is just what he did.

Knowing he was about to die, his thoughts formed something like a prayer. He sure could have been a better man than he'd been.

Knowing he was about to die, he conjured a picture of his young, pretty wife. He hoped that the afterlife wasn't just something ministers liked to talk about—he hoped he'd be seeing her soon.

And knowing he was about to die, he felt fear. It was shameful, this apprehension. It loosened his bowels and made his throat so tight he couldn't even swallow saliva. And it put tears in the corners of his eyes, too.

"I said for you to stop walking!" Walter Helms screamed somewhere back there in the darkness.

Soon enough, the shot would come.

Sleet cut his face like razors. Rain soaked his clothes and made them sodden. Ice gave his gait a comic aspect.

But he kept right on walking away from Helms.

There was but one shot, and the angry noise it made was mostly absorbed by the sleet and rain.

He expected to feel the bullet tear through his back and angle through his chest, ripping through his heart and lungs. A .44 could inflict a considerable amount of pain while it was killing you.

But the cry that slashed through the wind was not Kendricks's cry. It belonged instead to Walter Helms.

By the time Kendricks turned around to see what had happened, the kid had already fallen forward on his face. Several feet behind him, silhouetted in the yellow glow of the doorway, stood his mother. A rifle dangled from the fingers of her right hand.

Through the sleet and wind she called, "Will you help me get him inside, Mr. Kendricks?"

The vigil lasted till near dawn. Walter Helms was set in his bed and covered with two extra quilted blankets and given a seemingly unending supply of homeopathic medicines, including some of the herbs Grace had put in Kendricks's coffee.

But if any of it was doing any good the results weren't yet apparent, for Walter Helms looked as if he'd been laid out by a mortician. He grew more and more pale as the kerosene lamp flickered short on fuel.

Three times the widow got up and went to the door and stood in the blast of sleet and whining wind. And three times Kendricks could hear her sobbing quietly to herself before coming back to Walter's bed.

Kendricks saw him pass over. Or he thought he did, anyway. Walter lay there very still and then there was a twitch on his face and a long, deep sigh, and then he was still again but in a different and obviously final way. He had crossed over for sure.

Grace Helms had seen this, too.

For a long time she said nothing. She just held Walter's hand and stared at his face. Then she stood up and took pennies from the pocket of her muslin apron and put them on his eyes.

"It's time for you to go now, Mr. Kendricks," she said.

He started to talk but she stopped him.

"You know there's nothing to say, Mr. Kendricks, and so do I. So I'd appreciate if you got on your horse and rode."

There were so many things in her—anger, grief, melancholy—things he wanted to speak to somehow. But as she'd said, there was nothing to say.

By dawn, dry and golden in the east, he was three miles past the Helms place and riding fast to nowhere in particular.

Pards

1

Bromley always liked it when people asked him what he did for a living because then he could tell them he was a writer. He didn't mention his day job, which was being the only forty-nine-year-old bag "boy" at DeSoto's Supermarket; no, he just told them about his writing, and then showed them a copy of the one and only paperback novel he'd ever sold, a western called *Gun Fury*, which had been published by a company called Triton. He never mentioned that Triton had declared bankruptcy right after *Gun Fury* appeared, nor did he mention that Triton had been one of the worst publishers in history. Bromley's listeners didn't need to know that.

2

"Never seen anything like these before," the new mailman said on one of Bromley's days off (he usually worked weekends, which most of the teenagers refused to do, and so Sam DeSoto gave him two days off in the middle of the week). Bromley was sitting on the front porch of the aged Victorian apartment house where he lived, reading William Nolan's biography of Max Brand and sipping on a Diet Pepsi. In addition to losing his hair, Bromley had lately started to gain weight, one of the Chicano kids at the store even calling him "Fat Ass" one day, the little bastard, and so now it was Diet Pepsi instead of the regular stuff.

So Bromley was in the shade of the sunny porch, Mrs. Hanrahan's soap opera blaring through the lacy curtains, when the mailman said, "What exactly are they, anyway?"

"Fanzines."

"Fanzines?"

"Yeah, magazines that western fans publish themselves. There're fanzines for people who like the old pulp magazines and fanzines for people who liked the old Saturday serials and fanzines for people who like the old western stars."

The mailman, who was just old enough to remember, said, "Like Gene and Roy?"

"Exactly. Like Gene and Roy."

"So do you put one out yourself, I mean being a writer and all?"

"No; but I write for a lot of them."

"Yeah? Which ones?"

"The ones about the old cowboy stars." Bromley wanted to tell him about his dream he had sometimes; standing in this movie lobby in 1948 with all these great lobby cards showing Wild Bill Elliott and The Durango Kid (God, there was no getting around it; guys who wore masks were just great) and Gabby Hayes and Jane Frazee and Tim Holt and The 3 Mesquiteers, and how down on one end there was this table overflowing with pulp magazines, *The Pecos Kid Western* and *Frontier Stories* and *Thrilling Western Stories*; and then another table with an old 1946 table model radio with the sounds of "Bobby Benson and The B Bar B Riders" coming out of it; and yet another table with nothing but Big Little Books; and there was a church-like holiness in the air and Bromley was caught up in it, tears nearly streaming down his face; WAS NOT THIS HEAVEN? And he had this crazy urge to eat Cheerios, just the way Tonto did; or Ralston Purina, just like Tom Mix; or maybe even Pep, the way Superman was always telling him to.

"Those'd be the ones I'd be interested in, the cowboys, I mean," the mailman said. Then he shrugged and handed Bromley his mail. "You're really an interesting guy, Ken, you know that?"

3

He'd been married once, Bromley had, in the early sixties, already working at DeSoto's, to a pretty but dumb woman whom his mother did not like at all ("I don't see why you have to move out when you've got so much room here, especially since your father died, and anyway twenty-two is too young to get married, she's just looking for an easy ride if you ask me"), a waitress who seemed to know what all her customers made per hour at this-or-that factory, at this-or-that delivery service. "Four bucks an hour, Ken, you really should look into that." But somehow he never got around to it. Just down the block from DeSoto's was the city's largest used bookstore and he spent most of his lunch hours in there. The air was holy, the dusty air of Ace Doubles and Gold Medal books, of *All-Story Weekly* and *Star Western* and *Adventure*, the cocoon of paperbacks and magazines in which he'd spent his boyhood, never much caring that he didn't have many friends, that he was virtually invisible at school, or that the violent arguments of his parents caused him to shake uncontrollably for long periods of time behind his too-thin bedroom door. No, there were always the Saturday afternoon movies, or his books and magazines to escape into.

One night—this was a year or so into their marriage, the night one of those perfect late spring evenings shot through with fireflies and the scent of apple blossoms—right there in the same wedding bed Bromley would sleep in the rest of his life, right there in Mrs. Hanrahan's apartment house where he would live the rest of his life, his wife said, "I need to be honest with you."

"Huh?"

"I—did something."

"Did something?"

He was smoking a Lucky with the sheet just half on him and listening to the night birds at the window screen, and she was lying next to him in just her underwear.

"You know that Jimmy I told you about?"

"Uh, I guess so." She was always telling him about somebody.

"You know. He makes six-thirty-two an hour out at Rockwell."

291

"I guess."

"He has the red Olds convertible, remember, with the white leather interior?"

"Oh. Yeah. Jimmy."

"Well the other day he wanted to know if I wanted a ride home after the dinner rush."

"Oh."

God, now he knew what was coming.

"I knew I shouldn't have said yes but he kept pushing the subject. You know how guys get."

"Yeah, I guess I do."

"Well, anyway, I let him give me a ride home."

"Was this Thursday?"

"Yeah. Thursday."

"When you were late?"

She hesitated. "Yeah, when I was late."

"I see."

Neither of them said anything for a long time. He finished his cigarette and then just lay with his hands on his chest, in his boxer shorts which she was always asking him not to wear ("You're a young man, Ken, you shouldn't wear things like that").

Then she said, "But he didn't take me straight home."

"I see."

"I mean I told him to. But he didn't. He wouldn't listen to anything I said. He just kept driving out along the river road. He just kept saying isn't it pretty at dusk like this, with the sunlight real coppery on the river like this? I had to admit that it was."

"Did you let him do anything to you?"

"I let him French kiss me."

"Oh."

"And I let him feel my breasts."

"I see."

"But I didn't let him put his hand inside my bra."

He said nothing. He wondered if his heart would stop beating. Just *boom* like that and he would no longer be alive.

"And I didn't let him touch me down there."

He said nothing.

"He tried, Ken, but I wouldn't let him."

The tears came abruptly and without warning. There in the darkness he shook so hard—just the way he used to shake when his parents screamed at each other—that the whole bed shook. His wedding bed.

She leaned over and kissed him then, and it was a tender and pure kiss, and he recognized it as such, and she said, "You're more like my brother or something, Ken. I didn't want it to turn out this way but it did anyway. I mean you never want to go dancing or take me out to dinner or make love or—" She smiled there in the darkness. "You're more interested in your book collection than you are me, Ken. And you know that's the truth."

Later on after a long time of not talking, just lying there, her sometimes taking drags from his cigarette, sometimes not, she leaned over and kissed him and put her hand down there and got him hard, and then they made love with a purity and tenderness that broke his heart because he knew this would be the last time, the very last time, and when it was over and they were just lying there again, she started crying too, soft girl tears there in the darkness, her a girl as he was still a boy, and then just before she fell asleep she said—her only bitter comment during the whole night—"Well, your mother will be relieved anyway. Just don't move back in with her. I care about you too much to see that happen. OK?"

The next day she was packed and gone. Three months later he got proceeding papers from a lawyer in Milwaukee and six months after that he was divorced. Throughout the first year, she wrote him postcards fairly frequently. She mentioned different restaurants she worked at and she mentioned how hot Milwaukee was in the summer and then how cold it was in the winter and then one card she said she was getting married to a guy with a real good job (she didn't mention his name nor did she mention how much he made an hour) and then abruptly the cards stopped except, inexplicably, two Christmases later when she sent him a Christmas card with the snapshot of an infant girl inside. Her first child.

He stayed on at DeSoto's of course, spending his lunch hours at the used bookstore, and he did not move back in with his mother.

4

The odd thing was, Bromley learned about Rex Stone's moving not through one of the fanzines but when somebody at DeSoto's (Laughlin, the smirky guy in the meat department) mentioned that Stone was moving to Center City, a mere eighty miles from the city here. "That fuckin' cowboy guy, you know, the one when we were kids, the one who could make his horse dance up on his hind legs?"

Bromley could scarcely believe it. Sure, he'd known that Rex Stone (a.k.a. Walter Sipkins) had been born in this area but who could have guessed that after fifteen years of being a star at Republic (he'd starred in the studio's very last B-western, despite the fact that most film books mistakenly attributed this distinction to Allan "Rocky" Lane)—after fifteen years in movies and ten more in TV (usually in supporting roles but meaty ones), who could have guessed Stone would move back to where he'd come from?

About a month after Laughlin gave Bromley the word, the local paper ran a big photo of Stone in full singing-cowboy getup holding up a sweet little crippled girl in his arms. The caption read: "Cowboy Star spends sunset years helping others" and the story went on to detail how active Stone had become with Center City civic events. Retired now, he "planned to devote his life to helping all the little 'buckaroos and buckarettes' who need him."

Bromley couldn't believe it. Rex Stone. Only eighty miles from here. Rex Stone. The man he'd always measured himself against. Sure, Bromley liked Hoppy and Roy and Gene and Monte and Lash and Sunset but none of them had compared to Rex because, despite the fact that Rex sang a lot of sappy songs and could make his horse Stormy dance along at the same time, Rex was a *man*. The jaw and the eyes and the big hands and the deep voice told you that. He was a man not in the way of a Saturday afternoon hero but rather in the rough and somewhat mysterious way of, say, Robert Mitchum. That was why, back in the forties and fifties, Rex Stone had not only had a huge kids' following, he'd also managed to snag a major following of young women. (TV people had later tried to cast him as a he-man in a short-lived adventure series called *Bush Pilot* but the series had been on ZIV, and when ZIV went down—the other networks inevitably pushing it out—so did Rex's series).

And now, admittedly paunchier, gray-haired, and jowly, Rex Stone lived only eighty miles away.

5

"Is Mr. Stone there, please?"

"Who the hell is this?" The voice was female and old and accusatory.

Bromley did the only thing he could. He gulped. "Uh, my name is Bromley."

"Who?"

"Bromley."

"Spell it."

"Huh?"

"You deaf? I said spell it."

"B-r-o-m-l-e-y."

"Bromley."

"Yes."

"So just what the hell do you want?"

"I, uh, I'd like to speak to Mr. Stone."

"He's busy."

And with that, she hung up.

6

Six days later:

Dear Rex Stone,
    I know that you're probably too busy to answer all

your fan mail so let me assure you that while I'm a long time admirer of yours, this letter has to do with a professional matter.

As a published western author (GUN FURY, Triton Books, 1967 and hundreds of articles in western and popular culture magazines), I'd like to interview you for a forthcoming book about western stars of the forties and fifties called: INTO THE SUNSET (Leisure Books).

You may have noticed by my return address that I don't live very far from you. I'd very much like to come up for a day soon, bring my tape recorder, and spend several hours with you discussing your career.

I phoned several days ago but a woman answered and we seemed to have been disconnected or something.

I'd very much like to meet you and help bring your millions of fans up to date on your life. I know that you never attend any of the "Golden Oldie" shows that Gene and Roy and Lash and the others sometimes go to so this would be a particular treat for everybody who has followed your career.

Please let me know your answer at your earliest convenience.

> Sincerely yours,
> Ken Bromley

7

"Who?"
    "Rex Stone."

"Who?"

"Rex Stone. Don't you remember, I used to see all his movies?"

"Movies. Hah. Complete waste of time as far as I'm concerned."

And in fact, that had been his mother's opinion all the time Bromley had been growing up, and it was her opinion even now that she was eighty-seven years old and living in a nursing home thanks to the insurance her husband had left her.

But even in a nursing home, she had control of him. She was sort of like the Scarab in one of the old Republic chapter plays. All-knowing. All-seeing. Plus, she had him trained. He always checked with her on anything major, and certainly buying a Trailways ticket was major, even if it was only for eighty miles, even if it was only for a day. She was convinced that she was about to die of a heart attack at any moment and so she wanted him on call twenty-four hours a day. If he wasn't at DeSoto's then he'd better by God be in his apartment. And she certainly didn't like the idea of a trip to Center City.

"Why would you waste your money on him? He doesn't even make movies anymore."

"I want to write an article about him."

"Phoo. Article. They don't even pay you for those things. They only paid you $500 for a whole book. Talk about getting cheated. Why, I read that there Stephen King makes twenty million a year. It was right in *People*."

"It'll only be for a day, Mom. That's all."

"A day? You know how long it takes you to die of a heart attack?" She very impressively snapped her fingers. The sound was of twigs snapping.

They were on the veranda, late afternoon. She had a cigarette going and she was sipping a glass of beer. She'd raised enough hell with the nursing home people that they gave into her once every day. One cigarette. One glass of beer.

"I really want to go, Mom. It's real important to me."

How he hated his voice. His groveling. His begging, really. He was fifty, and nearly bald, and two or three of the clubs he belonged to gave him "senior rates."

And here he was pleading with this shriveled up little woman wound inside a black shawl despite the eighty-eight degrees.

"He have a phone?"

"Yes."

"You make sure you leave me that number."

"All right, Mom."

"It's all a waste of time if you ask me."

He leaned over and kissed her cheek. "I love you, Mom."

She snorted smoke through her nostrils and said, "You're more like your father every day."

He knew she didn't mean that as a compliment.

8

"Who?"

"Rex Stone."

"Guess I must be a little young to remember him or something."

"He was really popular."

"Yeah, I imagine."

Bromley caught the kid's sarcasm, of course. Twerp was maybe sixteen or seventeen and had an arm's length of blue tattoos (Bromley's mother had always insisted that a tattoo was a sure sign of the lower classes) and one tiny silver earring (which marked him as a lot less than manly, even if a lot of young men did wear them).

Bromley would've sat with somebody else but this was the 8:30 A.M. Trailways that went to the state capital and so it was packed with lots of old ladies in big summery hats and so there was no place else to sit. This was the last empty seat and the kid had come with it.

"He set an attendance record at the Denver rodeo," Bromley said.

"Oh."

"And in 1949 he came in right behind Roy Rogers as the biggest box office draw."

"1949, huh?" The kid shrugged and looked out the bus window.

Bromley put his head back and closed his eyes. The bus engine made the whole bus tremble. The smell of diesel fuel reminded Bromley of boyhood summers, walking down to the Templar Theater to see all the new Saturday matinee movies. It was easy to recall the smell of theater popcorn, too, and the way the sunlight blinded you when you emerged onto the sidewalk six hours later, and the way summer dusk fell, the birds somehow sad in the summer trees, and the girls you saw sometimes, always a little older than you and always blonde in a showgirl sort of way, and how they made you ache and how vivid and perfect they remained in your daydreams the whole hot school vacation. Not even after Dr. Fitzsimmons had convinced his mother it was just muscle cramps and not polio at all would she let

Bromley go to the movies again. Not until the following summer.

After twenty miles, Bromley opened his eyes again.

Next to him, the kid had this earplug in and his whole body was kind of sit-dancing to the music snaking from the transistor in his lap to the plug in his ear.

The way the kid moved around there, moving and grooving he thought it was called, struck Bromley as downright obscene.

Bromley closed his eyes again, and thought of the summer he got those funny aches in his legs and his mother went crazy and said he had polio for sure and lit candles to the Blessed Mother all summer and wouldn't let Bromley go to any movie theaters. She said that this was the number one place for catching polio germs and then she showed him a newspaper photo of a poor little kid inside an iron lung, a photo she always seemed to have handy.

The kid got off way before Center City, and Bromley had the rest of the trip to enjoy by himself. He'd been holding in gas for a long time and it was a pure pleasure to let it go.

9

"Here you go."

"You sure this is the right address?"

"Center Grove, right here."

"But it's a trailer park."

"That's right. Center Grove Trailer Park. See that sign over there?"

Bromley looked and there it was sure enough: green letters on white background, CENTER GROVE TRAILER PARK.

"Huh," Bromley said, "I'll be damned. A trailer park."

Somehow he couldn't imagine Rex Stone living in a trailer. He had an odd thought: Did his horse Stormy live with him in there, too?

He paid the cabbie six bucks, six sweaty ones that had been deep in his summer pocket, and got out, lugging his big old Webcor recorder along with him.

The place was dusty, hot and Midwestern, a high sloping hill covered with long, modern trailers of the sort that put on the airs of a real house. Lying east and west, bracketing all the metal homes gleaming in the sunlight, were pastures, black and white dairy cows grazing, and distantly a farmer on a green John Deere raising plumes of dust as he did some tilling. A red Piper Cub circled lazily over head, like a papier mâché bird.

Each trailer had an address. Just like a house. He supposed he was being a snob, he after all lived in an apartment house, he after all lived in a three room apartment, but he couldn't help it. People who lived in trailers . . .

And then he remembered: his mother of course. "People who live in trailers are hillbillies." She'd never offered any proof of this. That was not her way. She'd simply stated it so many times growing up that he'd come to believe it. At least a part of him had.

Hillbillies.

He found the trailer he was looking for. It was an Airstream, one of those silver jobs, and it looked to be a block long and it looked to be almost sinfully tidy as to shell and surrounding lawn. Indeed, bright chipper summer flowers had been planted all along the perimeter of the place. He wondered what his mother would make of that.

He went up and knocked and then there *he* was.

It was a strange feeling.

Here you'd spent all your life with an image of somebody fixed in your mind and then when you meet him—

Well, for him, Rex Stone would always be this tall, handsome, slender cuss in the literal white hat astride Stormy. His western clothes would have a discreet number of spangles, his hips would ride a pair of six guns always ready to impose justice on the lawless, and he'd just generally be—

—well, heroic. There was no other word for it. Heroic.

What he would not be was a) this old guy with a beer belly, wearing a t-shirt that said I'M AN OLD FART AND PROUD OF IT, b) this bald guy wearing a pair of lime green golf pants or c) this fat guy with a beer gut that looked a lot worse than Bromley's own.

"You Bromley?"

"Uh, yes."

"I'm Stone."

At least he had a strong grip. In fact, Bromley even winced a little.

Stone hadn't quite shut the door behind him. He said, "Be right back."

Not even inviting Bromley in or anything.

Bromley stood there listening to the noises of the trailer park: an obstinate lawn mower somewhere distant; a baby crying; a couple arguing and slamming more doors than you'd think a trailer could possibly hold; and a radio playing an aching country western ballad about heartbreak.

Bromley came back out. He carried two folded-up lawn chairs and a six pack of Hamms beer.

Ed Gorman

He didn't say anything, just nodded for Bromley to follow.

On the opposite end of the trailer was an overhang. Some tiles had been laid down to make a small patio. Here Stone flicked the chairs into proper position—his motions were young and powerful, belying his old fart appearance—and then he sat himself down and nodded for Bromley to do likewise.

"Beer?"

"Thanks," Bromley said. Actually, he didn't care much for alcohol but he wanted to be polite.

"That's an old one, isn't it?"

Bromley looked at his tape recorder. Indeed it was. A Webcor, a big heavy box with heads for reel-to-reel tape up top. Twenty-five years ago a friend of his had desperately needed money for some now forgotten reason. Bromley had paid him fifty dollars.

"It still works well, though. Just because it's old doesn't mean it can't do the job."

Stone laughed a slick Hollywood laugh and winked with great dramatic luridness. "That's what I tell the ladies about myself." Then he leaned forward and with a big powerful hand slapped the arm of Bromley's lawn chair. "Just because I'm old doesn't mean I can't do the job."

Bromley laughed, knowing he was expected to.

Stone seemed to relax some then, sitting back and sipping his beer. He studied Bromley for awhile and said, "Sorry, my friend."

"Sorry?"

"Sure. For being this old fart. You know, the way my t-shirt says."

"Well, heck, I—"

"Sure you did."

"I did?"

"Of course. You grew up seeing my movies and you've got this picture of me fixed in your head—this strong, handsome young man—and then you see me—" He shrugged. "I'm an old fart."

"No, you're not. You're—"

Stone waved a hand. "It doesn't bother me, son. It really doesn't. I mean, everybody gets old. Gene did and Roy did and Lash did—and now it's my turn."

Bromley wasn't sure why but he sort of liked it how Stone had called him "son." Made Bromley feel young somehow; as if most of his life (that great golden potential of youth) were still ahead of him and not mostly behind him.

"So you want to wind that puppy up?"

"That puppy?"

"The recorder. That big ole B-52 Webcor."

"Oh. Right. The recorder."

"And I'll tell you how it all started. And how it all ended."

"Yeah. Sure. Great."

So he wound that puppy up and Rex Stone started talking.

10

See, he'd never had any intention of being a movie star. He'd just been visiting in Los Angeles that day in 1934 when he was drinking a malt and having a ham sandwich in this drugstore when he happened to notice that, out on the sunny street, a group of people were standing there watching some kind of accident. Being naturally curious, and being from the Midwest and wanting to bring back all the great stories he could, he went outside to see what was going on, only it wasn't an accident, it was a movie, a bank robbery get-away was being staged, complete with a heart-stoppingly beautiful actress holding a tommy-gun and dangling an extra-long cigarette from her creamy red lips, and a fat bald little director who not only wore honest-to-God jodphurs but also carried a bullhorn and wore, if you could believe it, a monocle over his right eye.

That's how it started, how Presnell, that was the director, saw him standing there on the edge of the crowd, and between shots came over and started talking to him, and then had this very fetching young girl come over and take down his name and the address where he was staying, and four days—literally four days later—he was playing a six-line role in a western and singing as part of the cowboy singers who backed up the tone-deaf star.

Not that the rest of it came easy. It wasn't overnight or anything. By Stone's estimate he appeared in forty-seven movies (at least twenty of which came from Monogram, for God's sake) before it finally happened. One day Herbert Yates of Republic looked at sagging box office receipts for his westerns and then decided to give the singing cowboy movies one last try. Yates had been under the impression that singing cowboys had bit the dust about the time television started imposing itself on the American scene. Well, as usual, Herb's gut proved savvy: The Rex Stone pictures, eighteen of them in all, were the biggest-grossing Republic pictures of the era, and came in right behind Roy and Gene in overall grosses. Rex Stone was a star, at least in those small American burgs where the Fourth of July was still a big deal and where men, at least on occasion, still held doors for ladies.

As for Rex personally, he was not only a favorite with

the kids, he was also a favorite with the starlets, as Louella Parsons, then the country's premiere gossip columnist, noted with great delight. Rex was a big handsome lug and don't think he didn't take advantage of it. In one year he was hit with three fists (from jealous husbands), one champagne bottle (from a jealous fiancée) and two paternity suits. It was about then that he started marrying, a practice he kept up until the Rex Stone pictures started losing money and old Herb finally quit turning out westerns. Some movie historians had him marrying seven times; Rex himself claimed a mere five brides, though he did admit that there was one quickie Mexican marriage that might/might not have been legal. Anyway, the marriages didn't exactly help his popularity. Roy and Gene scrupulously kept their private parts in their pants; Rex seemed to be flaunting his and in those areas of the country where the Fourth of July still meant something, and where men still opened doors for ladies, his rambunctious behavior with starlets hurt him, and hurt him badly.

Then came the fifties and all those failed TV pilots and TV series. He started looking heavier and older, and then he started flying to Italy where westerns were being turned out faster than pizzas, and where Rex Stone, even with something of a gut and something of a balding head, was still a big deal. Meanwhile, he kept on marrying, two brides between 1955 and 1959.

By now, the marriages were no longer scandals, they were jokes, the stuff of talk show repartee, and Rex Stone was pretty much finished.

Nobody heard from or about him. Various organizations such as The Cowboy Hall of Fame, which tried to keep members up on news of all the old film stars, did their best to track him down but even when he got the letters, he just tossed them away. He didn't want to go on the rodeo circuit and be this sad old chunky guy on this big golden Palomino waving his white Stetson to a crowd of kids who had no idea who he was. He did not want to cut ribbons at supermarket grand openings, he did not want to be surrounded by dozens of sad grotesque aging fans (no offense, Mr. Bromley) at "nostalgia" conventions, he did not want to be featured in every other fanzine about old western stars, and brag in print about how good movies had been back then and what shit (relatively speaking) they were today.

So for the past twenty obscure years, what he'd been doing was just moving around the country in his Airstream and living in all the places he'd always wanted to live (North Carolina for the beauty and the fishing; Arizona for the climate; New Hampshire for the beautiful autumns and New England sense of tradition and heritage).

11

"Do you ever miss any of them?"

"Any of who?"

"You know, your wives."

"Oh."

"I mean, now that you're older and settled, isn't there one of them it would be nice to have along?"

At this point, Stone started glancing over his shoulder at the rear window.

Bromley hadn't noticed before, but despite the machine noise the air conditioning unit made, the back window was open about halfway. Bromley wondered why.

"Not really, I guess."

"You ever hear from any of them?"

"Uh, not really."

Then, unable to stop himself from asking this gushy question, Bromley said, "Wanda Mallory, was she as beautiful in person as she was on the screen?"

"She was a bitch and a gold-digger."

The thing was, Rex Stone hadn't said this. He'd just been sitting there holding his beer, with his mouth closed, and then out came the words.

Except the voice wasn't anything like Rex's at all. It was a crone's voice, a harsh cranky old lady's voice, and it had come wafting from the open back window.

Seeing how baffled Bromley looked, Stone said, "Why don't you try and get some sleep, Mother?" He was addressing the partially open rear window.

"You tell him what a little conniver she was. What a little conniver they all were."

"Did you take your medication this morning, Mother?"

"Don't try to change the subject. You tell him the truth about those little harlots."

"Yes, Mother."

"And I mean it."

"Yes, Mother."

"All that money you wasted on them."

"Yes, Mother."

"And I always had the smallest room. The very smallest room."

"Yes, Mother."

And then there was silence and Rex Stone just sat there sort of slumped over in his chair, whipped, beaten, this old man who looked as if some young guy had just delivered a killer blow to his solar plexus. He looked sad and embarrassed, and he even looked a little dazed and confused.

Bromley had no idea what to say.

The voice had reminded him a little of the mother's voice in *Psycho* whenever she got mad at Norman. Or actually (God forgive him) of his own mother's voice.

After awhile, still not looking Bromley straight in the eyes, Rex Stone said, "Why don't we hike on up to the rec room? It's a real nice place." One thing: he was whispering his words.

Then he looked nervously up at the open rear window and then he started making these big pantomime gestures that said Follow Me.

Obviously Rex Stone, cowboy star, singer of lush romantic jukebox ballads, wooer and winner of untold gorgeous starlets, was scared shitless of his mom.

12

Ping.

"Every one of them?"

Pong.

"Every single god damn one of them."

Ping.

"But how?"

Pong.

"Because she got me by the throat the day I was born, and she hasn't let go since."

Ping.

They had been in the recreation hall for twenty minutes. It was a big and presently empty room shady and cool on this hot day, with two billiard tables, a jukebox, a candy machine, a Coke machine, a sign that said I'M A SQUARE DANCER AND PROUD OF IT, and the Ping-Pong table on which Bromley and Rex Stone had been playing for the past ten minutes. Stone was good at it; Bromley not.

"Hell, they even started whispering I was queer," Stone said. "Just married all these women to make things look good, you know, the way some of the actors did but hell, I like girls, not boys."

"So you loved every one?"

"Every single one."

"And your mother broke up each marriage?"

"Every single god damn one."

"You couldn't get rid of her?"

"Hell, I tried, don't think I didn't, but about the time my bride and I would move into our new place, my mother would come up with some new ailment and force me to let her move in."

"Is that what she meant by always having the smallest room?"

"Yup."

"So she's pretty much lived with you all your life?"

"All my life, ever since my father died anyway, when I was eighteen."

"And your wives—"

"They'd just get fed up with how she controlled me and then they'd—"

"—leave. They'd leave you. Right?" Bromley said, thinking of his own wife, and how much she'd resented his mother.

"That's exactly what they'd do. Leave."

Ping.

Pong.

The game went on.

And then Rex Stone said it, "You aren't going to put all this stuff about my mom in your article are you, son?"

There was a definite pleading tone in his voice and eyes now.

"No, I'd never do that, Mr. Stone."

"When the hell you going to start calling me Rex?" said the old man at the other end of the pool table.

Bromley smiled self-consciously. "All right—Rex."

"You think you got enough?"

"Yes; yes, I do." Bromley said, and he did, more than enough for a good article about Rex Stone. The fanzine readers would love it.

"You play pool?" Stone said.

"Better than I play Ping-Pong."

"Good. Then let's try a game."

They were each chalking their cues when the black phone on the west wall rang.

Rex glanced at it with genuine alarm.

He shook his head and walked over to it.

"Yes?"

He looked back at Bromley and shook his head. "All right, Mother, so you found me. Now what?"

Now he turned to the wall and muffled his voice, as if he didn't want Bromley to hear a word of it.

"You know how embarrassing this is?"

Pause.

"I'll go to the drug store tonight. Not right now, Mother."

Pause.

"I get pretty sick of you telling me that I don't take good care of you, Mother."

Pause.

"All right." And then a huge, sad sigh.

Rex Stone hung up and turned back to the phone.

"Maybe I'd better go check on her," he said. "Maybe she really is sick this time. You mind?"

"No, Rex, that's fine."

So they left the recreation hall and went back to the trailer. Nobody, not the little kids, not the mothers pushing strollers, seemed to pay any attention to Rex at all.

Bromley wanted to say: hey, this is *Rex Stone* for shit's sake! Rex Stone!

On the way back, Rex told him a couple of stories about Lash Larue and Tim Holt but Bromley could tell that Rex was still embarrassed about his mother's phone call.

Bromley said, "I'll have to be leaving in twenty minutes. There's only one more bus back to town today."

"I've really enjoyed this, son."

"So have I." And then Bromley decided to ask him. Rex would probably just say no, that it was a dumb idea, but what could it hurt to ask.

"Rex?"

"Yup."

"How would you feel about getting dressed up in your cowboy duds and having me take your photo?"

"Ah, hell, son, I don't know about that."

"It'd really go great with this article. Your fans would really appreciate it."

"You think they would?"

"I know they would. They'd love it."

So Rex Stone chewed it over for awhile and then shrugged and said, "How about just standing next to the Airstream?"

"That'd be great."

When they got back to the trailer, Rex started whispering again. "Why don't you wait out here, son. I'll go inside and change my clothes and then come back out. All right?"

"Fine."

So while Rex went inside, Bromley went over and got his Polaroid all ready.

Rex didn't come out in five minutes. Rex didn't come out in ten minutes. Rex didn't come out in fifteen minutes.

Bromley could hear it all, oh not all the words exactly, but certainly he heard the tone of voice. She was chewing on him in a steady stream of rancor that managed to stun and depress even Bromley, who wasn't even directly involved.

Every few minutes, he'd hear Rex say, "All right, Mother," in this really sad, resigned way.

And then it ended all of a sudden and the trailer door opened and there stood Rex Stone in his cowboy costume, the big white hat, the fancy cowboy clothes with spangles and fringes, the big six-guns slung low on his hips, and his trustworthy guitar dangling from his right hand.

Bromley hadn't realized till this moment just how old Rex Stone was.

How the whole face sagged into jowls.

How the whole gut swelled over the gunbelt.

How the hands were liver-spotted and trembling.

"I sure feel silly in this get-up, son," Rex said.

"But you look great."

"You sure about that?"

"I'm sure about that, Rex." Bromley waved his hand a little and said, "How about a step or two to the right, just to the side of the door."

And it was at that exact moment that the trailer door opened and out stepped a little kewpie-doll of a woman, no more than four-eight, four-nine, no more than eighty pounds, no more than two or three hundred years old, buried inside of some kind of gaudy pink K-Mart wrapper, her feet swathed in matching pink fluffy slippers that went *thwap, thwap, thwap* as she came down the stairs and took her place next to her son.

"I forgot to tell you," Rex Stone said, "Mom asked if she could be in the picture, too."

13

He tried for the next six weeks to write the article. Every few days, Rex would call and say, "Just wanted to see how it was going, son," and would then say, "You, uh, haven't mentioned my mom or anything in it, have you?" and Bromley would say, uh, no, Rex, I, uh, haven't.

But for some reason he couldn't write the piece.

Every time he started it, it was just too bleak. Here was a guy who'd been in a very real prison all his life. (Not unlike Bromley.) Here was a guy who kept trying to break away and break away but couldn't. (Not unlike Bromley.) Here was a guy who had obviously wanted to spend his life with beautiful women but whose mother just didn't like the idea. (Not unlike Bromley.)

So how could you write a piece about a guy who'd been a hero to Bromley's whole generation . . . and tell the glum truth?

Because it was a pretty pathetic story.

14

Rex called two days after Bromley mailed him the article.

"Son," he said.

"Yes?"

"I—"

And then he made a familiar sound. "You know what that is, son?"

"You're blowing your nose?"

"Right. And you know why?"

"Why?"

"Because your article made me cry. And not cry for sad, son. Cry for happy."

"I'm glad you like it, Rex."

"I don't like it, son. I love it."

"I wasn't sure how you'd feel about it. I mean, I took certain liberties and I—"

"Son, you done good. You done real, real good."

15

The day the fanzine arrived, Bromley sat down in his recliner and started reading it, the way he did with all his own articles.

He turned back the cover and flipped through the pages till he saw the picture of Rex.

He'd stuck to the older photos. He certainly hadn't used the one with Rex's mother in it.

And then he read the caption under the photo of a young Rex as the cowboy star: "Here's a heartwarming article about cowboy film giant Rex Stone and how he's spent his life living on a horse ranch in Montana, sharing his bountiful life with his beautiful wife and three children."

Just the kind of life Bromley had always wished for himself.

A wife and three children.

Just the kind of life his generation would have expected Rex Stone to live.

16

"You haven't called me for a long time."

"I called you the night before last, Mother," Bromley said.

"I could be dead for all you care."

"Yes, Mother."

"Lying here on the floor while you're out running around."

"Yes, Mother."

And then he thought of Rex Stone's ranch in Montana, Rex and his beautiful starlet wife and their three perfectly behaved children.

He'd go visit Rex there someday soon.

Very soon.

That's just what he'd do.

"Are you listening to me?"

"Yes," Bromley said. "Yes, Mother, I always listen to you."

Someday very soon now.

The Long Ride Back

Soon as I snuck into his campsite, and kicked him in the leg so he'd jerk up from his blanket, I brought down the stock of my single-shot. 40–90 Sharps and did some real damage to his teeth.

He was swearing and crying all the time I got him in handcuffs, spraying blood that looked black in the dawn flames of the fading campfire.

In the dewy grass, in the hard frosty cold of the September morning, the white birches just now starting to gleam in the early sunlight, I got the Kid's roan saddled and then went back for the Kid himself.

"I ain't scared of you," he said, talking around his busted teeth and bloody tongue.

"Well, that makes us even. I ain't scared of you, either."

I dragged him over to the horse, got him in the saddle, then took a two-foot piece of rawhide and lashed him to the horn.

"You sonofabitch," the Kid said. He said that a lot.

Then I was up in my own saddle and we headed back to town. It was a long day's ride.

"They'll be braggin' about ya, I suppose, over to the saloon, I mean," the Kid said a little later, as we moved steadily along the stage road.

"I don't pay attention to stuff like that."

"How the big brave sheriff went out and captured the Kid all by his lonesome."

"Why don't you be quiet for a while?"

"Yessir. All by his lonesome. And you know how many murder counts are on the Kid's head? Why, three of them in Nebraska alone. And two more right here in Kansas. Why, even the James Boys walked wide of the Kid—and then here's this hick sheriff capturin' him all by hisself. What a hero."

This time I didn't ask him.

I leaned over and backhanded him so hard, he started to slide off his saddle. Through his pain and blood, he started calling me names again.

It went like that most of the morning, him starting up with his ugly tongue and me quieting him down with the back of my hand.

At least the countryside was pretty, autumn blazing in the hills surrounding this dusty valley, chickenhawks arcing against the soft blue sky.

Then he said, "You goin' to be there when they hang me?"

I shrugged.

"When they put the rope around my neck and the hood over my face and give the nod to the hangman?"

I said nothing. I rode. Nice and steady. Nice and easy.

319

"Oh, you're a fine one, you are," the Kid said. "A fine one."

Around noon, the sun very high and hot, I stopped at a fast blue creek and gave the horses water and me and the Kid some jerky.

I ate mine. The Kid spit his out. Right in my face.

Then we were up and riding again.

"You sonofabitch," the Kid said. There was so much anger in him, it never seemed to wane at all.

I sighed. "There's nothing to say, Kid."

"There's plenty to say and you know it."

"In three years you killed six people, two of them women, and all so you could get yourself some easy money from banks. There's not one goddamned thing to add to that. Not one goddamned thing." Now it was me who was angry.

"You sonofabitch," he said, "I'm your son. Don't that mean anything?"

"Yeah, Karl, it means plenty. It means I had to watch your mother die a slow death of shame and heartbreak. And it means you put me in a position I didn't ask for—you shot a man in cold blood in my jurisdiction. So I had to come after you. I didn't want to—I prayed you'd be smart enough to get out of my territory before I found you. But you weren't smart at all. You figured I'd let you go." I looked down at the silver star on my leather vest. "But I couldn't, Karl. I just couldn't."

He started crying, then, and I wanted to say something or do something to comfort him but I didn't know what.

I just listened to the owls in the woods, and rode on, with my own son next to me in handcuffs, toward the town that a hanging judge named Coughlin visited seven times a year, a town where the citizens turned hangings into civic events, complete with parades and picnics after.

The Long Ride Back

"You really gonna let 'em hang me, Pa?" Karl said after a while, still crying, and sounding young and scared now. "You really gonna let 'em hang me?"

I didn't say anything. There was just the soughing wind.

"Ma woulda let me go if she was here. You know she would."

I just rode on, closer, ever closer to town. Three more hours. To make my mind up. To be sure.

"Pa, you can't let 'em hang me, you can't." He was crying again.

And then I realized that I was crying, too, as we rode on closer and closer and closer to where men with singing saws and blunt hard hammers and silver shining nails waited for another life to place on the altar of the scaffold.

"You gotta let me go, Pa, you just gotta," Karl said.

Three more hours and one way or another, it would all be over. Maybe I would change my mind, maybe not.

We rode on toward the dusty autumn hills.

A Small and Private War

His nightmares once again woke her. She held his sweaty, trembling body until he eased once more into the embrace of sleep.

At breakfast, the maid Irene fed the two youngsters first. They were scheduled to be at Harvey Claybourne's all day. It was master Harvey's seventh birthday and festivities were to be daylong.

Aggie Monroe came down later than usual. She was a pretty, slender woman but this morning she looked pale and tired. She'd hoped to be fresh today. Needed to be. This was the day she was to follow her secretive husband and find out what he was up to. And Irene played a role in it.

Aggie was finishing her eggs when Sam came into the dining room. She noted that he'd stopped by the study and brought in a large bourbon glass three-quarters filled. She'd never seen him drink in the morning before. He came to her, kissed her on the forehead, seated himself across from her.

Before saying a word, he picked up the *Tribune* and scanned the front page. The Confederates had recently been routed near the Rio Grande. He sipped his whiskey. The second story he read dealt with President Lincoln sending an emissary here to speak the night before the election, the day after tomorrow. Lincoln wanted to make sure that only pro-war and pro-Northern candidates were elected. There was a small but ferocious band of Copperheads in Chicago, Northerners who sympathized with the South. They'd already shot a number of policemen, set a library on fire, and tried to smuggle arms into a prisoner-of-war camp not far from the city's outskirts. Jefferson Davis had already declared that the South could not win the war without the consistent help of the Copperheads.

Aggie said, touching his hand, "You had the nightmare again last night."

He nodded. "That's why I hope you'll excuse the bourbon. I was pretty scared when I woke up."

"Bourbon won't help you, dear." She hesitated. "You need to tell me what's going on. You need a confidante."

He smiled. "You and your theory that something's going on. *Nothing's* going on. I'm just having nightmares about my brother dying, Aggie, that's all."

The Monroe family was from Virginia. Sam had come up here after graduating from Vanderbilt. He hadn't any choice. He'd met the fetching Aggie at a governor's ball—the Monroe family owned a construction company in Illinois, and contributed to the governor's coffers—and since she was a self-described "unreconstructed Yankee," he had no choice but to move north, buy himself a small bank with a loan from his father, and set about starting a family with this woman who so obsessed him.

Then, six months ago, his older brother was killed in a battle in Kentucky; he'd died in the uniform of the South. Sam had felt guilty ever since. He couldn't even make love all the time anymore. He felt unmanned by his beloved brother's death. But worst of all were the nightmares. He'd described them to her. How he hovered just behind his brother, trying to warn him to hit the dirt before the bullet took him in the forehead. *Hit the dirt, Richard! Hit the dirt!* But in the nightmares, Richard never heard him. He always stood straight up, aiming his rifle as the bluecoats came streaming over a hill. Stood straight up. Angry that so many of his friends had fallen. Stood straight up. As if daring the bluecoats to kill him.

Irene poured him more coffee.

When she was gone, Aggie said, "The way you stay out nights these days, I'd swear you had a mistress."

This time he didn't smile. Nothing funny about taking a mistress. Aggie was the only woman he'd ever been with, the only woman he'd *ever* be with. He conveyed this to her by getting up and crossing over to where she sat and taking her hand and saying, "Never say anything like that again, Aggie. You're my wife and the mother of my children."

Aggie felt properly admonished. She could see how she'd inadvertently hurt him. Southern men thought of themselves as men of honor and principle. A Northern man might joke about having a mistress. But not a Southern one. Not an honorable one, anyway.

He drank very little of his bourbon and ate all of his breakfast. A very good sign as far as Aggie was concerned.

When he was finished, he came to her again and kissed her. "I need to get to the bank, Aggie."

"On Saturday morning?"

"Yes," he said gently. "On Saturday mornings when I've got all this work on my desk. I'll be home by evening."

She knew there was no point arguing. She'd argued with him many nights about him being gone. It was a dance they did now. Him saying he was sorry he had to go, her questioning *why* he had to go.

In ten minutes, dressed in a suit and the kind of heavy coat called a Benjamin, his slicked-down hair smelling of perfumed macassar oil, he once again kissed her good-bye and set off.

He didn't go to the bank. He drove his horse-drawn carriage to a small business building on State Street. He stayed there two hours, got into his buggy and drove to an isolated spot over by the packing houses and tanneries. Nearby were the tenements and small pine shacks where the workers lived. The stench of the packing-houses and tanneries was suffocating; the cries of the dying animals even worse. Chicago was a fine place to be rich in—a place to rival the infamous Calcutta if you were poor.

He had a Henry. He went to a clearing next to a wooded area and spent the rest of the day practicing on targets he affixed to trees.

He was quite good. Again and again he hit the bull's-eye.

He shot with feverish intent. He did not stop except to reload. The Henry was a breech-loading sixteen-shot rifle. The Union army was justifiably proud when they introduced it only a month ago.

He spent the afternoon this way. Then he got into his carriage and returned to the same small business building on State Street.

Cawthorne said, "Have you ever met Jim McReedy?"

Sam Monroe had been wondering who was sitting with Big Mike Cawthorne in Cawthorne's office.

McReedy, whose clothes were worn and whose expression combined anxiety and contempt, put forth a bony but strong hand. He and Sam shook.

Big Mike Cawthorne said, "McReedy here is my personal spy. I use him to make sure everybody in our little group is staying in line."

"I'm not sure I like that, Mike," Sam said.

"I don't like it, either," Big Mike said in his expansive way. Despite his 250-pound bulk, he was still a dashing figure. He wore custom-tailored clothes and moved with great strength and style. "But I'm not naïve, Sam. Our little cell has to worry about being infiltrated. Or having a double agent. Jim here just checks people out for me."

In every major Northern city there was a half dozen or so Copperhead cells. It had been decided that cells of six or seven were safer than one large one, each operating independently. This gave the Copperheads a stronger chance of surviving.

Sam had known Cawthorne long before his brother's death in Kentucky. They did a lot of banking business together. Cawthorne was in real estate. One drunken night Sam confessed to Cawthorne that he secretly favored the South in the war. Within days, Cawthorne had introduced him to the six other members of the Copperhead cell. Sam joined eagerly.

Cawthorne said, "Tell him, Jim."

"Today when you were practicing with your Henry?"

"Yes," Sam said.

"Somebody was following you."

"What? That's impossible. I would've noticed." His vanity was hurt. How could he have not known he was being followed?

"If Jim says you were being followed, you were being followed," Cawthorne said.

"Who was following me?"

"I don't know. A man. I didn't get a good look at his face. He wore this hat with a snap brim and very heavy clothes."

Cawthorne said, "This is serious."

Sam couldn't argue with that. "You think they're on to us?"

"Somebody's on to *you*, anyway," McReedy said.

"I don't like your tone," Sam snapped.

Cawthorne said, "Let's stick to the problem, all right?" His disgust with both of them was obvious on his face. McReedy liked to play the expert. Sam, with his money, education, and good looks, was all male vanity. "Jim has a solution."

McReedy was pleased he got to play the expert again. "You're going to go home right now and I'm going to follow you again. But this time I'm going to find out who's in the buggy behind you. I can run him off the road now that it's dark. In the daytime too many people could see and I could get arrested." And that, of course, could lead the police directly to Cawthorne's Copperhead cell.

Sam figured McReedy was probably getting a lot of pleasure out of this. A lower-class man like this getting to act superior to his social better.

Yet Sam didn't have much choice but to listen and go along.

Sam set off in his buggy. In the darkest of late afternoon on of November 1, there was a half-moon brilliant in its luminosity. It almost made the 28-degree temperature tolerable.

He could smell the slums on the carriage. He'd have to have one of the servants give it a good brushing and washing. When you were near slaughterhouses that big, you couldn't get the stench off for days.

He drove self-consciously, aware now he was being followed. He'd been stupid not to have noticed this earlier in the day. And behind, his follower, Jim McReedy, no doubt gloating. Waiting his chance.

He went ten blocks on Dearborn before the mansions and the wide estates began appearing. His neighborhood. His house was only six blocks away. He wondered when McReedy would make his move.

He passed estates from which he could hear wonderful music, a party in progress, wondrous European chandeliers casting starlight out upon the autumn-frosted lawns. Good brandy and jokes and— Or so it had once been, anyway, before the death of his brother, before the death at the hands of the Union army had reminded Sam about who he really was in his heart and soul. Southern. Very much in agreement with his own people and their traditions. By rights he should've been fighting right alongside his brother. Before, he could get along with Yankees, almost convince himself that he belonged here and was one of them. But now—

McReedy made his move.

He pulled his buggy up sharply behind the follower and then lurched right up alongside of him, swerving into the follower's vehicle as he did so. Horses crying in fear and anger; wooden wheels clashing against each other. Shouts, oaths. Sam half expected gunfire.

The paralleling buggies went on this way for half a block, McReedy finally forcing the follower's buggy up against the plank sidewalk.

McReedy pulled his own rig ahead of the follower's, then jumped down. The estate homes were far enough back from the street that nobody inside would see or hear any of this.

Sam, who had been watching this by leaning out of his own buggy, steered his horse over to the side of the road and hopped out. He was frightened. At this point in his life he had but one matter he wanted to take care of and he didn't want anything—or anybody—to interfere. He hoped this follower, whoever he was, could be dealt with.

McReedy had his Navy Colt pulled and was pointing it directly at the man in the buggy. The follower's face was lost in shadow. He said nothing.

"I want your name," McReedy said. "I'm a private investigator and I know you've been following this man all day. I want to know why."

At least McReedy had his lies down, Sam thought. He sounded very imposing. He just hoped he scared the follower.

"Your name," McReedy said again as Sam came up to him.

Sam looked at the man. He was lost in an inverness cape soiled and worn by time, a large theatrical-style hat with an enormous, floppy brim covering his face. He wore tanned gloves on his hands. If he had any weapon, it was concealed somewhere within the folds of his coat.

It was cold and dark here on the street. Fresh horse-

329

droppings scented the evening; a distant violin sang sweetly and sadly.

And McReedy, an obstinate little rat-terrier of a man, said, "Get down from there, and I mean now."

But the follower said nothing. Nor moved.

McReedy waited no longer. He lunged up the buddy step and seized on to the arm of the follower, yanking the man out of the vehicle with strength that startled Sam.

The man might as well have been a rag doll, the way he was jerked from the buggy and flung to the street without much resistance at all.

He lay at the feet of the men, his hat, remarkably, still on, his face still hidden. "Stand up," McReedy said.

But the man wouldn't cooperate even now.

McReedy didn't wait.

He leaned down and tore the hat away from the man's head.

All Sam could do was stammer. "My god, Aggie. Why're you following me?"

"You don't think I have a right to know?" Aggie said.

"I've told you, Aggie. It's just a gun club I belong to."

It was past dinnertime. They'd been arguing in the downstairs study for nearly two hours.

He said, "Do you know how embarrassing it is, having your own wife follow you around?"

"I only did it because I'm worried about you. You haven't been the same since your brother died."

"Not 'died.' Was killed. There's a difference."

"You seem to forget," Aggie said, "your side killed *my* brother. You aren't the only one who's lost somebody in this war."

She sank down on one of the French Victorian chairs. David's face came to her, fresh as it had ever been. Three years younger, he'd been. A long and distinguished career in law ahead of him, everybody said. Then the train car he'd been on had been dynamited by Confederate soldiers.

But Sam wasn't listening. He was lost in his own troubles. "How do I explain it to them? My own wife following me around."

"I'm worried about you and our family, Sam. And all you care about is losing face with some stupid gun club." She looked at him. "If that's what's really going on." She made her remark sound as suspicious as possible. "Maybe I'll have to start following you again if I want to find out the real truth."

"Oh, God, don't say that, Aggie. Promise me you won't follow me around anymore. Promise me." Instead of rage, her threat had inspired only a kind of half-pathetic pleading. She'd never seen her husband like this. His pleading was especially worrisome. Sam wasn't the kind of man who pleaded with anyone. When he wanted something, he simply took it. "Promise me, Aggie. Promise me."

What choice did she have? He looked so lost and miserable. She said, quietly, "All right, Sam. I won't follow you anymore."

But she had her suspicions, and she knew that she'd be following him again very soon.

When Sam returned later that evening, there was a stranger in Big Mike Cawthorne's office when Sam walked in. McReedy was there also.

"I'm sorry about your troubles earlier," Cawthorne said.

331

"There's nothing like a nosy wife. And believe me, I know what I'm talking about from personal experience."

"A fine-looking woman, though," McReedy said. "Mighty fine."

Sam didn't like the lurid implications in McReedy's voice. This man just didn't seem to understand his station in life, talking about a true gentleman's wife in this sordid way.

There was some more chatter during which Big Mike was his usual expansive self. He offered brandy and cigars and everybody partook. Sam noticed that he had yet to introduce the stranger.

The man was short, blond, goateed. His clothes were several cuts above those of McReedy's—especially the velvet vest—but he still gave an impression of the streets. Perhaps it was the feral quality of his blue eyes—an unsettling mixture of subservience and arrogance.

Big Mike Cawthorne, all blather at this point, suddenly looked uncomfortable. He glanced anxiously at the stranger and then at Sam. "Sam, this is Lawrence Dodd." He looked nervous. "He's going to take your place."

There. He'd said it. It was over. There would be anger and complaining but it was over. You could read all this on Big Mike's face.

"Take my place? You mean assassinating Kimble?"

"Yes, I'm afraid so."

"But why? I've been shooting every day. I've looked over the site several times. I know just how I'll get in and just how I'll get out."

McReedy said, "Your wife knows."

"She doesn't know anything," Sam snapped.

Cawthorne said, quietly, "She may not *know* anything, Sam. But she suspects something and that's enough."

"No, it's not enough!" Sam said. "And what's more, it's not fair. Not after all the work I've done."

The only way I'll ever be able to pay my brother back for deserting him the way I did. The only way I'll ever be able to do my duty the way he did his. And now they're trying to take it away from me. Dammit, Aggie, why did you have to follow me yesterday?

Cawthorne was his usual slick self again. His nerves were under control. The subject had been broached. "She's a Yankee, Sam."

"You think I don't know that?"

"One of her uncles back in New Hampshire is a colonel in the Union army."

"And," McReedy added, "her brother was killed by some of our people."

"No telling what she might do," Cawthorne said, "her loyalties being what they are. Mr. Dodd here—well, there won't be that trouble."

Sam was sure his name wasn't Lawrence Dodd. He'd been borrowed from some other cell. Probably from out of town, though not far away. He'd been summoned overnight. From here on out, Sam would be told as little as possible about things. His longtime fear that Aggie's Yankee loyalties would hurt him had come true. Big Mike saying he was no longer quite trustworthy. Sam had seen this happen before, cell members who were suddenly seen as suspicious in some way being subtly pushed out of the cell. Big Mike knew they'd never go over to the other side. Everybody in this cell had a personal reason for being part of it. They'd never betray the South. But that didn't mean Big Mike and the others would trust them with the inner workings of the cell.

But that isn't the worst of it. The worst of it is that I put every-

*thing into this. Killing Lincoln's man is the only way I'll ever be
able to make things up to my brother. Why can't you people see
that? To you, it's just one more killing. To me, it's my honor.*

"I'm sorry, Sam," Big Mike said, "I really am."

"She's a fine-looking woman," McReedy said, who must
have known he was irritating Sam.

"I'll try to do as good a job as you would have, Mr. Monroe," the man whose name wasn't really Lawrence Dodd
said. "I really will."

Aggie didn't have much trouble finding what she needed.
She almost smiled when she found it because it was so
sloppy of Sam to keep it in the bottom drawer of his desk.
Where anybody, including the police, could easily find it.

Several clipped newspaper stories about a Mr. Harper
Kimble, Esquire. Arriving by train in Chicago the day before the election to give a rousing public speech about why
it was so important to vote—and to vote for those politi-
cians who supported President Lincoln's handling of the
war. Several references to the large ballroom in the
Courier-Arms Hotel—one of the city's finest—were un-
derlined. Then there was a hand-drawn map showing the
front steps of the hotel—and a hotel room directly across
the street. And a circle on the steps inside of which appeared the word *Kimble*.

The secretiveness. The target practice. The newspaper
stories. Aggie might not be a genius but she was smart
enough to figure out what Sam was up to. She cursed the
Union soldier who had killed Sam's older brother. Because
in a very real sense he'd taken Sam's life, too. He no longer
cared about his wife and children. His only reality was

avenging his brother's death. And now she knew how he planned to do it.

Sam came home drunk. Not falling-down drunk but in-control, angry drunk. He stormed into the living room where she was sitting by the fireplace with their two daughters and said, "It's way past their bedtime—put them to bed! I want to talk to you!"

She had never seen him so angry. The girls, four and five, were terrified of the man who had once been their loving, congenial father. He stank of the streets. His eyes rolled wildly. His clothes were soiled. His right hand was clenched in a constant fist. "And I mean now!"

"What's wrong with Daddy?" said the youngest, Courtney, as their mother hauled them up to bed, one under each arm.

"He's pickled," said Jenny, the eldest. She loved words and picked up new ones constantly.

"Is he pickled, Mommy?" Courtney said, without having the slightest idea what the word meant.

Sam leaned against the fireplace, a cigar in one hand, a brandy glass in the other. He didn't look up when Aggie came back in. He said, "Sit down."

She knew better than to argue with him.

She sat in a Hepplewhite chair she'd had as a girl, entwined hearts carved on the chair back. All the time she was growing up she had wondered whose heart would be entwined with hers. Sam's, of course. She'd fallen in love with him the very first night she'd met him, even though she didn't realize it until a month or so later. Entwined hearts . . . and they *had* been entwined, until he'd lost his brother in the war. . . .

335

After a time, he spoke. He said: "They don't want me. They say they can't trust me anymore."

She wasn't sure exactly who "they" were. But she sensed that all this had to do with the newspaper stories she'd found in his drawer.

"So they're not going to let me do it. They got somebody else." For the first time, he looked at her: "And do you know why, dear wife? Because of you! Because you just *had* to follow me around! And because you're a filthy Yankee!"

He had never called her a "filthy" anything before and the word stunned her—shocked her, hurt her as he'd never hurt her before. A bond of faith was broken in that moment and they both knew it.

But she fought against her pain and anger and rose solemnly from the chair as she heard him begin to cry. Not even in all the early months of following his brother's death had he ever wept. But he wept now.

She went to him and tried to take him in her arms. He wouldn't let her. He jerked away like an angry child. But finally, finally, he needed her strength and solace and so he came within her arms and she comforted him.

"I know what you were planning to do," she said after a time, "but you would've destroyed our whole family, Sam. Think of what the girls would have to go through all their lives. Now you don't have to do it. Now we can be a family again and you can forget all this. The girls need you, Sam, need you the way you used to be. And so do I."

An hour later, in the gentle darkness of their bed, they made love with fresh ardor and succoring passion.

Sam slept in. He ate a late, good breakfast and then got up. It was a Sunday and he spent the entire afternoon playing with the girls in the living room, reading them stories, playing their favorite games, telling them about all the wonderful things winter would soon bring, including snowmen and ice-skating. It was as if he had survived a terrible fever that had not—thank God—killed him but had somehow burned itself out. He was the Sam of old.

He was that evening, too. He took Aggie out to dine. They took the fancy carriage with the liveried driver, and took in a show following dinner. Nothing about his friends at "the gun club" was mentioned. Nor was the war referred to in any way. When they went to bed, they made long and leisurely love.

On Monday, the day upon which Mr. Kimble, Esquire, was to arrive from Washington, D.C., Sam went to the bank and spent a busy morning catching up on the work he'd been neglecting.

At home, Aggie got the girls off to school and then went out in her buggy for some things she'd been needing at the store. She was only a block away from home when she realized she was being followed.

She went to the store, tied the reins of her buggy to a hitching-post and hurried inside. She wanted to make sure she was indeed being followed. Maybe her suspicions had gotten away from her.

But no. There he was. He'd pulled up to a hitching-post a quarter block away. He jumped down from his buggy and was now standing there and rolling himself a cigarette. Waiting for her to return.

Her boldness surprised her. She bolted the store and hurried back outside into the winds that lacerated everything on this drab, overcast day. There wasn't even any snow to make it pretty.

She walked right up to him. "I want to know why you're following me, sir."

He smiled. "It's people like you who make my work hard for me, Mrs. Monroe."

"Why are you following me?"

Her voice was sharp enough to attract the attention of people walking along the plank sidewalk. This was a block of shops and offices of various kinds, from a saddlery to a doctor and a dentist.

"Just had to make sure you didn't go see the police," he said in a quiet voice. "I've been watching you for three days now. You haven't left the house without Sam. We just wanted to make sure you didn't talk to anybody about what was going to happen."

She hated them all. And for one of the first times, they formed a monolith in her mind: *Southerners*. Devious, violent.

"Well, you can take this message back to your friends," she said. "He doesn't want any part of you anymore."

This time the smile was a smirk. "He's gonna be a good little boy, huh?"

She turned and stalked away.

She told Sam about all this before dinner but he only cupped her face in his hands and kissed her and said, "Let's just have a nice family dinner."

And so they did. Wind lashed the windows and made her thankful for the warmth and beauty of her home. How tall and proud it stood against the most furious of nights. The girls, too, seemed affected by this same sense of melancholy. Not only did they manage to look prettier than ever in the flickering lamplight, they also sat very close to each other and even gave each other hugs from time to time. Sometimes they fought angrily. But not tonight.

She watched Sam watching this. He seemed moved by everything. She even thought for a moment that she saw his eyes dampen with tears. It was one of those moments—so sweet, so peaceful, so tranquil. It seemed that nothing could possibly be wrong anywhere in God's world.

And then he was helping her up to bed. It was so odd. She'd been sitting at the table talking to the girls about snow—it had become their obsession—and then . . . And then Sam had to help her up the stairs. So queer. As if the wine for dinner had suddenly made her very, very drunk . . . sleepy. But she'd had less than half a glass.

And then she was in bed . . . sleeping . . .

Wind.

Panic: disorientation. *Where am I? What happened?*

Headache.

Dry mouth.

Drugs . . . yes.

Her inclination had been to think of the dinner wine. There was the culprit. She wasn't much of a drinker.

But no . . . this was more like the aftereffects of the sleeping-potion the doctors had given her after Courtney's birth. The grogginess . . . the slight feeling of nausea . . .

Wind again.

All she wanted to do was relieve her bladder and sink deep into sleep again.

He drugged me. Sam drugged me. But why?

Even through the blind, numbed, disoriented feeling of the moment the realization of it made her fight her way to wakefulness.

Have to wake up. Find Sam.

Walking was almost impossible. She kept slumping against chairs and bureaus and walls as she took one small step at a time. She found the pull cord for Irene the maid. Then she staggered on into her private toilet and began soaking her face in water standing in the basin.

Irene came quickly. And departed quickly, headed downstairs to make coffee, and a lot of it. . . .

Aggie found the letter in the study. Her name was on the front of it. She was just awake enough for it to make terrifying sense. . . .

Lawrence Dodd got to the hotel room a little early. He was always early. It was part of his professionalism. He'd assassinated seven men since the start of the war and he hadn't yet come even close to getting caught.

He kept the lamp off. He knelt by the window. It was cold enough for frost to rime the glass along the window casing.

He kept studying the place where Kimble would come out around nine, following his speech, on his way to the mayor's house where a reception was to be held. A carriage would pull up. Kimble would start down the front steps. And then Dodd would kill him . . . that simple.

An hour after he'd gone to the window, there was a knock on the door, startling him. Who the hell would be knocking? Who knew he was in here? He had a bad stomach. Acid immediately began scouring it.

The knock again. A soft knock. As if the caller didn't want to be heard beyond this one door.

Maybe something has happened. Maybe the police have learned about tonight. Maybe I'm not supposed to go through with it.

So many thoughts, doubts, suppositions prompted by the knocking.

Shit. He had to go to the door. Find out what was going on. For now, he had to hide the Sharps.

He looked around in the dim light from the street.

Another soft knock.

The closet. He'd put the Sharps in the closet.

He brought his Colt with him to the door but even with that, the other man didn't have any trouble slashing the barrel of his own handgun down across Dodds's face and knocking him back into the room. Nor any trouble knocking him out.

Nor any trouble tying him up and gagging him.

The buggy ride helped considerably. The harsh, cold weather completed the job of waking her up. The coffee had helped. The cold air was even better.

Downtown was crowded with vehicles of every kind. Police were everywhere. Bands could be heard in a variety of hotels. Both political parties were anticipating victory—or pretending to, anyway. She hitched her buggy, took her bag, and walked the remaining two blocks to the hotel. This was as close as she could get. Gunshots could be heard as she walked. The frontier mentality was still with them: when you were happy, you shot off guns. The police could arrest you but they had to catch you first.

The lobby was packed. Men in muttonchops and vast bellies stood about with huge glasses of whiskey in their fat pampered hands. Their women were almost elegant in gowns that displayed their bosoms to best advantage. The six-piece orchestra played one raucous tune after another.

Nobody noticed her. Just one more person. Pretty as she was, she was still unremarkable in this crowd.

Sam had been helpful enough to put the room number on the map he'd drawn. She had little trouble convincing the desk clerk that she was to meet her husband here. He gave her the spare key.

The hotel had emptied downward. All the rooms seemed to be empty. As she walked along the sconce-decorated halls, she heard nothing but the pounding music from the lobby. Not even New Year's Eve could be noisier than this.

When she reached the room, she paused. Took a deep breath. Said a hasty prayer.

For the first time, she was thankful for all the noise. It allowed her to slip the key in the lock and turn it without being heard.

The gun was in her hand as she walked inside.

A man was on the bed. Bound and gagged. Sam was just turning to her now. He sat in a chair at the window. A Sharps leaned against the wall. He'd have a good, clean shot from here. And in the clamor downstairs, he'd have an easy time getting away out one of the rear exits.

He'd planned well.

She shut the door. "I'm taking you home, Sam."

As she spoke, she thought of the words in the letter he'd left.

Dear darling Aggie:

I wanted to give you and the girls a good memory of me. The last few days have been wonderful. But now I have to be a man of honor and avenge my brother. Avenge my country which is, and will always

be, the South. I don't expect you to understand—
even though you, too, have lost a brother, you have
not lost honor. I should've worn the gray just as he
did. This is my only chance to make up for what I
failed to do. All my love to you and the girls

—Sam, forever.

"Go home, Aggie," Sam said gently. "Take care of the
girls."

"I'd rather kill you myself than have you disgrace your
daughters this way. They'll pay for this the rest of their
lives, Sam. You don't seem to care how it'll be for them to
have a traitor as a father."

"Traitor!" he said. "I'm not a traitor. I'm a patriot."

"You live in the North, Sam. Your girls are Yankees.
And they always will be."

He stood up. "I have to do this, Aggie. I have to."

But she stood unwavering. The gun pointed right at
him. "Don't fool yourself, Sam. I came here prepared to
kill you if I had to."

"You kill me here, the police'll know what happened
anyway."

"Not if I take the Sharps and let that man on the bed
go. I take it he's your replacement."

Sam started walking toward her. "You won't be able to
kill me, Aggie. I know you. You're not violent. And besides, you love me."

"Just stay there, Sam."

But he kept coming, obviously sure of what he was
saying. "You won't be able to do it. So why not just hand
me the gun and leave? I'm going to do this no matter
what."

She raised the gun so that it pointed directly at his chest. "Stay back, Sam. Stay back."

And then he lunged for her.

Overpowering her was easy. Getting the gun away was another matter. As they wrestled for it on the floor, she kept it tucked under herself so that his fingers couldn't quite reach it. He offered her no mercy. He hit her as hard as he would a man he disliked.

Then the gun sounded, muffled by the fact that he was lying on top of her when the weapon discharged. He knew almost at once that she was dead. The death spasm had been unmistakable. And now she moved not at all.

He pulled himself away from her. Felt her pulse. None. The gun had tired just as the band music had swelled. The sound of the firing easily would have been lost.

He stood up. Stared down at her. Wife. Mother of his children. He knew that he loved her but at the moment it was an abstract feeling, one far less vivid than the hatred he bore. Someday he would revile himself for what had just happened on this hotel-room floor. But for now, there was the task at hand. Kimble should be leaving the hotel in less than ten minutes.

He grabbed his Sharps and went to the window. He thought of his dead brother and his own disgrace.

Soon now, he thought. *Soon now.*

The Face

The war was going badly. In the past month more than sixty men had disgraced the Confederacy by deserting, and now the order was to shoot deserters on sight. This was in other camps and other regiments. Fortunately, none of our men had deserted at all.

As a young doctor, I knew even better than our leaders just how hopeless our war had become. The public knew General Lee had been forced to cross the Potomac with ten thousand men who lacked shoes, hats and who at night had to sleep on the ground without blankets. But I knew—in the first six months in this post—that our men suffered from influenza, diphtheria, smallpox, yellow fever and even cholera; ravages from which they would never recover; ravages more costly than bullets and the advancing armies of the Yankees. Worse, because toilet and bathing facilities were practically nil, virtually every man suffered from ticks and mites and many suffered from scurvy, their bodies on fire. Occasionally, you would see a man go mad, do crazed dances in the moonlight trying to get the bugs off him. Soon enough he would be dead.

This was the war in the spring and while I have here referred to our troops as "men," in fact they were mostly boys, some as young as thirteen. In the night, freezing and sometimes wounded, they cried out for their mothers, and it was not uncommon to hear one or two of them sob while they prayed aloud.

I tell you this so you will have some idea of how horrible things had become for our beloved Confederacy. But even given the suffering and madness and despair I'd seen for the past two years as a military doctor, nothing had prepared me for the appearance of the Virginia man in our midst.

On the day he was brought in on a buckboard, I was working with some troops, teaching them how to garden. If we did not get vegetables and fruit into our diets soon, all of us would have scurvy. I also appreciated the respite that working in the warm sun gave me from surgery. In the past week alone, I'd amputated three legs, two arms and numerous hands and fingers. None had gone well, conditions were so filthy.

Every amputation had ended in death except one and this man—boy; he was fourteen—pleaded with me to kill him every time I checked on him. He'd suffered a head wound and I'd had to relieve the pressure by trepanning into his skull. Beneath the blood and pus in the hole I'd dug, I could see his brain squirming. There was no anesthetic, of course, except whiskey and that provided little comfort against the violence of my bone saw. It was one of those periods when I could not get the tart odor of blood from my nostrils, nor its feel from my skin. Sometimes, standing at the surgery table, my boots would become soaked with it and I would squish around in them all day.

The buckboard was parked in front of the General's tent. The driver jumped down, ground-tied the horses, and went quickly inside.

He returned a few moments later with General Sullivan, the commander. Three men in familiar gray uniforms followed the General.

The entourage walked around to the rear of the wagon. The driver, an enlisted man, pointed to something in the buckboard. The General, a fleshy, bald man of fifty-some years, leaned over the wagon and peered downward.

Quickly, the General's head snapped back and then his whole body followed. It was as if he'd been stung by something coiled and waiting for him in the buckboard.

The General shook his head and said, "I want this man's entire face covered. Especially his face."

"But, General," the driver said. "He's not dead. We shouldn't cover his face."

"You heard what I said!" General Sullivan snapped. And with that, he strutted back into his tent, his men following.

I was curious, of course, about the man in the back of the wagon. I wondered what could have made the General start the way he had. He'd looked almost frightened.

I wasn't to know till later that night.

My rounds made me late for dinner in the vast tent used for the officers' mess. I always felt badly about the inequity of officers having beef stew while the men had, at best, hardtack and salt pork. Not so bad that I refused to eat it, of course, which made me feel hypocritical on top of being sorry for the enlisted men.

Not once in my time here had I ever dined with General Sullivan. I was told on my first day here that the General, an extremely superstitious man, considered doctors bad luck. Many people feel this way. Befriend a doctor and you'll soon enough find need of his services.

So I was surprised when General Sullivan, carrying a cup of steaming coffee in a huge, battered tin cup, sat down across from the table where I ate alone, my usual companions long ago gone back to their duties.

"Good evening, Doctor."

"Good evening, General."

"A little warmer tonight."

"Yes."

He smiled dourly. "Something's got to go our way, I suppose."

I returned his smile. "I suppose." I felt like a child trying to act properly for the sake of an adult. The General frightened me.

The General took out a stogie, clipped off the end, sniffed it, licked it, then put it between his lips and fired it. He did all this with a ritualistic satisfaction that made me think of better times in my home city of Charleston, of my father and uncles handling their smoking in just the same way.

"A man was brought into camp this afternoon," he said.

"Yes," I said. "In a buckboard."

He eyed me suspiciously. "You've seen him up close?"

"No. I just saw him delivered to your tent." I had to be careful of how I put my next statement. I did not want the General to think I was challenging his reasoning. "I'm told he was not taken to any of the hospital tents."

"No, he wasn't." The General wasn't going to help me.

"I'm told he was put under quarantine in a tent of his own."

"Yes."

"May I ask why?"

He blew two plump white perfect rings of smoke toward the ceiling. "Go have a look at him, then join me in my tent."

"You're afraid he may have some contagious disease?"

The General considered the length of his cigar. "Just go have a look at him, Doctor. Then we'll talk."

With that, the General stood up, his familiar brusque self once again, and was gone.

The guard set down his rifle when he saw me. "Good evenin', Doctor."

"Good evening."

He nodded to the tent behind him. "You seen him yet?"

"No; not yet."

He was young. He shook his head. "Never seen anything like it. Neither has the priest. He's in there with him now." In the chill, crimson dusk I tried to get a look at the guard's face. I couldn't. My only clue to his mood was the tone of his voice—one of great sorrow.

I lifted the tent flap and went in.

A lamp guttered in the far corner of the small tent, casting huge and playful shadows across the walls. A hospital cot took up most of the space. A man's body lay beneath the covers. A sheer cloth had been draped across his face. You could see it billowing with the man's faint breath. Next to the cot stood Father Lynott. He was silver-haired and chunky. His black cassock showed months of dust and grime. Like most of us, he was rarely able to get hot water for necessities.

At first, he didn't seem to hear me. He stood over the cot torturing black rosary beads through his fingers. He stared directly down at the cloth draped on the man's face.

Only when I stood next to him did Father Lynott look up. "Good evening, Father."

"Good evening, Doctor."

"The General wanted me to look at this man."

He stared at me. "You haven't seen him, then?"

"No."

"Nothing can prepare you."

"I'm afraid I don't understand."

He looked at me out of his tired cleric's face. "You'll see soon enough. Why don't you come over to the officers' tent afterwards? I'll be there drinking my nightly coffee."

He nodded, glanced down once more at the man on the cot, and then left, dropping the tent flap behind him.

I don't know how long I stood there before I could bring myself to remove the cloth from the man's face. By now, enough people had warned me of what I would see that I was both curious and apprehensive. There is a myth about doctors not being shocked by certain terrible wounds and injuries. Of course we are but we must get past that shock—or, more honestly, put it aside for a time—so that we can help the patient.

Close by, I could hear the feet of the guard in the damp grass, pacing back and forth in front of the tent. A barn owl and then a distant dog joined the sounds the guard made. Even more distant, there was cannon fire, the war never ceasing. The sky would flare silver like summer lightning. Men would suffer and die.

I reached down and took the cloth from the man's face.

"What do you suppose could have done that to his face, Father?" I asked the priest twenty minutes later.

We were having coffee. I smoked a cigar. The guttering candles smelled sweet and waxy.

"I'm not sure," the priest said.

"Have you ever seen anything like it?"

"Never."

I knew what I was about to say would surprise the priest. "He has no wounds."

"What?"

"I examined him thoroughly. There are no wounds anywhere on his body."

"But his face—"

I drew on my cigar, watched the expelled smoke move like a storm cloud across the flickering candle flame. "That's why I asked you if you'd ever seen anything like it."

"My God," the priest said, as if speaking to himself. "No wounds."

In the dream I was back on the battlefield on that frosty March morning two years ago when all my medical training had deserted me. Hundreds of corpses covered the ground where the battle had gone on for two days and two nights. You could see cannons mired in mud, the horses unable to pull them out. You could see the grass littered with dishes and pans and kettles, and a blizzard of playing cards—all exploded across the battlefield when the Union army had made its final advance. But mostly there were the bodies—so young and so many—and many of them with mutilated faces. During this time of the war, both sides had begun to commit atrocities. The Yankees favored disfiguring Confederate dead and so they moved across the battlefield with Bowie knives that had been fashioned by sharpening with large files. They put deep gashes in the faces of the young men, tearing out eyes sometimes, even sawing off noses. In the woods that day we'd found a group of our soldiers who'd been mortally wounded but who'd lived for a time after the Yankees had left. Each corpse held in its hand some memento of the loved ones they'd left behind—a photograph, a letter, a lock of blonde hair. Their last sight had been of some homely yet profound endearment from the people they'd loved most.

This was the dream—nightmare, really—and I'd suffered it ever since I'd searched for survivors on that battlefield two years previous.

I was still in this dream-state when I heard the bugle announce the morning. I stumbled from my cot and went down to the creek to wash and shave. The day had begun.

Casualties were many that morning. I stood in the hospital tent watching as one stretcher after another bore man after man to the operating table. Most suffered from wounds inflicted by minie balls, fired from guns that could kill a man nearly a mile away.

By noon, my boots were again soaked with blood dripping from the table.

During the long day, I heard whispers of the man General Sullivan had quarantined from others. Apparently, the man had assumed the celebrity and fascination of a carnival side-show. From the whispers, I gathered the guards were letting men in for quick looks at him, and then lookers came away shaken and frightened. These stories had the same impact as tales of spectres told around midnight campfires. Except this was daylight and the men—even the youngest of them—hardened soldiers. They should not have been so afraid but they were.

I couldn't get the sight of the man out of my mind, either. It haunted me no less than the battlefield I'd seen two years earlier.

During the afternoon, I went down to the creek and washed. I then went to the officers' tent and had stew and coffee. My arms were weary from surgery but I knew I would be working long into the night.

The General surprised me once again by joining me. "You've seen the soldier from Virginia?"

"Yes, sir."

"What do you make of him?"

I shrugged. "Shock, I suppose."

"But his face—"

"This is a war, General, and a damned bloody one. Not all men are like you. Not all men have iron constitutions."

He took my words as flattery, of course, as a military man would. I hadn't necessarily meant them that way. Military men could also be grossly vain and egotistical and insensitive beyond belief.

"Meaning what, exactly, Doctor?"

"Meaning that the soldier from Virginia may have become so horrified by what he saw that his face—" I shook my head. "You can see too much, too much death, General, and it can make you go insane."

"Are you saying he's insane?"

I shook my head. "I'm trying to find some explanation for his expression, General."

"You say there's no injury?"

"None that I can find."

"Yet he's not conscious."

"That's why I think of shock."

I was about to explain how shock works on the body—and how it could feasibly effect an expression like the one on the Virginia soldier's face—when a lieutenant rushed up to the General and breathlessly said, "You'd best come, sir. The tent where the soldier's quarantined— There's trouble!"

When we reached there, we found half the camp's soldiers surrounding the tent. Three and four deep, they were, and milling around idly. Not the sort of thing you wanted to see your men doing when there was a war going on. There were duties to perform and none of them were getting done.

A young soldier—thirteen or fourteen at most— stepped from the line and hurled his rifle at the General. The young soldier had tears running down his cheeks. "I don't want to fight any more, General."

The General slammed the butt of the rifle into the soldier's stomach. "Get hold of yourself, young man. You seem to forget we're fighting to save the Confederacy."

We went on down the line of glowering faces, to where two armed guards struggled to keep soldiers from looking into the tent. I was reminded again of a sideshow—some irresistible spectacle everybody wanted to see.

The soldiers knew enough to open an avenue for the General. He strode inside the tent. The priest sat on a stool next to the cot. He had removed the cloth from the Virginia soldier's face and was staring fixedly at it.

The General pushed the priest aside, took up the cloth used as a covering, and started to drop it across the soldier's face—then stopped abruptly. Even General Sullivan, in his rage, was moved by what he saw. He jerked back momentarily, his eyes unable to lift from the soldier's face. He handed the cloth to the priest. "You cover his face now, Father. And you keep it covered. I hereby forbid any man in this camp to look at this soldier's face ever again. Do you understand?"

Then he stormed from the tent.

The priest reluctantly obliged.

Then he angled his head up to me. "It won't be the same any more, Doctor."

"What won't?"

"The camp. Every man in here has now seen his face." He nodded back to the soldier on the cot. "They'll never be the same again. I promise you."

In the evening, I ate stew and biscuits, and sipped at a small glass of wine. I was, as usual, in the officers' tent when the priest came and found me.

For a time, he said nothing beyond his greeting. Simply watched me at my meal, and then stared out the open flap at the camp preparing for evening, the fires in the center of the encampment, the weary men bedding down. Many of them, healed now, would be back in the battle within two days or less.

"I spent an hour with him this afternoon," the priest said.

"The quarantined man?"

"Yes." The priest nodded. "Do you know some of the men have visited him five or six times?"

The way the priest spoke, I sensed he was gloating over

the fact that the men were disobeying the General's orders. "Why don't the guards stop them?"

"The guards are in visiting him, too."

"The man says nothing. How can it be a visit?"

"He says nothing with his tongue. He says a great deal with his face." He paused, eyed me levelly. "I need to tell you something. You're the only man in this camp who will believe me." He sounded frantic. I almost felt sorry for him.

"Tell me what?"

"The man—he's not what we think."

"No?"

"No; his face—" He shook his head. "It's God's face."

"I see."

The priest smiled. "I know how I must sound."

"You've seen a great deal of suffering, Father. It wears on a person."

"It's God's face. I had a dream last night. The man's face shows us God's displeasure with the war. That's why the men are so moved when they see the man." He sighed, seeing he was not convincing me. "You say yourself he hasn't been wounded."

"That's true."

"And that all his vital signs seem normal."

"True enough, Father."

"Yet he's in some kind of shock."

"That seems to be his problem, yes."

The priest shook his head. "No, his real problem is that he's become overwhelmed by the suffering he's seen in this war—what both sides have done to the other. All the pain. That's why there's so much sorrow on his face—and that's what the men are responding to. The grief on his face is the same grief they feel in their hearts. God's face."

"Once we get him to a real field hospital—"

And it was then we heard the rifle shots.

The periphery of the encampment was heavily protected, we'd never heard firing this close.

The priest and I ran outside.

General Sullivan stood next to a group of young men with weapons. Several yards ahead, near the edge of the camp, lay three bodies, shadowy in the light of the campfire. One of the fallen men moaned. All three men wore our own gray uniforms.

Sullivan glowered at me. "Deserters."

"But you shot them in the back," I said.

"Perhaps you didn't hear me, Doctor. The men were deserting. They'd packed their belongings and were heading out."

One of the young men who'd done the shooting said, "It was the man's face, sir."

Sullivan wheeled on him. "It was what?"

"The quarantined man, sir. His face. These men said it made them sad and they had to see families back in Missouri, and that they were just going to leave no matter what."

"Poppycock," Sullivan said. "They left because they were cowards."

I left to take care of the fallen man who was crying out for help.

In the middle of the night, I heard more guns being fired. I lay on my cot, knowing it wasn't Yankees being fired at. It was our own deserters.

I dressed and went over to the tent where the quarantined man lay. Two young farm boys in ill-fitting gray uniforms stood over him. They might have been mourners standing over a coffin. They said nothing. Just stared at the man.

In the dim lamplight, I knelt down next to him. His vitals still seemed good, his heartbeat especially. I stood up, next to the two boys, and looked down on him myself. There was nothing remarkable about his face. He could have been any of thousands of men serving on either side.

Except for the grief.

This time I felt the tug of it myself, heard in my mind the cries of the dying I'd been unable to save, saw the families and farms and homes destroyed as the war moved across the countryside, heard children crying out for dead parents, and parents sobbing over the bodies of their dead children. It was all there in his face, perfectly reflected, and I thought then of what the priest had said, that this was God's face, God's sorrow and displeasure with us.

The explosion came, then.

While the two soldiers next to me didn't seem to hear it at all, I rushed from the tent to the center of camp.

Several young soldiers stood near the ammunition cache. Someone had set fire to it. Ammunition was exploding everywhere, flares of red and yellow and gas-jet blue against the night. Men everywhere ducked for cover behind wagons and trees and boulders.

Into this scene, seemingly unafraid and looking like the lead actor in a stage production of *King Lear* I'd once seen, strode General Sullivan, still tugging on his heavy uniform jacket.

He went over to two soldiers who stood, seemingly unfazed, before the ammunition cache. Between explosions I could hear him shouting, "Did you set this fire?"

And they nodded.

Sullivan, as much in bafflement as anger, shook his head. He signaled for the guards to come and arrest these men.

As the soldiers were passing by me, I heard one of them say to a guard, "After I saw his face, I knew I had to do this. I had to stop the war."

Within an hour, the flames died and the explosions ceased. The night was almost ominously quiet. There were a few hours before dawn, so I tried to sleep some more.

I dreamed of Virginia, green Virginia in the spring, and the creek where I'd fished as a boy, and how the sun had felt on my back and arms and head. There was no surgical table in my dream, nor were my shoes soaked with blood.

Around dawn somebody began shaking me. It was Sullivan's personal lieutenant. "The priest has been shot. Come quickly, Doctor."

I didn't even dress fully, just pulled on my trousers over the legs of my long underwear.

A dozen soldiers stood outside the tent looking confused and defeated and sad. I went inside.

The priest lay in his tent. His cassock had been torn away. A bloody hole made a target-like circle on his stomach.

Above his cot stood General Sullivan, a pistol in his hand.

I knelt next to the cot and examined the priest. His vital signs were faint and growing fainter. He had at most a few minutes to live.

I looked up at the General. "What happened?"

The General nodded for the lieutenant to leave. The man saluted and then went out into the gray dawn.

"I had to shoot him," General Sullivan said.

I stood up. "You had to shoot a priest?"

"He was trying to stop me."

"From what?"

Then I noticed for the first time the knife scabbard on the General's belt. Blood streaked its sides. The hilt of the knife was sticky with blood. So were the General's hands. I thought of how Yankee troops had begun disfiguring the faces of our dead on the battlefield.

He said, "I have a war to fight, Doctor. The men—the way they were reacting to the man's face—" He paused and touched the bloody hilt of the knife. "I took care of him. And the priest came in while I was doing it and went insane. He started hitting me, trying to stop me and—" He looked down at the priest. "I didn't have any choice, Doctor. I hope you believe me."

A few minutes later, the priest died.

I started to leave the tent. General Sullivan put a hand on my shoulder. "I know you don't care very much for me, Doctor, but I hope you understand me at least a little. I can't win a war when men desert and blow up ammunition dumps and start questioning the worthiness of the war itself. I had to do what I did. I hope someday you'll understand."

I went out into the dawn. The air smelled of campfires and coffee. Now the men were busy scurrying around, preparing for war. The way they had been before the man had been brought here in the buckboard.

I went over to the tent where he was kept and asked the guard to let me inside. "The General said nobody's allowed inside, Doctor."

I shoved the boy aside and strode into the tent.

The cloth was still over his face, only now it was soaked with blood. I raised the cloth and looked at him. Even for a doctor, the sight was horrible. The General had ripped out his eyes and sawed off his nose. His cheeks carried deep gullies where the knife had been dug in deep.

He was dead. The shock of the defacement had killed him.

Sickened, I looked away.

The flap was thrown back, then, and there stood General Sullivan. "We're going to bury him now, Doctor."

In minutes, the dead soldier was inside a pine box borne up a hill of long grass waving in a chill wind. The rains came, hard rains, before they'd turned even two shovelfuls of earth.

Then, from a distance over the hill, came the thunder of cannon and the cry of the dying.

The face that reminded us of what we were doing to each other was no more. It had been made ugly, robbed of its sorrowful beauty.

He was buried quickly and without benefit of clergy— the priest himself having been buried an hour earlier— and when the ceremony was finished, we returned to camp and war.